The
HOUSE
of the
FOUR WINDS

~

DEDICATED TO THE MEMORY OF MY MOTHER,

JOYCE RITCHE

ALSO BY MERCEDES LACKEY AND JAMES MALLORY

THE OBSIDIAN TRILOGY

The Outstretched Shadow
To Light a Candle
When Darkness Falls

THE ENDURING FLAME

The Phoenix Unchained
The Phoenix Endangered
The Phoenix Transformed

THE DRAGON PROPHECY

Crown of Vengeance

ALSO BY JAMES MALLORY

Merlin: The Old Magic
Merlin: The King's Wizard
Merlin: The End of Magic

TOR BOOKS BY MERCEDES LACKEY

Firebird
Sacred Ground
Trio of Sorcery

DIANA TREGARDE NOVELS

Burning Water
Children of the Night
Jinx High

THE HALFBLOOD CHRONICLES
(WRITTEN WITH ANDRE NORTON)

The Elvenbane
Elvenblood
Elvenborn

The
HOUSE
of the
FOUR WINDS

~

BOOK ONE OF
One Dozen Daughters

MERCEDES LACKEY

AND

JAMES MALLORY

TOR®

A TOM DOHERTY ASSOCIATES BOOK · NEW YORK

This is a work of fiction. All of the characters, organizations, and events portrayed in this novel are either products of the authors' imaginations or are used fictitiously.

THE HOUSE OF THE FOUR WINDS

Copyright © 2014 by Mercedes Lackey and James Mallory

All rights reserved.

A Tor Book
Published by Tom Doherty Associates, LLC
175 Fifth Avenue
New York, NY 10010

www.tor-forge.com

Tor® is a registered trademark of Tom Doherty Associates, LLC.

Library of Congress Cataloging-in-Publication Data

Lackey, Mercedes.
    The house of the four winds : Book one of One dozen daughters /
Mercedes Lackey, James Mallory.
        p. cm. — (One Dozen Daughters; Book 1)
    ISBN 978-0-7653-3565-4 (hardcover)
    ISBN 978-1-4668-2420-1 (e-book)
    1. Daughters—Fiction.   2. Princesses—Fiction.   3. Pirates—Fiction.
    4. Magic—Fiction.   5. Fantasy fiction.   I. Mallory, James, 1945–   II. Title.
    PS3562.A246H68 2014
    813'.54—dc23

                                                            2014015447

Tor books may be purchased for educational, business, or promotional use. For information on bulk purchases, please contact Macmillan Corporate and Premium Sales Department at 1-800-221-7945, extension 5442, or write specialmarkets@macmillan.com.

First Edition: August 2014

Printed in the United States of America

0 9 8 7 6 5 4 3 2 1

The
HOUSE
of the
FOUR WINDS

PROLOGUE

~

THE PARLIAMENT OF CATS

THE DUCHY of Swansgaarde nestled in a tiny valley in the Borogny Mountains. South lay Turkey, north lay Poland. To the east was *Rossiyskaya Imperiya*—the Russian Empire—and to the west, the mighty and far-reaching Cisleithanian Empire. To be Swansgaardian, as Duke Rupert often said, was to be a mouse at a parliament of cats, for any of her large and powerful neighbors might at any moment take it into their heads to snap up such a tempting morsel.

But so far, Swansgaarde had escaped such a fate. Duke Rupert and Duchess Yetive had ruled Swansgaarde peacefully for many years. They were blessed with twelve beautiful daughters—and one son. Prince Dantan had been a happy surprise, for under the laws of inheritance, the throne of Swansgaarde could not pass to a daughter, only to a son—and before Dantan's birth the heir presumptive had been Duke Rupert's great-nephew Rudolf, who had never been east of Vinarborg in his life.

But the birth of the long-awaited heir also created a small problem.

On Prince Dantan's first birthday, the Duke and the Duchess gathered the whole of their family together for a family council.

All the princesses were there, from Clarice, the eldest, who would be eighteen in just a few months, to little Damaris, who was just six.

"Well, daughters," said the Duke, gazing around the comfortable parlor, "I am grieved to say this, but there are a great many of you, and our duchy is very small. I do not know how to provide for all of you, for twelve royal dowries would leave our country impoverished, and I do not like to think of leaving little Dantan an inheritance such as that."

"Nor would he have it for long," the Duchess commented drily.

While the Borogny Principalities had not gone to war with one another for as long as anyone could remember, an absence of war did not mean a presence of peace, and any of their neighbors would be happy to extend their realms if Swansgaarde were not in a position to prevent them.

For a moment all the princesses gazed at one another.

"We must go forth and seek our fortunes!" little Damaris cried, bouncing up and down with glee at the thought.

"I think," said Princess Clarice, after a moment's consideration, "that this is an excellent plan."

Now, perhaps if this were any other realm, such a declaration would have been met with scorn, rage, or dismissal. But the Duke and the Duchess were liberal minded and their daughters had been allowed to study whatever they liked—however unfeminine the subject might be. Moreover, the absolute, if covert, law of the royal family was that every one of them must learn some kind of trade. The history of Eurus was a history of countries, thrones, and even empires overthrown and lost—it was why the Borogny Principalities existed in the first place, for nearly all of them had been founded by exiles. A prince (or princess) in exile still needed to eat, and royal cousins might become royal enemies at any moment—but who would expect to see a prince behind the counter of a clockmaker, or a princess trimming fashionable bonnets?

"Expect the best and plan for the worst," Duke Rupert said, so each of his daughters, on her tenth birthday, was allowed to pick whatever "trade" she wanted to study. Clarice had chosen the sword.

Although it might seem this was stretching the definition of *trade* to the breaking point, no Duke of Swansgaarde had ever educated his children without the tacit assumption that one day one or more of them *might* actually need to practice it, and so it was decided. Each princess, on the day of her eighteenth birthday, would go forth to "seek her fortune."

1

FAREWELL TO SWANSGAARDE

THE EARLY-MORNING sunlight shone through the French doors that led out to the balcony of Princess Clarice's tower bedroom. From the balcony was the sweeping vista of the Borogny Mountains, spreading their pristine robes for admiration, their high peaks crowned in clouds and their slopes robed in snow year-round. They were the first thing Princess Clarice saw each morning as the sun rose over the Swanscrown.

I shall miss this. The thought came before Clarice quite realized she was awake.

There was no point now in trying to convince herself she was asleep. Throwing back the covers, she shrugged into her wrapper, tucked her feet into her slippers, and padded over to the French doors. Taking a deep anticipatory breath, she flung them open and stepped out onto the balcony. As always, the dawn chill made her catch her breath, but she had done this every morning for as long as she could remember. Today, she would do it for the last time. In the distance, she could hear the faint music of the bells at the university calling the students to their morning lectures. Any other day, Clarice would have watched the valley awaken until she was chilled clear through. But today was a day unlike any other in all her previous eighteen years, and she was in a hurry to meet it.

Breakfast was normally a noisy family affair, but today Clarice saw only three places set at the long oak table. Duke Rupert was seated in his usual place at the head of the table, but the Duchess was seated to his right, instead of at the far end, and a place was set for Clarice on his left.

"Come in, darling," Yetive said encouragingly.

"Where is everyone?" Clarice asked curiously, coming in and taking her seat.

"The ballroom," her father answered, taking a slice of toast from the toast rack and buttering it. "Today *is* your birthday, after all. Had you forgotten?"

"Of course not!" Family tradition was that the birthday child had breakfast alone with Mama and Papa. Even Dantan had had his special day, though then, on his first birthday, he had been much too young to appreciate it.

And Clarice would not be here for his next one.

"I was just so . . ." She stopped. She couldn't say exactly how she felt about leaving Swansgaarde. Preoccupied, absolutely. Nervous? Perhaps. Curious? Daring?

"Excited?" Mama asked.

Clarice smiled gratefully. "Yes. That. I can't wait to begin, but at the same time, it feels almost disloyal to be so happy."

"I shall call for the royal executioner at once," Papa said, helping himself to eggs and sausage from the silver chafing dishes on the table. The Duke had a particularly dry sense of humor and generally cloaked his stronger feelings in it.

"Don't you remember, dear?" Mama replied with a little smile. "Your great-grandfather pensioned the last one off and we haven't had one since."

"Drat," Papa said mildly. "What's the use of being a duke if you can't order anyone beheaded?"

"Oh," Mama said with a saucy wink, "you may *order* it as much as you like. . . ."

Clarice laughed, as she was meant to, at her parents' gentle teasing. Duke Rupert was the mildest of men, preferring a day of fishing on the banks of the Traza to a day of making ducal pronouncements. Clarice knew that other countries were ruled very differently—why, far-off Lochrin, which she had studied in her geography class, had a parliament and a prime minister and hundreds of people who did nothing all day but help Queen Gloriana rule her vast empire.

"So," Papa said. Breakfast was finished and the footmen had come in to clear away the dishes. "Today, Daughter, is your eighteenth birthday. Have you decided where you will go and what you will do?" He steepled his fingers. "Given your chosen 'trade,' I would become a very exclusive instructor, if I were you. I think you would excel at it."

Clarice refrained from making a face. Granted, she probably would make a good instructor—and eventually that might be what she would do. But not before she had a chance to see more of the world!

"I shall seek adventure, of course," Clarice said with a laugh. "Think how disappointed Damaris would be if I said anything else! But the best adventures come when one is not looking for them, so I have it in mind to see something of the world. Besides, the best instructors all have continentwide reputations, and I'm not going to get enough pupils to earn my living without one. I believe even traveling all the way to Lochrin itself will be far less costly than staying quietly in Swansgaarde." *And perhaps adventure will find me.* "It isn't as if I can't do without servants, after all."

This, too, was true. From the time they were fourteen, the princesses were required to spend a month of each year waiting on their sisters, and at sixteen, to spend three months living in the Royal Hunting Lodge without a single servant. It was one thing to be able to shoot a goose—any noble worth his salt could do that. But could he gut and skin it, then cook and serve it?

Duke Rupert's daughters could. And polish a pair of boots, make up a bed, or muck out a stable. It was excellent training, Duke Rupert always said, in case one had to go incognito among someone else's servants—or flee into the wilderness.

Clarice was unsurprised to see her mother nod. "An excellent choice," Yetive said.

"I thought that was what you would decide," the Duke added approvingly—but then, the Duke so trusted his wife's judgment that he was inclined to approve anything she endorsed. "I have made arrangements with my banker in Heimlichstadt for the necessary funds, so remember to see him before you go." While each of them would be expected to earn her own living, each princess would leave Swansgaarde with everything she needed to take up her chosen trade, and enough money to support her for perhaps a year. While it might seem like a great deal of outlay—especially since the entire purpose of this plan was to *not* bankrupt Swansgaarde—even the whole cost of sending twelve princesses forth to seek their fortunes was less than the cost of twelve royal dowries and twelve royal weddings.

The Duke got to his feet; Clarice and the Duchess stood as well. "And I wish you luck, love, and adventure, my darling." He hugged her tightly.

"Adventure most of all," her mother said, putting her arms around Clarice in turn. "And so you don't forget us on all your adventures . . ." The Duchess cocked an eyebrow at her husband.

The Duke reached into his pocket and drew out a small blue box. "What's a birthday without presents?"

Clarice opened the box. Inside, on a bed of royal-blue velvet, lay a golden brooch, perhaps as long as her thumb. Upon it, in silver and blue enamel over gold, were the swans and towers of Swansgaarde. As a proper princess, Clarice had had lessons on heraldry, and she could blazon the device as easily as the chief herald: argent and azure, shield quartered per chevron; center base, a swan swimming, argent; to dexter chief, a tower, argent; to dexter sinister, a mountain peak, argent. The arms were bordered by a double ring of diamonds alternating with pearls, and the back of the brooch was as ornate as the front, its smooth gold etched with an intricate drawing of Castle Swansgaarde. Engraved beneath was the family motto: *Je me promène là où je vais.* The first Prince of Swansgaarde had come from Wauloisene, and Waulois was still the official court language. *"I wander where I will."* *Perhaps it is a good omen.*

"Of course it is bespelled," Mama said. "So long as you have it, you will always be able to find your way back to Swansgaarde."

"I shall wear it always—and think of all of you," Clarice said proudly.

The Temese docks were a noisy, bustling place, even at dawn. Dockers and wharf rats were everywhere, carrying loads almost larger than they were. The air was noisy with whistles and shouts, and ripe with smells—some exotic, some merely foul. At this hour, mist still skirled over the surface of the river, like steam in a cook pot, adding a dreamlike aspect that would disappear as soon as the sun rose higher.

Clarice had been surprised to discover the capital of the Lochrin-Albion Empire was not a coastal city, and that Lochrin was many miles inland. The fountainhead of its vast maritime empire was the river Temese, which flowed through the city itself—or perhaps it was more accurate to say that the sprawling city bordered the Temese. It was the largest city she had yet seen in the half year since she'd left home.

Clarice had been in Albion for a sennight. In that time she had entirely ignored the shops and playhouses, and even the parks and menageries. The docks held her interest, with their bustle of ships coming up the river or setting off down it. She always came to watch the docks at dawn because ships sailed on the ebbing—morning—tide, when the flow of the Temese ran unimpeded toward the sea. Now, one of the ships had cast off, drifting leisurely into midchannel with the aid of a oar-driven towboat. As Clarice watched, someone in the towboat tossed the towrope loose. As the sturdy craft backed nimbly out of the way, the trailing rope was drawn up to the deck of the ship and its sailors hoisted narrow, triangular sails, which quickly caught the morning wind. The ship began moving with slow grandeur down the river.

I want to go wherever she is going, Clarice decided firmly. *Somewhere far from any of the lands I know.*

Lochrin-Albion was a wealthy and far-flung empire. And the cornerstone of that power was thaumaturgy.

Magery was said to have come from Ammon, the son of King Solomon, who had first learned, and then taught, the ways of magic to his people. But when the Age of Exploration dawned, the Cisleithanian and Albionnaise and Wauloisene and Rossiyskayan ships had discovered vast kingdoms that had never heard of King Ammon—Khemetia and Khitai and the lands of Ifrane. From theurgy, magery had become thaumaturgy, a science just like geomancy or astromancy. It had taken centuries and been neither simple nor bloodless—as Clarice knew full well from her lessons in both history and thaumaturgy. But the realization that magic was but one of the natural sciences and not a mysterious indication of divine favor—as Dr. Albertus Karlavaegen was so fond of saying—had laid the foundation of the modern world in which she lived. Thaumaturgy guarded the great empires, armored their soldiers, empowered their physicians, and made travel across the great oceans a commonplace thing.

Thaumaturgical power was the product both of innate gift and long training. It was no more mysterious than skill with a blade, which was also the product of both gift and training, but its products were primarily the purview of the Crown (of whatever land) and the wealthy. Thaumaturgy could heal a wound, cure disease, suspend decay—so that bread or flowers would remain fresh and pristine for months or even decades—and do many other wonderful and miraculous things.

It didn't take any particular magical ability to see magic, Clarice knew, because she certainly didn't have any aptitude for spellcraft. It was more a case of learning to *see*. Dr. Karlavaegen had taught languages and magic to the royal family of Swansgaarde for the past three dukes, and he had told his young charges that most people saw what they expected to see. He intended, so he said, to teach them to see what was really there instead.

Now Clarice watched closely as a lady in satin and velvet stepped from her carriage to ascend the gangplank of one of the merchant ships. The lady's trunks were being hoisted onto the deck in a net, and the lady was accompanied by a small parade of servants: maid, footman, bodyguard. The lady wore the highest of high fashion, with voluminous ground-sweeping skirts over an enormous hoop petticoat—but even through the dockside was far from clean, her skirts remained pristine. And no wonder: the yards of lilac silk had been bespelled—probably on the loom—to repel dirt and stains. It was easy to tell if you knew what you were looking for: the use of thaumaturgy gave its objects a kind of *hyperreality*, so that even at several yards' distance, Clarice could make out every pleat and seam of the garment, and every separate hair of the fur-lined capelet the lady wore over it. Even the rings on her fingers were sharp and distinct, probably bespelled with a Finding Charm so that if they were misplaced—or stolen—they could easily be traced. Such wonders came at a high price, when they could be purchased at all on the open market. Clearly the lady in lilac was a wealthy woman indeed. Wealthy—or well connected.

The lady and her entourage vanished in the direction of the stern of the ship—only the best passenger accommodation would do, clearly—and Clarice's attention was claimed by movement farther along the dock. Another ship was departing. She stepped forward, to the very edge of the quay, hoping to watch the departing vessel as it began its journey.

"Hi! You! Laddie!" An urgent shout caused Clarice to spring backward just in time to escape being flattened by a net full of crates being swung to shore. The man who had shouted at her glared. Then his eyes flicked to the sword belted at her hip and he contented himself with warning her to watch her head.

He would have been demanding to know where my brother or my husband was had I been wearing a dress, Clarice thought smugly to herself.

No one would have recognized the slender, blond-haired, young man standing on the docks as Princess Clarice of Swansgaarde. She had a man's height, and all that had been needed to transform the princess into Mr. Clarence Swann was an artfully cut suit of clothes and a specially made corset that flattened her breasts. The current fashion was for a full-skirted coat that fell to midthigh, and the waistcoat beneath it—worn buttoned up nearly to the throat—was almost as long. Her soft leather riding boots, flaring out at the knee, with their tidy spurs buckled across the instep, and wide-brimmed felt hat—fashionably turned up at three sides, and decorated with a stylish plume—completed her transformation from princess to adventurer. She had played the part of a boy in many of the family's amateur theatricals, and if Mr. Swann seemed to be nothing more than a beardless youth, the rapier he wore at his hip—and his obvious ability to use it—discouraged his fellow travelers from attempting to take advantage of him, a matter she'd proved to her satisfaction many times in the past six months.

Clarice had never regretted her decision to masquerade as a young man, for in all the tales she'd read, it seemed that the princes got to have the adventures while the princesses had to languish in a high tower or a woodland cottage and wait for something exciting to happen. As she'd made her way westward, no one had ever for a moment suspected she was other than what she presented herself as: a young man of good family and modest fortune out to see the world. Though she'd presented herself on several occasions as perfectly ready to duel, her confident assumption of victory had meant there was no opportunity to practice her skills.

Having reached this bustling island at the edge of Eurus, Clarice had been trying to resign herself to retracing her steps. But in the days she had spent watching the passengers board the ships and the ships set sail, Clarice realized she had made up her mind: excitement and adventure were to be found in the New World, and that was where she would seek them.

A quick trip to the portmaster's office and a small gratuity bought her the information that the next three ships sailing to the New World were the *New Prometheus,* the *Cutty Wren,* and the *Asesino.* Another small gratuity bought her advice on how to find their captains.

James Galloway was the first name on her list. *New Prometheus* was a fine new ship, the portmaster's clerk had told her, one that would suit Clarence Swann's needs admirably. Apparently it also suited the needs of a great many other people as well, for Captain Galloway told her regretfully that he had no space for another passenger. She thanked him courteously and proceeded to the next name on her list.

The *Cutty Wren* had a berth available, but she was primarily a courier vessel delivering mail and documents to New Hesperia, and her passengers sacrificed amenities to speed. Aboard her, Clarice would have to share her accommodations with as many as five other passengers. That sort of communal arrangement would make the preservation of her masquerade impossible. Captain Hawthorne was a cheerful man and took no offense at Clarence Swann's desire for more private quarters and suggested several ships that would admirably meet his needs. Unfortunately, none of them was sailing within the next fortnight.

"What of *Asesino*?" she asked. "She is sailing soon and was recommended to me." She was careful to keep her voice slow and low. *A woman speaks quick and high, like the flight of birds,* she reminded herself. *A man speaks with the low, measured bark of a hound on a scent.*

Captain Hawthorne frowned thoughtfully. "She's one of Bellamy's fleet and sails with a hired captain. I have not heard that Sprunt has any fondness for live cargo, begging your pardon, sir, but it will do you no harm to ask. You will find him at the Mandrake; it is his usual tavern. You'd best hurry; *Asesino* sails on the morning tide."

Thanking Captain Hawthorne for his advice, she paid for her shot and left the Mermaid's Locker.

All things in life had a hierarchy, she had discovered on her travels. Sometimes of money, sometimes of birth, and sometimes of inclination. She wondered which of the three was behind Captain Sprunt's choice of drinking establishment, for the Mandrake was clearly several steps below the Mermaid, where her first two prospects had been found.

Sawdust was on the floor, and from the look of it, it had not been swept out recently. The air was thick with the fumes of tobacco and the smell of stale beer. But by now she was no stranger to places even more dire than this; Clarice stepped boldly through the doorway and hailed the barkeep. "I am seeking Captain Samuel Sprunt of the brig *Asesino*. Is he here?"

"Depends on who's asking," the man replied.

"Why, someone who wishes to pay him money, of course," Clarice answered lightly.

That seemed to be the right answer; the barkeep jerked his chin toward the back of the tavern. "Table under the window, and you can tell 'im from me, 'e ain't getting another pitcher until 'e pays for the last three."

This comment did not seem to require an answer, so Clarice merely inclined her head and walked in the direction indicated. The position of the table—and the two empty pitchers upon it— were ample indication she had found the right man.

Samuel Sprunt was not the sort to instantly inspire confidence. In other circumstances, Clarice would have had little hesitation in dismissing him as nothing more than a common seaman, for his clothing was dirty and stained, evincing hard use and little care, and his thinning black hair was pulled back into a tarred rattail as was the curious custom of the sea.

She seated herself without waiting for an invitation, removing her hat and setting it on a portion of the table that, if not clean, was dry.

"Here, now. Who do you think you are?" Sprunt growled. "This is a private table."

"My name is Clarence Swann, and your ship was mentioned to me as one upon which I might purchase passage."

"We're not—"

At that moment the barmaid arrived, asking what the gentleman would have to drink.

"Bring me another pitcher," Sprunt said. "I'm dry as a dog's bone."

"Pockets empty as his dish, too, I'll wager," she said unsympathetically.

"I'll pay." Clarice took a silver quarter-angel from her pocket and set it on the table. It was the smallest coin she had on her, but from the barmaid's expression, it was a great deal larger than what was usually seen here. Sprunt and the barmaid both grabbed for it; the barmaid got there first and whisked it into her apron.

"Won't be a moment, lovey," she said, scooping up the empty pitchers and sauntering off.

"You're mighty free with your coin," Sprunt growled.

"I find it's easier to pay for what I want than to argue about it. More peaceful as well." Clarice put a hand on the hilt of her rapier.

"Well, as I was saying, my lad, normally I don't like to take passengers, but you seem like a good enough sort." She had no trouble deciphering the crafty gleam in Sprunt's eyes: he thought Mr. Clarence Swann was easy prey.

"Your ship is bound for the Hispalides and New Hesperia with a cargo of tea, spices, brandy, and wool. It sails tomorrow. I shall require a private cabin. Do you have one available?"

"Well, as to that, something might be arranged. I'm not sure it'd be up to the standards of such a fine lord as yourself."

Clarice gave him a mocking look and said nothing.

The barmaid returned with a tray that held a pitcher and a pewter tankard. She set the tankard in front of Clarice, leaning low over her to pour it full, then indicated the coins on her tray. "Two spaniels a pitcher. Less you want to pay for what he's already drunk."

It was forty silver angels to a gold angel, and a silver angel was worth forty spaniels. Clarice scooped up all but one coin deftly. "I don't pay for a man's drink unless I'm drinking with him," she said with a smile. She dropped the coins into her pouch and picked up her tankard. Sprunt had already taken possession of the pitcher and filled his own tankard.

"Grasping harpy," he said as the barmaid departed. "Do you travel on business, my lad? *Asesino*'s a good ship—the best—but she's not so fast as some. It might be you wouldn't see Lochrin again for a good half year. Won't your family miss you? A sweetheart, perhaps?"

He is fawning in one breath and bullying the next, like a fearful dog that is too cowardly to bite. And far too interested in her personal life for Clarice's taste.

"That's hardly a matter for your concern," she said repressively. "As it happens, I travel upon a small stipend bequeathed me by my late aunt. Alas, the whole of the principal vanishes into the hands of her lawyers at the moment I breathe my last, so I am determined to live a very long time." The story had served her well in the past, explaining her leisured lifestyle without giving the impression that any great sum of money could be extracted from her. "Now. We were speaking of the availability of a private cabin?"

Sprunt had already drained his tankard and refilled it. "Fine accommodations, fit for a fine lord such as yourself. You'll eat at my own table, same as my officers, and I'll see you dry-shod to the streets of New Hesperia."

"Then all we have to settle is the cost of such fine dining and fine accommodation."

"Five gold angels. Payable in advance, of course." The pitcher was empty once more, and Sprunt flourished it meaningfully in the air.

It wasn't a small sum of money by any means, but it was more or less what Clarice had expected to pay. She dug into her pouch and produced a gold half-angel.

"Take this in token of my desire to sail with you. I shall provide the balance, of course, before we arrive at our destination." Clarice had no intention of paying the whole of Mr. Swann's passage until they were within sight of the Hispalidean Isles, for she had received a quick yet thorough tutorial in the untrustworthiness of hired assistants during her memorable passage through the Borogny Pass.

The coin vanished swiftly.

The barmaid returned, and Captain Sprunt ordered another pitcher. Since he looked prepared to spend the entire day drinking at Mr. Swann's expense, Clarice rose to her feet.

"Then as we are in agreement, I will take my leave. There are a number of errands I must run before we sail."

Before Captain Sprunt could argue—or attempt to try to convince Mr. Swann that as another pitcher had already been ordered, he must pay for it—she collected her hat, bowed, and made her escape. She had nearly reached the door when a young man— clearly a ship's officer—entered.

No greater contrast with the slovenly captain Sprunt could be imagined, for the newcomer's coat and trousers were immaculate, and his soft brown hair was cut short, rather than tarred and pigtailed. Clarice stood aside to let him pass, then lingered in the doorway as he made his way to Captain Sprunt's table. He was roughly her own age, she judged, which was not uncommon, since many seamen of both naval and merchant fleets began their apprenticeships as young as eight. The young man approached Captain Sprunt and bent over to speak to him. Whatever the officer had to say was evidently not to the captain's liking, for apparently it took a good deal of persuasion before Sprunt heaved himself to his feet and stomped out. He attempted to rearrange his features into a pleasant expression as he passed Clarice and was not entirely successful. She watched him depart with mild curiosity, wondering if she should reconsider her choice of ship. A half-angel, even if it was gold, was a small price to pay for avoiding unpleasantness.

"Pardon me, sir, but are you the gentleman who has booked passage aboard the *Asesino*?"

Clarice turned, to find herself face-to-face with the young man who had spoken to the captain.

"I am." She frowned in puzzlement.

He held out his hand. "Then on behalf of *Asesino* and all her crew, I bid you welcome! I am Dominick Moryet, and I have the honor of sailing as her navigator. I should like to—" He broke off, blushing a little. "I should like to ask you not to mind Captain Sprunt's manner overmuch. He has a few odd ways, but he is one of the best captains to be had in all of Albion. And lucky as well—he has twice been boarded by pirates, and yet, as you see, he is still here."

Dominick held out his hand, and Clarice shook it firmly. His grip was strong and warm.

"I am Clarence Swann. He did not look at all pleased to see you."

Dominick grinned. "I came as the bearer of bad news, sir. We sail tomorrow, as you know, and I'm afraid I told him that he must go and buy our cook out of jail, if we are to have any feeding at all."

Clarice smiled back. "I should hate to starve all the way to the Hispalides, for that is a voyage of some weeks, is it not?"

"A month if the winds favor us, two if they do not. Have you sailed before?"

"No great distance," Clarice said dismissively. "Perhaps you will give me some idea of what I might expect—if you are not engaged elsewhere, of course." She gestured toward the table Captain Sprunt had just vacated.

"I should be pleased, Mr. Swann. I am of no use at all until we are at sea—and then, I flatter myself, I am vital. But may I suggest a change of venue? There is a coffeehouse not far from here that I am accustomed to frequent when I am in Lochrin. You might find it agreeable."

"Lead on, Mr. Moryet." Clarice gestured for him to precede her. "I have not been so many days here that I know the city well, and I would be glad of your instruction."

The establishment her new friend led her to was different in every way from the Mandrake. The Golden Wheel had large bow windows and was light and airy. Its bare wooden floor seemed to have been scrubbed within an inch of its life, and the brass footrail of the polished counter gleamed as brightly as new-minted gold.

The atmosphere inside seemed to be almost that of a private club. The tables at the back were all occupied by grave, bespectacled gentlemen who consulted together over stacks of paper and rolls of maps.

"They are assurance agents," Dominick said, noting the direction of her glance. "A ship cannot sail without being indemnified." He directed her to a table at the front. It could seat ten, and two of the chairs were already occupied by a man and a woman a few years older than Dominick, both reading the newspaper. The woman's skin was the same shade as the beverage she drank, its darkness a vivid contrast to the whiteness of her linen collar and russet wool gown.

The first time Clarice had seen someone with skin of such a color had been in Vinarborg, and for a moment she had been astonished, until she realized she was seeing her first Ifranian. Ifrane was a continent so large that all of Eurus could fit into it several times over. Since then she had become accustomed to the sight, for Ifranians lived in every great city of Eurus.

It seemed to be the custom to share tables here, for the woman looked up and smiled, gesturing them to the unoccupied chairs before returning to her reading.

"What do they assure?" Clarice asked as they seated themselves.

"Why, that a cargo and a ship should arrive," Dominick answered, sounding surprised. "What a ship carries is rarely her own property and has been bought and sold long before she leaves port. If she does not arrive—I assure you that is a rare occurrence—someone, the Cornhill Society in this case, must make good the loss."

The server arrived and presented the bill of fare. Clarice discovered that one could order tea or chocolate, call for a pipe of tobacco or a cup with dice, and even request bread, cheese, and oranges.

"There are many who arrive when the Golden Wheel opens her doors in the morning and do not leave until the lamps are lit," Dominick said with a smile. "They would starve were there not food to be had."

"It seems entirely convenient." Clarice ordered chocolate—for it was a luxury she had often missed on her travels—and bread and cheese.

"Enough to share," Dominick said, placing an order for a pot of coffee. "And a bowl of oranges, too. Fresh fruit is the thing I miss most on a long voyage, and I dare say you will, too, for we go weeks without it. You have said this is to be your first time at sea, Mr. Swann?"

"It is, and I look forward to the experience. But you must call me Clarence, Mr. Moryet, if only for introducing me to the pleasures of such a delightful establishment."

"And so I shall, Clarence. And you must call me Dominick," he said charmingly. "For we are no ship of the line, to stand upon formality."

"Dominick," she agreed. "Perhaps you can tell me what I might expect? I have the promise of a private cabin, but I understand *Asesino* does not commonly carry passengers."

"As to that, I cannot say," Dominick answered carelessly, "for this is my first voyage on her as well. But I know her type. She is a good merchant brig. We sail first to Cibola in the Hispalides and then on to New Hesperia, where we shall make port in Manna-hattan. I have been there many times; it is a vast island that lies near to the mainland, and its harbor is excellent."

Clarice repressed a smile. Just as a carpenter might look at a forest and describe it in terms of its excellent timber, she supposed a sailor might view all cities in terms of harborage. "You mentioned that Captain Sprunt has previously been boarded by pirates. Are they common upon this route?"

Their server returned, wheeling a small cart, and set out their food. The oranges were presented in a blue-and-white porcelain bowl that had surely come from Khitai, the bread was fragrant and still warm from the oven, the wedge of cheese still wrapped in its cloth. The fragrance of the coffee nearly made Clarice regret her choice until she picked up the wooden handle of her own pot and tipped it over her cup. The rich scent of the chocolate made her sigh with pleasure.

"I think chocolate is one of the best things to come from New Hesperia," Dominick said with a smile. "It is a great pity, of course, that both chocolate and coffee come from Iberian lands rather than Albionnaise. But you mentioned pirates. Permit me to put your mind at rest. They know that a ship sailing westward is less likely to hold much of value to them, and even on an eastward voyage, they are less likely to trouble a ship of Albion than one of the Hesperian treasure ships. They know our cargo is more likely to be furs, cotton, and sugar, rather than gold, silver, and gems. You may expect an uneventful voyage in both directions."

The war that had swept from Albion to *Rossiyskaya Imperiya* as Cisleithania and the Lochrin-Albion Empire fought for possession of New Hesperia had been fought on every battlefield: land, sea, and air. It had ended almost a generation ago, and then there was peace, but men who had reveled in the freedom and danger of privateering and blockade-running were not inclined to give them up simply because ancient enemies had now become wary allies. They'd struck the colors of the nations that had commissioned them and raised the Red Ensign in their place. And so piracy was something any sea traveler had to be concerned with, much as those on land would guard against bandits and highwaymen. It was possible, she knew, to survive capture and even sail away with one's ship intact, were ship and crew skilled or lucky.

Apparently Captain Sprunt was lucky.

"That is good to know," Clarice answered honestly, for though she sought adventure, she didn't feel she'd be likely to find it at the bottom of the ocean.

"I have been a sailor nearly half my life," Dominick said, "and I have never, I am happy to say, sailed upon a ship that was taken. You are more likely to find yourself a victim of boredom than of buccaneers."

They spoke for some time—about the conditions aboard ship and what she was likely to experience as a passenger. Dominick expressed no doubts that she would receive the private cabin she had specified, but warned her she must not expect it to be spacious: "There is not a great deal of room aboard a ship. Not as you landsfolk reckon it."

Clarice found him easy to talk to, willing not only to answer her questions, but to anticipate them. She told him much the same tale of her history as she had given Sprunt, about journeying to the New World to seek adventure. She added something she had not confided to the captain, that she was eager to increase her reputation so that she could set up an exclusive swordsmanship sallé when her adventures were complete—provided she had not found her fortune in some other way.

"I should think Cibola will suit you admirably, Clarence," Dominick said. "It is very much Iberia in miniature, and I have seen many duels there."

"Perhaps I shall fight some and make my fortune." She smiled, pleased with the success of her masquerade, for though they had spent more than two hours together, Dominick clearly had no clue as to her true gender.

At last he said, with some reluctance, that as they sailed at dawn, he must be off to his guildhouse to settle some necessary matters, and after a gentle wrangle over who was to pay the bill, he rose to go. As he did, Dominick offered one last piece of advice, which turned out to be the most useful of all.

"There is no reason you may not board as soon as you like. Better tonight than in the morning—it will give you time to get settled before we are on our way."

"I thank you, Dominick. I believe I shall do so."

She watched him as he walked from the Golden Wheel, a smile on her face. She liked Dominick Moryet, and a new friend would make the coming voyage even more pleasant.

It was early evening before Clarice returned to the docks. She rode in a carriage this time, for she had left her horse at the Borogynian embassy's stables—the seventeen tiny Borogny Principalities shared, out of convenience and economy, a single ambassador to Queen Gloriana's court—with instructions that it was to be returned to Swansgaarde when convenient. The next messenger to Swansgaarde would be glad to see such a sound beast waiting for him. Perhaps one day she and her faithful companion might meet again.

Her shopping had occupied much more of the afternoon than she had expected it to, but she had listened closely to Dominick's tales of seafaring life and made purchases accordingly. He had said that boredom was a great enemy, so she had purchased a portable chess set, a cunning thing little larger than a book. Each square of the board had a small hole drilled in its center, and each of the pieces had a corresponding peg in its base, for Dominick had said that storms were not uncommon, and that the ship might grow "lively" if it ran into weather. She'd also purchased a small selection of medicinal items that should serve against anything she might reasonably be expected to encounter, since she couldn't risk accepting the ministrations of the ship's doctor.

But her most expensive purchase—and the hardest to find—had been a spellmatch.

The spellmatch was a golden tube about the size and thickness of her longest finger. It was threaded at the middle so that the two halves could be screwed together, and when opened, one half contained a spindle the size and shape of a nail: the match itself. When removed from its case, it would burst into flame, burning until it was closed away again. It would do so forever, if the case was not crushed.

They had been common enough in the castle, and only when she found herself without one had she mourned the lack of its convenience, but she had never had a compelling reason to replace it until now. Clarice possessed, and had often used, humble flint and steel to start a flame. But that not only took time and tinder, but light to see by, three things that were not likely to be easily available on shipboard.

To contain her possessions, she had purchased a sea chest with strong brass strappings and a stout lock. It was broader at the bottom than the top to prevent its toppling over, and its handles were ring shaped, the better to lash it into place against the wall of her cabin against the possibility of heavy seas. The stout leather saddlebags that had previously contained her possessions would hardly be useful at sea, she had discovered: leather tended to mildew.

Her shopping and packing done, she ate a last meal at the inn and settled her account, then, as thoroughly prepared as she could render herself, presented herself at the foot of the *Asesino*'s gangplank.

In the twilight, the ship seemed nearly insubstantial, its great bulk illuminated by nothing more than a few lanterns. No one was in sight, but after a few moments a sailor looked over the side and saw her, and a few minutes later—just as she was wondering if she should have asked the coachman to carry her trunk on board—a man in a hastily donned coat, his hat askew, hurried down the gangplank to greet her.

"Are you Mr. Swann? I am Simon Foster, quartermaster. We do not sail for some hours yet."

"Indeed, I hope you do not, as your captain said you would leave on the morning tide. But Mr. Moryet told me I might board earlier, if I wished to."

"Yes, of course." Mr. Foster inspected her for a moment, clearly assessing her breeding and fortune. Clarice had become accustomed to this in her travels, and she was once again grateful that her dress proclaimed her to be a respectable gentleman of good family. She suspected that if it had not done so, Mr. Foster would have told her to carry her own luggage, but he nodded, as if to himself, then stuck two fingers in his mouth and whistled shrilly.

"Mr. Foster!" the response came from the deck, from the same sailor who had seen her before.

"Here's our passenger, Mr. Swann. Take the gentleman's trunk to his cabin, Neddy, and see him squared away!" Mr. Foster called up.

As Neddy hurried down the gangplank, Clarice saw that he wore only a shirt and breeches unbuttoned at the knee, and his feet were bare. He hefted a corner of the trunk to gauge its weight, then heaved it onto his shoulder with an ease that spoke of long practice and formidable muscles. Clarice followed him up the gangplank and onto the deck. There, Neddy paused to collect another sailor, an Ifranian, garbed in much the same dress as Neddy. The newcomer took up a lantern, then, carrying the chest between them, the pair went through a door and down a narrow flight of steps.

"Mr. Foster called you Neddy," Clarice said, hoping to start a conversation.

"That's right, sir. Ned Hatcliff's my name, and this here is John Tiptree. Best topsail man in the seven seas."

"Mind the ladder, sir," John said, and Clarice was glad of the warning, for the ship's interior was decidedly dark. By the time they stepped out again, they had gone down two decks.

The passageway was narrow, the ceiling so low that the heads of both the seamen nearly grazed it. At a door that seemed identical to all the ones they had already passed, the two men dropped the trunk to the deck. Ned opened the door. "Here you are, sir. Breakfast is at two bells forenoon."

At Clarice's look of incomprehension, both men smiled slightly. "Nine o'clock, as they say on the land. I'll send young Jerrold down to show you to the captain's mess. No fear you won't be awake. We'll be under sail by then."

Ned and John carried the trunk into the cabin. After a bit of awkward shifting about—Clarice had to move up the passageway before they could exit—she was alone. She entered her new accommodations with curiosity.

The cabin was so small it would have been overcrowded with the three of them present. The only illumination came from the lantern John had hung on a hook jutting out from the beam that bisected the ceiling—low enough, Clarice was certain, that she would have to resign herself to banging her head upon it at frequent intervals—and she was once more pleased at her foresight in purchasing the spellmatch. The bunk filled the whole of the wall to her left; to the right, a small table, apparently meant to serve as both desk and table, was built into the bulkhead, its low-backed chair fitting neatly beneath it. Her trunk had been set against the wall opposite the door, and also upon that wall were several pegs, as much of a wardrobe as the cabin possessed. The door was louvered, for which she was grateful, as there was no other means of ventilation.

Clarice latched the door, unbelted her sword and hung it by its belt upon one of the pegs, and seated herself on the edge of her bunk. Ned had seemed to think she would remain here until morning, but until the moment she sat down, she had planned to make her way back up to the deck to see something of her temporary home. Now, she decided it had been a long enough day without finding herself lost in the maze of passages. She pulled off her boots, debated with herself for a moment, then undressed (hanging her hat beside her sword), put on her night-shirt, selected a book on the natural history of the New World from her trunk, and transferred the lantern to a hook at the head of the bed.

Though the ship lay at anchor and had not seemed to be moving when she had gazed at it from the dock, she now sensed a tiny rocking motion and saw that motion reflected in the slight sway of the lantern. It gave her the odd feeling that the ground beneath her had suddenly become strangely insubstantial, though of course there was no ground beneath her now at all. The motion, though new, was not unpleasant, and she read barely a chapter before the day's excitement caught up to her. Blowing out the lantern, she was quickly asleep.

When she came awake in the dark, at first Clarice had no idea where she was. Everything was moving—apparently in several directions at once—and there were loud creaking noises.

She sat up and clutched dizzily at the side of the bed. *Oh,* she realized. *I am on the* Asesino. *She must be under way.*

The ship's motion wasn't extreme, but was enough to make her clutch at handholds as she groped her way to the table. She'd left her satchel there the night before. It took her a few moments to locate the spellmatch, but once she had, in moments the lantern was alight. She hung it back on the hook in the beam.

With the aid of the lantern, she made quick work of dressing. The special corset she wore to disguise her sex flattened her chest appropriately, and once she had laced it firmly into place and donned her shirt, vest, and coat, it was completely invisible.

Once she was dressed, she blew out the lamp and placed her hat firmly upon her head, ready to venture out into the ship.

Enough light came belowdecks for her to easily find her way back to the ladder and up. When she stepped out on the main deck, the sight she beheld caused her breath to catch in wonder for the first time since her last morning at home.

It was barely dawn. The *Asesino* glided down the river toward the sea. The air was filled with the brackish scent of the river and the sharp cleanliness of morning. The ship was not yet under full sail; the mainmast and foremast stood bare, their sails still furled. Wind filled the jibs at the bow. On either bank, Albion swept past, as quickly as if Clarice rode at a gallop. The deck was the highest point in the landscape; she could see for miles. She felt her heartbeat quickening; it was really happening, she was really going to sail to an entirely new world!

"A pretty sight, is it not?" Dominick had reached her side as she gazed entranced. "I love the sea, but I admit the land has its charms—when one is leaving it, anyway."

She turned toward him, smiling. He wore no hat, and his sandy curls danced in the sharp morning breeze. His blue eyes sparkled with excitement that matched her own.

"Oughtn't you be . . . ?" She gestured vaguely toward the bow. The great ships had a language all their own, just as they were worlds all their own, and Clarice was not yet fluent in it.

"At the helm?" Dominick asked merrily. "Mr. Greenwell would have my ears for such presumption. *He* is our helmsman," Dominick added, seeing her look of confusion. "I show him where to go, and he takes us there."

"You are the navigator," she said, remembering.

He nodded, pleased. "I won't have anything to do until we are at sea, and we must go some distance until I am of any use. Past the Scilly Isles at least, and that will be a day or two. Once we are in the Channel, we shall sail down the coast and past Lizard Point. Once we pass the Scillies, we shall be in open sea. I can show you on a map later, if you wish?"

"I should like that." Clarice was about to say more when a series of shrill blasts on a whistle interrupted her.

"We'd best get out of the way," Dominick said, taking her arm. "Come. There's a better view from the poop deck anyway." He gestured toward another set of stairs to her right, and Clarice followed him.

From here, she could look across the whole of the main deck. Its surface seemed oddly cluttered—barrels, crates, coils of rope, a coop full of chickens, and even a pig.

"The chickens are kept for eggs and turned into soup or stew near the voyage's end," Dominick said. "Mr. Squeal is fattened upon offal and garbage until he, too, is ready for the table. It is common practice. The less garbage we toss overboard, the less likely the sharks will follow us."

"I should like to avoid meeting any sharks." Clarice looked out across the deck. It was like a great roofless chamber, and upon it at least two dozen men were engaged in various mysterious tasks. Some seemed merely to be idling, though she doubted they were. They seemed to be drawn from every race that inhabited the globe; among the pale skins of Eurus burnt bronze by tropical suns and ocean wind, she saw coffee-dark Ifranians, honey-brown Caribe, the paler honey of Khemetia. . . .

"The sea is its own nation," Dominick said, accurately interpreting her gaze. "We sail with men born under the suns of a dozen nations, I'll wager."

"But no women?" Clarice asked boldly.

Dominick smiled. "I dare say a woman can be as bold a sailor as any man, but *Asesino* is Albionnaise. Only our naval ships carry female crew. But there. That is what you will be wishing to see," he said, pointing along the length of the deck.

Another raised deck was at the bow, where she could see the great spoked wheel that controlled the ship's rudder. It was at least five feet across, and its wood and brass gleamed in the strengthening light. A man stood before it, his hands upon two of the spokes, his back to them. Mr. Greenwell, she supposed.

"You will soon learn when and how to get out of the way,

Clarence," Dominick said encouragingly. "If you are ever in doubt, simply go to the rail. It is the deck itself which tends to be busy. As you may see for yourself."

He gestured, and she watched as the crew did . . . something . . . with lines and sails. The ship seemed to lunge forward. The swanlike elegance of a schooner under full sail was an illusion that held only at a distance. Up close, one could see that mystery of elegance and grace was bought with backbreaking human effort.

"We shall raise the mainsail when we are in the Channel," Dominick said. "That is something to see, I promise you."

"It must take a very long time to learn all one needs to know," Clarice said slowly. The more she studied it, the more the *Asesino* seemed to her like some vast machine, as if she had somehow found herself within the workings of a great clock.

"All your life. I first went to sea when I was eight, as a cabin boy on my father's ship. And I vow I am still as good a rigger as any soul aboard." He pointed upward, where the great masts seemed to prod the belly of the sky. "*There* is where the best view of all is to be had, a hundred feet above the water," he said fondly. "Perhaps you would like to go aloft with me in a week or so, once you have gotten your sea legs."

Clarice glanced down and realized she was gripping the rail at the edge of the deck. She forced herself to release it. "Perhaps I shall. You will find I am no coward."

"Why, Clarence, you sail with us on a voyage to the ends of the earth! I already consider you the boldest of fellows."

Dominick seemed content to oversee the work on the deck as if *Asesino*'s crew were the subjects of his own private kingdom. By now the sun had risen above the housetops, and they were already near the edges of the city. What had been outlying villages only a century before were being engulfed in the city's expansion, thatch and timber and ancient stone giving way to grand open squares and the palatial town houses of Lochrin's wealthy.

"It is so very large," she said, half to herself. "I think you could set all of Swansgaarde down within this city alone."

Dominick chuckled, recalling her to herself. "It is the greatest city in the world," he said proudly. "And I am delighted to leave it, for it is the most crowded as well."

"Do you—" She broke off at the sound of a bell being rung in a complicated rhythm.

"Five bells. Mr. Emerson may take pity on us and give us a stale crust to gnaw upon until breakfast time. You will do well to ingratiate yourself with him, for you will become tired of salt beef and salt pork, no matter how well they are disguised, and you will long for fresh bread even more than fresh fruit. It is his skill that stands between you and utter weariness of life."

"Mr. Emerson is the ship's cook," Clarice guessed.

"He is indeed, and we shall hope he is a good one. We will know by whether he gives us bread or biscuit. A ship's cook bakes bread when he has the ingredients, and ship's biscuit when he does not—if he has the skill."

"I see this is to be a dire warning of our future. Was he very drunk when Captain Sprunt arrived to collect him?"

"As drunk as a sea cook might be," Dominick said cheerfully. "But that is less important than that he and Mr. Foster do not like one another at all. I suspect he reported Mr. Emerson to the watch so as to get him out of the way while our supplies were being loaded."

"Mr. Foster is . . . ?"

"The quartermaster. He is one of our officers, so you will meet him at breakfast. He is responsible for purchasing every item used on a voyage."

"I believe I made his acquaintance last night. It was he who sent Ned Hatcliff to bring my trunk aboard."

"Which brings me to my next question. I meant to ask you if you found your accommodations satisfactory."

"Quite as small as you promised me, but entirely satisfactory."

Clarice followed Dominick down to the deck. "It does seem to move about a great deal, though."

"I will hope you don't find yourself afflicted with seasickness. But if you do, I believe our surgeon has an excellent cure for the ailment."

"I will hope I don't need it." The alchemist's shop in which Clarice had purchased her spellmatch had also sold talismans against seasickness, and she had thought of buying one. But they were dauntingly expensive, and the proprietor had told her honestly that no one ever died of seasickness, and its effects, though dire, passed within a few days. She hoped she would not regret her decision.

Dominick led her the length of the ship. As they approached the bow, she realized she smelled smoke. "Dominick—the ship is on fire!" she said urgently.

"What—? Oh. No, Clarence, that is merely the galley chimney. Mr. Emerson can hardly be expected to cook without a stove, now, can he?"

Clarice had never considered the matter before. But a kitchen—and a stove—aboard a wooden ship seemed like a recipe for disaster rather than dinner.

"It is entirely safe," Dominick said. "But the moment there is even a chance of bad weather, the galley goes cold, and there is no hot food at all to be had. It is something I hope we avoid."

The ship's galley was beneath the bow. They went down a set of steps—Dominick called it a "ladder." and Clarice made a mental note; everything on a ship seemed to have a different name than it did on the land.

The first thing she noticed was the heat. It was quite as hot as if she stood within the bake ovens she knew must be here, and so dark she could not imagine how anyone could see to do anything.

"Mr. Emerson!" Dominick called out. "I have brought our passenger to see your domain! We are both of us, I assure you, perishing of hunger."

"Perishing, is it? I'll give you perishing, my lads. And put you to honest work, too, see if I don't."

The figure to go with the voice appeared out of the gloom. It was certainly not what Clarice expected. For all that he spoke as if he had never been east of Lochrin, Emmet Emerson had the ink-black skin of a subject of the Wagadu Empire in distant Ifrane. He was short, and as round as he was short, with a fringe of curly, white hair bordering his gleaming scalp. He wore a cloth apron over his shirt and breeches, on which he now wiped his hands. His left leg ended at the knee, and below the joint was a long peg of wood, like a chair leg, held in place with straps. For all his grumbling, he was smiling.

"Admiring my furniture, are you, lad?" he asked Clarice. "Went afoul of a line these ten years gone. Took it right off, clean as any surgeon. Bam!" He clapped his hands together in illustration, and Clarice startled.

"This will be Mr. Swann's first time at sea," Dominick said.

"Then we'd better get some belly-timber into him before we're off the river," Mr. Emerson said firmly. "Here now, Jerrold!" he called behind him. "Bring out one of the fresh loaves and a couple of tankards!"

A moment later a young man appeared. Beneath the sun-bronzing of his skin he would probably be as pale as Mr. Emerson was dark; his eyes were gray and he had a shock of copper-red hair. One hand held a round baker's loaf, while the other held two wooden tankards. "Here, Mr. Emerson. What should I put in the tankards?"

"Why, the finest coffee with cream and sugar," Mr. Emerson said. "What do you think, my fine young cloudwit? It's hot ale I've got a brimful cauldron of."

Taking the loaf from Jerrold's hands, Dominick broke it in half, handed half to Clarice, and explained, "The morning watch is being fed. After that is done, Mr. Emerson will get our breakfasts."

"I see," Clarice said, although she wasn't sure she did.

"Enjoy it while you can," Dominick said, flourishing the bread before taking a hearty bite. "It's the first thing to go."

"There'll be biscuits and pancakes right along," Mr. Emerson said. "Fresh milk, if the nanny cooperates. If she doesn't, it's into the stew with her!" He chuckled at his own wit.

Jerrold returned, carrying the steaming tankards carefully. Clarice was used to the notion of beer served hot, for it had been common enough in the inns at which she had stayed, but any landlord who'd served beer as weak as this would have been soundly thrashed by his customers.

"It is watered, of course," Dominick said, seeing her expression. "You can't ask a man to go up into the rigging drunk."

Mr. Emerson made a rude noise. "Take more than a tankard of beer to get any of those layabouts drunk. It's for the water, same as the rum."

"I see I have much to learn about shipboard life," Clarice said, though she understood this. The water they carried, while drinkable, would be far from fresh in two weeks—or six. The charms to keep it fresh were beyond the budget of any vessels save rich merchantmen—or the Imperial Navy. "I hope you will be willing to instruct me."

"Put you to work, if you aren't careful!" Dominick said, laughing.

They returned their empty tankards to Jerrold and went back up on deck. The Temese, broad even where it flowed through Lochrin, had broadened farther still. The city was long behind them now; all there was to see on either side was rolling green meadows, flocks of sheep, and the occasional distant spire of a village temple. For the first time, Clarice could smell the sea.

"I had thought a ship was like, well, a sort of seagoing inn. Or a company of wagoneers. I mean to say, such an organization as . . . as . . ." She faltered, not quite certain of what she meant to say.

Dominick came instantly to her rescue, though her comparison of the *Asesino* with a tavern or a wagon train made him smile.

He had a dimple in his cheek, Clarice noted absently. "As is not put together from random dock sweepings at the beginning of each voyage!" he said irrepressibly. "But I assure you, dear Clarence, it is often the way of things—we are not the Imperial Navy, and our sailors only sign on for a single voyage at a time, being discharged when the ship reaches her home port. Though I grant you a captain is often the owner of his ship, with his officers taking a share in the profits from a voyage, such ships cannot easily compete with the companies which may own a dozen ships or more."

"So none of you have sailed together before?" It seemed to Clarice a haphazard way to arrange matters, especially if people were to be living in such close quarters for so long, with no way of going elsewhere if one found one disliked one's companions.

"Captain Sprunt has brought with him companions from other voyages, I believe," Dominick said. "Mr. Foster, whom you have met, and our ship's chaplain, Reverend Dobbs. And he has brought his own first mate, Freeman Lee, so you may be sure of a smooth and easy voyage. It is not the custom for a ship's captain to have a great deal to do with the crew directly, for the sake of discipline. It is the first mate who is their ruler when we are at sea. As for the rest of us, the ship's officers, we have come to our berths in the usual fashion: Mr. Greenwell, his apprentice, and I from our respective guildhouses, and Dr. Chapman from the Surgeon's College, I expect."

"Have you no apprentice, Dominick?"

"Captain Sprunt does not choose to sail with a navigator's apprentice, and that is his privilege. He has said there will be little for me to do, for he was once a navigator himself and prefers to take his own sightings, but the assurancemen require every ship to carry a guild navigator, and so here I am."

"And will you someday become a captain as well?"

It was an innocent question, but Dominick's expression darkened and he turned away. "I could not hope for such great fortune," he said briefly. "Come. I will conduct you to the captain's mess."

The captain's mess, when not being used for meals, served as the common room for the ship's officers, and, so Clarice was told, for paying passengers. She was welcome to spend as much of the day here as she chose, but could expect little company until evening, for everyone else had duties to occupy them.

It seemed to her to be a pleasant enough chamber for one in which she was to spend so much of the next six weeks. It ran the full width of the deck, with portholes on each side. The ceiling above her head, and the upper half of the bulkheads, had been given a good coat of limewash, so the whole effect was bright and airy. In addition to a large, round dining table beneath a wheel chandelier that held six oil lamps, the room held a smaller, round table that might seat four, a writing desk, and a sideboard, which flanked a second door—or hatch, as she had learned to call it. The sideboard looked much like the one she had seen in the Swansgaarde kitchens, meant to provide an additional working surface as well as to display fine serving pieces. It did not seem to perform either function here aboard *Asesino*.

Two members of the ship's company were already present when Clarice and Dominick entered.

"Ho, Dickon, are we to go upon the rocks while you stuff yourself like a glutton?" Dominick said. His momentary dark mood, she was relieved to see, had vanished as quickly as it came.

"In the Temese?" Dickon Greenwell answered in mock outrage. He was perhaps a year or two older than Dominick. His black hair was pulled back into a braided pigtail, but not tarred. He wore a coat of green worsted over a loose shirt, but neither weskit, lace, or bands. The *Asesino* seemed to be a somewhat informal ship. "If young Miles can put us aground here, he is a fellow of unsuspected talents! But who is this?"

"This is our passenger, Mr. Clarence Swann." Dominick's tone of voice indicated a *passenger* was an exotic rarity indeed.

"You will lose that fine hat overside the moment we're at sea," the second man present said. "And then your fine white skin will burn red as a boiled ham. Come see me then."

"Dr. Chapman, our ship's surgeon," Dominic said, seating himself, and added, by way of introduction, "He has come to us from the navy."

Dr. Chapman was a spare, sun-bronzed man of an age somewhere between forty and sixty. A life spent at sea made it difficult to tell his age, but his hair (worn sensibly cropped, but somehow still disheveled) was more silver than brown. He was dressed with more formality than either Dominick or Mr. Greenwell; his blue coat had clearly once been a part of a uniform, and the falling bands at his neck were crisply starched, as were the ruffles at his wrists. His weskit was curious, being made of leather rather than cloth, and an ivory-handled walking stick was by his side. Despite his gruff words, his blue eyes held both kindness and humor.

"I am no stranger to wind and weather," Clarice said, a bit tartly. She had been no stranger to the outdoors as a princess of Swansgaarde, and her skin had tanned a good deal since. She sat down between Dominick and Dr. Chapman; no one had said anything about assigned seating.

"To such wind and weather as you will encounter in the Hispalides, you are," Dr. Chapman replied with gloomy relish. "But suit yourself. It would be a great shame to lose such a fine hat, however."

"I shall take care that I do not. It has been my companion on many adventures, and I hope to have its company on many more."

"An adventurer, are you, Mr. Swann?" Dr. Chapman asked. "You will surely find adventures enough in the Hispalides. Why, once, when I was serving aboard the *Megara*—"

He broke off as the hatch opened once more, and the rest of their breakfast companions arrived.

Captain Sprunt she had already met, and she recognized Simon Foster from the previous evening. The other two must be Freeman Lee, and the ship's chaplain, Reverend Dobbs.

It was not hard to tell who was which. The reverend was garbed as if he were on his way to a funeral rather than a breakfast. Coat, breeches, weskit, were all of sober black cloth, as was his flat, wide-brimmed hat. He was of middle years, his complexion sallow with either ill health or dissipation, and his long, narrow face bore an expression of what seemed to be perpetual dissatisfaction. His eyes were dark, and he regarded those already seated with disapproval.

"On your feet for the captain!" his companion boomed out.

Everyone at the table rose quickly. Clarice did as well, removing her hat, though in her case it was merely a matter of courtesy. Freeman Lee's shoulders strained the seams of his faded blue coat. His thin, gray hair was scraped back into the same sort of tarred pigtail as the captain wore, and his nose had been broken several times. His hands were enormous, their knuckles, too, marked with the scars of a number of brawls.

This man is dangerous, she thought, looking at Mr. Lee. She'd learned to rely on her judgment to keep her out of trouble during her travels; she wondered, if she had seen Samuel Sprunt in the company of this group of his officers, if she would have been quite so quick to book her passage.

I suspect Reverend Dobbs of liking his whiskey far too much, and Mr. Lee is a bully. It is too soon to form an opinion of Mr. Foster, but he does not look as if he smiles overmuch.

Still, she told herself consolingly, *Dominick is nice, and I think I shall come to like Dr. Chapman and Mr. Greenwell quite well. And there is Mr. Emerson. . . .*

Everyone seated themselves again, and a moment later the inner door opened. A boy—he could not be more than eight or ten—entered, pushing a small wheeled cart. He began to lay the table for the meal, beginning with Captain Sprunt, and moving clockwise: next Reverend Dobbs, then Dr. Chapman, then Clarice. He wore only a shirt, and trousers instead of breeches, the first she had seen anyone wearing aboard ship. His skin had the paleness of a city-dweller, and his brown hair had escaped its queue, falling in locks about his face.

It did not conceal the large purple bruise upon his cheek.

"How do you fare, David?" Dominick asked quietly when the boy reached him.

"Quite well, thank you, Mr. Moryet," the boy answered softly.

"I thought I'd taught you to stop your chatter," Sprunt barked from across the table, and Clarice saw David flinch.

"Your pardon, Captain, but I asked the boy a question," Dominick answered as David moved on.

"How do you find shipboard life so far, Mr. Swann?" Dr. Chapman asked loudly.

"It is quite interesting," Clarice answered, just as boldly. If being a princess had taught her one thing, it was how to make small talk at a moment's notice—and to take control of a conversation when it suited her. "Far more convenient than traveling by land, for one need not leave one's lodgings to reach one's destination."

"And what is that destination, if I might ask? Permit me to introduce myself: I am the Reverend Philip Dobbs, of the One True Church, and all the souls who sail aboard *Asesino* are in my care."

"It must be a great deal of work for you," Clarice said mildly.

"A congregation of heathens, atheists, and Old Church heretics," Dobbs said darkly. "If sin and evil had worldly weight, this ship would sink before she left the dock."

"How dreadful," Clarice said, though she was one of the Old Church adherents he seemed to dislike. The Old Church and the New Church (the so-called One True Church) had broken more than three hundred years ago over the question of thaumaturgy: the Old Church had once held that only priests could practice what was then called theurgy. The New Church held that thau-maturgy was a mere science, and so priests must not practice it at all. The Old Church now recognized thaumaturgy as a secular science distinct from ecclesiastical theurgy; the New Church did not recognize either theurgy or the Old Church. It had been a long and bitter quarrel, and during the Protectorate, Albion had outlawed all magery entirely.

"But you have not answered my question," Reverend Dobbs repeated—rather rudely, Clarice thought.

"I go to seek my fortune in the New World. I am a swordsmaster by profession."

"A man of blood and violence," Reverend Dobbs said with gloomy satisfaction. "But you are young—there is still time to turn from your sinful path."

"I shall take that under advisement, to be sure."

While Reverend Dobbs had been lecturing her, David had finished laying the table and departed. Now he returned, his cart this time laden with serving dishes. Jerrold, the cook's mate, was with him. This menu was still much what she would have expected at any inn or tavern, but a month from now even the captain's table would lack fresh fruits and vegetables.

Once the dishes were set on the table, Reverend Dobbs embarked upon a lengthy prayer. It was cut short, to Clarice's secret glee, by Captain Sprunt's reaching across the table to help himself to the plate of sausages.

David, Captain Sprunt's cabin boy, remained to act as server. Captain Sprunt ate quickly. It put Clarice in mind of the custom of most royal courts, where no one at the table could continue eating once the ruler had finished. Papa had learned to dawdle outrageously over his food at formal banquets for that very reason, and Clarice hoped ships did not follow the same rules as courts, or she would probably starve. But she saw that Dr. Chapman was in no hurry to finish, even taking a second helping of eggs as the captain drained his tankard a final time and got to his feet.

When he stood, Mr. Lee jumped to his feet as well, and everyone once again followed suit, settling back into their seats a moment later. Lee remained on his feet, hesitated, grabbed up a sausage and a piece of bread from his plate, and followed the captain from the room, chewing as he went.

"What a tiresome custom," Dr. Chapman said, then took a sip of his coffee. "And to think, I thought I had put it behind me forever."

Clarice hid a smile. Mr. Foster simply ignored him. Reverend Dobbs glared at him with outright dislike. Dominick and Mr. Greenwell both looked uncomfortable.

"I suppose the Imperial Navy must have a great many formalities," Clarice said. Anything to break the charged silence.

"Traditions, dear Mr. Swann!" Dr. Chapman said cheerfully. "You may think our navy sails on timber and canvas, but it is tradition that keeps it afloat. Why, you might think yourself in Camelot Palace to see the young officers all lined up in their white gloves and silk stockings awaiting the morning inspection. And woe to him who has tarnished buttons or a run in his stocking, for he is doomed to go hungry. Fine customs—for a ship of war. But that puts me in mind of a time when I was surgeon's mate on the *Stormcrow,* Neptune bless her, and we had just sailed into harbor in Khitai to pull the Great Cham's beard . . ."

The story that followed was as amusing as it was improbable, and soon Dominick and Mr. Greenwell were smiling and exclaiming at each new twist in the tale. Dobbs, seeing nobody was paying attention to his glowering, threw down his napkin and stalked off, leaving his breakfast unfinished. Foster continued to eat as if he were entirely alone, but at least he gave Dr. Chapman the courtesy of a bow when Foster, too, departed.

Dr. Chapman drew his tale to a close as soon as the hatch had closed behind Mr. Foster. "Chaplain!" Dr. Chapman said, nodding toward where Dobbs had sat. "What in the Seven Oceans does a ship need with a chaplain? I ask you."

"I would not expect—" Dominick said, and stopped abruptly.

"But who would lead services if we did not carry one?" Clarice asked.

"Why, the captain, of course," Dr. Chapman said. "Who else?"

Dominick's refusal to finish his sentence suddenly made sense. *He does not wish to criticize the captain, and it seems as unlikely to him as to me that Captain Sprunt has any familiarity at all with the* Prevailing Book of Prayer.

"I suppose he feels it more practical to leave such things to an expert," Dominick said carefully. "And they have sailed together before. Perhaps Reverend Dobbs is his luck."

"Do you think so?" Mr. Greenwell asked. "*Sirocco—Aglaia—Queen Gloriana—Pride of Londinum—Atlantis* . . . Do you suppose Reverend Dobbs was with him on all of them?"

Dominick had told her Captain Sprunt had survived several maritime disasters. These must be the names of the ships involved.

"If he was, then we sail with two lucky men, and that is lucky for us," Dr. Chapman said firmly, and Mr. Greenwell nodded .

"Mr. Swann, I am pleased to have made your acquaintance," he said formally.

"As I am yours, Mr. Greenwell. But you must call me Clarence. For we are to be shipmates."

"And I was churched Richard, but my friends call me Dickon" came the quick reply.

David came forward—he had been standing in the corner so silently Clarice had forgotten he was there—and began to clear away.

"Come down to my surgery when you are done with your duties, young Appleby, and I will give you a liniment for those bruises," Dr. Chapman said gruffly. "I am afraid it is too late to do much for your eye, but a cold compress should take down the swelling a bit."

"I fell, sir," David said, not meeting Dr. Chapman's kindly gaze. "I am not yet used to the motion of a ship at sea."

"Yes," Dr. Chapman said dryly, when David had turned away.

"Sea! We shall reach the Channel in another turn of the glass or so, I wager."

"Sprunt hit him," Clarice said accusingly.

"And that is his affair. You will do nothing to stop it, nor will I," Dr. Chapman said. "Nor will any man aboard this ship. The sea is not the land, Mr. Swann. You must not try to apply your landsman's rules here, or you will come to grief. And now, I shall return to my proper place." Dr. Chapman got stiffly to his feet. "I shall welcome company, should you find yourself at leisure."

"Thank you," Clarice answered. "I am told I shall have nothing *but* leisure."

Dr. Chapman chuckled. "That is why so many seafarers gamble, you know. Sailors are not great readers, and it is a good thing, for if a ship were to carry enough books to serve her crew, there would be no room left for cargo! Do you play cards, by any chance?"

"Indifferently. But I have brought with me a chess set. Do you know the game?"

Dr. Chapman beamed with honest pleasure. "A man after my own heart! Bring your set when you come, and I shall give you a game you will not soon forget!" He moved toward the door, leaning heavily on his cane. His right leg, Clarice noted, was held stiff and did not flex at all.

"I suppose that is my cue to return to my cabin and immerse myself in a book." Clarice was oddly reluctant to leave, but Dominick surely had work to do if she did not. "Though I may bring it back here to read. The light is better."

"It is better still upon deck," Dominick answered. "Nor is there any reason you should not go there. Ah, but I forgot! You must have a care for your hat!"

Clarice retrieved her hat from her knee, where it had rested during the meal, and swatted Dominick with it. "My hat has weathered storms and great battles. It laughs at a mere sea breeze."

"Does it?" Dominick's eyes danced with mirth. "Then perhaps you—and your hat—would like to accompany me on a stroll about the deck?"

"With pleasure," Clarice said instantly. "If your duties permit?"

"What a landlubber you are, Clarence!" he said teasingly. "I am hardly called upon to perform my duties—as you call them—yet. But come, and I will show you how it is done, if you are interested."

"With pleasure!"

After a pause in his cabin to retrieve his instruments—it was no larger than hers, but he shared it with Dickon—they proceeded to the deck, and then to the bow.

"We tell our direction by the compass, and our longitude by means of the chronometer," Dominick said. "It is a good enough instrument, but it is not spellset, so it is not entirely accurate. To discover our latitude, we use this."

He opened the large, flat case of waxed and oiled canvas and drew out something that bore a faint resemblance to a gigantic geographer's compasses. It was a long, straight rod with two smaller rods set into it at right angles. Each of the smaller rods bridged the gap between the main staff with wide, curved pieces of engraved metal that had a sliding marker.

"I have never seen anything like it!" Clarice said.

"Nor would you have—on land. It is a Davy's quadrant. With it, I can tell you the angle of the sun above the horizon. From that, and my tables, I can tell our position. Every place on the surface of the earth can be described as the intersection of two points, its latitude and its longitude. Simple enough to determine ashore—and the craft of a lifetime at sea."

He took up the quadrant, with the largest curve toward him, and held it up in the manner a huntsman would hold a bow. He put his eye to the sliding marker, then sighted along the long axis for a moment. "There is a good deal of finicking involved." He lowered the quadrant with a smile and returned it to its case. "But no matter how good your charts, there are no landmarks to be found at sea."

"Except the land itself."

"And it is easier to miss than you would think. Now come, and we will take our constitutional."

Later, she was to look back upon this as the last moment of unalloyed peace and happiness she was to find upon the *Asesino* and wonder if anything she might have done could have made a difference.

2

THE CRUCIBLE OF TREASON

IT HAD been spring when they sailed from Albion, but their course had taken them far south in the last seven days, and the noon sunlight was hot. During her first memorable night in open sea, Clarice discovered that a ship before the wind never moved just in one direction, but *all* of them, and had spent the following day in her bunk, drinking brandy and nursing a headache and an uncertain stomach. But once that had passed, it had been easy enough to fall into a routine. Breakfast, a stroll about the deck, a few hours spent reading in the common room or playing chess with Dr. Chapman.

More and more she found herself in Dominick's company. He sought her out as often as she looked for him. He said as little as he could when the captain was present, but outside those times, he was a merry and cheerful companion.

Or he had been. At first.

It's amazing, Clarice thought bleakly, *what a difference a week can make.*

She was not quite certain when she noticed the temper of the ship begin to change. A few days out, crewmen who had greeted her with smiles and teasing questions as she walked around the deck began to turn away silently as she approached.

She had already formed the habit of departing the captain's mess as quickly after dinner as she could without giving insult. She knew it was the custom on ships such as these for passengers and those officers who did not have other duties to entertain one another with games or stories each evening after dinner, but Sprunt's malign, toadlike presence made that unthinkable. When the table was cleared and the smoking lamp was lit, Sprunt called immediately for brandy; one such evening spent in his company had been more than enough to make her decide there would not be two.

For a few days, she had spent her mornings or her afternoons in the common room, for it was deserted between meals—at least it had been until the Reverend Dobbs began to make it his special mission to relentlessly seek her out. He seemed to have only two topics of conversation: Mr. Clarence Swann's history, family, upbringing, and prospects, and the sinfulness of everyone who was not an adherent of the New Church.

He also took quite an ungodly interest in her finances, pointing out several times that she had not yet paid the balance of her fare. She ignored such remarks completely, save to say Captain Sprunt would be paid in full before she went ashore. She knew her quarters had been searched more than once in her absence, but a caution learned in months of travel ensured that every item she did not carry upon her person was safely locked in her sea chest. Its stout lock had so far defeated all attempts to force it.

As Dominick grew more silent, she relied more heavily upon Dr. Chapman's company. She had taken to him instantly, sensing in him a kindred spirit, and had spent many hours in the *Asesino*'s surgery playing chess with him. He was an expert player and delighted to find she could give him a good game. In addition to its other charms, the surgery was one of the few places she could be sure neither Sprunt nor Dobbs would come: Dobbs, because of his unwavering enmity to Dr. Chapman; Sprunt, because he, like many others of the crew, believed a place where men had died was unlucky, if not outright haunted.

The surgery had delighted her from the first moment she had seen it, for it was fitted out with the neat complexity of a piece of furniture, its bulkheads fitted with cunning drawers and shelves and a small desk and chair tucked into a corner. Light filled it not merely from its open windows, but through the latticed hatch cover in the ceiling, for the surgery was situated on the deck below the main deck. The center of the room was dominated by a large table, its surface covered with a sheet of tin. Thick, ominous leather straps dangled from its edges at six points, ready to be buckled into place over a struggling patient.

But despite the grim stains and scratches of the operating table, the cabin was oddly cheerful. Its floor was scrubbed white with sand and lye, and it even possessed windows. Dr. Chapman had told her that on the rest of the deck, these were not windows but gunports, for the merchantman carried eight cannon to defend her.

She had retreated once more to its sanctuary, for the mood on deck was ugly. Freeman Lee ruled his kingdom by intimidation and did not hesitate to use his fists. He had called all three watches up on deck—the crew was divided into four parts, one of which was asleep at any given time, so that a portion of the crew were always awake—and had them drilling in the rigging, running up the ropes to the main brace and back down as quickly as they could. Any who slipped or fell or merely begged for a moment's rest could expect to be struck by the first mate's huge fists.

She reached the doorway of the surgery and peered in.

"At his tricks again, is he?" Dr. Chapman said, setting aside the book he had been reading. "Come in. It is just as well for you to be out of sight until he tires of it."

"But it is cruelty!" Clarice burst out. "Why do you not stop it—if Sprunt will not? He beats David for no reason—you saw those new bruises today as clearly as I did—and you say nothing!

All you say is that no one can do anything. I do not believe it. Those men are being mistreated—"

"And a sailor's life is a hard one. There have been no floggings yet, but I expect one soon. Sit down, and I will explain to you why there is nothing to be done but endure."

"What explanation could possibly convince me?" Clarice demanded bitterly. "I thought you a humane man, a man of healing, but—"

"Mutiny," Dr. Chapman said simply. "Now sit, my hot-blooded young fighting cockerel, and learn from one who has stood where you stand now.

"I was twenty-one years of age when I saw my first man flogged. Newly graduated from the Physician's and Surgeon's College, bound to serve ten years in the navy to repay the cost of my education, and surgeon's mate aboard the *Gallowglass*. I thought myself a very fine fellow indeed, ruler of all the ship, for there are some instances in which the ship's surgeon can overrule the captain, and I thought myself above such trifling rules as applied to lesser men. And so, when the captain ordered forty lashes given for a cause I thought unjust, I stepped in front of the first mate and told him not to do it."

"What happened?"

"This." He rose to his feet and removed his coat and weskit, then pulled his shirt from his belt, pulled it up under his arms, and turned his back.

His back was covered with fine white scars.

"I got ten lashes that day for insubordination. The captain was a fair and forgiving man: I could have gotten sixty and a hanging to follow it, for it wasn't insubordination I'd committed, but mutiny."

"Mutiny!" Clarice exclaimed. "But—"

"I had tried to overturn the captain's order." Dr. Chapman tucked his shirt back in and reclothed himself. "That is what mutiny is. It is treason, for the captain of a ship is the monarch of all who sail in her. And so it is penalized as harshly as if someone were to raise his hand against the Queen herself."

"But is there nothing that can be done?"

Dr. Chapman smiled coolly as he turned to the liquor cabinet and pulled out a long, black bottle. Whiskey was both food and medicine aboard ship—and sometimes anesthesia as well. Dr. Chapman had told her many tales of operations he had been forced to perform, both during and after a battle. Without the resources of a land-based hospital, amputation was often the only way to save a sailor's life. He drew the cork and poured a generous measure into each of two silver cups, then handed one to Clarice while he downed the other in a single gulp.

"Nothing," he said, refilling his cup and gesturing for her to drink. "The ship is Samuel Sprunt's to rule over as he sees fit. Have I ever told you of how ships such as these gain their crews?"

Bemused at the abrupt change of subject, Clarice shook her head silently. She raised her cup and sipped its contents.

"Well, the way of it is this. As I have said, the captain's word is law on a ship under sail, and some captains are, let us say, easier to please than others. To sail with an unknown captain is a risk every sailor takes when he signs aboard a ship, as he well knows, and for that reason, your common seaman will sign only with a master he knows, or upon the word of others who know of him. It is common practice for a captain or his first mate to recruit a crew upon the strength of their own reputation. That is, for many, as great an asset as any skill of seamanship. I think you might find, did you care to inquire, that a full third of the crew we set sail with are old cronies of Captain Sprunt or Mr. Freeman. A ship's roster is filled by hearsay and by reputation. To my great regret, I knew few of my shipmates this voyage."

And if word is spread of how Captain Sprunt and his officers behave, no one will sign with them again. That is what he wishes me to understand.

It was poor comfort.

"Do you think Captain Sprunt's employer also takes . . . reputation . . . into account?" Clarice asked carefully.

"I know little of Barnabas Bellamy, who owns the *Asesino*, save that he has half a dozen ships and sails none of them himself. But I promise you: Shipping is a business like any other. A hired captain who can bring a cargo to port at the least cost to the owner is a man who will never lack for employment."

"That sounds ruinous!" Clarice exclaimed. "It is as if—as if a man were to lease a farm and then go traveling, leaving behind himself a hired overseer with orders to squeeze every last penny out of the land!"

"A landsman's simile, but apt," Chapman agreed. "I know not what countinghouse or academy disgorged you, young Mr. Swann, but permit me to enhance your education. A ship owner who has bid upon a lucrative route, such as ours—and been confirmed in its lease by the Sea Lords—must do all within his power to earn back not only the money he has spent upon the bidding, but to take a profit while he can. His ready capital goes into his hulls, and hire-captains sail his ships, for it is more economical to hire a captain at a flat wage and thus retain all the profits of any voyage."

"I can see I would have been well advised to inquire more closely about my ship before I booked passage," Clarice said quietly. But in her heart, she knew it was a lie. Even knowing the difference between a hired captain and a captain-owner, it was Dominick's presence that would have decided her. She could not regret a voyage that had given her the chance to meet him.

A young sailor suddenly appeared in the doorway, panting as if he had been running. *George Lamb*, Clarice thought, recognizing him. *Called Geordie and Lost Lamb by his shipmates*. His lank blond hair was plastered to his skull with sweat, and the fresh red of new sunburn made his eyes startlingly blue.

"Captain says you're to come at once." His eyes were wide—not with exertion, Clarice realized, but with terror. "There's to be discipline."

"Who is it?" Dr. Chapman said, getting to his feet and reaching for his medical bag.

"It's Kayin, sir," Geordie gasped. "Mr. Lee is doing for Kayin Dako."

"Give Captain Sprunt my compliments and tell him I shall be there at once," Dr. Chapman said imperturbably. He turned to Clarice.

"Mr. Swann, I give you this advice in the strongest possible terms. Go to your cabin and stay there."

At the grim note in his voice, she could do nothing but nod.

But if she could escape seeing the first flogging, she was not so lucky again. Sprunt had begun to punish the crew harshly for the tiniest infractions, and Freeman Lee made certain there were plenty of them to be found. No accident or error escaped the most draconian correction.

Today, Kayin Dako was being flogged again, the second time in a week.

Kayin's "crime" had been to leave an empty bucket unattended upon the deck. Geordie had been responsible—he had been holystoning the deck and had gone to put those tools safely out of the way before dipping up a bucket of seawater to finish the patch. But when Freeman Lee demanded to know whom the bucket belonged to, Kayin had stepped forward.

Kayin Dako made Freeman Lee look like a small man. His skin was as black as Mr. Emerson's, and his scalp completely hairless—by design, Clarice suspected, for he was a young man.

Only someone young and strong could survive such treatment.

He smiled mockingly at Freeman Lee as he stripped off his shirt and tossed it aside. The welts of his last flogging were still raised and raw, and his skin glistened with the oil he had used to keep them from sticking to his shirt. He stepped forward and placed his hands at the top corners of an uptilted hatch cover propped against the mainmast. As Mr. Lee stepped forward to tie the hands in place, she saw Kayin's teeth flash whitely as he spoke. She was too far away to hear what was said, but Mr. Lee's face darkened alarmingly, and he reached for the long-tailed cat Mr. Foster handed him with relish.

All the ship's officers were present, save young Miles Oliver, who took the helm. They stood in a line just before the foredeck, a line of silent witnesses. The crew was gathered in the center of the deck, opposite them. Captain Sprunt stood on the foredeck itself.

"You may begin when you are ready, Mr. Lee!" Captain Sprunt called down.

Mr. Lee raised the whip. Clarice turned her back, staring resolutely out to sea, to avoid seeing what was happening, but she couldn't stop the sounds that reached her ears. The dull, remorseless *thwack!* of leather against flesh followed wherever she went. Her gorge rose at the sound, but she didn't dare show it.

To make her avoidance of the sight of the brutal punishment less obvious, Clarice turned her attention to the captain. As always on these occasions, he paced back and forth on the foredeck, to all intents and purposes oblivious of what was being done in his name once it had begun. While he was still as slovenly a figure as he had been at the dockside tavern, once the *Asesino* had reached open sea, a new and incongruous item had been added to his dress: a large pendant on a heavy golden chain.

She hadn't gotten a close look at it, for Sprunt was careful to keep it tucked inside his shirt when he dined with his officers and lone passenger. From a distance it appeared to be a disk of green stone perhaps four inches across, elaborately surmounted by a design in golden metal. While she was utterly at a loss to divine its purpose (clearly it was not for its wearer's beautification), she was certain it was magical, for not only did it closely resemble such items in the Swansgaarde Treasury, its numinous aura of hyperreality would have given away its true nature regardless.

Captain Sprunt had a magical talisman or amulet.

Such items were hardly unknown among seafarers: amulets to

conjure a fair wind, to save their wearer from drowning, to keep a wound from turning foul; talismans to bring luck or a true course, to alert the wearer to the thousand dangers of the high seas. The thing was—Clarice frowned, happy enough to attempt to divert herself with this puzzle—such items were either family heirlooms or the expensive purchases of a wealthy shipowner, and in either case, they were usually displayed proudly. Why did Sprunt conceal his?

A fortnight ago, Clarice might have asked him directly. Now, even though she was hardly likely to become its victim, she wished to do nothing that might provoke Sprunt's increasingly erratic temper.

She closed her eyes briefly as another *thwack!* was followed by a muffled grunt. Behind her, Clarice could hear voices raised in argument—Dominick's and that of the quartermaster, Simon Foster. Mr. Foster had the authority to recommend to the captain that punishment be halted or deferred if it would render a man too injured to work. Each day Dominick argued for mercy, urged Mr. Foster to ask for clemency for the newly chosen victims. Each day Dominick was refused. Once, when his arguments had irritated the captain, Sprunt had threatened to flog him as well—for making noise. All Dominick could do was stand and watch. Even so much as a thrown punch—whether it landed or not—would be considered an act of rebellion. And rebellion—mutiny—was punished by death.

It began to seem to Clarice as if Dominick was the secret target of the captain's punishments, as if his true agenda was to goad Dominick Moryet into rebellion.

At last the sounds of leather on flesh stopped. Even over the other sounds, the murmuring of the men, the creaks and moans of the wooden ship, the singing of the wind in the ropes and the flapping of canvas, Clarice heard the graveyard thud as Mr. Lee dropped the cat-o'-nine-tails to the deck. She willed herself to turn around and look. Even before she had boarded the *Asesino*, her long months of imposture had taught her that she must always appear unmoved by the misfortunes of others if she was to continue her masquerade unsuspected and unmolested.

Dominick was the first to reach Kayin. She saw the flash of a knife blade as he cut loose the cords that bound Kayin's hands to the hatch. Kayin slumped, but caught himself before he fell to his knees.

Geordie Lamb came forward with a bucket of water. Kayin leaned forward as Geordie poured it over his back. Red runnels of water dripped to the deck.

Dominick handed Kayin his shirt. His face was carefully expressionless. The man shrugged and tied it around his waist by the sleeves.

"Is he ready to work, Mr. Foster?" Captain Sprunt called.

"I say he is!" Simon Foster called back.

"Then put him to work!" Sprunt bellowed. "I'll have no slackers aboard my ship!"

Clarice found herself shaking with rage.

This ship was edging, day by day, ever closer to mutiny.

They were three weeks into the voyage now, and Dominick said that if matters continued as they were—by which he meant wind and weather, nothing aboard the ship itself—they might expect to reach Cibola in three more.

Clarice found herself longing for that landfall.

At the beginning of middle watch the ship was as quiet and still as it ever got. Even if most of the crew were asleep, even in the middle of the night men would be standing watch or sometimes even sleeping upon the deck, where the air was fresher and cooler. Clarice had been surprised, a few days into the voyage, to discover that over eighty souls made their home aboard *Asesino*, but there were four watches to man, and in foul weather the whole of the ship's complement might be needed on deck to sail her. Clarice had quickly discovered that Dominick, too, relished these moments of peace and relative privacy.

"I think this is my favorite time of day," Dominick said.

"And yet, it is not day at all," Clarice answered lightly. She stood beside him at the wheel, for she sought him out as often as he did her. Though there were many things he would not—must not—speak of, she drew solace from his company and hoped he found the same in hers.

"Day contains night as well."

"A philosopher's distinction," Clarice scoffed, and saw Dominick smile. Clearly he enjoyed this jousting with words. Well, if that was what he wanted, she would give it to him. Certainly she could contribute little else to his welfare and that of the crew.

"And yet, if I said this were my favorite time of night, that would imply I also had a favorite time of day," he answered. "And this is my favorite time of all, day or night."

"And so you miscall it and hope to escape your just punishment."

Dominick laughed. "Look around you and tell me I am wrong."

It was after midnight, and the waxing moon hung low and golden in the sky before them. The sea was a featureless, black plain that stretched all the way to the low horizon, but above it, the heavens were brilliant and the sky was the deepest possible blue. The night air was cool and soft, streaming over her skin with the motion of *Asesino*'s passage through the night. The familiar song of the ship was joined by the hush of water streaming past the hull, and if the ship's lanterns had been extinguished, Clarice might have fancied herself some magical night bird, flying through the darkness under her own power.

"In truth, I cannot," she admitted.

Dominick chuckled warmly. "We shall make a sailor of you yet, Clarence. It is clear the sea is in your blood, even though you have come to it late indeed."

"If by 'late' you mean I had never even seen it until six months ago, then you are quite right. I never thought I would find anything to compare with the mountains of home, but . . . this is beautiful."

"I've never seen a mountain. At least, not a proper one, with snow on it. Is your home very far away?"

"Very." For just a moment Clarice was filled with such a pang of homesickness it was like a heavy weight in her chest. "You must cross both Wauloisene and Cisleithania before you reach it. As for mountains, the Swanscrown is the highest peak in all the Borogny Mountains and is covered with snow all year round. Some people climb it for sport, but that is dangerous, and I have never done it."

"Swanscrown! What a wonderful name."

"It is said that, long ago, the Swan King had two daughters named Wealth and Victory, who were stolen from him by a wicked sorcerer. He sought all over the world for them, and when he found them, Wealth was a princess, and Victory was a scullery maid. He carried the scullery maid off to his kingdom west of the moon, but her twin sister was betrothed and would not leave her kingdom. For love of her, he watched over her and her descendants in a magic lake high in the mountains, and one day he saw that her kingdom was beset by enemy armies. He dared not leave his kingdom again, but Victory came to him and said, 'Papa, lend me your magic crown, and I will fly to rescue my sister.' And he said, 'I will do so gladly, but if you take it from your head before you return to Swansgaarde, you must remain in swan form forever.' And she promised to remember his words and took his crown and flew far over the mountains to her sister's realm, where she found her sister, and her sister's husband, and their three small children. 'Get upon my back,' Victory said, 'and I will fly you all to safety.' But there were too many of them for her to carry, so Wealth said, 'Loan me our father's crown, Sister, so I may carry my husband to safety.'

"And so she did, and they all flew safely back to Swansgaarde, together. But when they arrived, Wealth discovered the price her sister had paid to save them, and so she, too, chose to remain a swan forever."

"Hard on her husband and children, I should think," Dominick said after a moment. He nodded to Miles, who took the wheel again.

Clarice shrugged. "It is only a fairy tale. They always end sadly. But I have told you a story, and now you must tell me one," she finished quickly.

"I have no head for stories," Dominick protested. "All the stories I know are true ones."

They walked to the railing. Dominick rested his forearms on it, looking down into the sea. Clarice stood beside him.

"Then tell me one of those," Clarice said promptly. "Have you lived in Lochrin all your life?"

Dominick laughed. "Certainly not! I have lived at sea! I've spent very little time on land, truth to tell. I was cabin boy on my father's ship from a very young age. Our housekeeper was glad enough to see the back of me, and I— Well, I was delighted not to be sent off to school. Of course, wouldn't you know that Father had planned for that as well—our purser was a former schoolmaster, and so I got my lessons anyway." He paused, as if stabbed by a sudden thought. "I was to have had the *Sea Sprite* someday," he said softly.

"I was teasing you, Dominick, you know that. You don't have to speak of things you'd rather not talk about," Clarice said quickly.

"But you are my friend," Dominick answered instantly, "and it is an old injury. And I suppose it is rather like one of your fairy tales after all. My father was Daniel Moryet, a captain who sailed all the Seven Oceans. He had grown rich from the sea, and when he took a wife, she sailed with him. But a ship is no place for a woman about to have a child, so when they discovered I was to be born, he bought her a fine house and sailed away again."

As Dominick spoke, he began to walk the length of the deck, and Clarice followed. There was nothing but moonlight to see by, and the deck was far from uncluttered. But Dominick moved across it with graceful sureness, occasionally touching Clarice's arm to guide her around an obstacle.

"And when he returned, there was only I, and my nurse, and the housekeeper, and a stone in the churchyard, for my mother had died giving me life. After that, he lost all taste for the land and sailed away again. We were strangers when we met again; I had not seen him in all my eight years of life. But I grew to love him, as much as I grew to love the sea."

Even in the dimness she could see Dominick smile with love and remembered affection.

"By then he had a fine fleet at his beck, for he had been fortunate in his voyages and spent his wealth to buy ships. He needed someone to look after things while he was at sea, and that was Barnabas Bellamy, who was my father's employee, not his partner. Father was determined that I should have the *Sea Sprite* and the business as well. For his long service, Bellamy was to have a third share in it, enough to make him a wealthy man. So I would learn the skills I would someday need, I was 'prenticed to Mr. Bellamy as soon as I was of an age, and for a long time I spent half the year on the land, and half at sea."

"Then—" Clarice began. Dr. Chapman had said *Asesino* was owned by a Barnabas Bellamy. Surely, if the two were the same, Dominick should be her captain, and not Samuel Sprunt. But before she could ask, Dominick continued his tale.

"I was at my books when we learned that the *Sprite* had been lost with all hands. That was tragedy enough, and Bellamy, whom I still believed to be my friend, told me the sea was the best cure for a wounded heart. He found a berth for me on another of our ships, which sailed within the sennight. And like a fool—I went."

This time Clarice said nothing. She could hear the weary bitterness in his voice, though he did his best to keep his tone light.

"We were gone a year. The navigator took an interest in me and taught me all he knew. When we returned to Albion, I found that the house had been sold, months earlier. So I went to our offices, where I discovered that Barnabas Bellamy had been determined to be my father's sole heir. All they had possessed in common . . . was now his."

"But surely that was not legal!" Clarice burst out. "You could have gone to the courts—claimed your inheritance—"

"Oh, aye." Dominick seated himself on a crate halfway down the deck and motioned for her to join him. "Had I not been a fool a second time. Bellamy assured me it was merely a legal convenience, done because I had been at sea and unavailable, that tomorrow we would go to his lawyer to sign the papers that would make me a full partner in the firm. He told me the sale of the house was an accident made in the settling of the estate. It sounded plausible enough. Then he offered me a drink by way of an apology for all the worry he'd caused me. And I drank, to show I bore him no hard feelings." Dominick laughed shortly, but it was not a happy sound. "The next thing I remember was awakening in the hold of a ship bound for Khitai, press-ganged like a common sailor. It was three long years before I saw Lochrin again, and by then I'd learned better sense. I took my wages and bought my membership in the Navigator's Guild, and lucky I was that Guild-mistress Watson remembered Daniel Moryat's son, for she waived half the fee."

"That was kind of her," Clarice said quietly. Her heart broke for Dominick's recounting of his history, and more, for the way it had been delivered, as if the string of tragedies and disasters had been a matter of no account. The wounds were deep, and the carelessness cloaked true bitterness. Yet she knew that she could not show him any of what she felt. It was, in the most absolute sense of the word, unmanly.

"She was, and is, a good woman, fair and kind. She took me into her own home and gave me a bed, for I had spent every last coin I possessed to gain membership in the guild. And that was my second stroke of fortune, for when she asked my intentions, I told her I meant to confront Bellamy again, this time with the guild at my back. Should a ship be blacklisted by the guild, no navigator will sail upon her, and should any guildsmember be unjustly harmed, the guild will investigate. Thus I thought myself safe from Barnabus Bellamy's clever tricks, for I was no longer alone, you see.

"But that protection had come too late. While I'd been out of the way, he'd married one of the Sea Lords' daughters. Small chance the courts would have given me a fair hearing before, but Bellamy is now the son-in-law of a Sea Lord and very likely in line to be appointed one of them himself as soon as there is a vacancy. I might as well try to overthrow a crowned monarch as go up against him at law."

"But—you said the guild—"

"Would sanction a ship or a captain, yes. If I were flogged, or starved, or forced to labor as a common seaman, or deprived of my wages. But it would not pay the costs of a court case. I might as well throw a thousand golden angels into the Temese and spend them upon a lawyer—if I had them. And I did not. And so I make my own way in the world, and if it is a different one than my father hoped for me, it is still a good one. But what of your story, Clarence? I am certain there is more to it than swan kings and magic crowns."

She could not imagine how he'd survived such disasters and betrayals to become the sweet, generous friend to her that he now was. All she could offer him was her acceptance of his confidence, and what distraction she could provide. So she gathered her wits to recount her own tale. She had perfected her false history during her months of travel, and it came easily to her lips now.

"When I spoke to you of Swansgaarde, I spoke of my home, but it is no mythical land. It is one of a dozen or so tiny principalities in the Borogny Mountains. The people there live by farming and herding. The only town of any size is called Heimlichstadt. It lies a few miles from Castle Swansgaarde and contains a university of some renown. And there my tale begins. I was born within the sound of the great carillon of the university to a prosperous lawyer's clerk."

She had chosen such a background for herself because she'd watched her father preside over the quarterly sessions of the High Court since she was a child, and even in the unlikely event someone questioned her about some obscure point of Swansgaarde law, she could answer with assurance.

"I was the eldest child, and my parents saw to it that I lacked for nothing. I learned to ride, to hunt, and to fence, and for some time my father hoped I would read for the law, to become a clerk, as he was, or perhaps even a lawyer myself. But I had no head for the law, nor for clerking, and so, seeking to broaden my experience, I took to travel. For the last several months I have traveled. I spent nearly two months in Vinarborg before I came to Lochrin. By then I had discovered the trade I wished to follow, one at which I have some skill. But to earn my bread as a master of swords, I need a formidable reputation, a goodly store of tales of my adventures, and a great deal more practical experience. No one will go to a swordsmaster whose expertise, however vast, consists in merely taking lessons himself."

"Well, perhaps you will find what you seek in Cibola, or in Manna-hattan, or in Avignon, or Valois, or in some other city of New Hesperia."

"Perhaps I shall. These are all great ports, I imagine?"

"What sailor knows anything of land save where it meets the water? And now, the hour grows late. I give you good night, friend Clarence."

"And I, you." Clarice got to her feet and swept him an elaborate courtly bow. She was rewarded with a small but genuine smile as Dominick turned away.

Clarice watched him go, feeling troubled.

Suddenly she was glad she had taken the time to send a letter home on her last day in Lochrin. She had made up a packet of her diaries and sent them along with a letter. There was nothing in the diaries her parents might not see, and her letter was meant to be read to everyone. In another month at most they would receive it and know she was safe and well. She could imagine how everyone would respond, from Anise's complaints that she did not include more history of the lands she visited, to Damaris's disappointment that she had not slain at least a dozen highway-men.

As the eldest child of a large family, she had not lacked for playmates and even friends. But for the first time in her life Clarice had a friend whose life was a mystery to her imagination. She could not visualize the street upon which he had once lived, could not imagine the bedroom in which he'd slept, could not consider his days and know them to be similar to her own, for they were not.

Clarice had never been able to give her friendship freely, and certainly not her heart. A ruler could have no favorites, and a princess consort must wed for duty.

Clarence Swann's life, she discovered, was as much a mystery to her as Dominick's was. She wondered how long *Asesino* would remain in Cibola. Perhaps he would show her the island.

The thought of him went down with her into sleep that night.

Clarice woke, as she did each morning, to a soft double tap on her door. Dominick's quarters were nearby, and he rose early to take a dawn sighting—though he'd spoken no more than the truth when he'd said that he would have little to do on this voyage. If she slept through breakfast—and she had, once or twice—nothing was to be had until lunch, and so he'd appointed himself to give her a wake-up call. The days when she might have gone to Mr. Emerson to tease out of him a late breakfast were long gone. The last time she had tried it, Simon Foster had seen her. She'd received a long lecture about the parts of the ship a mere paying passenger was to stay strictly away from. For herself, she didn't mind, but she wished to add no fuel to the feud between Mr. Foster and Mr. Emerson, lest it end in more punishment.

Lighting her lamp, she uncorked a bottle—a former wine bottle, now repurposed—and poured her washbasin full of fresh water.

Giving herself a quick scrub, she toweled herself dry and prepared to dress for the day.

The first item, as always, was the so-necessary corset. Clarice regarded it with a faint regretful sigh. It had seemed so light and comfortable before she'd come on this tropical pleasure cruise!

She dusted the inside of the corset with talc, then slipped it over her head. Once she'd snugged the lacings down tight and tucked them carefully away, she picked up her shirt, sniffing it experimentally.

She wrinkled her nose. *Not too bad,* she decided judiciously. She could pay one of the sailors to wash her clothes—those items that could be washed, at least, for velvets and embroidered satins required expert care—but the washing would be done in salt water, not fresh. She intended to put that off as long as possible.

After the shirt and drawers and breeches came the weskit. The gray linen one was the lightest weight—she would certainly have items more suited to the climate made when they reached Cibola! She picked up the brooch that had been her parents' parting gift to her and kissed it, just as she did each morning, before pinning it carefully to the inside of her weskit. She did not wish to display it openly, but she wanted it close.

She considered her choices, thinking with momentary longing of the chests and wardrobes full of gowns from which Princess Clarice could have chosen, before selecting the mustard-colored broadcloth. Young Mr. Swann traveled light, as befit an adventurer: the mustard, a blue wool, and the green velvet were the only coats she had; and the green velvet was . . . rather more formal than she thought breakfast warranted, especially on this ship.

She took down last night's stockings from the peg over which she'd hung them to dry—those, at least, she had been able to rinse each night in her washing water—and tucked them into her trunk, selecting a fresh pair. She pulled them on, buttoned the legs of her breeches to keep them from rolling down again, and pulled on her boots. The transformation from Princess Clarice to Clarence Swann was complete in all but a few incidentals. She brushed out her hair, tied it back with a broad length of black ribbon, and shrugged into her coat. Fortunately, the style for men had not required her to cut her hair. As she did every morning, she hesitated over the swordbelt and baldric before slipping the baldric free of the belt and buckling the belt into place. The baldric was ornamental—more advertisement that its wearer was armed—and under other circumstances, she might have left the items locked in her trunk.

On this ship, she thought it was a good idea to remind her companions that she could defend herself.

This far into the voyage, breakfast had become oat porridge, sausages, and stewed fruit. If it was monotonous fare, it was hearty and filling, and both the coffee and the tea that were served at breakfast were hot and strong. She contented herself with coffee and porridge this morning, for it was already sultry, and the thought of a heavy meal was intolerable.

David moved around the table like a silent ghost. No matter how often Dr. Chapman warned her there was nothing she—or any of them—could do, the sight of the cowering, terrified child filled her with anger. Dominick had said that the boy's family had undoubtedly signed an indenture with Captain Sprunt—if he had any family at all.

It was the only ray of hope, for Clarice well knew Captain Sprunt's love of gold. An angel or two, she was certain, would be enough to pay him to break the indenture as soon as they made port—and she would be certain the entire matter was overseen by a lawyer *she* chose. After that . . . Well, that could be decided once she'd freed him.

David filled Sprunt's tankard, careful not to spill a precious drop. He began to back carefully away. The pitcher was nearly full, and heavy, and all his attention was focused on it. Suddenly he went sprawling backward. The pitcher slipped from his hands and fell to the deck.

Captain Sprunt leaped to his feet, roaring in fury. "Clumsy half-wit guttersnipe! That's a pitcher of beer wasted, and the deck filthy!"

Freeman Lee folded his hands ostentatiously in front of him.

He tripped David! He did it on purpose!

Her hand went to the hilt of her sword, and she began to rise to her feet.

Dr. Chapman's hand came down on her forearm, his grip like iron, forcing her back into her chair.

"But, Captain, sir, I—" David said, his voice shaking with terror.

"Clumsy, wasteful, and insubordinate!" Captain Sprunt snarled. "A taste of the cat will cure that—will it not, Mr. Lee?"

"Indeed it will, sir." Mr. Lee grinned nastily.

Clarice opened her mouth to protest. The hand upon her arm tightened, the grip punishingly strong. She looked toward Dominick. His face was white with rage, his jaw set.

"I have found it to be a sovereign remedy for many evils that afflict the spirit of young boys," Reverend Dobbs said fulsomely. "Beat them regularly, and they are all the better for it. Do you not agree, Mr. Moryet? Mr. Greenwell? Mr. Swann?"

Clarice swallowed hard. "It is not the custom where I come from to beat children." She kept her voice level with an effort.

"Then perhaps you will learn something of value," Dobbs answered gleefully. "Dr. Chapman? I am certain *you* will agree with me."

"My dear Reverend Dobbs," Dr. Chapman answered tonelessly. "How can you ever be in any doubt about the extent with which I agree with you?"

"Get that mess cleaned up," Captain Sprunt said to David. "And then bring a fresh pitcher."

Neither Dominick nor Dickon had any further appetite for their breakfasts. Neither did Clarice, but she was the only one who could possibly leave before the captain did, and she did not wish to desert her companions—or to give Sprunt more fuel for his anger. He had not yet decreed the number of lashes. Sixty could kill a grown man. David Appleby was just ten years old.

After breakfast, Mr. Lee mustered the crew to witness punishment. Clarice would have gladly been anywhere else, but Dobbs stuck to her side like a shadow. She could not slip away unnoticed, and she was certain Dobbs would call her departure to Sprunt's attention.

Kayin Dako led the terrified boy out of the ranks, speaking gently to him as he did. He helped David remove his shirt—the boy would have forgotten to otherwise—and tied his wrists to the edges of the hatch cover. Bruises were clearly visible along his ribs.

Mr. Lee took up the cat and gave it an experimental swish. Clarice saw David flinch, his eyes wide and staring with terror.

"You may begin at your pleasure, Mr. Lee!" Captain Sprunt called down.

"With pleasure, Captain!" Lee called back. "What is to be the count?"

"Why, that's correct, Mr. Lee; we had not decided that, had we?" Captain Sprunt said cheerfully. "Well, now. What should it be?"

He is playing with David, as a cat with a mouse! Clarice's fury was so great it nearly choked her.

"I should say—purely as a medical man, of course—that your lesson will be well taught with five strokes of the cat." Dr. Chapman managed to sound—and look—completely indifferent. "Naturally, sir, the matter is entirely in your hands."

There was a moment of breathless silence, and Clarice saw Sprunt about to agree.

"Five lashes!" Reverend Dobbs exclaimed, turning ostentatiously to Clarice. "Why, my dear Mr. Swann, that will barely be enough to tickle!"

He pretends to speak to me, knowing Sprunt can hear every word! The knuckles of her hand gripping the hilt of her rapier ached with the effort it took not to draw it.

"Ten lashes, Mr. Lee!" Samuel Sprunt bellowed.

On the second stroke of the whip, David Appleby screamed, high and shrill.

On the fifth, he stopped screaming.

Dominick was arguing furiously with Mr. Foster. Clarice saw Foster smile mockingly as he pulled his sleeve free of Dominick's impassioned grip, shaking his head.

The beating went on. Six—eight—ten.

It was done.

Blood dripped from the boy's back where the lash had cut. The welts were already rising, darkly purple with congested blood. Dominick motioned to Kayin, who came forward and held David Appleby upright as Dominick cut the ties that had bound him to the hatch cover. David's arms dropped limply to his sides. Kayin looked to Dominick, unspeaking.

"Is he ready to work, Mr. Foster?" Captain Sprunt called.

Mr. Foster picked up the bucket of seawater that stood ready. "Will be in just a moment, Captain!" he called back. "Stand aside, you Ifrane lout!"

Clarice saw Dominick nod fractionally. Kayin laid David, face-down, upon the deck and stood back, picking up David's discarded shirt as he did.

The seawater struck David squarely between the shoulder blades. He did not move.

But Dr. Chapman did. He stumped forward across the deck, his cane thumping sharply on the planks. She saw him motion to Dominick, who lifted the boy to his feet. "I shall have him back in service as quickly as possible, Captain," Dr. Chapman called over his shoulder.

As they walked away, Clarice saw Dominick turn a look of burning hatred on Simon Foster.

Mr. Foster saw it, too.

When Clarice had finally been able to escape Dobbs and visit the surgery, she found Dr. Chapman sitting with his patient. A pallet of blankets had turned the operating table to a makeshift bed. David lay on his stomach, bandaged from armpits to hips, still unconscious. The bandages were spotted with scarlet.

"Opium," Dr. Chapman said simply. "And I wish, by Neptune's beard, I could keep him insensible all the way to Cibola."

"Is it very bad?" Clarice asked softly.

"Bad enough. Ten lashes for a man is an uncomfortable business—and as you know, I speak from experience—but it is laid over a man's bone and muscle. Young Appleby was laid open to bone. It will be a miracle if his wounds do not turn septic. He is already running a fever."

"You did as much as you could," Clarice said quietly.

"Oh, aye," Dr. Chapman said irritably. "But did I do as much as I should have?"

"How is he, Clarence? Pray, tell me the truth."

Dominick had met her at the ladder to the deck. After the events of that terrible day, Clarice had been counting the hours until she could slip out of her cabin to seek out Dominick. His company was the only bright spot in an increasingly dark voyage.

"I will tell you what I know. It is not much. Or good."

She moved to step past him, but he put a hand on her arm. "I do not know if is safe for you to be seen in my company. I am a marked man now."

Clarice remembered the expression on Simon Foster's face and repressed a shudder. "But they cannot force you to . . . commit a crime? Can they?"

"No," Dominick said in a low voice. "But if they say I have . . .
There is little I can do. And soon I— But we were speaking of
David," he said firmly.

Clarice told him what Dr. Chapman had said.

Dominick looked away to hide his expression. "If that boy
dies, it will be murder," he said in a low voice. "And I swear I will
see justice done." He took a deep breath, obviously trying to
compose himself. "And now I bid you good night, my dear friend.
As good as it can be under such circumstances."

He turned and walked quickly away, clearly intent upon leaving her behind.

Clarice stared after him for a few moments, then walked to the
rail as if she had come topside for nothing more than a breath
of air.

It was all she could do for him.

It had been a week since David Appleby's flogging, and the boy
was still under Dr. Chapman's care. His wounds had, as Dr.
Chapman had feared, turned septic, and David raved and muttered with fever.

Clarice had offered up her few nursing skills, bathing David in
hopes of reducing the fever and helping Dr. Chapman to change
his bandages, but neither of them could do much to combat the
infection that ravaged the boy's starved and mistreated body. Dr.
Chapman did not want to say so, but Clarice could read the truth
in his face. It was only a matter of time.

The tension Clarice felt was well-nigh unbearable; she could
not imagine what it was like for the crew. Dobbs moved constantly among them; Clarice had overheard him, time and again,
counseling the *Asesino*'s crew to bear their fate with scriptural
meekness: "—for the sons of Ammon have no part in the theurgy
which is the birthright of the lastborn and must resign themselves
to servitude." Thanks to Dr. Karlavaegen, Clarice could have
capped that verse with half a dozen about mercy being the duty

of princes, but it would have done little good. Floggings had become constant, and Sprunt had ordered half rations until further notice as an additional disciplinary measure. But neither floggings nor near starvation could stop the crew from whispering together. Just this morning, Sprunt had ordered that three or more sailors gathered together on deck would be considered insubordinate and disciplined accordingly.

He could not stop them from gathering together belowdecks or talking together there. But he could have them beaten if they did. No one knew who would report a conversation to Mr. Lee and who wouldn't.

Gone were the days when she could spend a few precious nighttime hours on deck with Dominick. She had not dared to seek him out since the day David was flogged. It was too risky. A walk in the night air meant a risk of being drawn into—or overhearing—the wrong sort of conversation. She was terrified that she would be asked by Sprunt or his cronies to report any mutinous overtures made to her—and she did not think any of them would believe her when she said she'd heard nothing. Guilt was not necessary. Only the appearance of guilt.

And so she had taken to a self-imposed imprisonment in her cabin, where she counted the days until the *Asesino* might reach landfall. And with each passing hour, *Asesino* slipped closer to open mutiny.

Tonight, as usual, she left the captain's mess the moment she could. Even the isolation of her cabin, cramped and stuffy as it was, was preferable. She latched her door—there was no lock—and wrote a few lines in her diary, but it was hard to come up with anything that was both true and that she would ever want her parents to read. So she undressed and resolutely composed herself for sleep. Tomorrow would be no better than today, but it would bring them one day closer to landfall.

But sleep, it seemed, was to be presented tonight with an intermission.

She sat up, straining to discern what had wakened her. She wasn't sure how long she'd slept. The hiss of the water against the hull, the rhythmic creak of a hull under sail, were all familiar sounds. But there was more, some discordant element in the customary symphony. . . .

She heard the distant ring of steel on steel.

Her first thought was pirates. But a pirate ship wasn't a troop of horse, and the open ocean offered no form of concealment—to close with the *Asesino* it would have needed to chase them for hours or even days, and the ship's lookout would have seen them.

No, the violence on *Asesino* came from within. Mutiny. Everyone involved would be hanged—or worse.

Dominick! He will be with them!

Without thought Clarice sprang to her feet, fumbling in the little desk for her spellmatch. In the lantern's dim gleam she dressed quickly, yanking the laces of the corset tight, flinging on a coat chosen at random, her ear tuned to the growing discord of armed combat above. She buckled her swordbelt over her coat and seated her rapier firmly in its sheath.

The passage to the deck was both deserted and darker than usual: Clarice realized that several of the lanterns in the corridor had gone out for lack of oil, apparently abandoned—or sabotaged—by whichever crewman was in charge of filling them. As she climbed the ladder to the main deck, the sound of steel on steel grew louder, and she caught the scent of blood on the night wind. The smell sent her up the last steps of the ladder and through the hatch before she could think further.

The forecastle was ablaze with light. She could see men—dark, anonymous figures at this distance—holding torches. The torchlight flashed from the drawn blades, though she couldn't see who was fighting. The only good thing was that nobody on the *Asesino* was paying any attention to anything but the scene before them.

She cut sharply to the left as she approached the foredeck. Men lined the rail and stood on the ladder and she couldn't get past them without being seen—or stopped. Thankfully the construction of the ship left her many other routes to the upper deck. First to the railing, where she balanced for a precarious moment before springing upward. Then she clutched at the spindles of the half rail, swinging her body back and forth until she could find purchase for her feet. She didn't know what it was, but it was enough to allow her to make the last lunge that took her over the foredeck rail.

A sight from her nightmares greeted her gaze. The deck around the wheel was choked with the wounded and the dead. Captain Sprunt stood with a cutlass in his hand. Its blade was dark and wet. Lee, Foster, and Dobbs stood at his back—Lee with an enormous bludgeon, Foster with a musket, and the reverend with a saber. The three of them held the rest of the mutineers at bay as Sprunt closed with his prey. Of all of them, Clarice recognized only Kayin Dako, Emmet Emerson, and Dr. Chapman. Dr. Chapman held his arm as if it was broken, and his face was badly bruised. Most of the others were in similar shape.

A spreading stain was at Dominick's left shoulder where the heavy cutlass had struck him. His face was white and his eyes glittered with exhaustion and pain. Sprunt loomed over him like a great bear, his piggish eyes gleaming with triumph and bloodlust. He had the advantages of size, reach—and skill, for even in the split-second glimpse Clarice had gotten as she vaulted the railing, it was plain to see that Dominick was no swordsman. Sprunt must know it. If Dominick was still alive and so lightly wounded, it was clear the captain had merely been playing with him, as a cat would a mouse.

And now, as a cat with a mouse, he meant to deliver the coup de grâce.

Clarice's feet skidded on the deck as she sprang into the little space between them. Sprunt sprang backward as she drew her sword.

"This is not your fight, Swann!" he shouted. "Or do you cast your lot with the mutineers?"

I have no choice, Clarice thought. "Shut up and fight!" she snarled, lashing out at him with her sword.

He laughed—a wordless shout of rage—and raised his own blade.

The world narrowed to the clash of blades. Sprunt had strength and reach and the heavier blade; Clarice dared not block his attacks directly, for she risked her rapier being broken by the bludgeoning weight of the heavier blade. But she had speed and skill, a skill honed by a master swordsman over her whole life. And not just any master, but one who taught the skills of the street brawler along with those of court fencing—and the means of countering the former with the latter.

Again and again she slipped away from Sprunt's attacks—out of reach, or merely dodging the few inches that led him to cleave air instead of flesh. She shut out the sounds around her. Her heart raced, blood roared in her ears, her spine was etched with chill— and she ignored all these symptoms of the deadly peril she was in. There was nothing in the world but this deadly midnight dance on a bloodstained deck. Parry, attack, riposte, remise. Classical training and deep knowledge against back-alley brawling and brute strength.

Slowly, Clarice saw the way to win. Sprunt was a thug and a bully, relying on terror and main force to gain him the victory in any encounter. He knew nothing of pacing himself, of blade-work that was as much science as art. She did not know how many he had slain already tonight, but now he was tiring. And this opponent was not afraid.

It seemed to take hours before he gave her the opening she sought. Hours of stamping her boots against the deck as she danced out of reach, hours of measuring success or failure by the ethereal ting of steel against steel, hours of slitting her eyes against the blaze of torchlight and hoping she would see the next attack as it came. In reality, of course, bare minutes—if that—had passed.

Clarice stepped back, as if seeking a way to flee, and dropped her guard. Sprunt roared out his triumph and lunged for her, blade held high.

And she struck upward, the sharpened point of her rapier shearing through his filthy shirt, and transfixing his heart.

Only because the disengagement that followed that stop-thrust had been drilled into her, month after month, in the sallé at Swansgaarde by the exacting von Karstetter, did she jerk her sword free and step back, automatically falling into first position once more. With an effort, she stopped herself from reflexively raising her sword in salute to her opponent. This was no salon bout, where the loser would cheer the winner's skill and they would shake hands afterward. Her opponent was dead and only now realizing it.

Sprunt crashed to his knees and fell forward, a look of astonishment still on his face.

She looked around wildly as the night was split by the roar of the musket.

"Captain Sprunt is dead!" she heard someone shout. "The ship is ours! Throw down your weapons and you will not be harmed!"

So I am a mutineer now, Clarice thought numbly. *Whatever shall I tell Mama and Papa?*

All around her, from every corner of the captured ship, sailors began to cheer.

3

~

A Pirate's Life for Me

THE SUN that rose that day illuminated a far different ship from that over which it had set the day before. Clarice sat down on the nearest barrel and sighed in weariness. It had been a long night.

The *Asesino* carried two ship's boats, used to reach shore when the ship dropped anchor some distance from land or dock. Each boat could carry twenty people in the usual way of things, of which twelve to fourteen were the rowers needed to propel the heavy, narrow hull through surf or rough water.

Today the boat being lowered over the side held over thirty people. It might even hold the long oars that propelled it. But it was being launched into the open sea.

"Ship's boat away!" Dominick shouted.

"Ship's boat away!" Kayin Dako echoed.

"Damn you, Moryet—this is murder and you know it!" Simon Foster cried.

"You had your chance!" Kayin shouted back. "It is a better one than Sprunt gave any of us!"

Dominick, stripped to the waist, his shoulder bandaged, watched as a dozen sailors began to lower the jolly boat to the sea. The boat's passengers seemed resigned to their fate now; they sat quietly as the boat began to descend.

"I imagine this was not what you expected when you booked passage on our fine ship, is it, Mr. Swann?" the Reverend Dobbs said with a meaningful smirk.

Dobbs had been firmly in Sprunt's camp. He'd fought at Sprunt's side last night in a most unchurchly way, but now he wouldn't share the fate of the captain's cronies. His vows protected him from retribution.

And what danger can one man present to us? Aside from getting all of us hanged the moment we make port and set him ashore . . .

"I did not think I would be sailing with a monster, it is true," she said, looking up to meet his eyes. She had learned only a few hours ago that David Appleby had died last night of his injuries. His death had been the spark laid to the tinder of unrest.

"I doubt you are in any position to judge, young man," Dobbs said repressively. The ropes creaked as the boat began its descent toward the surface of the ocean. Dobbs glanced toward it. "Their fate is hard, but it may yet be sweeter than what awaits these wayward souls."

"If it's as sweet as all that, you've still got time to join them," Clarice pointed out acerbically.

Her remark was received with a tiny bow of acknowledgment. "I believe I may do more good here," Dobbs murmured. "And there is still the last office I must perform for the victims of these misguided men. And of yourself, of course," he added with a malicious glitter in his dark eyes.

Clarice kept her face smooth with an effort. Even though she knew she had made her choice when she entered the fight, the awful finality of Sprunt's death was something she saw afresh every time she closed her eyes.

"Of course," Clarice echoed, rising to her feet.

She glanced up the deck, to where the bodies of the dead lay, shrouded and anonymous. They had barely begun to stiffen and certainly had not had time to putrefy, but she could have sworn she caught a whiff of charnel odor from them, and she repressed a shudder. There was no place to bury them save in the sea, but Dominick had said they would wait until the jolly boat was well away before putting the bodies overboard. The wait would give its passengers as good a chance as possible, though their only true chance for life was to be rescued by another passing ship—an unlikely possibility.

And if they were, their rescue would seal *Asesino*'s doom.

As he hauled to lower the boat, Kayin began to sing. First one voice took up the song, then another, until at last all of them were singing. The tune, in despondent antiphon, wafted up from the lowering boat:

> *Oh, the times was hard and the wages low*
> *Leave her, Enoch, leave her*
> *And the grub was bad and the gales did blow*
> *And it's time for us to leave her*

> *Leave her, Enoch, leave her*
> *Oh, leave her, Enoch, leave her*
> *For the voyage is done and the winds do blow*
> *And it's time for us to leave her . . .*

Clarice had heard the mournful song, and others like it, many times in the past several weeks. A few moments later, the song broke off and the sailors released the ropes. Far below, she heard a splash as the jolly boat fell the last few feet to the sea. A few moments more, and the work party began drawing the ropes up again.

"*Set sail!*" Dominick shouted, and the etiolated crew sprang to obey. All around her, the *Asesino* exploded with mysterious calls and orders transformed into the rhythmic squeal and creak of ropes drawn through pulleys, the snap and rattle of canvas as it opened and caught the wind. The great white sails filled, making the

Asesino look almost unbalanced, and suddenly Clarice felt the ship come alive as it leaned into the wind. Soon the jolly boat became an anonymous speck in the distance.

The sea was wide.

"I do hope Mr. Moryet doesn't have ambitions of becoming captain," Reverend Dobbs murmured. "He is far too young to be selected for the post."

"I am certain that is a decision that does not rest with either you or I," Clarice said repressively, deliberately turning her back on Dobbs.

Dominick was one of only three ship's officers who had not been set adrift in the aftermath of the mutiny. But the *Asesino*'s new captain would be chosen by a vote among the crew, and only one sort of ship on all the wide ocean chose its captain by election.

A pirate ship.

She returned to her cabin to clean her sword and to make herself more presentable. The ship was restoring itself to its familiar routine. Only a few last tasks remained.

She shrugged off her coat, noted that the shirt beneath was blood spotted, and tossed it away with a weary sigh. She took out a cloth and a bottle of oil, then sat down to clean her sword. When it was gleaming once more, she tucked away the cleaning supplies, washed her face and hands, and brushed her hair out thoroughly—the sea wind had tangled it—before tying it back in its customary ribbon once more.

Once she was dressed, she searched among her belongings until she found a black kerchief. She folded it into a mourning band and tie it firmly around her left arm. She had not liked Captain Sprunt, but that did not mean he deserved to be dishonored in death.

Her last act before she left the cabin was to place her rapier carefully into her sea chest and lock it away.

At a little before noon she returned to the deck. If she'd been asked a month ago, she would have said that seamen, deprived of their master, would quickly devolve into idleness, just as any laborer deprived of an overseer might. Yet everywhere around her, Clarice saw evidence of industry, from sailors scrubbing down the deck with buckets of salt water, to the pennon of smoke lacing backward from the chimney of the galley. She supposed the difference between this and some farm somewhere was that if the farmhand idled, the crop wouldn't flourish—but if the sailor idled, the very thing that preserved his life upon the bosom of the sea would vanish beneath it.

She glanced around herself for people she knew. Dr. Chapman stood at the rail, looking out to sea; he wore his coat capelike over his shoulders, his broken arm thoroughly strapped and in a sling. Dominick (now wearing a shirt) stood beside Dickon at the helm, taking a sighting. Everyone was going about his business in a perfectly normal way.

It was Dobbs's attempt to be furtive that drew her attention.

When she saw him kneel beside the shroud-wrapped bodies, she thought at first he was praying over the dead and wondered why, for he could gain nothing by doing so. Then she saw him surreptitiously draw a tiny penknife from his pocket and begin to cut through the stitches on the topmost shroud.

Clarice moved toward him slowly and carefully, taking as much shelter as she could to keep him from noticing her advance. But Dobbs was intent upon his task. Finally, when he had opened the shroud, Clarice saw why. The body was Sprunt's, and Dobbs's goal had been the curious pendant Captain Sprunt wore. She watched as he eased the neck chain free. Whatever magic the pendant possessed, it had not been linked to Sprunt's life, for the green-and-gold disk was as sorcerously vivid as ever.

Dobbs had folded the shroud back into place and was just about to tuck the pendant into his pocket when Clarice plucked it from his hand and held it out of his reach.

"Robbing the dead, Reverend? I wonder why."

"Give that back!" Dobbs snarled. "You do not know—"

"—what it is for? Do you?"

"It is a keepsake, nothing more, Mr. Swann. In fact, it is owed me, for Samuel pledged it at cards and lost, and I was to have it when we reached the Hispalides."

What a very bad liar you are, Reverend Dobbs, Clarice thought to herself. *Of course, you know I was not in the common room of an evening, and so you feel you may say what you like. And yet . . .*

He made as if to reach for it.

"I am sure coin would be more useful to you than the talisman of a seafaring man," Clarice answered implacably. She dropped the pendant into the pocket of her coat. "And there must be some in Sprunt's effects. When they have been examined, I am sure the crew will look favorably upon your claim—should you choose to present it."

Dobbs sneered. "You do not know what you face, Mr. Swann!"

"Do you?" Clarice turned and walked away.

"Will you join me in a small libation, Mr. Swann? I'm sure you'll agree—the last several hours have been trying ones."

The dead had been committed to the sea, and Clarice had urged Dr. Chapman to rest a little and accompanied him to the surgery. She thought she had never seen any man look so exhausted. The pain of his injury and the long hours without sleep had made his face white and drawn.

Clarice smiled faintly. "When I took ship for the Hispalides, I was in search of adventure, I admit. But perhaps not this much adventure?"

Dr. Lionel Chapman returned her smile as he reached, one-handed, for the bottle. "God grant you never see true adventure," he said with a sigh, pouring himself a cup of whiskey.

"I think I have little choice about it now."

It did not seem likely she would reach her original destination. She had written to Papa and Mama before she sailed. Her fate would be set before her letter reached them, and months more would pass before they truly began to worry. *But whatever fate may be mine, I shall not simply say yes to whatever it sends!* she vowed stubbornly. *If it is not to my liking . . . then it is not my fate.*

"But these poor sailors! What is to happen to them? Dobbs says they will all be hanged should they fall into the hands of the authorities."

"I'm afraid he is right." Chapman sank heavily into a chair. "The law of the sea is harsh and unforgiving. I have been at sea these twenty years, and I have seen men bear up under harsher treatment than what Sprunt meted out here," he said slowly. "I believe I am telling the truth when I say that these men could have borne it all—save poor Appleby, God rest his stainless soul!—if not for the fact that they were goaded toward mutiny day and night. But now it does not matter into whose hands we fall—our own navy, that of the Iberians, or even of the Waulois—we have become outlaws of the sea. You alone might escape."

"I?" Clarice said, startled. "How?"

Chapman gestured with the cup he held. "You did not swear to obey Sprunt's orders, and so you cannot mutiny against them. Once we have made port, wherever we make port, you must go immediately to the governor-general and tell him your story. If a pardon is needed for those actions you committed here, surely he can write you one."

So long as I do not include in my story the fact that Captain Sprunt died by my hand, Clarice thought. *Though perhaps I might confess even to that without penalty, for certainly the enchanted brooch I carry would be sufficient to establish my true identity. And Princess Clarice of Swansgaarde is unlikely to face the same penalty as plain Clarence Swann.*

"But what of you? It must—" She paused and cleared her throat, remembering to keep her voice pitched low. "It must have cost you a great deal to throw in your lot with the mutineers."

"It would have cost me a great deal more if I had not," the doctor answered with the ghost of a smile. "Some voyage would have been my last. This is as good as any to go out on. There is much work for a medical man in the Hispalides, and few questions asked. I shall say I am from Scotia, or Hibernia, or some other place, and soon enough Dr. Lionel Chapman will vanish, to be replaced by I know not whom. Leonard, perhaps. Leonard DeForrest. I have always liked the name Leonard."

"Then that is two of us who are safe, out of nearly three score souls," Clarice said wryly. "What of the others? What will be their fate?"

Chapman sighed again. "The rope and the gibbet. Save of course for the good reverend," he added with a sour smile. "*He* shall be covered in glory."

"Dobbs!" Clarice exclaimed. Suddenly she was reminded of the talisman she carried. She dug in her coat pocket and drew it out. "He was trying to get this from Sprunt's body, but I stopped him. He swore he had won it from Sprunt at cards—but I doubt that very much."

This was the first opportunity she'd had to get a good look at it since she'd taken it from Dobbs. The disk was about a hand span across and perhaps a finger's width thick. At a distance, it had seemed to be made of green stone—perhaps nephrite, or jade—but now she thought it might be glass, for tiny threads of gold went all through it and seemed to have been placed with some conscious purpose. The green disk was held in a flat gold bezel that covered its sides and extended a little way across the front.

She turned it over. The back was completely covered in gold, with a thin groove near the edge, so that a round, golden disk was set in the center of the bezel. The disk's entire surface was engraved with delicate lines, and its edge was covered with a forest of odd broken markings. Her inspection revealed that the bezel around the rim was meant to rotate. She held the disk between thumb and forefinger and twisted the rim experimentally. On this side it, too, was covered in odd markings.

Though she could make out neither top nor bottom, a ring was set in its edge, through which ran a substantial golden chain, long enough to pass easily over the head. She set the object down upon the table.

"It's bespelled, isn't it?" Dr. Chapman asked, regarding it dubiously.

"Yes. I have no idea what it does. All I know is that our good Reverend Dobbs very much did not wish anyone to know he was after it. He might have removed it from the body openly before the body was prepared for burial, then made his claim."

"Clearly he did not wish anyone else to get a close look at it." Chapman picked up the medallion and studied the back intently. "For any sailor worth his grog would recognize a map," he finished, sounding pleased.

"A map?" Clarice asked, bewildered. "But there is no—"

"Land?" Dr. Chapman asked with a smile. "No there is not. Navigational charts, you know, rarely include land," he added dryly, and Clarice grimaced. "Nor could I tell you where it leads. It is a mystery."

"Perhaps. But if it is in some way a sailing chart, surely we should consult Dominick?"

When she returned to the deck, Dominick was nowhere to be seen. Ned Hatcliff told her he was in Sprunt's cabin, taking possession of the charts, and called Geordie Lamb over to show her how to find it.

"Just down the corridor to the left, sir," Geordie said. "Last door."

"Thank you, Mr. Lamb. But there is no need to be formal. We are shipmates now. Please call me Clarence."

Geordie blushed red to the tips of his ears. "Oh, no, sir! My mother wouldn't like that at all! Taking liberties, she'd call it. But I'll call you Mr. Swann—if that's all right? And you can call me Geordie, same as everyone."

"Thank you, Geordie," Clarice said gravely. "I shall be honored."

Geordie turned even redder—if that was possible—and turned to leave so quickly he walked into the hatch instead of through it. Clarice most carefully did not laugh as she stepped down the hallway. The door was ajar when she approached, so she pushed it open and entered, thinking it unoccupied.

Then she stopped, blinking in surprise. She had become used to the idea that all the spaces aboard ship were small and cramped. This space was not. It was at least twice the size of the common room and had surely been built for a captain who was also owner and master. The ceiling sloped upward from the doorway, and the back wall was an immense bank of windows that looked down upon a bed whose mattress was nearly twice the width of Clarice's narrow bunk. The sides and base of the bed were fitted out with drawers. Above, instead of a peg for a lantern, she saw an entire chandelier waiting to be lit; along the walls were mirrored brackets that held unlit lanterns. In one corner stood a desk, and in another, a pair of comfortable chairs that wouldn't have looked out of place in any library in Swansgaarde. The center of the room was dominated by a great square table of standing height.

The initial impression was one of luxury, but that was an illusion. The furnishings were worn and shabby, the wood dull and dry. A light rectangle of decking indicated where a carpet had once covered the floor, but no longer. The windows had fixtures for curtains, but no curtains, and even the wooden shutters, folded back to admit light, were splintered and broken. All this could be nothing more than hard use and long neglect, but over it lay, like a noisome cloak, the evidence of Samuel Sprunt's tenancy. Even the sea air couldn't wholly banish the fetid reek of an unwashed body. The sheets upon the bunk were greasy and stained, and the corners of the room were filled with litter. She could not decide whether this was the fault of the former occupant or evidence of a truly thorough search.

"Kayin, if you would be so kind, you may tell Mr. Greenwell that the navigational materials and sailing charts are all here and in good order," Dominick's disembodied voice said. A moment later, he rose from behind the standing table.

In the middle of all this disorder, Dominick appeared like a creature from another world. He was freshly shaved and had changed his soiled shirt for a fresh one. Dark smudges of weariness beneath his eyes and a bruise upon his cheek were the only visible signs of what had transpired the night before. He stood at the table, studying the items that covered its surface: several thick, leatherbound books; a personal journal; a telescope in an open case; and a number of navigational instruments that must have belonged to Sprunt lay atop several enormous charts.

"Clarence!" he exclaimed. "Forgive me. I thought you were Kayin coming to see if I had been lost—or perished of poison." He grinned at her crookedly.

"I would hardly be surprised if you had, now that I have seen this place. But I am pleased to hear that we are not lost."

It was a strange and refreshing thing, Clarice reflected idly. If she were here in her own person, being alone in a room with a handsome young man would inevitably lead her to wonder (or worry) if he meant to make romantic advances at her. But as Clarence Swann, she had no such concerns at all.

"Oh, we wouldn't be lost in any event," Dominick said offhandedly, "for the ship's compass and chronometer are in good order, and while I couldn't undertake to reach our destination without instruments—did I not have my own, and kept far better than these, for that matter—we could certainly reach Hesperia itself. An entire continent is a difficult thing to miss."

"I am glad to hear it," Clarice said wryly.

"And I am glad to have this moment alone with you, for in all the confusion, I don't think I have properly thanked you for saving my life."

"I . . . I did only what needed to be done," Clarice answered awkwardly, trying to control her flush of embarrassment. "You seem to me to be quite an expert sailor, Dominick, but I do not think you are any sort of swordsman."

That made him laugh. "Perhaps you will be willing to give me lessons, since I can see it is a useful skill indeed. Though I do not know if there is another rapier to be found aboard ship. A sailor's weapon is the cutlass—" He broke off suddenly, and Clarice knew he was remembering, as she was, the blood-slick cutlass in Sprunt's hands.

"Why, then, we will begin as I began, with wooden swords," Clarice answered. "You will soon get the hang of it. But will you have time for your lessons?"

"Plenty of it. We do not make port for another month—should we continue on our charted course. And yet . . ." Dominick peered at the topmost chart again and then took up a book from the stack upon the table.

Clarice moved around to his side of the table. The other books were printed—navigational tables and ephemerides—but this one was handwritten. The ship's log. She couldn't read Sprunt's crabbed writing, but most of the penciled entries seemed to consist of columns of numbers and dates.

"I shouldn't trouble you with this, Clarence," Dominick said, favoring her with a weary smile.

"How not? You are my friend," Clarice said honestly. "And I have been getting quite the education in naval matters from Dr. Chapman. If I understand him aright, I am the only person aboard ship you can speak frankly to."

"It would be true if I were captain," Dominick answered modestly, "for the captain, whatever his doubts—or hers—must not share them with the crew. But at the moment we have no captain, though we are to hold elections as soon as I have checked our heading and made sure we need make no corrections for a while. Though where we are to go, and what will become of us . . ."

"Must we turn pirate? Is there no other option?" It seemed to

Clarice that she had been asking that same question since the moment Sprunt had fallen dead on the deck.

"Only one," Dominick answered grimly. "We must find a port where the *Asesino* is not known, put the crew ashore, and sink her in the tide. Only then can any of us hope to end our lives as free men. And that is more easily said than done. We are sailors. We have no other trade or livelihood." He sighed again. "I still cannot imagine how we came to this situation. Samuel Sprunt was an experienced captain. He could not have so misjudged the temper of the crew. Not easily."

"I do not think it was a misjudgment. Dr. Chapman believes the crew was driven to mutiny. Led to it. Intentionally."

"Why?" Dominick demanded. "What could he possibly have gained by it?"

"Would this tell us?" For the second time that day Clarice drew out the medallion and laid it upon the chart table.

If she had placed a scorpion there, it could not have caused a greater sensation. Dominick flinched back instantly, then reached out a cautious hand to pick it up. "Dear Lord," he whispered, inspecting it carefully. "Was this Sprunt's great secret? Who knows you are in possession of it now?"

His abrupt change in manner disoriented her. "Reverend Dobbs. And Doctor Chapman. And you. Dobbs was trying to take it from the body without being seen."

"Then Dobbs will not speak of it—though he will certainly try to take it from you—and Dr. Chapman is trustworthy. As am I," he added with a faint smile.

"But what is it?" Clarice demanded in frustration. "Why should I conceal it?"

"It is a map," Dominick said simply. He held it over the chart, gold side facing up. "And to sailors, there is only one sort of map—a treasure map. Treasure fever has destroyed more good ships than pirates or mutineers."

"If I have a choice between being a treasure hunter or a pirate, I know which one I'd pick," Clarice muttered, yet she felt her breath and heart quickening. "But how can you say it is a treasure map when you do not know even what it is a map *of*?"

"I do not say it is a treasure map, Clarence," Dominick answered pedantically. "I say that anyone who discovers a secret, hidden, and enchanted talisman with a map engraved upon it will instantly assume it is the key to a great treasure."

"I assumed no such thing," Clarice said stiffly.

"Ah, but you are a landsman, not a sailor." Dominick was still holding the pendant, absently turning the moving rim with his thumb.

For a moment she felt a wave of irritation flare up within her and held her tongue with an effort. Everyone aboard this ship seemed to feel that a ship was not merely a convenient mode of transportation, but some sort of floating kingdom in which they were all princes.

"Perhaps so, but I am smart enough to see that a map one cannot read is a useless map," she said tartly.

"Of cour—" Whatever Dominick had meant to say died unuttered. He had been about to hand the object back to her when he had glanced down at it a final time. "But if one has latitude and longitude, one has little need for a map," he said in a stricken voice.

He held the talisman out to Clarice. The decorative curves and loops around the border were no longer merely decorative. When the ring and the disk were properly aligned, they became a series of numbers.

"Is it a— Do you know where it goes?"

"Give me a moment," Dominick answered, reaching for his tools.

In fact, it was closer to half an hour before he had turned the ring of numbers into a location on one of the charts, and when he had done so, it was nothing more than a faint penciled X in the middle of a vast expanse of blue.

THE HOUSE OF THE FOUR WINDS · 99

"But there is nothing there!" Clarice exclaimed in disappointment.

"We would have to go there to be certain of that," Dominick answered. "Whatever is there, it is about four days away from Cibola. The Hispalides are a chain. There could be an island that had been overlooked. Or a reef."

"Cibola is where we are—we *were*—going, isn't it?"

"Yes." Dominick's voice was thoughtful and grave once more. "But . . . look." He took her arm and drew her closer to the table. "This is what I was puzzling over before you arrived. Each evening, I took a sighting to determine the number of miles we sailed that day. I gave my reckoning to Dickon, and Dickon gave it to Sprunt, and Sprunt marked it upon the chart. See? It is here." He pointed, and Clarice could see a faint penciled line upon the chart, and along it, a series of Xs and dates. "And then each morning, he would check the heading and make any corrections he deemed needful. And so I have never seen our whole course laid out upon the chart until now. And it is . . . not the course I would have plotted myself."

He laid out the charts until they covered the whole surface of the table, then reached into a small carved-bone box she had not noticed before and picked up a handful of tiny metal objects. "See? There are the Hispalides at the edge of this chart—and see? There is Cibola. But . . . look. Were I choosing our course, it would be . . . so." He set the small pyramids upon the charts in a long arc stretching from Cibola all the way across the map.

"This is hardly a reason for you to look so worried when you are inspecting a chart you have said is perfectly fine," she said.

"Yes, but that was before I knew about our mysterious island. And it is true Sprunt might have chosen a course to sail us wide of some danger—marauders, or rival merchantmen, or great whales, or storms, or kraken. The sea is a thousand roads, and none. But . . . here is the place indicated by the talisman." He set down another triangle. "And this is the course we have been sailing." He indicated the penciled marks.

"Your course and Captain Sprunt's are not at all the same. But you said he might choose a different route for any number of reasons."

"True. But if you extend our present course in a logical fashion . . ." Dominick set more of the tiny gray pyramids onto the charts, starting at the last mark on the map.

"Then that was his destination all along," Clarice said slowly. "And not Cibola at all. But what's there? Should we go and see? I think—"

"It is not my decision to make," Dominick said firmly.

Clarice opened her mouth to argue. Not only was Dominick one of the few officers still on board, he was the only one who could sail the ship.

Then she changed her mind. For all her brave talk (even if the only audience was herself and her diary), she was utterly unprepared for the situation in which she found herself now. It was one thing to decide, in the comfort and safety of Swansgaarde, to leave home and go adventuring. She'd been prepared for highwaymen and dishonest innkeepers. Perils she knew how to easily cope with or could leave behind. But her current situation was a kind of trouble beyond anything she'd imagined . . . and it was not hers alone. Everyone in *Asesino*'s crew was in just as much danger—and though it certainly wasn't her fault, she could not help but feel their safety was her responsibility.

And the worst thing about all this was that she suspected Dominick had no more idea of how to get them out of this mess than she did.

Even so, you are not helping matters by sticking your head in the sand like, like—like an ostrich! You must . . . advise him. Somehow.

Just then there was a quiet scratch upon the door, and a squeak as it was pushed all the way open. Clarice quickly dropped the talisman into her pocket. Kayin Dako was standing there, his enormous bulk filling the doorway.

"It's time, Dominick. If you're ready."

"Yes, of course," Dominick said absently. He swept the course markers back into the box and began to roll the charts on the table into neat cylinders. "Tell Mr. Greenwell our present heading is good. We'll be right there."

4

~

THE CASTING OF LOTS

YOU ALL know me, lads. And I'm here to tell you what's to be done."

Emmet Emerson paced back and forth behind the foredeck guardrail like one of his own chickens. Of the fourscore souls who had sailed from Lochrin a few weeks before, a little over three dozen now remained, and nearly the whole of them were gathered here.

By rights Clarice did not belong here at all, as she was only a passenger, but no one had objected when she stepped onto the deck with Dominick. And after all, she'd taken part, however haphazardly, in the ship's liberation.

"We're mutineers, and there's no point in dressing it up to make it look better than it is. Captain Sprunt was a bad 'un, and we sent him packing, so who's to be captain now? A ship without a captain is like a body without a heart, and that's the plain truth."

"You!" Geordie shouted before Emerson could continue. "You be our captain, Em!"

The rotund cook stopped and glared. "And who's going to get your dinner for you if I'm running this ship, Geordie Lamb? It's plain to see you were standing behind the door when they gave out brains." There was general laughter. "Let that be a word to you all," Mr. Emerson said firmly. "I can captain this tub, or I can cook, but I can't do both. But soonest begun soonest done. So oil up your tongues and let me hear you."

It swiftly became clear to Clarice that the idea was to put up a slate of candidates who would then be voted upon. Some of the choices were obvious. Dr. Chapman was one of the candidates, as were Kayin Dako, Ned Hatcliff, and Rogerio Vasquez, the armorer's mate, a man with the dark eyes and dark skin of an Iberian. When each was nominated, he went to stand behind Mr. Emerson on the foredeck. Even Jerrold Robinson, the cook's mate, was nominated, and whether or not it was a joke, he took his place beside the others.

"Dobbs!" someone in the back of the crowd shouted. "Let us have Dobbs! Reverend Dobbs!"

Clarice craned around, trying to see who it was, but the crowd was packed too closely. The first voice was joined by a few others, and then the crowd parted as Dobbs came forward, walking toward the ladder. His head was down, and his hands ostentatiously gripped his prayer book. But he could not repress a small smirk as he passed Dominick and Clarice.

"Dominick!" Clarice whispered. "They cannot mean to elect Dobbs!"

"I will not vote for him, you can be sure," Dominick answered. "But any man on this deck may be nominated."

"Now that's a fine tally, and any one of them a good captain," Mr. Emerson said firmly. "Now, mark well the method that you will use to signify your choice. As I call out each name—"

"What about Dominick?" Ned Hatcliff shouted suddenly. "Without Dominick none of us'd be wrangling over this now! He can captain us and navigate both!"

"I—" Dominick began, but whatever protest he was about to make was drowned out by the shouts and cheers around him. Everyone seemed to think Ned Hatcliff's notion was a good one.

"Clarence—I can't possibly!" he said into her ear.

"Come on, Dominick!" Dickon said, taking his arm and pulling him forward. A moment later he stood with the other candidates.

"Now, is there anyone else you layabouts think can do this job of work?" the cook asked. "Or shall we go about picking one of these fine fellows?"

More laughter and demands that he get on with it greeted this speech.

"I'm not stirring my stump until I can hear myself think!" Mr. Emerson shouted back. When there was quiet once more, he addressed the crowd.

"Here's the way of it. I'll call out a name, see, and every one of you man jacks who wants to stand for him moves back over there by the rail, see? And I'll count heads and mark down the number here on the bulkhead with this stick of chalk. And when all the votes is tallied, that's *Asesino*'s new master. Now! All of you as thinks young Jerrold should be the captain, declare yourselves!"

And so the election began.

Clarice had never thought to see an election of any sort, even though she'd read about them in books. She had received a brutal education in how much power the captain of a ship could wield if he chose. It seemed near to madness to put such power into the hands of one selected by the mere casting of lots.

And what if the Reverend Dobbs was chosen? His first act would surely be to force her to surrender the talisman. Map it might be, but Clarice did not think that was the whole of its secret. A string of numbers might be concealed on a slip of paper, a length of ribbon, a leather belt, a ring, without needing sorcery to place it there. So the talisman was more than the hiding place for a destination. Perhaps . . . a key?

To what? she wondered in exasperation. *Treasure, as Dominick thinks? If it is, why did Sprunt not claim it and buy a ship of his own? Or a fine house and servants, if there was enough of it?*

She could hardly ask him now, could she?

With good-natured horseplay the men jostled about to take their places for the voting. Unsurprisingly, Jerrold Robinson did not receive many votes, but he took it in good part, laughing and blushing as he was teased. Rogerio Vasquez garnered only a few more supporters than Jerrold had, but swore he considered it an act of pure kindness that anyone who knew him would wish him to stand for captain.

To Clarice's surprise, at this point Mr. Emerson announced that, as both candidates had clearly lost, those who had voted for them must choose again. Dr. Chapman made a good showing; between them, he and Ned Hatcliff accounted for a dozen votes, with Dr. Chapman receiving the majority of them.

Two dozen votes yet to be cast, and three possible candidates.

Dominick's was the next name to be called, and Clarice found herself clenching her fists tightly as the men—including Dickon—moved across the deck to be counted. He made a good showing, but two names were still to be called after his, Kayin's and Dobbs's.

Kayin Dako was well liked among the crew, and there were cheers when he came to strut and swagger before the rail, grinning broadly. When his tally was called, for a moment Clarice was certain he had won, especially after Ned Hatcliff sprang over the rail, to her astonishment, to join those voting for Kayin.

"I— Can he *do* that?" Clarice asked, astonished.

Her remark was not directed toward anyone in particular, but Dickon answered, "A man's vote is his own, to cast any way he sees fit."

"But—he is one of the candidates!"

"And he could vote for himself, if he wished," Dickon answered.

When Kayin's tally was called, it was a scant two votes shy of Dominick's.

"You'll have me for your first mate then, Dominick?" Kayin demanded irrepressibly.

"I should wish for no better," Dominick answered.

"And yet, your encomiums may well be premature," Reverend Dobbs said smoothly, stepping forward. "For the last tally has not been made. Gentlemen of the *Asesino*! I present myself, humbly and with God's guidance, as your new captain, should the Almighty in His wisdom cause you to choose me." He gazed down on the quarterdeck and the men gathered there as if he were already their master.

There was an uneasy silence. Clarice had already learned that sailors were as deeply superstitious as a medieval peasant—how not, when their very lives were at the mercy of forces they could neither control nor predict?—and oddly, for that very reason they avoided, whenever possible, clergymen and magicians.

For an instant nobody moved. Then the group began to divide itself.

It had been nearly impossible for her to keep track of who'd voted and who hadn't, especially since Jerrold Robinson and Rogerio Vasquez's voters had been allowed to recast their votes, but anarchic as the process was, those directly involved seemed to have a clear understanding of the proprieties. Nobody raised an objection as the votes mounted.

"Thirteen souls for Reverend Dobbs," Mr. Emerson said, sounding as if the words tasted bitter.

One more than Dominick! Clarice thought in horror. She could not imagine what inducement he'd offered the men who had voted for him. Surely a few hours' time had not been enough for them to forget he had been Sprunt's crony, spared only for the sake of his holy orders.

Perhaps that is the reason. If Dobbs sails us into Cibola and vouches for the men who voted for him, they will be spared. I do not think the crew will willingly sail into a hangman's noose, but a pardon must be what he has offered them!

"And that means—"

"Oh, but wait! I have not yet cast my vote," Dr. Chapman said, stepping forward.

"Be silent!" Reverend Dobbs snapped.

"You ain't captain until all the votes are in," Mr. Emerson snapped. "Who're you going to cast your vote for, Doc?"

"Why, for young Mr. Moryet of course," Dr. Chapman said.

"Me, too!" Kayin announced loudly. "I mean, it completely slipped my mind to cast a vote and all, and . . ."

"And me! I mean, Mr. Emerson, I don't think I voted, did I?" Jerrold asked anxiously.

"Why, no, young Jerrold, I don't believe you did," Emmet said blandly. "Do ye wish to stand for Mr. Moryet?"

"Yes!" Jerrold announced. "I mean—"

"This is outrageous!" Reverend Dobbs said. "This unseemly attempt to contravene the will—"

"I hope your next words aren't going to be *of God*, Reverend," Emmet Emerson said softly. "As I don't think a man who claims he knows what's on God's mind is the sort of man I'd want to have as captain. And so I'm voting for Mr. Moryet—and that gives him a proper majority."

Clarice glanced toward Dominick.

He looked more stunned than pleased. "But I—" He had won, but only by three votes.

"Why, you have all my votes—and Dr. Chapman's, too!" Kayin said firmly. "What say you, Ned?"

"And mine!" Ned Hatcliff said stoutly.

"And that is a goodly two-thirds of the souls afloat," Emmet finished. "And no one could argue with that. Could they, Reverend Dobbs?"

Dobbs took a deep breath and forced an unconvincing smile. "It is the law of the sea, Mr. Emerson. No one can argue with that."

Despite his protests of inadequacy, Dominick seemed to have a good idea of what a captain needed to do. He redistributed the watches, as they had lost over half of their crew now, and ordered the contents of the now vacant cabins and lockers turned out and made available to all. He appointed Kayin as first mate and Rogerio as chief armorer. Dickon was confirmed as helmsman, and Mr. Emerson as cook, and of course there was no question about Dr. Chapman's remaining as ship's surgeon. Mr. Emerson suggested Geordie Lamb as their new purser, and Dominick ordered a full inventory of their supplies, with Mr. Emerson to draw whatever he wished from stores to prepare a good hot meal for everyone.

Clarice found herself working as hard as anyone else, making lists of what was found and how it was handed out. Together she, Kayin, and Dominick finished the search of Captain Sprunt's cabin; they found a great deal of liquor, sweets, and tobacco—if Sprunt had starved the crew, he didn't stint himself.

"That ends now," Kayin said firmly, and Dominick nodded. "Yes, as does unjust and excessive punishment, though I expect you to deal with slacking and bad conduct, Kayin, for all our lives depend on the seaworthiness of *Asesino*."

At Dominick's direction, Clarice turned over the liquor to Dr. Chapman, the candied fruit to Mr. Emerson, and the tobacco to Kayin, who promised that every man who wished should have a share.

Coats, stockings, breeches, shoes, and shirts belonging to Sprunt, Lee, and Foster were added to what Dominick called the slop chest, from which the crew could replace their own worn, tattered, or (in some cases) bloodstained clothing. The discarded rags would be boiled, then divided between bandages and polishing cloths. The only exception was a fine brocade vest and a tricorne hat lavishly trimmed with plumes—formerly Sprunt's property—for if Dominick was called upon to act the captain in front of strangers, he'd better be able to look the part.

Kayin announced that he would move Dominick's possessions to his new quarters at once—Clarice thought it had not occurred to Dominick he would have to move—and Clarice said it had to be cleaned first. Kayin had laughed and called for a work crew and said she must oversee it. Under Clarice's guidance—consulting

Ned Hatcliff carefully about what should be thrown over the side and what should be saved for reuse—the bunk was stripped, the mattress turned, the piles of litter and detritus collected, and cabin aired out thoroughly. Clarice called for oil, candles, and rags, took off her coat, rolled up her sleeves, and cleaned the furniture herself, to the great delight of the sailors. It felt good to be doing useful work at last, and Mr. Emerson contributed a basin of precious lemon peels—"So the job is done right and fitting," he said.

Now the wood gleamed, and the air smelled pleasantly of lemon and beeswax, and every trace of Sprunt's occupancy had been erased. Dominick's sea chest stood upon a stand at the foot of the bed, and all that remained was for the deck to be scoured and scrubbed.

Clarice washed her hands in a basin and rolled down her sleeves. A glance toward the windows showed her it was nearly twilight. She regarded the splintered shutters with disfavor. Perhaps someone could remove and repair them—if anyone among their reduced crew had the skill or the time—but dealing with them was beyond her skill.

"Good Lord," Dominick said, stepping inside as she reached for her coat. "I would think myself suddenly transported to the finest inn Lochrin possesses! Surely you did not learn these skills from your fencing master?"

Clarice thought, with a brief pang of longing and homesickness, of the hunting lodge at the foot of the Swanscrown. Maria Gantzer had been its mistress since the Old Duke's time and had taught each and every one of her royal charges to wash and clean and polish as rigorously as if they were the newest housemaids entrusted to her tutelage.

"From our housekeeper," Clarice answered. It was not quite a lie. "My parents believed there was no shame in servants' work and made sure I knew what it was, so I valued it as I should."

"If you cannot make your way as a fencing master, you should consider becoming an innkeeper, I think." He glanced at a newly gleaming chair, then flung himself down to sit on the bunk instead. "I still do not know how this happened, Clarence," he said in bewilderment.

"Kayin wanted you to be captain if he was not chosen," Clarice said reasonably. "Dr. Chapman did not want to be captain at all. Mr. Hatcliff lost fair and square, as did young Jerrold and Mr. Vasquez—"

"—and I am not certain how Reverend Dobbs was nominated at all," Dominick said slowly.

"I am sure we are all better off not knowing that," Clarice said gravely, though she had a pretty good idea. The gap between her and Dominick, she saw, was not one of age—for they were much of an age—or, really, of birth, for Dominick thought Mr. Clarence Swann to be a fellow such as himself, and Swansgaarde's royal line was neither particularly grand nor particularly ancient. The difference between them was in how they had been trained. Clarice had been raised to look for both enemies and advantages everywhere, for if she had not been expected to rule Swansgaarde, she had still been trained to lead. But Dominick seemed to take the world at face value and to think everyone was ready to be his friend. Even now.

Is that a good quality in a pirate captain—or a bad one? Clarice wondered. *When I set off to seek my fortune, I certainly did not expect it to lie in piracy, but everyone says that is our only choice now.*

"Well, I can't put Dobbs in chains," Dominick said exasperatedly. "If anyone would have stood for that, we would have set him adrift with the others."

"You could have him watched," Clarice said quietly. "Him, and the men who voted to make him captain. I am certain Mr. Emerson could tell you their names."

"All we need is another—"

Just then Jerrold Robinson entered with a mop and a sloshing bucket. "Begging your pardon, Captain Moryet"—Jerrold was unable to stifle his grin of delight—"but I didn't know you and the other gentleman would be here. Kayin says I'm to scrub the deck right and proper, until anything that doesn't shine, squeaks." He beamed at Clarice, then leaned his mop against the bulkhead and tossed the contents of his bucket to the deck. In a moment, the cabin was awash with seawater.

"Very . . . efficient," Clarice said, watching Dominick struggle to keep a straight face.

"Indeed," Dominick agreed. "And we will leave you to your work. I shall be in the common room if you need anything, Jerrold."

"Yes, sir, Captain Moryet!" Jerrold said enthusiastically.

"I think he believes he is in the Royal Navy," Dominick said, when they were out in the corridor.

"I think he must enjoy your captaincy more than you do," Clarice agreed.

"It is an office I had hoped to attain by more legitimate means." Dominick gestured for Clarice to precede him.

"I know you are tired of being asked the question, but now you are captain, and—" She broke off as they passed one of the sailors. *Now I shall have a chance to learn everyone's name,* she thought randomly. *And make friends without fearing I am earning someone a flogging.*

Dominick opened the door to the common room. It was still enough before dinner that it was deserted. She thought of David Appleby with a brief pang of sorrow. But at least if his life had been a misery, his last days had been spent in gentle hands with gentle care.

"I would like—" Dominick broke off, looking stricken. "I am going to need a cabin boy, I suppose. I was about to say I would like a mug of tea, but I can hardly go to Mr. Emerson and demand one."

"He would chase you out of his galley for lèse-majesté," Clarice agreed solemnly. "And part your hair with a ladle into the bargain. Why not ask him if he will give up Jerrold to be your cabin boy? I think Jerrold would be delighted to enhance your dignity among the crew. And it is certainly a step up from . . . scullion?"

"I think I'd rather have a less eager acolyte," Dominick said, laughing. "Even if it is only a temporary post."

"How so?" It seemed that Dominick was finally going to broach the subject that she desperately wanted to discuss: What do we do now?

"We have very few choices," Dominick said seriously. "We're outlaws now. There's no real way to disguise *Asesino*. Or any of us, really."

"But—"

Dominick shook his head, as if he'd already guessed her next words. "Say the longboat never makes port. Say we sail into harbor in Cibola, and Reverend Dobbs never says a word about what happened here. Say that all our crew walk free and take berths on other ships, as I would urge them to do if I dared. We would be safe only for a little while. When the *Asesino* is reported missing—as she will be in time, for the Cornhill Society will investigate her disappearance before paying out the assurance money—anyone discovered to have been of her crew on this last voyage will be questioned closely. A record is kept at the Charterhouse of our roster—it is one of the documents a ship must provide to be indemnified. When a ship vanishes, the souls lost with her go upon a watch list. Once someone who sailed upon our "lost ship" is found, he will be made to tell all he knows. And in that moment, we are all outlaws. Hunted men. If we are not to turn pirate in truth, our only hope is either to find a haven so far from the Cornhill Society that we're never discovered, or—"

"Or find a treasure great enough to convince the Admiralty to pardon you all," Clarice said firmly. "It can certainly be done. Pardons are bought and sold like turnips—or so I hear."

"Yes, perhaps," Dominick said gently, though she could tell he did not believe it was possible. "But meanwhile, we can't simply sail into Cibola, so this evening I will consult our charts and

THE HOUSE OF THE FOUR WINDS · 113

choose a new destination. If nothing else, we can find some deserted isle where we can lay up for a while and decide our fates.
All we need is—"

Suddenly the door flew open. Dominick and Clarice both
sprang to their feet.

"Dom—I mean, Captain," Kayin said.

"Close the door," Clarice said sharply. "If it's bad news, keep it
quiet."

"It won't be quiet for long," Kayin said grimly, doing as she
said. "I've told Geordie I'll sew his mouth up with sail twine if
he breathes a word, but—"

"About what?" Clarice asked.

"He was doing an inventory of stores," Dominick said, dawning
horror in his voice.

"That he was," Kayin said. "Best you come and see for yourself."

Clarice had never been down in the hold of the ship. The floor beneath her feet was faintly damp and covered with straw. All around,
in the moist, odiferous darkness, stood wooden crates, and barrels,
and chests; anonymous cloth-shrouded bundles and piles of canvas and burlap sacks. They were stowed in labyrinthine balks and
spires, secured with nets and straps and pulley ropes.

I shall never look at goods in a shop in the same way again,
Clarice thought. *Now that I know what they went through to get
there.*

Kayin and Dominick carried lanterns. As they reached where
Geordie stood, the light of the lantern Kayin carried fell upon the
new purser's face. Clarice felt her heart sink at his woebegone
expression.

"Found four more like it, Kayin," Geordie said forlornly. "Didn't
have the heart to go on." He gestured to a tall pile of sacks. Clarice
could see that several had been cut open. Sand had spilled from the
breaches across the deck.

"That should be our flour," Dominick said quietly.

"Aye," Kayin said. "And this"—he kicked the side of a barrel, which rang hollowly—"should be salt pork. I wonder how many of them were in on it?"

"In on what?" Clarice asked blankly.

"It is a common enough practice, Clarence," Dominick said. "The captain, or the purser, takes the money he is allotted to buy provisions, pockets most of it, and buys bad or meager supplies. To make it look as if he is not doing that, containers full of wood or sand or sawdust are loaded in place of what he should have bought."

"But can't the crew complain to the owner?" she asked.

Kayin laughed harshly. "As if the likes of us would be let to see him! Oh, they like their gold well enough—so long as they don't have to see where it came from. But there's worse."

He led Dominick to a line of enormous casks that were lashed to the bulkhead. The most vital provision a ship carried was water, for the desalinizing charms that could turn a barrel of seawater into a barrel of fresh were prohibitively costly. "Green wood."

Even Clarice could see that the barrels were leaking.

"How—" Dominick swallowed hard. "How much is left?"

Kayin met his eyes squarely. "Enough for a fortnight, if we go on half rations. After that, we must have water."

There is no landfall to be made within that time, Clarice thought, feeling suddenly cold.

Command was like rulership, and her father had always said a crown was a heavy weight to bear. In that moment she saw the truth of it, as Dominick's shoulders sagged momentarily with the realization that Kayin was waiting for orders.

Then Dominick straightened and smiled. "Then we have no problem at all," he said easily, "for the destination I have in mind—I was showing it to you earlier today upon the chart, Clarence, if you recall?—is barely a week's sail from our present position. And I dare to swear we can reach it faster if we try. There is no need at all to go on half rations, though I will tell Dr.

Chapman and the others that we must save all our freshwater for drinking."

She saw the fear in Kayin's and Geordie's faces ease and made sure her own countenance gave nothing away.

"We'll be there before you know it, Cap'n," Geordie said. "But . . . what am I to do . . . ?"

"Inventory what there is," Dominick said. "Make a list. There's a few days' worth topside, is there not?"

"Aye, Mr. Emerson's most particular about having his victuals to hand," Geordie said eagerly. "Three days' worth. Maybe four. He was always—" Geordie broke off for a moment. "He was always fighting with Mr. Foster about it," he finished quietly.

And now we know why, Clarice thought. *And I imagine the sailors Mr. Foster sent down to fetch Mr. Emerson's provisions went into the sea this morning—one way or another.*

"Then we won't starve and we won't thirst," Dominick said with firm cheer. "If Mr. Emerson needs anything from stores, one of you two fetch it for him. I shall make an announcement when I've had time to go over Geordie's tally, but in the meantime, I won't have anyone panicking. So I must ask you to keep what you have discovered to yourselves."

"Oh, that should be a simple matter," Kayin said darkly.

Supper in the captain's mess that night was an unreal occasion.

Gone was the atmosphere of tension as Sprunt swilled his liquor and Dr. Chapman and Reverend Dobbs baited one another with exquisite indirection. Tonight—despite the discovery in the hold—the atmosphere was one of celebration.

In honor of the occasion, Clarice had come dressed in "Mr. Swann's" best: embroidered silk weskit and fine lace-trimmed shirt instead of her plain and serviceable everyday broadcloth and linen. She'd even unpacked her best coat, the one of bottle-green velvet with gold silk lacings and yellow silk facings.

Dressing had taken her longer than she'd expected, for the coat had needed brushing and the lace had needed careful handling. She had mourned the absence of a decent mirror, but the one she carried with her was tiny and her cabin had none. When she was finally as presentable as she thought she could make herself, she departed for the captain's mess and found she was the last to arrive.

The lamps were lit, and the compartment looked just as it always had. Kayin and Geordie looked a little uncomfortable at their sudden promotion. And one soul who should have been there was missing.

"Where is Reverend Dobbs?" Clarice asked as she settled into her place.

There was a brief silence.

"Our minister of God has been called to a period of quiet meditation in his quarters," Dr. Chapman said blandly. "I do not believe he will be joining us at table for the duration of the voyage." He attempted to accompany this speech with a gesture, caught himself, and winced.

"You locked him up?" Clarice blurted. Hadn't Dominick said just this afternoon that he could take no action against Dobbs?

"Caught him down in the hold," Kayin said bluntly.

"I suppose all of us know—" Dickon broke off as the door opened to admit their dinner, carried, on this special occasion, by Mr. Emerson himself, accompanied by Jerrold Robinson.

"There you are, Cap'n," Mr. Emerson said proudly as he set the soup tureen on the table. "All right and tight. And a chicken to go on with. On account of the occasion."

"And the crew?" Dominick asked.

Mr. Emerson beamed. "A pleasure, sir. Good thick stew and honest biscuit—no more of that gruel! Plenty of meat in 'er, too. And a double ration of grog, just as Geordie here ordered. Or p'rhaps, I should be calling him Mr. Lamb now? Him being an officer now."

Dr. Chapman chuckled.

Geordie blushed. "Oh, no, Mr. Emerson. My mother would say it was a liberty. I couldn't possibly."

"You must feed the crew as you would feed us, Mr. Emerson," Dominick said. "I'll have no one under my care go hungry if I can prevent it. I've been hungry myself," he added, in such a low tone Clarice did not think anyone was meant to hear.

"Anyone does a better day's work on a full belly," Kayin said, sounding satisfied.

Once Mr. Emerson had left, Jerrold poured the wine. Kayin regarded his glass with suspicion, then drank its contents down in one gulp as if it were medicine, clearly trying not to make a face.

"Latch the door, Dickon," Dominick said quietly, and Dickon got up quickly and barred the door. Once he had seated himself again, Dominick resumed, "I am sorry to bring up such subjects at our meal, but we all know our situation—and I may rely, I am sure on Jerrold's discretion . . ."

"Oh, yes, sir, Captain Moryet!" Jerrold said.

"I am entirely certain the good reverend knows it as well," Dr. Chapman said with grim relish. "And knew it before he made his ill-advised journey to the nether regions of our fair vessel to 'discover' it."

Dominick cleared his throat. "That is not the issue at hand," he said tactfully. "There is a deeper mystery here. As you all know, it is another three weeks before we could have hoped to reach Cibola. Geordie tells me our food would have been gone before that—it would have run out already, I think, if not for the starvation rations the crew has been kept on—but the thing that concerns me is the water. It, too, would have run out at least a week before we would have reached our purported destination."

"This is, as you all know, my first time at sea, and while I cannot claim to be a sailor, I am not a fool," Clarice said slowly. If Dominick did not want her to mention this, he could interrupt her before she continued, but he didn't. "Sprunt never meant to sail to Cibola at all. He meant a mutiny to occur—and he timed it pretty neatly, too. Dominick, if you had died that night instead of him, what would have happened next?"

Dominick thought carefully for long moments. "The mutiny would have failed, I think. We were hard-pressed already when you came to our timely rescue. Captain Sprunt would have resumed his command and executed the surviving mutineers."

"Which would have been most of the crew," Dr. Chapman said dryly, reaching for his wineglass with his good hand.

"He might pardon a few," Dickon said. "*Asesino* can be sailed with perhaps half the crew she carries—as we now have to. We must all pray the weather continues clear," he added with a faint grim smile.

"And his navigator would be dead," Clarice pointed out. "And there would be no one to wonder at the course he took. You would not know, would you, Dickon?"

"Not in the least," Dickon said promptly.

"And no one would breathe a word of reproach against such a *lucky* captain." Privately Clarice thought that the catalog of disasters he'd survived didn't make the late Samuel Sprunt lucky so much as a lightning rod for misfortune. But there was no reason now to say so.

"Only he never meant to make port in Cibola and tell that tale," Dr. Chapman said.

"No," Dominick said slowly. "He meant to go precisely where I am taking us." He paused for a moment, then smiled. "And that answers one question. Wherever we are bound, there is both food and water there. So we may all rest easier."

"Except we're all pirates now," Geordie burst out suddenly. "My mother won't like that. She won't like that at all."

"And I suppose you're planning to write home and tell her so?" Kayin asked with heavy sarcasm. "It's plain to see there's no room in your head for common sense—it's too full of facts and figures."

"We'll worry about that later," Dominick said firmly, as Geordie opened his mouth to vigorously defend himself. "After we have made landfall."

The talk continued through dinner—chicken and potatoes, a side dish of vinegar cabbage, buttered carrots, and pickles— most of it to do with the ship. Kayin spoke of this thing and that thing that must be mended, improved, or changed. Though Clarice could follow few of the particulars of their discussion, she hardly cared. Even Dr. Chapman offered suggestions, and if they were not to his taste, Kayin was not shy about telling him so: "—for it is plain to me you've been an officer all your life," he said.

That made Dominick grin and make some incomprehensible joke that made Kayin shout with surprised laughter.

When the dishes were cleared away, the port and the walnuts were set out, and for a change Clarice did not rise to her feet to leave. Even facing an uncertain future and sailing to an unknown destination, the atmosphere around the table was so much freer and cleaner than it had been when Sprunt had presided that she wanted to bask in it a while longer.

What a great difference, for good or ill, one man can make. It is something Papa always said, but it is so very different when you see it for yourself.

Dominick called for a pitcher of ale as well—to Geordie's and Kayin's obvious relief—and said they might smoke if they wished. Both Kayin and Geordie began enthusiastically filling their pipes; Dickon extracted a plain silver snuffbox from his pockets and took several pinches, sneezing violently after each. Clarice reached into her cuff for her cigar case, one of the many props she used to turn herself into Clarence, for the chiefest art of disguise was misdirection. She offered the case to Dominick, who shook his head with a smile.

"It's a vile, disgusting, dirty habit that shortens men's lives," Dr. Chapman said sourly.

Clarice stood to take a light from one of the lamps above the table. "Spoken like a true man of medicine," she teased, puffing the narrow cylinder alight. "You would have us all living on nuts and berries if you could." She allowed her mouth to fill with the bitter, fragrant smoke, then blew it out. She'd come to enjoy the taste—so long as she didn't actually inhale it. The one time she'd tried that, she'd coughed until she'd gagged.

"You'd all be healthier for it," the doctor grumbled, though he reached for the port at the same moment.

The port had made only two circuits of the table when Dominick got to his feet. Everyone else rose as well, just as they had for Captain Sprunt, and Clarice thought Dominick looked a bit taken aback to be receiving the same deference. Then he rallied and said, "Gentlemen, I leave you to your pleasures. As for me, it has been a long day and it will be an early morning, and so I bid you good night."

"I, for one, will be glad of my bed," Dr. Chapman grumbled, turning toward the door.

"Let me assist you to your cabin," Dickon said cheerfully. "It is a difficult thing for a one-armed man to move about a ship."

"Puppy!" the doctor growled. "I was wise in the ways of the sea when your greatest frontier was your mother's knee."

Dickon laughed, and even Dominick smiled, though Clarice could see that he looked tired.

"That's it for us, too," Kayin said. "I'll just make sure everyone's settled, then see if I can find my new bunk."

Dominick was not the only one to have moved today; Kayin had moved his sea chest to Freeman Lee's cabin, and Geordie had taken over Simon Foster's.

"Clarence, if I could beg your company for a moment longer?" Dominick asked as good-nights were being said. "There is a bit of unfinished business I would like to take care of before bed."

"Of course," Clarice said, smiling.

The experience was as odd as any she had had since leaving Swansgaarde—being alone in a bedroom with a man who was preparing himself for bed and giving her no more notice than if she were another item of the furniture.

No. It is not that. He is treating me as if I am precisely who I appear to be: Clarence Swann, gentleman adventurer.

Dominick flung his coat onto the nearest chair. His vest and shirt quickly followed, though he winced a little when he pulled off the shirt. The bandage, Clarice was relieved to note, was still white and clean.

"It feels good to have those off!" he said with a laugh. "Whoever laundered that shirt last had a heavy hand with the starch!" He smiled at her, inviting her to share the joke, and Clarice found herself smiling back.

"Surely you didn't invite me here just to complain of your laundress?"

"No. I meant to ask you . . . is the talisman safe?"

Clarice reached into the pocket of her coat and produced it, holding it out to him. But Dominick did not take it.

"I know I should take it," he said with a sigh. "It is why I asked you here. But now, seeing it once more . . . I think I would prefer you to keep it—if you are willing."

"Gladly," she said, dropping it back into her pocket. "But why?"

"It is bespelled," he said simply. "And I have less experience of the thaumaturgical arts than you, I wager. Besides . . . if I wear it, it will cause talk, and I cannot simply keep it in a pocket, for if I were to go aloft, it might fall into the sea and be lost. Nor is my cabin an entirely private place." He nodded toward the chart table.

"And Dobbs will probably assume I've already given it to you," Clarice observed. "But won't you need it?"

"Not to take us to the place Sprunt meant *Asesino* to go. I have already plotted our course. But if it is needed once we get there . . . I should like to have it in hands I can rely on. I know of no one I trust more than you."

The simple statement, its praise offhand and matter-of-fact, warmed Clarice in a way she had not expected. She smiled, hoping the sudden rush of blood to her cheeks would be taken for the effect of the wine. "You may always rely upon me, Dominick."

"Then that is well. And now I shall bid you good night, friend Clarence, and we shall each seek our bed. Spirits and Powers grant that tomorrow will be a quieter day than this has been."

"Quiet and peaceful both," Clarice answered quietly. "I bid you good night."

But as weary as she was, it took her a long time once she had reached her cabin to fall asleep.

And when she did, Dominick's face followed her into her dreams.

5

~

FAIR WIND AND FOLLOWING SEA

THE NEXT day, Dominick called a captain's mast, held just before
breakfast, the one time of day when all four watches were
gathered on deck.

Dr. Chapman had told Clarice that captain's masts were not
usual aboard a merchant vessel, but they had become a daily fea-
ture of life under Samuel Sprunt, for it was then, the whole crew
gathered before him, that he had announced new punishments
and restrictions.

Kayin, Geordie, and Dr. Chapman stood beside Dominick, and
he had asked Clarice to join them. Whether it was out of friendship or from a desire to remind the crew she was a valued ally,
she did not know, but she was glad of it. Both for the chance to
show her support—and because it gave her an excellent vantage
point. The medallion Clarice now wore beneath her shirt seemed
suddenly heavy; when she'd returned to her cabin last night,
she'd found that someone had searched it, but though its lock
sported several new scratches, her sea chest remained unopened.

*I wonder if it was Dobbs? It would have been a busy day for
him—trying to pick my lock, skulking about in the hold . . . I
imagine he took his imprisonment as quite the vacation!*

But he had been released from his confinement to attend the captain's mast. Dressed in his storm-crow black, Dobbs was easy to spot. He stood at the center of a small knot of sailors. Clarice did not know what he was saying to them, but she was willing to bet they were the devil's dozen who had supported his bid to become captain.

"Gentlemen!" Dominick said, stepping up to the rail. "I know you all have many questions, and I, or any here, stand ready to answer them. As you know, one of my first acts as captain was to order an inventory of our stores"—the men who had gone hungry for far too long cheered and laughed—"and I regret to say that Mr. Foster did no more than we might expect of him and sold off many of our supplies before they were loaded—"

"We will all starve!" someone shouted from the back. "The food is gone! And the water!"

Confused and angry muttering rose at that, and Dominick was forced to gesture several times for quiet before he could continue, "No! We have enough food and water to make landfall without anyone going either hungry or thirsty. You may ask Geordie or Kayin—we have two weeks of food, at full rations, for all on board. You are all men of the sea and know as well as I do that we cannot raise Cibola in that time—and you also know we dare not go there as mutineers. I have called you together to tell you I know of another place we can drop anchor. Upon my review of the log and our course, I found evidence that Captain Sprunt was making for that destination. I believe he had visited it before and meant to provision there."

"If he could do it, we can do it!" Kayin shouted, stepping up beside Dominick. "Fresh water, fresh fruit, pigs and goats—and no busybodies asking questions!"

There was another cheer at that, though not as loud as before, and Clarice could see many worried faces in the crowd below. The men who had been standing with Dobbs were working their way through the crowd now, whispering in ears.

"We are mutineers now," Dominick said. "There is nothing to

be done to change that, for it is a fact. When we drop anchor, we shall have a breathing space to consider what that means, and what we shall do. For the moment, I am your captain, and I shall do all I can to keep all of us safe."

He nodded to Kayin, who stepped back and rang the ship's bell to dismiss the company. The men began to disperse, gathering in small groups to discuss what they'd just heard. Geordie and Kayin headed down to the main deck.

"Dobbs means to make another mutiny, Dominick," Dr. Chapman said quietly as Dominick stepped back to join him.

"I know," Dominick said. "And I know he has supporters. But I do not think he can do it in a week's time, and by then we shall have reached landfall."

"And what then?" Clarice asked quietly. It was strange, she reflected, how calm she felt. Even lighthearted. It was as if their danger had still not sunk into her mind enough to bring alarm or even panic. Perhaps it was that Dominick seemed so certain that the "danger" would be little more than an inconvenience, and she was reacting instinctively to his surety.

"I do not know," Dominick said. "Marooned, if we are lucky. Shot, if we are not. It will depend on what we find."

"And how many of the men believe whatever scandal-broth Dobbs is brewing," Dr. Chapman said grimly.

"And that is a matter entirely beyond my control," Dominick said lightly. "So I will not worry about it until—and if—that day comes. For now, I am hungry for my breakfast. Let us go and see what wonders Mr. Emerson has performed today."

If not for the Reverend Dobbs lurking everywhere like a bird of ill omen, the next days would have counted as among the happiest of Clarice's life. Dobbs had not chosen to rejoin the Asesino's aristocracy in the common room. When questioned, Mr. Emerson rewarded Clarice's curiosity by saying that the reverend ate with the crew. Let him eat what he chose where he chose to and try to spread his poison as he chose as well—as Dominick said, there was nothing to be done about it. So she did her best to emulate his easy way of living only in the moment. Having made friends with Mr. Evans, the ship's carpenter, she persuaded him to craft her a pair of wooden swords and began to give Dominick the promised fencing lessons.

"It is a sword, not a bludgeon!" she called as Dominick trudged across the deck, once again, to retrieve his fallen weapon.

He was stripped to the waist, for the day was warm, and his soft brown hair had darkened with sweat, breaking into a riot of curls. The cut Sprunt's cutlass had inflicted the night of the mutiny had been no more than a deep scratch, and he had stopped bandaging it two days before.

"Oh, I know that—if it were a bludgeon, I might be of some use with it!" Despite the faint red marks along his forearms and shoulders where her attacks had struck home, he was laughing as he retrieved his practice sword and brandished it theatrically. He trudged back again to face her, straightening himself with a conscious recollection of her lessons, and made a sketchy salute. "Ready when you are, maestro."

Clarice shook out her sleeves as she returned the salute. Though Dominick could strip to the waist for this exercise, she certainly could not. Fortunately for her, this lesson did not involve much exertion—on her part anyway. He was flailing away, wasting energy and strength, while she was countering him with a few lazy movements of her sword arm. Administering counterblows was even simpler. She hadn't even worked up a single drop of sweat.

Now she knew how Count Albrecht had felt during her first lessons.

"This time, try to remember not to block with your free arm," she advised. "It is not a good habit to have when you are facing live steel. Attention!" she said formally, and Dominick raised his weapon to the guard position.

Once again she called out the positions she wished him to

take—the five basic parries that were the foundation of swords-manship—as she attacked. Though she moved slowly enough for him to parry, she struck with her full strength.

He retains his grip on the hilt by strength alone. His wrist is far too rigid. As soon as he tires . . .

Just as she predicted, once she began to speed up the moves, she quickly knocked the practice weapon from his hands—again. It fetched up against the railing—again.

"You are still holding it as if it is a belaying pin!" she cried in exasperation.

"I am a sailor, not a marine!" He strode quickly toward the rail, but this time he did not pick up the sword. Instead, he kicked off his shoes as he unwound a rope from a bight on the rail. With a fluidity of motion Clarice had in vain tried to get him to use with a sword in his hand, Dominick wrapped the rope around one wrist and ankle, and then, to her astonishment, he flew up into the air. In moments he was standing on what she now knew to call the mainsail yardarm.

"You've called me clumsy all morning," Dominick called down, laughing. "Come up here and say that!"

"You think I won't!" she shouted back, suddenly angry. *Idiot! What's he trying to prove?*

She sat down on a barrel to pull off her boots and set them aside, along with her coat. The full-skirted weskit should be enough to conceal her corset and protect her secret. She turned to the nearest ratlines and began to climb.

It was easy enough—like climbing a fishing net strung taut between two points—save that the farther from the deck she got, the more pronounced the movement of the ship seemed to get.

Oh, Papa always told me my hotheadedness would get me into trouble, and I am very much afraid he was right.

Within moments her flare of temper had subsided, for though Clarice angered easily, her anger cooled just as fast. By then she had climbed so far that a fall to the deck would have disastrous consequences—if not death, then certainly the unmasking of her deception. She gritted her teeth, forcing herself to look up instead of down, and met Dominick's eyes.

The expression of delighted shock on his face made it all worth it.

He did not expect me to take his dare! she thought in sudden glee.

He reached out and grasped her wrist. She grasped his in turn, and he lifted her the last few feet to the beam. He was holding to one of the buntlines for safety, but his whole manner was as easy as if he stood on the deck so far below. To her great relief, he shifted his grasp from her wrist to her arm and gestured her toward the comforting haven of the mast. With something solid—though hardly still—to cling to, Clarice turned her gaze outward.

The deck below them had dwindled to mere table size, and the rocking motion of the ship placed open sea beneath their feet every few seconds. But if the position was precarious, the view was worth it. *No wonder a seaman will not give up the sea,* she thought suddenly. *To relinquish all this would be as if one were to give up an entire kingdom. . . .*

The sea stretched sparkling to a horizon that had to be miles and miles away. In the distance, she could see a bright line of foam against the water. It appeared as if things were leaping into the air from it from time to time. Like very distant fish leaping from the water—except at this distance, they must be large fish indeed! She pointed toward it questioningly.

"Dolphins," Dominick said. "They mean good luck. They like to play in the bow wave—once they notice we're here, they'll probably accompany us for a while."

She bit back an exclamation at their beauty—such a response belonged to Princess Clarice of Swansgaarde, not plain Mr. Clarence Swann—and took a deep breath. "I still say you handle a sword as if it were a club."

He grinned in unfeigned delight. "Why, if you say that after following me up here, I am forced to believe it. I present myself to you in all humility and ask your pardon."

To Clarice's horror, he swept her an extravagant bow—and slipped from the beam. But he had never released the buntline he held, so he merely swung a few feet out into space before regaining his perch. Laughing the whole time.

"You fool! You cannot risk your life so!" The words burst out of Clarice before she thought.

Dominick's expression quickly sobered. "I . . . You are right, of course. I am no longer a mere member of the crew."

"I—" Clarice began, not knowing what she was about to say. Apologize for destroying the merry mood of the day? Confess that the outburst had not come from any consideration of *Asesino*'s future—but from the realization of how she would feel if she saw his body broken upon the deck below?

A fine time to think of yourself as Clarice instead of Clarence! she scolded herself.

But was it that? Princess Clarice had exchanged kisses with the handsome young men at her father's court. She had learned to flirt just as she had learned to dance and had done a good deal of both. But those partners had been acquaintances, not friends. It had all been in fun.

She had never expected friendship.

Dominick was perhaps the truest friend she had ever made. He was honest and open with her, taking her at face value and enjoying her company as much as she enjoyed his.

But she was not being honest with him, and that had gone from a simple fact, to a minor annoyance, to a nagging irritation. She wanted to be as straightforward with him as he was with her—and she could not be.

What if she told him she was not Clarence, but Clarice? Would they still be friends? Companions? Comrades?

Or would he only see that she had lied to him? Deceived him?

She glanced to the deck. It was a long way below. But there was more than one way to fall. . . .

Movement caught her attention. Reverend Dobbs had stepped out onto the open deck and was looking up at them.

Dominick saw him, too. "Let us go down," he said quietly.

"Yes," Clarice answered, low. "Let us go down."

Clarice was still brooding over the matter when she retired to her cabin that night—after dinner, after a merry evening of playing cards in the common room, after a last stroll on the deck with Dominick.

In the short weeks the *Asesino* had been at sea, he had become a good friend.

No, she thought stormily. *He and* Clarence Swann *have become good friends. But Clarence Swann is a shadow, a figment. A mask I hide behind. And, oh, it did not chafe until . . .*

Until today, when she had looked at Dominick and wanted him to see *her,* not the mask she wore.

She'd never felt this way before. Not this combination of nervous and self-conscious and giddy and *terrified.* Dantan's birth had freed her from the tyranny of having to live for Swansgaarde . . . but she had given no thought to living and loving for herself. Not until now—when the situation was more tangled and hopeless than when she had spent her days knowing she must marry Swansgaarde's next prince.

Not because she was aboard a ship full of mutineers who had little choice in their futures save to turn pirate. And not because they sailed toward an unknown destination filled with possible dangers that was likely only the first step on an even-more-peril-filled journey.

No.

The situation was hopeless because Dominick Moryet had absolutely no idea she was a woman.

And so she had absolutely no idea if he could come to care for her, too.

She was falling in love with—might already *be* in love with—a man who didn't even know she existed. Literally.

You must tell him, she told herself sternly. *Oh, not that you are in love with him—Mama has said that men do not like to be surprised by declarations of that nature. What you must tell him is that you are not Clarence, but Clarice, and then hope that his friendship remains true.*

But not right now, she added in a hasty mental footnote. *Not when we sail toward Spirits and Powers know what! When we have seen what's there . . . then I shall find a moment when we may be private, and I will tell him, if not all, then at least that I am Clarice, not Clarence.*

I know he will understand the reason for my disguise. That I am certain of. What I do not know is . . . will he like "Clarice" at all?

No answer was to be found within the pages of her diary, or the four walls of her cabin, and brooding on the unknown was a useless occupation at the best of times. With a sigh, Clarice returned her diary to her chest and got to her feet.

Time for bed.

Perhaps tomorrow would be as glorious as today had been.

But of course the idyll could not last.

That evening, they had barely taken their seats for dinner when the door opened again and Reverend Dobbs entered. It was the first time he had come to the common room since the mutiny. He gazed around the table with a tight, triumphant smile, and Clarice tried to stop herself from thinking of him as a feral cur that no amount of loving-kindness could tame.

"I hope I am not unwelcome?" he asked silkily.

Immediately, Clarice's suspicions rose to a fever pitch. What did he want? Was he here to gloat? What did he know that they did not?

Dominick had risen to his feet when Dobbs entered. "Why, of

course not. Jerrold, fetch a chair. I shall have another place laid for you."

Jerrold had made himself Dominick's cabin boy simply by virtue of being constantly underfoot, until Mr. Emerson had given up trying to keep him in the galley.

"For your guest?" Dobbs asked, still in that same mild, treacherous tone, as Jerrold brought a chair and set out plates and glassware from the store now displayed in the sideboard. "Or do I put words in your mouth you were not about to speak?"

Dominick didn't answer.

"You know you do, you canting gallows-bird," Dr. Chapman said roughly. "I can't say I welcome your presence here, speaking only for myself, but you have every right to be here. I wish you *were* here under the guise of a guest. A guest can be disinvited. If you were a guest, I'd throw you out myself," he added in a lower tone.

"Ah, honesty, at least," Dobbs said, seating himself and reaching for the bottle to fill his glass.

"That's ironic, coming from you," the doctor growled.

"Gentlemen," Dominick said, "I will have no quarrels over our food. Reverend Dobbs, I am sorry if you thought you must avoid this place, but perhaps I might ask, why come back now?"

"Why, to experience the company of gentlemen, of course," Dobbs answered, turning the remark to a slur on Kayin and Geordie by the direction of his glance.

Geordie flushed dark. Kayin affected not to hear. Jerrold finished laying out Dobbs's place. "I'll go and get the dinner now, Cap'n, I mean, if—"

"Yes, of course, Jerrold, thank you," Dominick said. "Whatever your reason, please consider yourself welcome," Dominick added to Dobbs.

The presence of Reverend Dobbs cast a chill over the meal. No one was in the mood for jokes or stories, and everyone seemed preternaturally cautious of his or her words. At last the plates were cleared away, the port was set on the table, and the smoking lamp was lit.

When Clarice took out her cigar case, Dominick leaned toward her and asked, "May I beg the favor?"

She opened the case and held it out to him; he took one of the small, black cigarillos.

He has never done that before, she thought. *But Reverend Dobbs would be enough to make anyone turn to drink—or worse.*

When Dominick had puffed the cigarillo alight, he paused to sip from his wineglass. Clarice realized he was stalling. Or . . . gathering his courage?

"As some of you know—and more of you guess," he said with a bland look in Dobbs's direction, "tomorrow we shall reach our destination. As you are aware, it is no more than a mark on a chart to me. I know nothing more of it than that Mr. Sprunt, our late captain—"

"Foully slain by you all," Dobbs said with quiet force.

"No," Clarice said strongly. "*I* alone ended his life. Do not place that blame on anyone else here."

"I still do not know what reason you had to interfere in a matter that had nothing to do with you," Dobbs sneered.

"As much as anyone on this ship, with our provisions—and our *water*—meant to run out midocean. We have enough to reach our destination *now,* but with a full crew, we would have been perishing of thirst days ago. But"—she reined in her temper with an effort—"I am afraid I have interrupted our captain, and for that I beg pardon."

Though Dominick managed to keep a smile from his face at her utterly mendacious segue, his eyes danced with merriment. "As I was saying, before Clarence's unconscionable rudeness, tomorrow we shall reach our destination. I hope, as we all do, to find it uninhabited, but I know not what may lie in this place Mr. Sprunt wished to sail to. So I will issue weapons to the crew, and our guns will be run out and ready."

There was a pause.

"Let us consider that one man at this table may know more of our destination than he has yet seen fit to confide in us," Dr. Chapman said with heavy irony.

Amazingly, Dominick laughed. "Why, my dear doctor! I am certain he does! And I am equally certain he will not tell us anything of any earthly use. So let us go on as if we had put him over the side with his cronies—do you not think this a wise plan, Clarence?"

"Certainly it is the easiest one," Clarice answered, a bit startled at being asked. "Though I dare to say he has filled the crew's ears with all manner of nonsense tales about the horrors that await us."

"Do you think so?" Dominick said, as if he were much struck by the idea.

The Reverend Dobbs now looked decidedly uncomfortable. "You malign me," he muttered halfheartedly.

"Not I," Dominick said virtuously, and Kayin snorted rudely. This time, it was Clarice who was forced to conceal a smile. "At any rate," Dominick said, rising, "I shall bid you gentlemen good evening. Tomorrow will be a day of great interest to us all."

"Interest," Clarice thought sourly, *is far too mild a word for it!*

The morning dawned bright and clear, and Dominick called a captain's mast to tell the crew he expected to reach their destination by midafternoon at the latest. He detailed his plans for preparing the guns and issuing weapons, reminding them that he knew as little of what they could expect to find as they did.

Things went well enough until a voice shouted out of the crowd, "And what of the treasure, Captain? What of that?"

I see the Reverend Dobbs has not given up hope, Clarice thought sourly.

"Why, Gil Morley—is that you? Stand forward so I can answer you fairly," Dominick said.

After some pushing and shoving, at last Morley came—or, rather, was thrust—forward. He didn't look happy to be the center of attention and stuck his chin out belligerently.

"Whoever has put this rumor of treasure into your head clearly knows more of our destination than I, and I invite him to present himself and give us all the benefit of his wisdom," Dominick said.

Most of those listening took this for a joke and laughed appreciatively.

"I know nothing of our destination, and I know nothing of any treasure," Dominick went on, "but I do know this: whatever we find at our destination, we will all share in it equally, as comrades and shipmates. This I vow, before you all, and before *Asesino* herself." He placed a hand on the wood of the railing before him with a gesture very like a caress.

To nobody's particular surprise, most of the inventory of arms they should have been carrying was missing, but Kayin assured Dominick that the remaining weapons would be ready by two bells of the afternoon. Clarice had been aboard long enough to translate that into an hour past noon.

With Dr. Chapman still unable to use his injured arm, Clarice was pressed once again into service as surgeon's mate. She and Dr. Chapman inventoried the contents of the surgery and arranged everything so it would be easily and quickly available. She sharpened all of Dr. Chapman's tools and hoped desperately they would not be needed, for if any surgery must be done today, she would have to be his hands.

As she worked, she traced the progress of the ship's getting ready by the thumps, crashes, and muffled swearing she heard faintly through the deck and the bulkheads.

"You're lucky you're a passenger," Dr. Chapman said. "Else they'd be putting you to work."

"And you aren't?" She chuckled.

"You're the only one left on this tub who doesn't faint at the sight of blood," he answered cheerfully. "Other than Dobbs, and

I'm certainly not trusting him within a day's sail of my equipment." He glanced toward the porthole, frowning. "God help us if we are forced to fight," he said as if to himself.

At her look of inquiry, he sighed. "We have eight twelve-pounders with untrained gun crews. I doubt that means much to you. The gun's rating is for the weight of the cannonball it fires. A first-rate ship of the line—a military vessel—might carry a hundred guns. Forty-eight pounders with gun crews trained until they can get off five shots a minute, and a captain who understands that the whole of his ship is another weapon."

Clarice had never seen their cannon, but she knew that polishing them had been Freeman Lee's favorite form of extra work, though he'd liked all of them. *Asesino* had been as sparkling and scrubbed as a prince's toy, though the men whipped to the work had been half starved and exhausted.

It does not matter how pretty we are, or how pretty the cannon are, if we must fight, Clarice thought uneasily. *But Sprunt would never set sail for a harbor he would have to fight his way into,* she told herself encouragingly.

"But surely we are not likely to encounter an enemy in these waters?" Clarice asked, swallowing hard, her mouth suddenly dry. Dr. Chapman had been a naval surgeon once. Perhaps he had even been involved in such battles as he described so offhandedly.

"If we do, I hope Dominick has the good sense to surrender at once," Dr. Chapman said dryly. "Hanging is a cleaner death than gangrene—and quicker than drowning. But never mind. All you need to know is that any ship we meet is likely to carry at least sixteen guns to our eight and know how to use them."

"Then why are we armed at all?" Clarice asked in exasperation.

"Because a salvo or two will actually discourage some people." He glanced toward the porthole. "It looks as if we are losing the sun," he added mildly. "Let us go up on deck and see."

When they emerged into the air, Clarice saw that the sky had taken on a pewter sheen.

"High mist," Dr. Chapman said, squinting at the sky. "Odd time of day for it."

"I suppose any sort of weather is possible."

That comment earned Clarice a rude snort. "Not at sea, my fine young landlubber. Not at sea."

An hour later the high mist had grown thicker, blurring the horizon and softening the shadows until they could barely be seen. Three times Dickon had gone to Dominick to confirm their heading, and a few minutes ago Dominick had given the order to take in their sails. They were continuing along their previous course, for it was that or stop where they were—something Clarice was not even sure was possible—until the mist lifted. She was no longer certain it ever would.

Clarice stood beside Dominick on the foredeck as he paced and peered into the mist before them, checking both ship's compass and ship's clock every few seconds. The horizon grew closer minute by minute as the mist closed in—she hadn't had the nerve to ask how far away it was now. Dominick's mouth was set in a grim line, and all of the crew lined the rails to gaze out to sea. Even Kayin's best efforts to order them to sword drills and musket drills had little effect. The tension in the air was palpable. It seemed to thicken with every breath Clarice drew into her lungs.

"Kayin, please find Reverend Dobbs and bring him here," Dominick said abruptly.

Clarice looked at him questioningly as Kayin hurried to obey.

"It seems we must question our upright man of God after all," Dominick said grimly.

Another quarter hour passed before Kayin returned. From the look of him, Reverend Dobbs hadn't wanted to come. His coat was distinctly rumpled, and from the look of it, the collar had been used as a handle.

As soon as he'd mounted the steps, Dobbs began, "I demand to know—"

"You make no demands on the deck of this ship," Dominick said quietly, and something in his voice made Dobbs stop in mid-sentence.

"Now," Dominick said briskly. "You were in Sprunt's confidence. You helped him drive this ship to mutiny. You know we sail toward the same destination he intended to make for. Tell me what is there."

"I will tell you nothing," Dobbs said with a smirk. "Save that your one chance for life is to deliver this vessel into my hands at once."

Glancing toward Kayin, Dominick raised one eyebrow. "And what do you suppose would happen then?" he asked mildly.

"Nothing I want to see," Kayin said bluntly.

Dominick heaved a theatrical sigh. "Very well then! Take him below. And Kayin? Lay him in irons on the orlop. It is below the waterline, you know," Dominick said to Dobbs, as if this might be something Dobbs was unaware of. "It will be the first to flood if we sink."

Dominick turned his back as if the matter were settled. Clarice caught her breath. To leave a man to drown in cold blood was a very different thing from killing one in the heat of a battle.

But sure enough, Dodds had not gone three steps before he turned back. "Wait! I only meant that there are reefs ahead. Yes. And you will go aground upon them without my aid. I can guide you through them. For that I shall need Captain Sprunt's talisman, of course."

Clarice was carefully looking anywhere but at Dominick, but she did not miss the flash of surprise that crossed Kayin's face, as if what he had just heard was unbelievable.

"Dickon!" Dominick raised his voice a little. "Could you tell me, have you gone deaf in the past quarter hour?"

The surprise in Dickon's voice was a mirror to the look on Kayin's. "Why . . . no. How could I have? I heard you perfectly plainly."

"Then it is possible you would also hear the sound of surf

upon a coastline—or breaking upon a reef large enough to run us aground?" Dominick asked mildly.

"Why, I do believe that is not beyond my powers." The mockery in Dickon's voice was plain—and not directed at Dominick.

"So," Dominick said, turning back to face Dobbs, "you are perfectly safe. It is just as well, since I do not have Sprunt's talisman."

"Where is it?" For the first time, Dobbs's composure seemed truly rattled.

"I could not tell you where it is at the moment," Dominick said, and Clarice knew this was the truth, for he had not once asked her where she kept it. "Have you anything more to say? . . . No? Then you may go below. Kayin, please place the reverend in his own cabin. Securely."

"No irons?" Clarice thought Kayin sounded rather disappointed.

"Not right now," Dominick said.

"We know more than we did," Dominick said as soon as Dobbs had been escorted away. He stood shoulder to shoulder with her, his voice so low that no one standing three feet away could have heard.

"What?" she whispered back. "He told us nothing."

"He told us that the talisman is vital to making a safe landfall. You had best go and get it."

"I am wearing it right now."

His teeth flashed briefly in a grateful smile.

Another hour and the mist pressed against the flanks of the ship itself. Dominick had taken in even more sail.

"Can we stop?" Clarice asked him in a low voice.

He shook his head. "We could drift, but I do not like that either. Our safest choice is to send out the jolly boat on a long line.

It is a technique for getting through a fog bank. I have seen it done once." He turned to give the order.

"Wait." The medallion around Clarice's neck had suddenly grown icy cold. But before Dominick could ask a question, or Clarice could tell him how little she knew, the fog began to billow and melt away as if it were steam.

In another instant, they saw the ships waiting for them.

6

~

Down the Throat of the Dragon

HE TWO ships stood perhaps a mile off *Asesino*'s bow. The motley and colorful garb of the figures crowding their rails left even Clarice little doubt that she was looking at . . . pirates.

Both ships were clearly waiting for *Asesino*—they had their guns run out, and she could see they bristled with cannon. Dozens of them. Large ones. Ones that the crews of the ships were clearly expert in the use of. So transfixed was she by the horrible sight that Clarice barely registered that the fog was gone. The snap of *Asesino*'s mainsail filling with wind made her jump. The ship picked up speed, sliding smoothly forward.

Directly toward the other two ships.

"What are you *doing*?" she demanded, her voice high and sharp.

"Sailing into harbor," Dominick said, his voice flat.

He pointed, and at last Clarice was able to raise her gaze past the dazzle of weapons directly ahead to look beyond them.

There was land.

Quite a lot of it, in fact.

Magic, she thought in a daze. *Magic to conceal this island from passing ships, magic to summon the fog . . . What more? What worse? Sprunt must have known. . . .*

Beyond the arms of a rocky breakwater, a bay as round and perfect as a coin lay mirror still. The breeze eddying toward them brought the scent of flowers and oranges. Across the bay was a white crescent of beach, and beyond that the buildings of a town straggled up the side of a green-forested peak. A lazy curl of smoke eddied from its top. *Volcano,* she thought automatically. *I have read of them.*

"Oh," she said inadequately.

They were close enough to the pirates now for her to read the names painted on the bows of the ships as they passed: the one to port was the *Vile Vixen* and the one to starboard was the *Horrid Hangman.* The *Vixen*'s crew seemed to be mostly or entirely female; they hooted and shouted as *Asesino* glided by.

"I don't think our poor ship is properly named to keep this company," Clarice said, trying to make a joke of it.

"You're wrong," Dominick said quietly. "Her name means 'murderer' in the Iberian tongue. But it is bad luck to change a ship's name, so she sails as she was named."

After that, Clarice could think of nothing more to say.

The entrance to the harbor was bordered by two half-circles of black boulders half the height of a man. She didn't need to look at Dominick's expression to know this was hardly a natural formation. She could see two enormous rings bolted to the rocks at either side of the harbor, each with a chain attached that was as thick as her leg. The chains vanished into the water, but the hyperreality of them told Clarice that they were bespelled: they would probably go taut on command.

Just as they entered the harbor, one of the ships behind them fired a single shot. The sound echoed across the water like a thunderclap, and a moment later an answering flash and boom came from somewhere far above the town.

"I think it would be a very good idea if you were to display the medallion openly," Dominick said, nodding back the way they'd come. The *Vixen* and the *Hangman* were coming about, sliding with predatory grace in *Asesino*'s wake. With shaking hands, Clarice did as she was bid, fumbling the heavy gold chain from beneath her shirt to hang exposed about her neck.

"I wonder what Mr. Dobbs would say if he were here?" she said, pleased that her voice did not tremble at all.

"Undoubtedly he would say he was the captain, and we must all be hanged at once. And for just such reason, I think it would be a very good idea, Clarence, if you stopped being a passenger. I do not think this is a port that welcomes random visitors. You must become my first mate. It is enough to explain why you carry the talisman and not I," Dominick added. "I will tell Kayin privately as soon as I may."

"So long as you also tell him it is only a masquerade." *Another masquerade.* "I know nothing about ships."

"I suggest you learn very quickly. If they discover the truth, it will not go well with any of us." He turned away and began shouting orders to Kayin.

Though the situation was utterly terrifying, *Asesino*'s crew dropped anchor smoothly. Within the harbor, the air was utterly still.

"Stay here," Dominick said, heading for the main deck.

"But—" Clarice said. The *Vixen* and the *Hangman* were both lowering jolly boats, and she had no doubt what their destination was. Dominick merely waved a hand as he vaulted down the steps.

He is rallying the crew, she realized. *Telling them what to expect, as far as we can imagine it.*

But her unreasonable pride in his coolheaded cleverness was overshadowed by an equally unreasonable anger. They were likely hours, if not mere minutes, from death, and she felt irrationally cheated. Cheated of a future, cheated of the chance to tell Dominick the truth, cheated of all the hours and days and minutes she could have spent at Dominick's side . . .

If this is love, it is the most inconvenient thing in the world!

"They'll be here in a few minutes," Dickon said, his voice tight with fear.

"Then we will welcome them with as much proper style as we can manage," Clarice answered. "See? Even now Dominick is seeing to it."

Down on the deck, a section of the rail hinged like a gate was being swung back, and a rope ladder lowered over the side.

Dickon smiled. "You are so calm about all this," he said gratefully. "I'm sure . . . I'm sure all will go well."

"Of course it will," Clarice said stoutly. *I am as terrified as you are, Dickon. The only difference between us is that I have had years of training in never showing it—or anything else I do not mean to show.* That discipline had made her masquerade not only possible, but easy. The thing she most feared was that she would never have the chance to learn if she could set it aside and simply *be.*

"Ahoy, the *Asesino*!"

The first of the jolly boats—the one rowed by an all-female crew—had reached them. Clarice moved over to the rail for a better look and Dickon followed her.

The woman in the bow was dressed in men's clothes, but unlike Clarice she had made no attempt to conceal her sex. Her hair was a mass of fiery-red curls pulled back into a tail that cascaded halfway down her back, and the style showed off to great advantage the enormous gold hoops—several of them—that pierced each ear. She wore a necklace of rough-cut emeralds about her neck, and beneath her coat of scarlet velvet she wore a short leather vest held closed with a row of gleaming buttons that Clarice suspected were gold coins. She had a cutlass belted at her hip, and a brace of holstered pistols balanced it on the other side. She looked up and caught Clarice's gaze.

"Hello, boy! Is your mother at home?" she called.

"I'll ask," Clarice answered dryly. "Who shall I say is calling?"

That made the woman laugh heartily. "Why, tell her that

Melisande Watson, Queen of the Seas from Albion to the Hispalides, has come for tea!"

The woman's cocky self-assurance made Clarice smile. "I'm
afraid my mother is away," she called. "You will have to settle for
my captain!"

"I rarely settle for anything!" Captain Watson shouted back
gaily, and then her boat was at the ladder, and she sprang up it
with catlike agility.

Clarice saw, with increasing gloom, that two of the other
women in the boat followed her. One had skin as black as ebony
wood, and the other, the flat, golden features of the Hispalideans.
Both were dressed in the fashion of sailors, and both were excessively armed. *Really, is there the least need to carry quite so many
knives?* Clarice thought waspishly. *Only think what would happen if they fell overboard.*

She'd wondered if all fifteen of the boat's company would be
joining the *Asesino*'s crew on the deck, but apparently the others
were just there to row, since as soon as the three women were
safely aboard, the jolly boat moved smoothly away.

The second boat approached quickly. Compared to Captain
Watson's flamboyance, the attire of the *Hangman*'s captain was
decidedly sober. He might have been mistaken for the Reverend
Dobbs's sartorial soul mate—save for the hangman's noose he
wore about his neck, the knot trailing down his chest like a grisly
fall of lace. His crew, if not as colorfully attired as Captain Watson's, were equally well armed.

"Topper Harrison, captain of the *Horrid Hangman,* requesting
permission to come aboard, all shipshape and prayerbook fashion!" he called.

*At least we have now been properly introduced to the people
who are going to kill us all,* Clarice thought with dark humor.

"I'm surprised to see a new face here at the House of the Four
Winds," Captain Harrison was saying as Clarice approached. "I

thought I knew everyone in our particular line of work. But I don't know you." For a man who wore a hangman's noose as an article of dress, he seemed remarkably ordinary. Scary, but ordinary.

"But perhaps you know this," Clarice said, before Dominick could answer. She slipped the chain over her head and held the medallion up so both he and Captain Watson could see it. "Forgive us if we considered it an invitation."

"My first mate, Clarence Swann," Dominick said.

"Mr. Swann looks as if he has many sterling qualities," Captain Watson purred, and despite herself Clarice found herself blushing. "Would it be too forward of me to ask where he came by that particular *carte d'invitation?*"

"I took it off a man I killed," Clarice answered with absolute truthfulness. *So it is not just a guide to a location, but a passkey of sorts. And that means Samuel Sprunt was either very wicked . . . or very stupid.*

"They disagreed about some matters to do with the running of the ship," Dominick added innocently. "I do hope he wasn't a friend of yours."

"I have no friends," Captain Harrison said smoothly. "Well then. Enjoy your stay, gentlemen. The liberty of the House is yours. Drink—women—dice—whatever you fancy—"

"—and have the gold to pay for," Captain Watson finished with a cool smile. She turned and gestured to her two companions. The ebony-skinned one drew a small silver pipe from her pocket—a bosun's call—and piped a warbling call. Out on the water, one of the jolly boats raised its oars in response, then began rowing toward the ship. Captain Watson's departure was accomplished with as much speed as her arrival, and as soon as one jolly boat was away, the other began to approach.

"A word of advice," Captain Harrison said as he turned to follow his men down the ladder. "You'll want to be careful here. This might not be the sort of place you're used to."

"You might be surprised at what I'm used to," Dominick answered coolly.

Harrison bowed slightly. He swung over the side and began to climb down, then stopped. Clarice had no doubt the pause was calculated; being a pirate apparently required a theatrical disposition. "Oh. Just one more thing, you being new here. Sailing in, that's easy enough. Sailing out . . . not as simple." He tipped his hat and vanished down the ladder.

In silence, the crew of *Asesino* watched the two boats return to their ships. "Well," Clarice said, once the pirates were safely out of earshot. "Nobody shot us."

"Yet," Dominick answered.

The senior officers—and Clarice, in her dual roles as "useful passenger" and "first mate"—were gathered around the table in the common room. Clarice's thoughts were dark, tangled, and very, very personal.

She must tell Dominick who she was—or more precisely, *what* she was. The longer she delayed, the more awkward it would be for both of them. But their arrival at the House of the Four Winds had complicated matters. It would have been easy to tell him—and to make sure no other overheard—on an unpopulated tropical island. But this crowded pirate haven was most definitely *not* the place for such a confession. Indeed, Clarice realized with a start, nobody at all had better discover the truth about her.

"We must have the barrels," Dominick repeated, running a hand through his hair. "If nothing else, those—and water to fill them. And we can get them here."

About half the *Asesino*'s cargo was still intact, and Sprunt had been carrying a young fortune in gold in his cabin strongbox. During the voyage here, they'd discussed the possibility of making for a known port to buy what they needed; both Dominick and Kayin thought there was sufficient gold to pay for new—and properly made—water barrels, but they'd meant to settle those matters once they'd reached safe haven.

Only there was no safe haven.

"And the crew will want liberty," Dickon said. "Most of them heard what that hangman said, and those as haven't will have heard tell by now."

"It will be impossible to keep them aboard," Dr. Chapman pointed out. "Especially once we dock—or off-load cargo."

"Kayin? Geordie?" Dominick said. "We've said we're pirates, and this is clearly a pirate haven. How much of the crew can you trust to keep to that story?"

"Any of them—when sober" was the swift reply. "Pour a bottle of drink down their throats and they'll give the game away to anyone who asks."

"Well . . . can't you tell them not to drink?" Clarice asked.

Everyone at the table stared at her. "As well tell them not to breathe," Dickon said at last. "Everyone knows where a sailor will be at the end of a voyage. In the nearest tavern—or in a room above it."

Beyond that lay the unspoken truth: the crew had elected Dominick captain—and could depose him just as quickly if he gave enough unpopular orders.

"So let us marshal what facts we have, and see if there are enough of them to weave us a cable tow that can extract us from these doldrums," Dominick said.

There was a moment's pause.

"Dr. Chapman," Clarice said. "Didn't you once tell me that Mr. Sprunt was a very lucky man to have survived so much misfortune? And you, Dominick—didn't you say he'd been twice boarded by pirates?"

"Yes." Dominick frowned, thinking. "He lost his cargo each time, and some of his crew—kidnapped or killed—but he was let to go free."

"What if he wasn't?" Clarice asked. "What if, on those voyages, he brought his cargo here—and sold it? And the other ships—"

"*Atlantis,* too, was taken by pirates, but with a less fortunate outcome," Dr. Chapman said. "Or so he said when he reached shore, claiming to have been set adrift in one of the jolly boats— but near enough to the islands that he reached shore. *Sirocco* and *Aglaia* were lost in storms—again, he and many of the crew escaped in boats and managed to make landfall. *Gloriana* and *Albion* burned to the waterline and sank near deserted stretches of the Hesperian coast; Sprunt and the other survivors built a signal fire and waited for rescue from the fort nearby."

"And in each of those cases, there was only Sprunt's word for what had happened," Clarice said. "And I will wager anything you like that the crew members who survived the 'boardings' of those ships were the same ones we set adrift. Who would doubt their story when they reached port to tell it? If Reverend Dobbs was with them, I'm sure he confirmed it."

"You think Samuel Sprunt was a pirate?" Dominick asked, as if this were the most unbelievable thing he had ever heard.

"Why not?" Clarice answered. "He had the medallion. This is a pirate haven. Pirates steal ships and cargoes, and I suspect that is just what he did. Perhaps the ships that were boarded and released were those where he could not manage to induce the crew to mutiny. Or perhaps there was some other reason they were spared."

"But—see here, Clarence, that doesn't make sense," Dickon said. "If you're right, why didn't those two recognize our ship? Or the medallion?"

"Ah, but Sprunt was a hired captain, who might be master of any ship—and he could hardly have written to tell them he was coming! As for the other, they *did* recognize the medallion," Clarice said. "But I am sure there is more than one in existence, and they cannot know whose this once was, for I did not tell them the name of its former owner."

"Dobbs will, right enough," Geordie said gloomily. "As soon as he's within shouting distance."

"Which we will all take great care to make sure he is not," Dominick said firmly. "Though I would not object overmuch if we could somehow manage to leave him behind here when we sail."

"Leave that to me," Dr. Chapman said. "When you're ready to sail, I can mix up a dose that will keep him asleep for a week. All you'll need to do is get him ashore at the right time."

"Then that's what we'll do," Dominick said decisively. "As for *Asesino*, no one here will recognize the ship as having been Sprunt's—if he has come here before, he has come on a different ship."

"So much to the good," Dr. Chapman said. "And if only we could swear on the Bell and the Book that we had sunk a dozen or so helpless ships on our way here, we might be perfectly at ease. As it is, sooner or later the secret will get out that we're—"

"Honest, virtuous, law-abiding mutineers?" Clarice asked with feigned innocence.

Her remark made everyone at the table shout with laughter.

Even Dr. Chapman voiced an approving chuckle. "Quite so, my boy. Do you think that will be enough to save us?"

"Well, it might." The only thing she knew about pirates was that they were outlaws—and no laws meant no rules. They might do anything at all. "At least it couldn't hurt."

"Then let us go ashore and see what we can do to make our ship ready for sail," Dominick said firmly. "Clarence, I hope you will accompany me?"

"Of course," Clarice answered instantly.

Kayin picked a crew, and soon enough Clarice and Dominick were being rowed across the lagoon in *Asesino*'s remaining jolly boat. Upon arrival, Kayin had the men drag the boat up onto the sand, and after drawing lots to see who would stay behind with the boat, the others headed for the nearest tavern.

At least, Clarice told herself, Kayin was with them. Not that he would nursemaid them, but he could remind them they needed to be capable of rowing back to *Asesino* when she and Dominick had finished their exploration. For that was what this was in truth—a reconnaissance, to see what might be possible here.

"Perilous as our greeting was," Dominick said as they walked toward the street, "it was not nearly perilous enough. Any warlord of Khitai would have demanded bribes and probably killed a few people to make sure he was taken seriously. All they did was wish us a good day."

"They wanted to see the talisman," Clarice reminded him. "I don't think they'd have been nearly as accommodating if we didn't have it."

"Yes," Dominick said thoughtfully, "but they didn't seem to care too much about where it had come from. I don't think we've passed all their tests yet. Be on your guard."

"Always good advice." *And much easier to follow when I am not gawking like a tourist.*

But it was difficult to avoid in such an exotic location. While her reading had told her what to expect from the Hispalides, the reality was far more vibrant than she'd imagined. The air was filled with the scent of flowers, and the source of that scent twined over walls and even roofs in profligate display. The town was mostly made up of one- and two-story buildings of stone and limewashed brick facing hard-pounded-dirt streets along which goats and chickens—and the occasional pig—ambled with perfect ease. From the talk aboard the ship, Clarice had expected to be confronted by little more than a vista of taverns and brothels, but in fact there were barbers and surgeons, tailors, jewelers, and even a candy store.

"This is not what I expected," Clarice said, lingering in front of a shop whose window display wouldn't have been out of place in Lochrin or Vinarborg—or Heimlichstadt. The window displayed a full-rigged four-masted ship, completely made, so far as she could tell, from glistening spun and colored sugar—hull, deck, rigging, sails, and even the ocean it sailed over. In the shop's interior, she could see rows of cabinets and display cases, just as in any other sweet shop.

"I suppose buccaneers have a sweet tooth, too," Dominick said. "Come on, let's see what they have."

Before she could come up with a good reason why they shouldn't, he'd taken her arm and walked into the shop. The bell over the door jingled.

"Good morning, gentlemen. What can I get you?" The proprietor emerged from the back of the shop at the sound the bell. He wore the voluminous white apron of his profession and looked . . . perfectly ordinary. Clarice wasn't sure whether she was relieved or disappointed. This was a pirate haven after all. Shouldn't it be more . . . dramatic?

"Something sweet," Dominick said. The proprietor smiled slightly at the small joke. "We've just made port, and my friend and I were seeing the sights. That ship in your window is certainly one of them."

Now the shop's owner smiled widely. "Yes, indeed. My own work. A copy of one I did for a party at the House of the Four Winds—the original, of course, did not survive the evening. It is not for sale, I fear—but if you wish something similar? A copy of your own ship perhaps?"

"Perhaps later," Dominick said. "For now . . ."

"Candied ginger?" the shopkeeper asked. "Or candied limes? Very popular those, and not sour at all. Rock candy, marchpane, sugarplums . . ."

As he listed his wares—samples of which were on display in a small glass case on the counter—Clarice tried hard to keep her mouth from watering. Her family had always teased her about her sweet tooth, and all of it looked so good.

"Candied ginger for me," Dominick said. "And my friend will have a loaf of marchpane." Clarice looked up at him, startled, and couldn't help grinning back when Dominick winked. "At least if our money's good here." He drew out a gold coin—an

Albionnaise double angel. It could probably buy the entire contents of the shop.

"Well, gold spends anywhere," the shopkeeper said. "So if
you'll give me a moment, young fellow, I'll bring out my kit and
see what she's worth."

"What are you doing?" Clarice whispered as soon as the man
had disappeared into the back of the shop.

"Buying sweets," Dominick whispered back. "I need to see
what the rules are. If any."

A moment later the owner returned with a touchstone, a bottle
of aqua fortis, and scales. "You'll have to trust they're honest," he
warned as he set Dominick's coin in one of the pans. "But then,"
he said, laughing, "you'd have to do that anywhere."

"Of course we trust you," Clarice said mendaciously. "After
all, you want us to come back."

"Just so, young master," the proprietor said with a chuckle. He
scraped the coin against his touchstone, then carefully added a
couple of drops of aqua fortis to the golden scratch marks. The
purity of the metal could be told by the color the acid left behind.
The acid bubbled and foamed, but did not destroy the gold. "Ask
anywhere in Dorado. They'll tell you Peter Robinson is as honest
as the day is long."

"Dorado?" Clarice asked. "Isn't this the House of the Four
Winds?"

"Ah, young master, it is and it isn't. This town, now, this is
Dorado. And in a general way, this whole area of ocean is the House
of the Four Winds. But if you mean to get particular, the House is
up there." He jerked his thumb in the direction of the mountaintop.
"No doubt you'll be seeing it soon enough, never fear."

Not if I can help it, Clarice thought firmly. But she had the
uneasy feeling that her resolution and the reality of the situation
were going to have little to do with one another.

It took only a few minutes for Mr. Robinson to measure out
their purchases and wrap them up in brown paper and string. It

took slightly longer for him to make change for the purchase, and Dominick ended up with a pocketful of coins. A large pocketful.

"Serves you right for paying for a bag of candy with a double angel," Clarice said heartlessly as they stepped back into the street. After the dimness of the shop, the sunlight struck with the force of a blow; she reached up to tip her tricorne farther down over her eyes.

"But now we know that we can spend what we have and have some idea of the prices"—he paused to hand Clarice her package of marchpane; she tucked it into the sleeve of her coat—"and we know that we are fine, upstanding freebooters in the eyes of the townspeople."

"But not, alas, in the eyes of the pirates."

Dominick tipped her an ironic bow.

"How did you know I was partial to marchpane?" Clarice asked curiously.

Dominick looked sheepish. "It is the first thing you reach for in the candy bowl. And the night we had almond custard, you ate two helpings. It is these small things, I think, that form the basis of true friendship, not the great secrets."

"But I would think it would be just the other way around."

Dominick smiled. "Why, you might tell anyone the great events of your life—a casual acquaintance, even an enemy. Or the information might be stolen from you. But matters like your favorite sweet, or how you take your tea . . . those are things only a friend would know. No one else would care."

"I suppose there is a certain wisdom in that." *I know you prefer coffee to tea, that you drink it unsweetened, that you prefer fiery flavors to mild ones—just as you bought candied ginger at the sugarbaker's—that your favorite color is blue, that you once had a pet marmoset . . .* "But I think it is a mark of friendship to not simply seek out the truth about someone, but to believe the best of them."

"To know the best," Dominick corrected. "As I know you, my friend. You are far kinder than you want anyone to see. Far braver. And . . . far more reckless." The glint in his eye belied the sobriety of his voice.

"Reckless, am I?" Clarice demanded, swatting at him with her hat. "You'd dance a hornpipe on the mainsail yardarm if you took a notion."

Dominick danced backward, laughing, and Clarice pursued him, swatting at him with her hat until he threw up his hands and begged for mercy.

"It is a formidable hat!" he cried. "A well-traveled hat! A hat that has fought off perils uncounted! Peace! Mercy!"

"Idiot," Clarice said fondly, settling her hat upon her head again. "Anyone would take you for our cabin boy and not our captain!"

"Do you think so?" Dominick fell into step beside her once more. "Thus, my cunning plan of misdirection prospers," he said cheerfully. "But on to the chandlery, where further adventure awaits! Once we find it, at least."

"I could help you with that—if I knew what it was."

Dominick laughed. "This way, I think." He gestured at the largest building Clarice had seen here so far. "If that is not it, I don't know what it is."

The building was a shopfront before and a warehouse behind, and two stories tall. What looked like the figurehead from a ship was mounted over the door: one of the heraldic spaniels from the Albion royal arms, its wings outstretched in flight. Its gilding gleamed against the gray-weathered wood.

"But to continue your education, my fine young 'prentice, every proper established port has a chandlery. It's a place where you can buy anything you could possibly need—or want—or use. From chisels to calico, from potatoes to pitch—and in one place."

"Convenient."

"Necessary," Dominick corrected. "While you may dally as you like over the initial outfitting of a ship, a working ship must be re-provisioned as fast as possible, whether to keep to a schedule, or to go to the aid of another ship of the fleet. And now, we have arrived at our goal."

He opened the door and walked inside, where everything gleamed with cleaning and polishing. A wooden counter ran the length of the back wall. Behind it was a doorway leading to the warehouse—where larger items were stored in quantity—and along the walls were display cases and shelves. Clarice stopped to stare. It was as if someone had taken all the shops in every market town in all of Swansgaarde—or even all the Borogny Mountains—and somehow combined them all within one building. She could recognize less than half the items on display: a shelf full of lanterns, a wall-mounted display of saws and axes. Suspended from the high ceiling was an entire jolly boat.

"Ahoy, the chandler!" Dominick shouted.

"Prepare to come about!" a Caribe-accented voice responded.

A dark-skinned man came out of the back of the shop, smiling broadly in welcome and followed by two young assistants, a man and a woman. It was a dazzling smile indeed, as his teeth were gold. She remembered something Dominick had once said to her: *The sea is its own nation.* Certainly that must be the nation the chandler and his children claimed as their own, for their features were not Ifriqi, not Caribe, not Iberian or Hispalidean, but all of them, and none. Perhaps more to the point, the gentleman looked far more as if he belonged in a pirate haven than Peter Robinson had, as he was missing one arm from just below the elbow, and the scar that crossed his face and had taken his right eye seemed to have been made with a large ax. Despite these cosmetic modifications, his assistants were plainly his offspring. It was odd to imagine a pirate having a family. Perhaps he was an ex-pirate. Could someone be an ex-pirate?

"Rollo Thompson, present and ready. And whose acquaintance is it I have the pleasure of making?"

"I am Dominick Moryet, captain of *Asesino*, newly arrived. And this is my first mate, Clarence Swann."

Clarice took her place beside Dominick.

"Well, here's a pretty young gentleman," Mr. Thompson exclaimed cheerfully. "A bit of dash never hurts, when one sails upon the account, does it? A pleasure to welcome the both of you to the House of the Four Winds, and the liberty of Dorado. My boy, Randolph, and my girl, Alumeda. There's nothing we can't provide to those with the gold to pay for it."

"We need a number of items," Dominick said. "But our most pressing need is water barrels. Sound ones, and as soon as possible."

Mr. Thompson gestured back toward the warehouse. "Water barrels, cannon and shot—anything from eggs to anchors. Only tell me your list, and it will be on your deck quicker'n a fat merchant can cry for quarter!" He chuckled appreciatively at his own wit.

"Mr. Swann will return tomorrow with a full list of the supplies we need, but I wished to be certain you would be able to supply the tuns," Dominick said.

"We'll have the old ones off and the new ones on in two shakes," Mr. Thompson said. "Filling them's your lookout, but there's a pump just outside, and I won't charge you for the water, seeing as you're buying your barrels here."

"Done," Dominick said, sounding relieved. They shook hands. "I admit, the thought of just heaving them over the side wasn't one I thought would go over well. Not in a harbor."

"Why, bless my soul, you'd be hanging in chains in the town square not an hour later," Mr. Thompson said blithely. "No, you bring her on in and tie up at my dock. Good deep water—the Lady wouldn't have it any other way. You can go from deck to land dry-shod—so long as we're in the way of business together."

"Speaking of business, I wonder if you will know who I should see about my cargo? It's nothing much, but I am a sailor, not a shopkeeper. I'd as soon have it off my hands."

"Why, my dear Captain Moryet, Rollo Thompson prides himself on providing every service a gentleman of the trade could need. Look no further, for you've come to the right port o' call! What are you carrying?" Clarice noticed a sudden crafty gleam in Mr. Thompson's eye.

"As Captain Moryet says, it is merely what was in the hold when *Asesino* . . . came into our possession," Clarice said blandly. "Some wines and brandies, a few crates of tea. Spices. Beads and trinkets to trade with natives. And a good many bales of good Albionnaise wool—though I doubt you have much of a cloth trade here."

Mr. Thompson smiled faintly at her small joke, and Clarice was glad she'd managed to imply that *Asesino* was a prize ship. It would explain their lack of . . . whatever pirates considered suitable plunder.

"You'd have the right of that, Mr. Swann, but Rollo Thompson knows those who do, never fear! Randolph will be pleased to value your cargo for you while he's aboard. That way, you'll know what tithe to pay to the House of the Four Winds. And the credit might well pay for the whole of your supplies. Have we a fair bargain?"

Dominick was about to agree. Clarice stepped on his foot. "We're more than willing for you to value our cargo *and* to take charge of it. Pay the tithe to the House on our behalf, and we will be happy to take the balance in credit, here at your fine establishment."

She thought Mr. Thompson did not look quite as pleased by this plan as by his original one, but Clarice was wise enough in the ways of crooked innkeepers—and surely, a ship's chandler was an innkeeper of a sort—to know that while he would probably have given them a reasonable assessment of the worth of the cargo to avoid trouble in calculating the amount that must be paid to Dorado's masters, all their ready coin would have gone to pay that fee, while the credit he so generously offered would somehow vanish into the cost of their supplies.

"You're a right clever lad," Mr. Thompson said. "Done and done. A drink on it? 'Meda! Go and get a bottle and some tankards!"

The young woman smiled and went to do as she was bid and, a few moments later, returned with a silver tray containing five tankards and a squat, black bottle. Dominick watched her carefully as she filled all of them and did not raise his own tankard to his lips until Mr. Thompson and both his offspring had drunk theirs down.

When Dominick drank, Clarice followed suit. It was a dark rum, so heavily spiced that she was hard put to swallow even a mouthful without coughing.

"Until tomorrow, then," Dominick said, placing his tankard back on the tray. "We'll tie up at your dock and then my crew can get to work."

"And so can we," Mr. Thompson said. "Fair wind and following sea, Captain Moryet."

"And to you as well," Dominick said.

"You are excessively cautious," Clarice said when they were outside again and walking toward the dock just beyond the end of the chandlery. She had not missed how carefully Dominick had watched to see that the Thompsons drank before he did.

"Thus speaks the beardless youth. Were you not listening to Mr. Robinson—and to Mr. Thompson, with his merry talk of men being hung in chains for displeasing this island's rulers? The talisman's enchantment may have gotten us here safely, but this island and even the waters about it are enchanted. We cannot even sail free without satisfying some authority, for the harbor chain is enchanted as well. How can anything I do prevail against an enemy I cannot see, sense, or fight?" All the tension—the fear—that had been absent from his easy manner at the chandlery was in his voice.

"Just as you would against any other natural force," Clarice answered calmly, ignoring the gibe about "beardless youth." She'd never mentioned her age, but a woman dressing as a man could not help but look young. He probably thought Clarence Swann was a few weeks shy of fifteen, instead of a man's age of eighteen. "You deal with the wind all the time, for example."

"I can feel the wind," Dominick growled in frustration.

"And you can see thaumaturgy, even if you cannot feel it."

"I'm not a withered professor in an ivy-covered university tower."

"Nor am I. But I can teach you. Here, for example. Come with me."

A well-traveled footpath led inland past the chandlery. Clarice had no idea where it led, but beside the path stood an enormous tree. Someone had kindly circled its trunk with a wooden bench. It looked like a comfortable place to linger out of the day's glare. The two of them walked toward it.

"Sit down, and hold out your hands, palms up."

Dominick sat at Clarice's command, and she seated herself beside him.

"Here is my pocket watch." She placed it in his hand. "It was a gift from my father, so pray do not drop it." In fact, she'd purchased it from a pawnshop in Kalindagrad as she had journeyed west, and it could reveal nothing about her true identity no matter how closely Dominick inspected it.

"I won't." Dominick closed his fingers lightly around the smooth heft of the silver case.

"And here"—Clarice slipped the chain over her head and placed the talisman gently in Dominick's other hand—"is an object that we know to be magical. The watch, by the way, is not. Now. Please regard them both carefully. When I was very young, my tutor, Dr.—well, let us just say my tutor—began with an exercise very much like this one."

The castle schoolroom was warm and sunny. Clarice felt a thrill of pleasure at the start of this new lesson. Normally she and her sisters took their lessons either all together (geography, mathematics, history, drawing, and languages) or entirely separately (fencing and riding, for example). But only she, Anise, and Talitha—the three oldest princesses—were to undertake this course of study just now. Clarice was twelve, and Talitha was barely ten. The others were too young.

"Pay close attention, Your Highnesses. As you will know from reading the third book of Kings, Solomon was beloved of God and possessed of a clever mind. And in the nine hundredth year of his reign, his studies at last bore fruit. He discovered magic. And what is magic, pray tell?"

"It is the after-echo of the Divine Word which created the world," Princess Anise said promptly. Anise had been fascinated by thaumaturgy for as long as Clarice could remember. "And as it retains certain characteristics of its genesis, magic—or more properly, thaumaturgy—can be used to alter the created world."

"Just so," Dr. Karlavaegen said, sounding pleased. "And since the act of enchanting an object brings it more into harmony with its perfect self—as the Magus Plato taught in ancient times—it is only logical that it should appear as a different order of reality than its mundane counterpart. As sight is the most sublime and perfect of the senses, it is the only sense that thaumaturgy will reliably affect. So it is easy to determine a bespelled object due to its brightness and sharpness to the unaided eye."

"So you can't feel an enchantment, or smell it, or taste it?" Talitha asked.

Anise gave her sister a long-suffering look for asking such a stupid question.

"A science whose purpose is to redefine natural laws in a very small area is not one in which questions have yes-or-no answers," Dr. Karlavaegen admonished. "All you will ever hear from me, or from any reputable teacher, is 'generally' or 'rarely.' And in this case—as a general rule—you are correct."

In the comfort of the tree's shade, Clarice gave Dominick a much-edited summary of Dr. Karlavaegen's lecture. His intention had not been to teach the young princesses thaumaturgy, but to explain its underlying principles, for that was a skill that would be a great deal of use to them.

After studying the items for some time, Dominick had grudgingly agreed that the talisman and the watch looked distinctly different. "As if one is under strong sunlight, and the other is not. But if magic comes from God, how can it be used for evil purposes?" Dominick said, sounding frustrated.

"We, too, come from God, and our purposes are often ungodly, Dominick." Clarice smiled, for she had asked the same question more than once. "Thaumaturgy is merely another of the noble arts—like medicine, or law, or astrology. As such, it can be turned to good purpose—or ill. Now"—she tucked away the watch and slipped the chain of the talisman over her head again—"here is another object. Tell me, is it enchanted, or not?"

"You ask a lot of me upon half an hour's lesson," Dominick grumbled as he held out his hand for her penknife. It was not magical, but it was beautifully made, and it took him a moment to pronounce it mundane.

"Correct. You make an excellent student despite my poor teaching. Now this." Clarice placed her spellmatch into his hand.

"Magic, of course," Dominick said promptly, rolling the slender cylinder between thumb and forefinger. "What is it?"

"Open it and see." Clarice smiled at Dominick's exclamation of wonder as the tip of the match burst into flame.

"What a handy thing," Dominick said, smiling. "Why, it would be easy to light any lantern anywhere, no matter how strong the wind." He gazed at her inquiringly, clearly uncertain what to do with it now. Clarice took the match and its cap away from him and doused the flame. The metal was still cool. She tucked the intricately made tube back into the pocket of her vest. *I suppose, considering everything, I shall need to keep on the lookout for pickpockets while I am here,* she told herself.

"Well then, are my tests done?" Dominick asked. "And do I gain my laurel and the title of 'Prentice Thaumaturge?"

"Even I do not have that, and I have not told you the whole of what I know yet," Clarice said lightly. "But one more test, and I will happily rate you an Entered Apprentice."

Her fingers were busy as she spoke, unpinning the jewel that she wore, well concealed, on the inside breast of her long, high-necked vest. She placed it in Dominick's outstretched hand, keeping the object concealed until the last moment.

"This. Magic or not?"

"This is a jewel of great price," Dominick said slowly, staring at it as if it might suddenly bite him. "It is not such a thing as I would look to see in the possession of a young man traveling upon his father's indulgence."

The moment Clarice had seen Dominick's expression, she regretted the impulse to display the brooch that had been her parents' parting gift to her. It had been foolish, and she could not decide whether she had done it because its enchantment would be a good test of her teaching—or because she hoped, somehow, that Dominick would guess what she did not dare tell him.

I must tell him something, for I can see that he is trying hard not to wonder how I came by it. "It was a gift. That isn't either an excuse or a lie. It's the truth. It is not an heirloom of any sort—so far as I know. It was given to me by the royal family of Swansgaarde. I've already told you I came from there. It is a very small country. I was very close to the princesses; we grew up together and shared tutors."

So far everything she had said was the absolute truth, but she was very much afraid that Dominick's next question, whatever it was, would force her to lie. Or to tell him the truth, which was not something she wished to do before weighing the consequences carefully.

The moment might have become an awkward, save for the approach of a young woman. She was barefoot, with a silver bangle around one ankle, and her skirt and shift were knotted at her hip, dragging the hemline of the garment perilously high. Her skin was a dark caramel color that owed nothing to the sun, and she wore her chestnut hair loose and flowing, rather than tidily braided or knotted up at the back of her neck as a respectable woman should.

Well, I suppose it is too much to expect a lady buccaneer—if that is what she is—to embrace respectability .

Dominick slowly got to his feet at her approach. To Clarice's intense irritation, the woman stopped to brush her hair back from her shoulders, clearly striking a pose so Dominick could ogle her. The bracelets on her wrists glittered in the light.

"Can I . . . ?" He took a breath and began again. "How can we help you, mistress?"

The woman smirked and took a swaying step closer. "Ah, it's clear you're a fine gentleman, not like *some* here." She darted a speaking glance at Clarice.

"That's nice to hear, but who are you and what do you want?" Clarice said sharply, resting her hand on the hilt of her saber.

"My name is Fleta, and my business isn't with a boy too young to shave," she said scornfully. "I'm here to speak to your fine, handsome young captain."

I wonder who sent her, and how they knew to find us? Clarice thought. *The chandlery is the logical first stop for any ship that comes here, and so it is a reasonable place to look, but that does not explain why she came looking for us.* Clarice fought to control the flash of jealousy that even *she* knew to be irrational. As far as Dominick knew, Fleta was the only woman standing here right now. And any man, high-minded or low, was going to stare at someone like Fleta.

"Well, his fine, handsome young captain is right here," Dominick said mildly. "And I'm all ears."

"Perhaps we should go somewhere more . . . private . . . for our talk?" Fleta purred, taking another swaying step closer. The breeze brought Clarice the smell of Fleta's perfume, something flowery and heavy.

"Oh, ah, actually, I don't think so." Dominick sounded a little harried now. "This is fine."

Fleta pouted, folding her arms beneath her breasts. But to Clarice's relief, she stopped where she was. "Think yourself too good for the likes of me, do you? Imagining you can come waltzing in here and charm the Lady—just as if she'd even look at someone like you!"

This is the second time someone has mentioned "the Lady," Clarice thought. "This 'Lady'—who is she?" Clarice asked. "Your sovereign?"

Fleta scowled at her. "You'll find out. And you won't like what you find."

"Did you come looking for us for a reason?" Clarice asked. "Or just to be mysterious?"

"Do you let your cabin boy do your talking?" Fleta demanded, turning to Dominick.

"When my *first mate* says something I disagree with, I'll be sure to speak up. I have nothing to say to you that cannot be said in front of him. And if your 'business' cannot be settled here and now, well . . . I have little interest in what I presume is your usual trade," Dominick said coldly.

"You'll regret your high-and-mighty ways!" Fleta said furiously. "Hear the Council's word then! Captain Moryet is bid to appear at the House of the Four Winds to give an account of himself and his ship, tonight at moonrise. And you'd better be ready to spin a good yarn," she added viciously. "Bring your pretty boy with you if you like. He'll see some things he hasn't seen yet, I'll wager."

"The—? Where—? Wait!" Dominick said, but it was too late. Fleta turned her back and stalked away. In a few moments she'd vanished into the trees.

"Excitable, isn't she?" Dominick said with a sigh. Clarice saw him realize he was still holding her brooch. He held it out to her. "You wouldn't want to lose such a precious keepsake."

"Magic or not?"

"Magic," Dominick said, smiling.

"You are an excellent pupil, young master Dominick, and are

hereby raised to Entered Apprentice at thaumaturgy." Clarice pinned the brooch back into its place. "I can't imagine why she expected you to just go wandering off with her," she added tartly.

Dominick raised an eyebrow. "I imagine she isn't used to being told no when she makes that suggestion."

Clarice raised an eyebrow. "I suppose not. But I feel her messenger skills leave a great deal to be desired. Where is the House of the Four Winds, and how do we get there?"

"As to that"—Dominick flung an arm over her shoulders and began walking back toward the chandlery—"I am certain our new friend Rollo Thompson will be happy to tell us everything we need to know."

"Assuming we have the gold to pay for it," Clarice said dryly.

7

SEEKING THE HOUSE OF THE FOUR WINDS

"THIS IS going to be a problem," Dr. Chapman said.

He, Dominick, Kayin, and Clarice were gathered in the captain's cabin. Kayin had a battered and sea-stained roll of parchment containing the list of *Asesino*'s original (alleged) supplies, with additional scribbled notes made by Geordie. Kayin and Clarice would be taking that back to Rollo Thompson tomorrow. When Thompson had learned of their summons, he had offered them the loan of a skiff, which meant she and Dominick could keep their appointment without bringing a crew to man the jolly boat.

Dominick had sailed it back to *Asesino,* which turned out to be a good thing, as the shore party had done as much shopping as drinking, and the jolly boat had been laden down with supplies—fresh fruit, bread, beef, ale, and tobacco—so the crew should not find a night spent aboard too much of a hardship.

Clarice had tried to talk Dominick out of keeping his appointment at the House of the Four Winds, but Dominick had pointed out that failing to appear would strip away what little protection they had. Right now the pirates were giving them the benefit of the doubt, more or less. Ignore the summons, and their masquerade would be over. Unfortunately, Clarice was unable to fault his reasoning, though she tried hard.

"We suspected something like this was coming," Dominick said. "Captain Watson and Captain Harrison might have given us permission to drop anchor, but Dorado is too . . . orderly . . . for there not to be some form of government."

"A government of pirates," Dr. Chapman said bitterly. "And this House of the Four Winds taking a tenth part of their plunder to provide them with a safe harbor where they do not need to fear discovery."

"Well, look at it from the pirates' point of view," Clarice said reasonably. "They don't like being shot at—or chased—or hanged—any better than anyone else does. And whoever is running Dorado deserves *some* recompense for all the trouble he—or she—has gone to."

"Spoken like a true pirate," Dr. Chapman muttered.

"We can't just bolt," Dominick said. "You both saw the chain across the harbor mouth. If it was a matter of just sailing out, I think they would be guarding us more closely."

Dr. Chapman gestured eloquently toward the window, where the *Vile Vixen* and the *Horrid Hangman* were clearly visible as they sat at anchor.

"Even so," Dominick said, dismissing the ships. "Our only chance is to keep acting as if we belong here—and that means going to this meeting tonight. I'm sure it's only a formality."

"Oh, of course. What else could a meeting of pirates be? I am certain it will be so well mannered and civilized that you should bring a canister of tea along so we can all drink it," Clarice said dourly. "Well, don't think you're going to this meeting alone. She said I could come. And I'm not letting you out of my sight."

"Oh, thank God," Dominick said, laughing with relief. "You're a much better fighter than I am. Ah . . . not that this meeting will lead to fighting, of course. I'm sure we can continue to bluff them."

"I don't think that will actually be that hard," Clarice said thoughtfully, propping her chin on her hand. She'd been letting the whole incident stew in the back of her mind since Fleta had flounced off, and a number of things had occurred to her. "Think. If you were, oh, the Queen's Council in Albion, and you wished to take a message to someone, would you send someone like Fleta? She was far too easy to anger, and then she blurted out her whole message and went storming off."

"We *hope* it was her whole message," Dominick said.

Clarice nodded in agreement. "But even if it was not, consider. Wouldn't it have been sensible for her—acting on the Council's orders, or just in her own interests—to have found out everything about us she could? The best way to do that usually isn't by snarling threats and storming off in a sulk. She could have smiled and spoken soft words and been sympathetic. Such winsome treatment has been known to induce gentlemen to offer up confidences," Clarice finished dryly.

Dominick's expression plainly showed he couldn't decide whether to be insulted by Clarice's opinion that flattery would make him give up his secrets, or impressed by her analysis of the matter.

I have been trained from the cradle to see the world this way, Clarice mused, *against the day I might rule—or at least guide— Swansgaarde. Perhaps that will be enough advantage for us tonight.*

"So you will give them a jolly tale, told in confidence," Dr. Chapman said thoughtfully. "With just enough truth in it to—"

There came a frantic scrabbling at the door, and without waiting for permission Jerrold Robinson burst in. His face was white with terror.

"Oh, Cap'n!" he wailed. "The reverend has gone and escaped!"

Reverend Dobbs's cabin was a bit larger than Clarice's, and surprisingly neat—she had somehow expected Dobbs to be the same sort of sloven as his master.

It was also quite empty.

"Locked him in, just as you said," Kayin said, gazing around in confusion. "Duff fitted a hasp for a padlock, and Rogerio gave me one of the padlocks off the arms chests for it. I kept the key around my neck—I gave it to Jerrold when we came aboard so he could take him his meal."

"And I did!" Jerrold wailed. "Didn't I go straight to Mr. Emerson and get his food, same as we have ourselves? See? The tray's still here!" He pointed, as if to confirm his story, at the tin tray with the mug of watered grog and the bowl of congealing stew that sat in the corridor. "And then didn't I unlock the door and say, 'And here's your meal, Reverend?' And . . . he wasn't here!"

"Well, he didn't go out through this," Clarice said, indicating the porthole. She could open it easily enough, but could not imagine fitting herself through it, and Dobbs was much larger. With the porthole for ventilation, the cabin had the luxury of a solid door—there were no slats, and so no possibility he'd been clever enough just to remove them and step out.

"And you had the only key?" Clarice asked.

Kayin frowned, as if her question were absurd in the extreme. "No," he said slowly. "How could I? Mr. Emerson would be asking after it a dozen times a day to get into stores, or Dickon, if he was wishing to use the instruments, or young Miles, if he was to see to the chronometers. . . ."

"You mean every lock on this ship is keyed alike?" Clarice asked, barely able to keep the horrified indignation from her voice.

"Nearly," Dr. Chapman said with a sigh. He produced a key that he wore around his neck upon a ribbon. "I have my own locks on the cabinets that hold my remedies."

"And there is a strong room in the captain's cabin which has its own key as well," Dominick said, "but for the rest . . ." He shrugged in mute apology. "It does not matter if the key was easy to get. Someone would still have to have come and let him out."

"And it looks as if somebody did," Clarice said, shaking her head. "But where is he now?"

"If I were him, I'd have gone overside as soon as I could and swam for it," Dr. Chapman says. "It's not far, and the water is calm. We all know he's got friends aboard, but there are damned few places a man can hide on a ship this size. For any length of time, at least."

"I'll go about and have a quiet word with some of the men," Kayin said meaningfully.

"No," Dominick said. "Whoever did it isn't likely to say so, are they? All you'll do is set them at each other's throats. And spread panic, if they think Dobbs is ashore and spreading tales about us."

"Well, isn't he?" Clarice asked reasonably.

"Maybe," Dominick said. "Or maybe he's hiding down on the orlop right now, hoping to work some sort of mischief. He can't imagine that telling a bunch of pirates that this is a ship full of mutineers and murderers is going to offend them."

No, merely cause them to do I know not what, my dear, Clarice thought forlornly. *I mocked Fleta for not trying to worm information out of us when I should have tried to do the same thing to her. If only there were some way to know where the wretched man has gotten to!*

"We must hope—if it comes to it—that my skill at spinning a tale exceeds his," Dominick said.

Clarice was dressed in her finest clothing, and Dominick wore Sprunt's embroidered vest beneath his blue jacket and had donned a plumed tricorne hat. He'd wound a long sash around his waist and stuck a set of pistols into it; Clarice hoped they wouldn't need to use them. Or her sword.

They sailed to shore as the last light of sunset faded from the sky.

Mr. Thompson had given them directions to their meeting place. As Clarice had suspected from the moment of their arrival, the House was high on the hill. *It must have a good view of the*

*harbor from that height. And yet it cannot be seen. Soon enough,
I suppose, we shall discover how that trick is managed.*

They beached the little skiff and found the path Mr. Thompson
had indicated. The dockside establishments were noisy and full
of people, but as they climbed, they passed into what was clearly
a residential district and left the noise behind. The path became
a road lined with houses that were clearly the permanent resi-
dences of well-off individuals. Lights were on in some of the
windows, and once Clarice heard the tinkle of a piano. But they
saw no one.

Who lived in these grand houses? Who supplied their needs—
everything from wine to candles to beef? If Dorado was more
than a free port for pirates, how much more? Were some of the
people who lived here not actually pirates—nor involved with
them? And if so, who were they and what did they do? Clearly
they had no objections to being ruled by pirates, or they would
not be here . . . would they?

And most of all, precisely *how many real pirates* were they
dealing with?

"And here we are," Dominick said. "Or . . . we're somewhere,
at any rate."

Clarice looked up.

The road ended in a set of gateposts. Atop each pillar of them
stood a lantern that burned with a waving blue flame; not sorcery,
this (though any viewers might be tempted to think so), but lamps
burning alcohol instead of oil. Between the gateposts, a narrow
path led into the jungle. Nothing could be seen beyond, and the
track itself vanished into the shadows after just a few feet.

"Charming," Clarice said. "But not very welcoming." *At least
nobody is waiting here to pounce on us and take us prisoner,* she
thought hopefully. *But why would they bother? After all, we intend to walk right into their den.*

"Perhaps there are better accommodations farther on." Dominick offered her an ironic bow, doffing his hat and sweeping it
low. "After you, my dear fellow."

"You just want to see if they're going to shoot at me," Clarice said archly, and strode forward.

The path rose steeply upward. Once her eyes had adjusted, Clarice could see it was marked, after a fashion. Masks were attached to trees at the edges of the route. They (like the lamps) were meant to frighten; they glowed with phosphorescence and bore a family resemblance to the gargoyles that graced the heights of Swansgaarde Cathedral.

"Demon masks," Dominick said dismissively. "And no magic needed to make them glow, either, but I imagine they'd scare off anyone with a guilty conscience."

"Fortunately ours are clear," Clarice said dryly, and Dominick chuckled.

The undergrowth rustled as they passed, and Clarice kept her hand on the hilt of her sword. After a few more moments' walk, they saw the glow of firelight up ahead, and shortly thereafter, they stepped out into a clearing.

"Well," Clarice said after a moment's pause. "If the masks and the lanterns didn't scare everyone off, this certainly would."

The courtyard was ringed by flaming torches. Among them, the figureheads of dead ships stood like watching demons. The building at the far end of the courtyard was made not of stone or planks, but of whole logs that raised it twenty feet off the ground. The enormous tree-trunk pillars were decorated with garlands of human skulls interspersed with bizarre and disturbing trinkets. A child's doll. A lady's hat. The remains of a clock. Light spilled from the building's open windows, the shutters were thrown back. The window frames held no glass, but though Clarice could see the shadows of moving figures within, the night was eerily silent.

And that is thaumaturgy, she said to herself. *Dr. Karlavaegen spoke of such enchantments, and I think there was one on the council chamber in the castle, though of course I never tested it. But no one outside will be able to eavesdrop upon anything that goes on within. Or even know what it might be.*

She looked to see if Dominick had noticed, but his gaze was

fixed on the open level above the building proper. It was nothing more than a roof supported by pillars with a low wooden rail around the edge. As she followed his gaze, she saw the barrel of the enormous signal cannon jutting outward over the edge of the rail, a spyglass on a tripod beside it. She'd known this must be some sort of vantage point, and she'd expected the signal gun, but she had not expected the smaller guns that flanked it. She could see that those could be aimed toward the courtyard below.

"My," Dominick said mildly.

"Courage," Clarice muttered under her breath as they started forward.

At the top of the stairs two enormous doors flared in the torch-light like mirrors, for they were covered in pure gold wrought in a design of piled skulls. As they reached the doors, the right-side one swung open, flooding the night air with the sound of talk and laughter from within. The door was held by a man who might have sprung out of a picture-book drawing of a pirate. The monkey on his shoulder bared its teeth at them and shrieked; the man smiled, exposing a gap-toothed expanse of brown teeth.

"Welcome!" he said, bowing them inside with a theatrical gesture.

"Ah! Here's the pretty captain and his pretty boy!" Melisande Watson called.

Clarice was about to remove her hat as she entered, but seeing that Dominick did not remove his, left it as it was. The interior was dominated by the largest table Clarice had ever seen. The building must have been created around it, for it filled the room—and the room was thirty feet across.

The table was round, and in its center was a golden compass rose, the twelve points of the compass marked out. Save for that, the whole surface was a map made in colored stones, but a map such as Clarice had never seen, for the continents seemed like af-terthoughts. She recognized the coast of New Hesperia, and the scatter of the Hispalides that led to it. A single crystal struck hot fire from the lamps hanging overhead; Clarice was certain it marked the island upon which they now stood. But the map was dominated by the sea, depicted in a thousand shades of blue and green, filled with fanciful sea monsters and ornamented with personified winds.

She'd taken in the table and its surface with no more than a glance, for the table was surrounded by a score of chairs, and more than half of them were filled.

But there are only two ships in the harbor besides ours! she thought in panic. *When I heard we were to come and give an account of ourselves, I thought it would be only Captain Watson and Captain Harrison, and a few people from the town, perhaps. Oh, I was so confident that we would be able to fool a little handful of people, even pirates, but this is . . .*

She wanted to think Dominick was as aware of the danger as she was, but he gave no sign of it as he made for a chair in the center of the empty side of the table. Clarice quickly sat down beside him. *At least I see no sign yet that they mean to kill us out of hand,* she told herself hopefully, striving for calm. *And I do not see Reverend Dobbs, either, which is more to the point.*

"I am Dominick Moryet of the brig *Asesino,*" Dominick said coolly. "Who is it who asks me to give an account of myself?"

Four women were here besides Captain Watson. One of them was enough like her to be her twin. The other three were far less flamboyant, and if not for her own practice in disguise, Clarice might have taken at least two them for youths. All of them regarded Dominick with cool professional interest.

"Why, it is the House of the Four Winds itself which asks, my fine young fighting cockerel." The man who spoke wore opulent, even princely, garb, from a gold-laced coat of claret velvet to the ransom in gems that gleamed upon every finger. If Clarice had seen him on the streets of Albion or Vinarborg or Heimlichstadt itself, she would have been certain he was some visiting prince.

"Edmund Bell Fairfax, master of *Sirocco,* at your service, sir," he added. "And these are my fellow Sea Lords—and Ladies, of course." Six other men were seated at the table—Ifrani, Caribe, even one with the unmistakable copper-bronze skin of a Hesperian. As Clarice surveyed them, she noticed that each displayed a talisman identical to the one nestled under her own shirt.

Captain Watson nodded, smiling at the acknowledgment. "Let us introduce ourselves to our new brother, and then we can all be friendly. I have already made myself known to him. And here is my sister Aubrianna, mistress of the *Lusty Leman*."

Melisande's twin nodded slightly, her unsmiling gaze fixed on Dominick's face. "And yet, I ask which of them is our brother, for our good Captain Moryet seems a bit . . . underdressed," she said at last.

"This is what you want to see," Clarice said, taking the talisman from around her neck and setting it on the table between her and Dominick. "As for why I carry it and not he, I do not think that is any concern of yours."

"Well spoken, young sir!" Fairfax said. "He shows a proper spirit, doesn't he? Let us drink to his health!"

There was a general roar of assent, and as if that were a signal, Fleta appeared at Fairfax's side, carrying a silver tray with tankards stacked upon it in a precarious pyramid. Behind her came the doorkeeper, his arms full of bottles, and another man behind him, his arms wrapped around an enormous cut-crystal punch bowl nearly large enough for Clarice to bathe in.

"The punch!" Captain Harrison roared, and the cry was taken up by everyone in the room. "The punch!"

At first Clarice had regarded the bowl with relief, thinking that at least she would not be called upon to drink an entire quart of rum. But as the ingredients were added to the bowl, she began to wish that simple wholesome rum was what was being offered.

First, a boxful of golden sugar lumps was thrown into the bowl. The ingredients must have been prepared beforehand, for next, the doorkeeper returned with a kettle of boiling water and poured it over the sugar. Next came a bowl of fruit—lemons, limes, and oranges—all cut into chunks.

Then Fairfax began pouring in the liquor. Clarice lost count of the number of bottles it took to fill the bowl, but she caught the scents of brandy and rum, and even a couple of bottles of claret.

"We should have brought them a few bottles as a guest gift," Dominick murmured, leaning close to speak into her ear.

Then came a platter of something diced too small for Clarice to identify. It looked like roots. She hoped it was ginger—and not mandrake.

At last the bowl was full to brimming. Fairfax got to his feet and gave it an enthusiastic stir with the barrel of his pistol—slopping a good portion of the dark liquid onto the table—then reached into his coat for a small bottle that gleamed black in the lamplight. He drew out the cork with his teeth.

"And now—" He upended the bottle over the steaming, swirling liquid. The bottle's contents splashed out. Though it looked like nothing more than water, at its addition the surface of the bowl burst into flames. The others, who seemed to expect this to happen, cheered.

It is only a small enchantment, Clarice told herself firmly. *A party trick. I have seen similar things a score of times.*

The flames had not yet begun to die down when the tankards were plunged into the bowl, their holders heedless of the flames. As the tankards were filled and passed around, the other members of the council made their own introductions. None of their names meant anything to Clarice, but from Dominick's expression she was alone in her happy ignorance.

Since the bowl was on the far side of the table—or perhaps because they were guests?—Captain Fairfax filled a pair of tankards and shoved them across the table. The heavy objects slid freely across the slick, wet surface, and it took an alert pounce on Clarice's part to keep both herself and Dominick from getting doused in punch.

When she raised her tankard to her lips and sipped, she could barely discern any hint of alcohol. The punch was warm and tasted of oranges and—oddly—cherries. But she'd seen what had gone into it and intended to be cautious. *At least no one intends to poison us,* she thought hopefully. *Only to get us very drunk.*

"Now, here we are all matey," Captain Fairfax said heartily. "And our ears itching, one and all, for a rousing sea story, full of blood and adventure!" He regarded Dominick expectantly.

"Then I'll tell you one." Dominick took a deep breath. "Once upon a time, in a far country, there lived a very wicked man . . ."

The pirates leaned forward, with varying expressions of interest or malice on their faces.

The story Dominick told seemed, at first, to be a nursery tale, for it involved a great pirate who had no ship at all, and yet was the most successful buccaneer in all the Nine Oceans. After a few minutes, Clarice realized he was telling these people the story of Samuel Sprunt.

Who survived the sinking—or loss—of five ships: Aglaia, Queen Gloriana, Pride of Albion, Atlantis, *and* Sirocco. *Captain Fairfax's ship is named* Sirocco! *Oh, Dominick, I do hope you know what you're doing.*

All she could do was keep her face still and smooth as he spoke. He held the medallion in his hands now, turning it over and over in his fingers as his voice went on, as light and cheerful as if he really were telling a story fit for children. The heavy gold chain slithered and twisted against the stone table.

". . . and the wicked man, a sea captain of broad fame and noble repute, plied his trade wherever he chose, and the joke of it was, men paid him good gold angels to take their ships from them. He had a handpicked crew, and a merry one, and for their sport he would incite the good, honest men on his stolen ships to mutiny. But you know the rest of the tale, I'm sure . . ."

"I do not!" Captain Fairfax said instantly. "Pray conclude it, my good friend. What became of this terrible, wicked man?"

"He talked a great deal," Dominick said with a feral smile utterly unlike his normal expression. "And in the wrong places. You see . . . to take ships here in the West is a dangerous thing—

though rewarding, I grant you. But sail East, and turn your guns on the ships of the Great Cham, or the argosies of the princes of Hind, and you may sail West again just as you please, your hold full of spoil and yourself nothing more than an honest trader. And so my master did these many years—you may ask after him in Albion, for he sails for Barnabas Bellamy, whom all men know."

Oh, that's a nice touch, Clarice thought sardonically.

"But I regret to say my master and I fell out," Dominick said. "I wanted a ship of my own, and he swore I would not have it while my skills were of such great use to him. It was then I chanced, by happy fortune, to make the acquaintance of . . . the late Captain Samuel Sprunt."

"And is this the terrible, wicked man of whom you spoke?" Captain Watson asked with bright interest.

Dominick smiled at her. "Why, the very same, dear madam! I knew of him by reputation, of course, and thought that to congratulate him on his seafaring luck might cause some of it to attach to me. And . . . he told me it was not luck at all."

"That seems unlike our dear Samuel," Captain Harrison murmured gently.

"He was a friend? My condolences," Dominick said with fulsome insincerity. "But knowing him as you do, you will agree he was a man of great appetites."

"He drank like a porpoise," Aubrianna Watson said flatly.

"Why, so he did!" Dominick agreed cheerfully. "And he had been drinking all that day, you see, and after I heard what he had said, we drank together all that night, with me pressing him for his story the entire time. I let him know enough to know I had been in the same trade, and that oiled his tongue nicely. He said the Eastern trade my master had founded was all well and good, but that a man might also sail the Western seas and do just as he liked . . . if he had a good port to call home. Why, I signed articles with him that very day! *Asesino* sailed not a week later, and . . . here we are. He meant to sail *Asesino* here, after all. I thought my friend and I would save him the trouble."

"Just like that?" It took Clarice a moment to recollect the speaker's name. Nigel Brown, captain of the *Tamerlane*. In this company, his clothing, though of fine quality, was subdued to the point of dowdiness; he wore a blue coat with modest gold piping, and a buff weskit beneath it, and no jewelry other than the medallion. He looked like a kindly grandfather. She doubted he was one.

"He didn't object much after I put a yard of steel in his gut." Clarice needed to convince these people that she, too, was a hardened pirate. "Of course, in my own defense, he was trying to put us all over the side at the time."

Captain Fairfax nodded as if this all made perfect sense. "And what of his companions, little man? Did you slay them all?"

"Certainly not!" Clarice said, pretending indignation. "We set them adrift."

"They might still be out there," Dominick said helpfully. "Ah . . . somewhere. I didn't make any particular note of where we left them. But you might be able to find them if you cared to look."

"To the locker with them!" Captain Harrison said roundly. "They were fool enough to be taken. Let the sea be their fate. And it's better than swinging." He fingered the noose about his neck. "I can say that for certain."

So much for the "brotherhood" of the Pirate Brotherhood! Clarice thought.

"A pretty story," Captain Watson said, "from a pretty lad. But . . . ladies and gentlemen of the Four Winds, what proof is there of it beyond his bare word? He and his companion come bearing the proper token, but . . . there are other ways of coming by one of these." She fingered her own medallion.

"Yes," Clarice said. "I could have bought it in a pawnshop." She plucked it from Dominick's hands and slipped the chain over her head again. "But I didn't."

"No . . ." Another of the brethren sat forward. He wore no hat, and his head was shaved clean. His white teeth were brilliant against his black-coffee skin as he smiled. "You might have had it from the hangman—or from one of the Albion Sea Lords, along with your commission. Sad to say, drink isn't the only thing to make a man sing. The whip—the rack—hot irons—any of them will do, you know."

Clarice wasn't certain whether the man was saying Sprunt might have given up his secrets under torture, or suggesting that she and Dominick be tortured to encourage them to do so. It didn't matter. What mattered was that the council didn't seem to have been completely persuaded by Dominick's clever story. *Even though parts of it are very nearly true,* she thought. *They think we're pirate hunters, not pirates.*

"True enough. Look at him. He stinks of manly virtue." It was Aubrianna again. "Look at how upright he is. How clean-limbed. How terribly noble! And far too familiar with how we manage our affairs. He's just the sort they'd send."

"Well, we really aren't," Clarice said, doing her best to sound both convincing and patronizing. "Sprunt was luckier than he should have been—*five* ships? People were starting to talk, you know. It was the medallion that cinched it, though. If you don't want people to come here, why hand out maps?"

"It's true the medallions can be passed on without a vote from the council." A woman who hadn't spoken before wrapped her fingers around her tankard. "If possession alone could condemn someone, we'd all have to hang ourselves."

"Given," Captain Watson echoed in grudging agreement. "Or lost. Or stolen."

"Thirty-six of them there were, when they were forged," Captain Harrison said. "Three for each of the wind's twelve quarters. And how many now?"

"Seventeen that we know of—as you know," Fairfax said. "The rest have gone to the bottom, where we are honorbound to send them if there is a chance of their capture. And when they are all lost, why—what then?"

"Why . . . then I shall make more, my darling. Never fear that the House of the Four Winds will lie empty, its enchantments broken."

The mocking female voice came from the shadows at the back of the room, and for a moment Clarice thought it was Fleta, for it possessed much the same lilting Caribe accent, but the woman who walked into the light was exotic in a way Fleta could never hope to equal. She carried herself with the haughty grace of a queen, and everyone in the room turned to regard her approach in respectful silence. She was a tiny thing, barely five feet tall, and so lushly female that no corset in the universe could let her pass as a boy. Her hair was a shining blue-black mass of curls held back from her face by a bright scarf tied about her brow. She wore a sleeveless bodice of black silk that barely covered her breasts, and her skirt was a thing of fluttering tatters in a hundred shades of blue that left her legs nearly bare. Dozens of multicolored bead necklaces were looped about her throat, and she wore sparkling gold bangles on her wrists and ankles. Her skin was honey dark, and as she approached, Clarice could see that her eyes were quite strange: large, almond shaped, and yellow-green, like a cat's.

"You said that was impossible when you made them, Lady Shamal," Fairfax said deferentially. He rose from his chair, clearly to offer it to her.

"With what I have here to work with," Shamal agreed. "But Dorado is not the whole world."

She ignored the chair and walked slowly around the table. Dominick was openly staring at her, his expression suggesting he'd just been struck by lightning. His mouth was hanging slightly open. Clarice wasn't sure he was actually remembering to breathe. Then at last her mind kicked in, and both surprise and irritation vanished under a flood of primal fear.

Everything about Shamal was hyperreal. Not merely her jewelry or her clothes or even her artfully tousled hair. *Everything.*

Oh, dear Dr. Karlavaegen, how I wish I had paid more attention to your lectures! Everyone here has spoken of "the Lady." Is she a powerful thaumaturge—or a creature of magic itself?

"But that isn't talk for a pleasant gathering such as this," Shamal said with a throaty laugh. She stopped halfway between Dominick and Fairfax. "We are here to welcome the newest member of our company, are we not? Of course you have suspicions of him—rightfully so, for are we not surrounded on every side by enemies? And yet . . . there are always good men to be found."

From the direction of Shamal's gaze, she clearly felt she'd found one in Dominick. Clarice fought to keep her head through the swirling emotions of jealousy and fear. Shamal unsettled people— she could see it in the way the council members held themselves. *At least, if I am not alone in my reaction to her, it can hardly be noticed, can it?*

"Oh, aye, just as you say," Aubrianna Watson said, a bit too sharply. "But Sprunt was a cunning old dog, and I don't think he'd spill his secrets to the first man who bought him a bottle—or six. I say this tale of Moryet's is a lie, and a liar has something to hide. Cut his throat, take his ship—and if I am wrong, then I shall make a pretty apology the next time our paths cross." She smiled triumphantly.

"You were always so wasteful, Sister," Melisande Watson said reproachfully. "Take his ship and his crew, of course, but Captain Moryet and Mr. Swann would fetch a pretty price if we sold them on—and cut their tongues out first, of course," she added conscientiously. "So they won't talk about what they oughtn't."

"Alas, dear ladies," Fairfax said, sounding regretful, and not shocked in the least, "that would be against the Code of the Brotherhood. Any who sail into our harbor have immunity from all quarrels until they sail out again." He paused to drink from his tankard. "Unless, of course, there's some proof they're out to do us harm. . . ." He gazed at them expectantly.

The dark-skinned man with the clean-shaven head spoke again. "Ah, Edmund, my dear friend, how many times have I told you one cannot prove a negative? No, this line of reasoning won't hold water. Not in the least."

"And how do you propose to find the truth then, Alec, my dear?" Fairfax asked mildly.

"We could let them sail away and chase them down in open sea," Captain Watson said.

Her sister sighed. "Cleaving to the letter and not the spirit of the Code as always."

"I know!" Alec said, beaming. "They must show us the true color of their hearts."

"Black, of course," Topper Harrison drawled.

"How?" Clarice said boldly into the laughter that followed. She had the crawling sensation that this was a play, and only she and Dominick didn't know their lines.

"A prize," Captain Fairfax said. "Take a rich prize, bring it here, and prove yourselves beyond all doubt."

"Well, I suppose we could—" Dominick began.

It did not take any mystical insight for Clarice to feel the jaws of the trap close about them.

"Of course!" Shamal said, clapping her hands in delight. "The very thing! It will solve Captain Moryet's problems and our own! He will go in search of the Heart of Light, and when he returns with it, I will have all I need to cast a new set of medallions! The Brotherhood shall reign over a fleet of corsairs that can scour the Hispalides and New Hesperia herself bare of treasure!"

Everyone was smiling now. Dominick turned to Clarice with an expression of baffled fear. Clearly he could tell that something bad had happened and had no idea what.

"And why hasn't anyone else done this?" Clarice asked.

For a moment an expression of surprise flitted across Shamal's face, turning her beauty to ugliness. Then she laughed. "Why, it is fearsomely dangerous, child! The Heart of Light is guarded by so many dangers that none have passed through them alive, and it lies in uncharted seas! To seek it is a quest so fraught with peril that no one here will undertake it—though the rewards would be . . . great indeed. The moment I saw his face, I was certain the dashing

Captain Moryet was the one to succeed where so many others have failed."

Suddenly Dominick pushed back his chair and got to his feet. After a startled moment, Clarice joined him.

"Captains," he said with a bow. "Lady Shamal. I thank you for an entertaining evening, but the hour grows late, and we must take our leave. Before we do, permit me to congratulate you on a rare joke. Why, first you say it is obvious I am your sworn enemy and so must be executed at once, and then you say I and all my crew may sail freely forth to a destination from which we are not likely to return! Well played, my brothers! I salute you!" He doffed his hat in an ironic salute and turned to go, tucking it under his arm.

Oh, Spirits and Powers, let this work. Clarice was certain, as she knew Dominick must be, that nobody here tonight had been playing a joke on them. But let the two of them get out that door alive, and . . .

"I told you he was a clever fellow." Shamal's voice at his back made Dominick hesitate. From her own vantage point Clarice could see the sorceress moving toward them. "And see, he has spotted the flaw in the argument. But it is no flaw, and I have the proof."

Dominick had turned toward Shamal as she spoke. She swayed toward him with a cat-footed tread, and as she came, she teased one of the necklaces about her throat loose from its fellows and flung it into the air.

Automatically, both Dominick and Clarice looked upward. The necklace was a delicate thing of beads, blazing bright and sharp with sorcery.

It should not have been able to pass over Dominick's head as neatly as a lariat's loop, but it did. He should have been able to tear it off again or break the slender strand. And he could not. It was as if his fingers passed through the beads as he clawed at them. The circlet of green stone beads slowly turned red, as if they drank his life's blood.

"Here is a binding only true love can break," Shamal said with a triumphant smile. "And while you wear it, Dominick Moryet, you must do Shamal's bidding. And so you shall seek my treasure, and do all I ask of you."

"Faithless enchantress!" Dominick snarled. He turned to face Fairfax, his expression of fury enough to make the smile fade from Fairfax's face. "So this is the legendary hospitality of the Brethren, is it? To leash me as if I were a hound, and—"

"Hush, my darling," Shamal said, and to Clarice's barely concealed horror, Dominick stopped speaking at once. "Now. Come. The hour is indeed late and the road uncertain. I shall see you safely back to your craft. And we shall go as friends, will we not?"

She tucked her arm through his, smiling, *smiling*. Dominick's eyes glittered with the effort he was making to refuse. Instead, he bowed slightly. "I thank you for your courtesy, Lady Shamal," he said, sounding, to Clarice's horror, as if the words were not forced from him by sorcery. "Indeed, I think you are the first friend I have found in this place."

The walk down the mountain was nerve-racking, for if Shamal's enchantment could exert such control over Dominick, all she had to do was ask him to tell her the truth, and he would have no choice but to do so. But Shamal's attention was apparently focused on other matters entirely.

"This is a lovely island," she said to Dominick. "I hope you will be able to see something of it before you must sail. You do not have to leave immediately, I trust?"

As if when we leave is up to us! Clarice snarled mentally.

"We must take on supplies if we are to travel any distance," Dominick answered. "I have made some inquiries at the chandlery. Mr. Thompson assures me *Asesino* will be seaworthy again within a sennight."

"Then you and I will have time to become great friends," Shamal said. "And you will tell me of the great city which you call home. I am eager to hear of your Albion and its queen."

I just bet you are, Clarice growled to herself. But she had larger worries just now. *Shamal could have forced the truth from Dominick at the meeting, if they wanted it. They don't care whether we are pirates or pirate hunters—why should they? Their true and only purpose is to send us sailing off after this Heart of Light, whatever it is. If we die sailing after it, they win. And if we come back, Shamal has another weapon to control us, a weapon none of us can use.*

At least . . . At least there is a way out. Shamal said true love could break her spell. Perhaps . . .

"And here is the heart of our pretty town," Shamal said.

Ahead was an open space lit by moonlight and a few hanging cressets. The cressets gave a dim and uncertain light, but it was enough to show Clarice what occupied the center of the square: a wooden platform, raised only a few steps above the ground. It held two posts about twelve feet tall, spaced their own height apart, with a crosspiece connecting them. Several sets of shackles hung from the crosspiece by their chains.

And one set that was not empty.

The corpse hung limply, bloated and sagging. Though its head was bowed, Clarice could see its face, slack-jawed and ghostly pale. The dead man's long, black coat fluttered in the breeze.

It was Reverend Dobbs. Or at least what was left of him. Suddenly the scent of decay was overpowering. He must have been killed soon after he reached shore.

She should be sickened. Outraged. But all Clarice could think was *What did he say before he died?*

Shamal kept walking, acting as if the gibbet and its occupant weren't even there.

"You can find your way from here, I think," Shamal said, stopping in the archway of the road that led down to the harbor. She spoke as if they had not passed a dead man on a gibbet to reach it, a man whose death Shamal must have known about before she led them here.

"We can, Lady Shamal," Dominick answered with colorless politeness.

"Then I will leave you." She turned away. "For now."

Clarice barely stifled an entirely unmasculine squeak of alarm as Dominick seized her arm and began to run. When they were halfway down the path, he staggered to a stop, clawing at his neck. After a moment, Clarice realized he was trying desperately to remove the necklace.

"Clarence! Do something!" he gasped.

She knocked his hands away and grabbed at the necklace. She could see it plainly in the moonlight, a dark line against the white of his shirt. But no matter how hard she tried to grasp it, the thing seemed to slide through her fingers as if it were smoke.

It wasn't an illusion. It had tangled itself in the lapels of his coat as he ran. But neither of them could touch it.

"I'm sorry," she whispered, and Dominick sank to his knees in despair.

She knelt beside him, putting her arm around him, fighting to be Clarence and not Clarice, because it was clear that Clarice didn't love him enough to break the spell. *If this isn't love,* she thought wildly, *what is? How will I know it? Do I watch him die and know it's because I . . . wasn't good enough?*

Nothing in her life had prepared her for the desperation she felt. The fear that wasn't for herself, any part of it, but for someone, *Dominick,* whom she couldn't protect.

Maybe this was love after all. But it clearly wasn't enough.

After long, tense moments of charged silence, Dominick pushed himself from under her arm and got to his feet.

"Let's get back to the ship," he said, his voice rough.

Kayin, Dickon, and Dr. Chapman were waiting in the common room.

"As you see, we return hale and whole, and none of us is likely to be slain anytime soon," Dominick said. He'd poured himself a glass of wine as soon as he'd walked in and drank it down as if it were water.

"Encouraging," Dr. Chapman said. "And it took them four hours to say so?"

Clarice pulled out her pocket watch. She hadn't thought nearly so much time had passed, but it had.

"They implied it, rather," Dominick said. "They said a great many other things."

He told them most of it—the meeting with the Brotherhood, his story, their suspicion. He told them about Shamal and the Heart of Light, but he didn't mention Shamal's spell. He'd concealed the necklace before they'd come aboard by the simple expedient of opening his shirt. He could not touch it, but it answered to the pull of gravity as if it were an ordinary string of beads—except that nothing he could do would make it fall off.

"They must want this thing badly," Dr. Chapman said, when Dominick stopped. "Whatever it is."

Clarice had waited for Dominick to tell all of the truth and now realized he wasn't going to. She opened her mouth to add the ensorcelling to the tale, then stopped. *Perhaps he has a plan,* she thought hopefully. *Spirits and Powers know we need one.*

Or perhaps it was part of Shamal's spell. Clarice hoped there was some way to find out.

"I wouldn't've thought of pirates as trusting souls," Dickon said. "I suppose they're going to hand you a set of charts and expect you to use them. But why would anyone in his right mind, well, either go or come back?"

"D'ye think they're selling you a bill of goods?" Kayin frowned, puzzling it out. "I'd say ambush, but it makes no sense."

Here, Clarice could comment without violating Dominick's

trust. "Apparently there's a rule against killing us while we're in port unless they have absolute *proof* we're going to betray them."

"Ah, the nebulous and elastic Code of the Pirate Brotherhood," Dr. Chapman said sourly. "I certainly wish I'd been there to hear that cited. Unfortunately, as soon as Dobbs surfaces and starts to tell the tale of the voyage, they'll have their proof."

"He won't," Dominick said flatly. "He's dead. We saw the body on the way back."

"What?" Dickon said. "Dead? When? How?"

Dominick just shook his head. "Maybe since midday. The body was pretty high. 'How' could be anything. I didn't get a good look."

"But we know he'd been to Dorado before this voyage," Clarice said thoughtfully. "He as much as told us so. And he would've gone first to someone he thought could help. Or who could do us the most damage."

"Shamal," Dominick said bitterly.

"Do you think she had him killed?" Dickon asked blankly. "Why? And he must have told her . . ." He trailed off in confusion.

"Any tale Dobbs told would match pretty closely with what I told the Council," Dominick said. "Except for Clarence being passenger and not crew."

"And the part about you being a hardened and experienced pirate," Clarice said.

"Well, as a medical man, I can say this much: dead is dead," Dr. Chapman said. "The question is, do we do anything about it?"

"Why of course we do," Dominick said. "We hold a funeral service for our upright man of God."

The meeting was over soon after that. Clarice waited for Dominick to ask her to stay behind, but he did not. But she could hardly demand he entertain her—if she was weary, he must be truly exhausted after the evening's events. So she went off to her cabin as if it were any other night and prepared herself for bed. She spent an hour in her bunk tossing and turning before deciding that no matter how grueling the evening had been, sleep was not going to come. She dressed herself again and went up on the deck.

The moon had long since set, and the night sky was choked with stars. *Asesino* rocked gently at anchor.

Dominick was on the forecastle, sitting on the deck with his back to the rail looking up at the stars. "I thought you'd come, Clarence. You want answers. Thank you for keeping my secret even without them."

"Is it you who keeps the secret, Dominick?" Clarice asked boldly. "And not . . . another?"

"The secret of the magic necklace that turns me into a dancing dog?" Dominick said bitterly. "I think it is my own choice—but how can I know? You do not know how hard tonight I struggled to be something—anything!—other than what she wished me to be. It was as if I lived through a dream from which I could not awaken."

"But you did nothing you need to regret," Clarice said helplessly. Small consolation to a man enslaved by magic!

"Not yet," Dominick said bleakly. "I think I am only compelled to follow direct orders. But if I am commanded to sail *Asesino* to the ends of the earth and back again, apparently I shall. Though I have tested the length of her leash tonight, and I think there is a way to save you all."

For an instant Clarice's heart sang with joyous hope. There was an escape, and Dominick had found it. "Tell me!"

"As I say, I must do all I am told to do, but I think I may also do anything I have not been forbidden to. And so, when we are in open sea, I will put myself over the side. And you will all be safe—Dickon is no navigator, but he has wit enough to find Cibola—"

"But you will drown!"

"Keep your voice down," Dominick snapped. "There are still

talebearers among the crew." He got to his feet and stood staring down at her. "What else can I do? If we survive the voyage, we will not survive the homecoming," he added as Clarice still said nothing.

"How—? How can you possibly . . ." *Kill yourself? Leave me?* There was no possible way to finish that sentence.

"At least I will die by my own choice—and free you all with my death. It is the lot I have drawn. I should be grateful I've been left that much freedom. I thought you would be happy for me—for the sake of friendship, if nothing else."

He walked away, leaving Clarice alone.

At least there was no one near to hear her furious weeping.

8

QUEEN OF HELL

KAYIN HAMMERED on her cabin door far too early the next morning, waking Clarice from an uneasy sleep. For a baffled moment she listened to him shouting they were late, then realized she and Kayin were supposed to go to Rollo Thompson's today to arrange for *Asesino*'s refitting. She scrambled into her clothes and hurried up on deck, blinking in surprise. The island had moved.

Then she shook her head in exasperation at her obtuseness. Dorado was exactly where it had always been. It was *Asesino* that had moved. While she had lain, furious and grieving, in her narrow bunk, the ship had been conveyed to Mr. Thompson's wharf, and the gangplank led to the landing stage below.

She looked around. *Asesino* seemed lifeless with all her sails furled, and the deck seemed oddly deserted. *Of course the crew have all gone ashore,* she told herself chidingly.

"Where is Dominick?" she demanded, and flinched inwardly at the sharpness she heard in her voice.

"Gone ashore right after breakfast. Four bells, that'd be," Kayin said. "An, er, a lady called for him."

"Was she half-naked and barefoot?" Clarice asked spitefully.

The surprise on Kayin's face was nothing to the shock she felt at her own words. Last night she'd wept at the thought that Dominick could see no solution to their problem but his own death. Now, she'd gladly strangle him herself. To go off alone with Shamal! Of all the *stupid* . . . !

"She was a fine lady," Kayin said, his expression clearly indicating he had no idea whether that was the right answer. "Dressed up like rich folks in Albion. She had a parasol," he added hopefully. "And a fine carriage."

At least that didn't sound like Shamal after all. "Fine," Clarice said shortly, trying not to ask herself the question of just what fine lady would have come for Dominick; she could somehow not imagine either Aubrianna or Melisande Watson with a parasol and a carriage. "Let's go and see how badly Rollo Thompson is going to cheat us."

Kayin clapped her heartily on the shoulder. "There's the spirit, laddibuck!" he said in obvious relief. "We'll make a sailor of you yet. Only . . . ," he said slowly. "Our Mr. Thompson's going to be all over *Asesino,* isn't he? And prying into every nook and cranny, I'll be bound. He knows where the first mate bunks as well as anyone, I guess. And it's going to look odd if your things aren't there, what with Dominick telling all of them you're that, and all."

Privately, Clarice doubted Thompson could tell one sea chest from another. Still, it was plain Kayin wanted to make the change. And everything Clarice owned was safely behind a stout lock even Dobbs hadn't been able to pick.

"Dobbs?" she blurted out.

"Crew's been told. We'll say out a service for him come Sunday. We don't have a body or any place to put it, anyway."

"I suppose that's best," Clarice said slowly. She wondered what they did with the dead here. *Perhaps they cart them up the mountain and throw them into the volcano,* she thought giddily.

Kayin was still looking at her, clearly waiting for her answer to the question of changing cabins. "Are you sure you don't mind?" she asked carefully.

He grinned at her. "And me with a cabin of my own and a door to it either way? We can shift around again once we're out to sea if you like. But the captain depends on you, and there's no mistake about that. And, well, stands to reason. You and him, you're two of a kind, see?"

I'm not the one plotting to throw myself over the side and calling it a plan! She took a deep breath and pulled the tattered cloak of her masquerade about herself once more. "I'm sure you're right, Kayin. I'll get my trunk moved as soon as we get back."

"No need to trouble yourself." Kayin stuck two fingers in his mouth and whistled shrilly. "Hoy! Neddy! See you get Mr. Swann squared away before you go ashore!"

From the far end of the deck, Ned Hatcliff got to his feet and semaphored his agreement.

Well, Clarice thought. *That's a nice tactful,* circumspect, *undercover way to handle things.*

Rollo Thompson was not precisely a thief. Nor was he any more dishonest than many innkeepers Clarice had met in her travels. It was just that he encouraged his clients to make assumptions, and the inevitable misunderstandings always worked in his favor.

Clarice spent hours with Thompson in his cramped and sweltering cubbyhole office, going carefully over pages and pages of lists containing all the things *Asesino* needed. Each and every item and amount held a trap for the unsuspicious, and Mr. Thompson was tireless in his attempts to hurry her along. But he was dealing with someone who had been trained by an expert—her mother—in ferreting out those who thought selling to the Crown meant a license to enrich oneself, so she was equally tireless in her insistence on plodding slowly and carefully through a full discussion of each and every item.

"Now then. This cost for salt pork seems quite low," she said.

After several minutes of discussion, it transpired that this was the cost per dozen barrels, not the cost of the six dozen barrels they meant to order. Clearly not even a mistake—how was he to know Mr. Swann wasn't entirely familiar with this utterly commonplace method of reckoning costs?

And so the true figure was reckoned and written into the margin, with Mr. Thompson grumbling indulgently.

If a price wasn't too low, it was too high: the cost for twelve when they needed six, the cost for lemons when they'd ordered limes, or bread instead of biscuit, lard for butter, mutton for bacon—and those were only the things she knew the use of! All she could do was question everything, for if Mr. Thompson was a swindler and a cheat, he was at least an honest one and would not tell her a flat-out lie.

When they were nearly finished with the manifest, Randolph returned with the inventory of the ship's cargo, for he and his sibling had boarded *Asesino* as soon as Kayin and Clarice had arrived. The inventory had been countersigned by Geordie, so that information, at least, was not in dispute. Since the numbers were beyond reproach, Clarice and Thompson argued instead about the quality of the items—resolved by consulting *Asesino*'s manifest, with its dangling seals from the portmaster of Albion, the guildmaster of the Provender's Guild (tea and spices), the seal of the Vintner's Brotherhood (wine and brandy), the seals of the Glassmaker's Guild and the brass foundry where the beads had been made, and the seal of the Chief Cargomaster in Ordinary (who'd verified the crates as they were loaded).

By then, Clarice had a pounding headache, and even Mr. Thompson looked weary. "You're a sharp lad and no mistake," he said admiringly. "Well then! And here's the two tallies—what I'll offer for your goods and what you'll offer for mine. And see? They match right up."

"Of course you've already figured in the tithe to the House," Clarice said, rubbing her temples. "And paid it."

"Of course!" Thompson said, looking wide-eyed and innocent.

"And will give me a letter to that effect. So there can be no confusion, you understand. And then you will take ten percent off your charges for wasting half my day, and you will give that to me in silver, not gold, so my crew can spend it here without getting cheated in the exchange. And do please be very clear on one thing. If I discover that your material is not entirely to the standards we have agreed upon, I will leap over the side of my ship, swim back here, and cut your throat as you sleep. I trust we have reached a full and complete understanding?" She should have been shocked at her own words. Surely they were nothing either Princess Clarice or Mr. Swann would have considered saying.

But she was becoming someone else. Someone she'd once been unable to imagine.

"Full and complete." Thompson was beaming at her, which made Clarice think she should have demanded he take even more off the price. But she found it hard to convince herself it mattered. Either they'd be safely away from here with a hold full of what they needed . . .

. . . or they'd all be dead and nobody would care anymore.

Mr. Thompson accompanied her as she left the chandlery. The wharf was a busy place now; *Asesino* was being unloaded. The sight before her was the Albion docks in miniature—save that the laborers on the Albion docks did not bear whip scars on their backs and brands upon their cheeks. Or wear the iron collar about their necks that marked them as slaves.

Beasts of burden in coincidentally human form.

Clarice stopped, staring. Well, here was the answer to one of the questions she had asked herself last night: Who did the work? *Slaves!* She ground her teeth, feeling sick at the sight.

Slavery was illegal in every other place she knew.

"Ah, admiring my fine ladies and gentlemen, are you?" Thompson asked. "You'll be needing to take on crew before you sail, you looking a bit shorthanded, if you don't mind me saying so. I could let you have some of them at a good price. Fine workers. Strong. And no trouble about finding wages for them, eh?"

And when they come and slay us in our beds, how could I even say it was wrong?

"I imagine the captain has made other plans," Clarice said, and moved toward the gangplank. The slaves moved quickly aside to let her pass.

Slaves.

I wish I had never been born, Clarice thought miserably.

The following morning she spent hours following Kayin or Geordie about the ship as they oversaw Mr. Thompson's slave laborers. Kayin had tried every tongue he knew, but he had no language in common with them and was reduced to issuing his orders in pidgin Albionnaise.

Everyone was engaged in the hundreds of tiny tasks a ship's crew dealt with in port. Geordie was having a jacket made at the tailor's. Dickon had found a bookshop. Duff Evans, the ship's carpenter, was seeing to the sharpening and repair of some of his tools at the blacksmith's.

Everyone had something to occupy him but her. Following Kayin through the bowels of the ship hardly counted. He would have done the same things whether she was there or not. Her presence was just another masquerade.

That evening she dined with Dr. Chapman, Dickon, Kayin, and a few others from *Asesino*. Mr. Emerson was one of those at liberty, which meant that everyone had to take meals ashore. Dr. Chapman was in a merry humor, for he'd found a thaumaturgical physician to speed the healing of his broken arm. The cost was high, he said, but worth it entirely.

Dominick wasn't there.

"I asked him to come along," Dickon said, "and he said he was 'stuffed as a tick' and didn't think he could bear the sight of food—possibly for several days."

There was general laughter at that, for Dickon was an excellent mimic, and it prompted a story from Dr. Chapman about the dangers of gorging the moment one made port. Of course, Rogerio responded with a story of his own, only to be capped by Kayin, and the meal passed merrily enough.

But when Clarice returned to *Asesino* afterward, Dominick was nowhere to be seen. She lingered on deck for an hour or so, but he did not appear, and short of going and knocking on his cabin door . . .

No.

So she went to bed.

In the morning, she was already ashore before she remembered she hadn't looked for Dominick before she left. He was in neither of the two taverns that were open during the day to serve food, so she breakfasted and returned to the ship to continue watching over its refitting. By the end of the day, she was quite certain she knew every nook and cranny of *Asesino* intimately, and Dominick wasn't in any of them.

Nor did he join them at dinner, though tonight the whole of the *Asesino*'s new-minted officers and senior crew had commandeered the large table at the back of the Bucket O'Blood. In the midst of the boisterousness of the impromptu dinner party, she felt not merely alone, but lonely. As if the presence or absence of one man made the difference between companionship or isolation.

She couldn't ask where he was. No one else at the table seemed the least worried, and Dr. Chapman, if no one else, was always expecting disaster. If Dominick's absence were unusual, he would be the first to speak up.

But she had no heart to remain once she had finished her meal.

When she stepped aboard the ship, Ned Hatcliff greeted her and assured her all was quiet. "Pirates," he said sagely, "are your quiet and peaceful sorts, Mr. Swann." At her skeptical look, he grinned. "Stands to reason, don't it? Murdering and pillaging is their business, like. Who'd do a job of work without getting paid? Why, it'd be like a soldier starting a war while he was on leave."

"I suppose you're right," she answered doubtfully.

She circled the deck, trying not to look—or feel—as if she was dawdling in hopes Dominick would magically appear. (A bad choice of words, that, she told herself, in this place where thaumaturgy seemed to be as pervasive as rain.) At last she admitted to herself that his arrival was unlikely, but a stubborn glimmer of hope made her lean her hip against a barrel propped against the rail and take out her cigarillo case. A touch of her spellmatch and the tip kindled. She blew out a cloud of smoke.

If anyone were to look in my direction, they'd see the perfect image of a young gentleman swashbuckler—sword at hip, hat on head, taking a moment's ease before his next adventure.

She wished with all her heart it were the truth. Her sister Jennet was addicted to such stories. In them, the wicked were confounded, the virtuous triumphed . . . and the dashing hero never spent chapters wondering whether he'd fallen in love with someone . . . and if he had not, why was he so miserable?

"Dearest Mama," she said silently, mentally composing a letter she would never write and had no way to send, *"I know that when I left Swansgaarde, you expected me to seek adventure in some civilized place from which I could send regular letters and receive them as well. I know yours would have been filled with good advice. And when I met a young man and wrote to you of him, you would have been able to tell me whether it was love or merely infatuation. You would have been able to tell me how I might know if his heart was true, and if mine was as well. You would have said I must bring him to Heimlichstadt, so that you and Papa could meet him. . . ."*

The fantasy was too painful. Clarice threw her half-smoked cigarillo over the side and went below.

But tonight she did not sleep well.

The loading, Kayin said next morning, was nearly done. This afternoon he and Geordie would go about the town to collect a work party so that they could see the supplies safely put away by their own people.

"Never trust a man to stow a cargo who won't have to sail in the ship afterward," Kayin said grimly. "It won't turn out well at all."

"'The eye of the master maketh the ox fat,'" Clarice said, quoting the old proverb.

"That's true enough. Still, once we've done with Mr. Thompson and his little ways, there's no reason you need to stand about with us. And probably far better you don't," he added darkly.

"Why?" Clarice looked around carefully before she spoke, but no one was close enough to hear. "You know precisely how much I know about seamanship, but—it doesn't look as if it would take much work to secure the cargo."

"Oh, as to that, not so much work at all. But there's all those hogsheads to be filled with freshwater, and each to get a bottle of good whiskey poured in to keep it sweet—which means a bit of whiskey poured into us as well, and rightly so, for you'll see there's no river in sight to pump the water out of."

"Then . . ." Clarice stopped. Mr. Thompson had mentioned the pump outside the chandlery. "You're going to fill them with buckets," she said in realization.

"That we are." Kayin sighed. "And a very great many of them. Times like that, it's just as well there's nobody in sight but those doing the work. And if the captain was here, I'd tell him the same."

"Wise counsel," Clarice said gravely. "And I will take it."

Kayin's offhand comment had brought Dominick to the forefront of her thoughts again.

More for something to do than out of any desire to go on hunting for Dominick, Clarice wandered about Dorado. She tried not to think how this expedition would have been a thousand times more fun if she'd been able to share it with Dominick. She imagined their conversation: what she'd say, how he'd answer. The stories they'd share of their adventures—hers on the road, his on the sea. She thought of his shy smile, of the wicked sense of humor he kept so concealed. She wanted to see Dorado through his eyes.

But he wasn't here. And all she could think of was the last words he'd spoken to her.

"At least I will die by my own choice—and free you all with my death. It is the lot I have drawn. I should be grateful I've been left that much freedom. I thought you would be happy for me—for the sake of friendship, if nothing else."

"But how can I be happy if you're dead?" she whispered softly.

In a bleak mood she reached the town square. Dobbs's body was gone, of course. Not even a suspicion of stink remained—just an open square with a gibbet in the middle, looking like nothing more sinister than a quaint, archaic ornament to a picturesque locale. It was all so very tidy and civilized. Somehow that made everything worse when Dorado was neither tidy nor civilized, but chaotic and feral beneath its lying surface.

But at the far corner of the square she spotted some familiar shapes displayed in a window. Books! Just the thing to raise her spirits. The little jingling bell that she heard when she opened the door of the shop was enough to make her ache with homesickness. Nothing bad had ever happened to her in a bookstore.

Yet.

She removed her hat and tucked it under her arm as she moved farther into the store.

"Are you looking for something in particular, sir?" the man at the desk asked.

"Just to see what there is," she answered briefly.

"Let me know if there's anything I can help you with. Matthew Pratchett's my name. Owner and sole proprietor of Pratchett's Fine Books."

"Thank you, Mr. Pratchett," Clarice said automatically.

The books were a random collection: poetry, essays, plays, sermons.

She was hesitating between a collection of plays by the False Marlowe and an epic poem about the founding of the Cisleithanian Empire when her attention was summoned by movement outside in the square. A carriage—the first she'd seen here—was arriving, a light chaise of the sort usually drawn by a single horse. But no horse was in sight. The chaise was hitched to four men—Cisleithanian, by their skin color—and each pair was bound together by a light yoke that kept them side by side. Each of the four wore a collar and had a branded cheek. Slaves. It was as if Clarice had wandered into a nightmare thinking she was still awake.

A lady was seated in the chaise; she was dressed all in pink silk, in the latest and most fashionable Wauloisene mode, and the color glowed warmly against her dark skin. Her hair was swept up, and she wore a tiny hat perched as if to swoop down across her forehead. The lavish ostrich feathers that adorned it—dyed pink to match her gown—were larger than the hat itself. Clarice watched as the fashionable lady twirled a tiny lace parasol and leaned over to address some companion walking on the far side of the chaise.

Then that companion stepped around to the near side of the chaise, to help its passenger down.

It was Dominick.

Distantly, Clarice heard a thud as the books in her hands hit the floor. The woman dressed in the highest style of Old World fashion was Shamal.

Kayin's words from the other day echoed through her mind, mocking her. *"She was a fine lady. She had a parasol. And a fine carriage."*

And what—who—was drawing her carriage when you saw it, Kayin?

Clarice swallowed hard, tasting bile. In the square, Dominick offered Shamal his arm, and they began to stroll away. After a moment Shamal looked back and gestured. The slaves turned the carriage about, heading back the way they'd come.

"Are you all right, sir? Sometimes the sun takes a body un-
awares. Come and sit down for a moment." Mr. Pratchett had
come out from behind his desk, his expression anxious.

"I'm fine," Clarice said gruffly, but she came along.

Behind the desk was a mahogany bench along the wall. She sat
down and leaned her head back against the wall. She felt . . .
Bruised.

A moment later Mr. Pratchett came back. He had her hat in
one hand, and the books she'd dropped. Whatever they were.

"I'll take them both," she said, reaching for her hat.

But as she did, she realized she could not leave yet. She'd lost
sight of Dominick and Shamal, and the last thing she wanted was
to encounter them.

"How did you come to open a bookshop here, if I may ask?"
she asked, almost at random.

"You're new come to our fair isle, I take it?" Mr. Pratchett
asked shrewdly.

Clarice hesitated, but she could do little but answer. "I came
with the brig *Asesino*."

"And soon you will sail away again. And meanwhile, you walk
the streets a free man."

She frowned faintly. It seemed an oddly obvious observation.

"Ships of the Brotherhood are the only ones who sail into the
House of the Four Winds and sail out again. If you'll permit an
old man a word of advice: when you sail free again, forget you
ever made landfall here. Or, out of pity, bring no one here alive."

"But surely it is better to live than to die," Clarice said with a
bitterness that surprised her.

Mr. Pratchett chuckled darkly. "Thus speaks youth! Hear my
tale, and judge for yourself, for I see you are not entirely aware of
what being a client of the House of the Four Winds entails." He
seemed happy to have a fresh audience for his tale, and Clarice
was cravenly glad to have an excuse to linger.

"When the *Morning Calm* was taken, I assumed I and my fellow passengers were spared to be held to ransom. But no. We

were to be enslaved. Most of the Ifranes you will see here have been kidnapped into slavery in their homeland and brought westward. The lords and ladies of the House of the Four Winds do not trust them not to seek revenge, but our great nobles must have servants. And that is our fate." Mr. Pratchett paused for a moment, polishing his spectacles upon a lace-trimmed handkerchief. "We serve for seven years—to repay the cost of our capture, we are told. And then we are free, those of us who survive. Free to starve or to sell ourselves into slavery forever. Only a few of the luckiest manage to find some trade to ply. But no matter how we may prosper here, we may never leave. We are bound to Dorado forever."

It was a terrible story, but Clarice had no doubt of its truth, and once more she had the sense of something missing. Why did the pirates preserve the passengers and bring them here? Why not enslave them once and for all instead of offering them the tantalizing chance of freedom?

It was another riddle, and she doubted Mr. Pratchett had the answer to it. So she thanked him for his time and care and left the shop. Dominick and Shamal were nowhere to be seen.

Where were they? Where was *he?* Until now, Clarice had thought Shamal had only as much interest in Dominick as a cat might in a mouse. And yet . . .

And yet, it is clear she has forced him to bear her company these last three days as if he were some besotted swain, and she the apple of his eye! What could she want—what more *could she want—than control of* Asesino *and her captain?*

Her handsome young captain, Clarice thought bitterly. Her steps slowed. Something in this was not right. Lady Shamal was the most powerful woman on Dorado. Dorado was a haunt of pirates.

Pirates elected their captains.

True, Dominick meant to end his life the moment they were at sea, but Shamal could not—Clarice prayed—know that. Yet, Shamal could not believe Dominick could manage to do her bidding once *Asesino* sailed free of here. *Dominick is well liked, that is true. But no captain of mutineers is well liked enough to sail his ship to certain doom.*

There is another string to her bow. And I need to know what it is.

Her first thought was to seek Dr. Chapman's counsel. The thought of violating Dominick's trust in her made Clarice wince, but she could not let Dominick keep this secret at the cost of so many lives. She struggled with her conscience all the way back to the ship, and the best she could manage was to confront Dominick before she went to Dr. Chapman and hope he would agree to speak.

If he did not, she must do it anyway.

But confronting Dominick was easier decided than done. He was still gone when she checked his cabin. Kayin, finding her there, said the water barrels were full and their supplies delivered and checked. Some minor work remained to do, but they could sail the day after tomorrow.

"Or any day past the day we're given our direction," Kayin said darkly. "And where are we meant to sail for? Any honest port is closed to us."

"No," Clarice said. "Sprunt was a pirate, and we overthrew him, and so we are not mutineers after all. All we need do is tell our tale—Dorado itself is our proof of innocence. As for how the House of the Four Winds has convinced itself we will sail at their bidding, I think Dominick can answer that better than I."

Kayin nodded. "I hope he'll speak soon. I don't like it here."

"Tonight, I am sure," Clarice promised recklessly. "I shall go to him myself the moment he's aboard."

Kayin smiled, his teeth a bright flash against his dark skin. "And I'll be sure you know when that is."

But Kayin's assistance was unneeded, for when Dominick walked up *Asesino*'s gangplank, Clarice was on deck. She'd spent the afternoon there pacing, trying to look as if she weren't. Fortunately only a handful of people were aboard to see.

Dominick was alone, which was a relief, and his shoulders slumped with tiredness. He greeted the watch briefly, but went below without looking around.

Clarice followed him.

She tapped at his door and opened it without waiting for an answer. Dominick was standing at the washbasin, coat off, pouring the contents of the ewer over his head.

"Dominick?"

He startled, dropping the pitcher. It hit the deck with a thud.

"Clarence! This is . . . I mean, I am very tired, and—"

"We have to talk." Clarice closed the door behind her. "Kayin says we are nearly ready to sail. We need to make our plans. And to find out how Shamal means to make us go after this Heart of Light. What has she told you?"

Dominick's expression was a mixture of hurt and puzzlement. "You heard her. You were there."

All Clarice's fear was turned to rage—a transmutation that did not require thaumaturgy. "You've spent the last three days wandering the island with her! I saw you! She holds all our lives in her hand—and yet you see nothing wrong with becoming her— her *lapdog*!"

For a moment Dominick gazed at her blankly, then confusion gave way to horror. He staggered back a step, his face gone white.

Clarice caught him before he fell. He clawed at her shoulders, trying to regain his balance, and for a moment she supported his whole weight. It was wrenching and unsettling in a way she had not imagined: she wanted to put her arms around him, to embrace him, to comfort him . . .

To tell him who she was.

To ask him why Shamal had wanted him to pretend he was her lover.

Shamal.

The thought of her silenced Clarice in this moment when she

might have told Dominick everything. Shamal considered Clarence Swann a minor annoyance at worst. But *Clarice* . . . ?

"Here is a binding only true love can break."

Clarice would be an active threat.

"I forgot *Asesino*, I forgot all of you—she said—she said—"

Clarice helped him to the bed, where he collapsed on the edge and lowered his face into his hands with a groan.

"You didn't know?" she asked gently, her anger burned away by his reaction.

"The morning after we had been to the House of the Four Winds, I awoke early. I could not sleep. I went ashore. I had some notion of going back to the House of the Four Winds, hoping to speak with Captain Fairfax. To discover more about this mysterious quest I had bound myself to. I heard a woman—Shamal—call my name . . . Nothing more. Oh, Clarence—what have I done?"

"Nothing," Clarice said firmly. She could not imagine what he must be feeling, to have had mind and will and memory all snatched from him. All she could do was offer him another illusion: that it did not frighten her. "You went on picnics, I think. And walked beside her carriage."

And were kept from speaking to anyone on the Pirate Council, and I wonder why?

"And asked no questions." Dominick sighed and tilted his head back to look at her. "And there are a good many I should have asked, Clarence. As you know."

"I know," Clarice said softly. "And that is one of the reasons I wanted to speak with you so urgently. There must be more to this madness than Shamal bespelling you, for the crew won't stand for sailing to nowhere. I think you must tell the others the whole truth. Tell Dr. Chapman, at least."

"No!" Dominick's protest was immediate and automatic. He bit his lip. "I . . . Clarence, if the crew does not think I am to be trusted . . . I would not leave my worst enemy here, let alone those I am sworn to see safe home. Let us but sail free of this harbor, and

I swear, I will tell anything to anyone you like. I swear it!" he repeated hoarsely.

"As soon as we're away," Clarice said warningly. She didn't know what the results of a panic among the crew while they were sitting here in the harbor would be—and she didn't want to. "But tonight you must speak to Kayin and your other officers—of more mundane matters at least. We still do not know where we are sailing, or when, or how the pirates mean to make sure we go there."

"Good questions all." Dominick's voice was rough with exhaustion. "And I have no answers. You might as well gather them so we may pool our ignorance."

"They have gone ashore to supper."

"Then so must you," Dominick said firmly. "And bring them back here when supper is done. And there is one thing more you can do for me, dear Clarence."

"Anything. You know that," Clarice said instantly.

"If Shamal summons me tomorrow—if her spell is somehow recast—do not let me answer her call."

"Certainly not. I shall lock you into your cabin myself. And soon enough we will sail away from here, and the problems we face will at least have the virtue of novelty."

"You make it sound simple." Dominick laughed, as she meant him to.

"Analysis usually is. It is execution that is the problem. Now lie down and rest for a while."

Dominick sighed and lay back on his bed. To her relief, the words Clarice expected to hear next did not come.

She did not think she could have stood to be called a "good friend" just now.

9

~

Voyage du Mal

I WAS late, and *Asesino*'s officers were gathered in the captain's cabin.

Clarice spoke first, summarizing the conversation she'd had with Matthew Pratchett, and the light it shed on the practices of Dorado, but omitting any mention of Shamal. "Law is for sale," she said bluntly. "And slavery is . . . common." She swallowed hard. The thought of the slave trade was still horrible.

"Aye," Kayin said quietly. "In my great-grandfather's time, we'd say the death prayers over those loaded onto the ships—or taken for them—because they were dead, or as good as. It's better now, but"—he shrugged—"if some will buy, some will sell."

"Mr. Thompson kindly offered to sell me a crew," Clarice said tightly.

"And that's another matter we have to settle before we sail," Dr. Chapman said. "No matter where we're to sail, who's to sail us?"

"We've loaded supplies for eighty men," Geordie said. "But . . . we don't have eighty hands."

They were less than forty now, and while forty hands could

sail *Asesino* in good weather, it meant extra work and longer watches—and a storm would doom them.

"We will sail as we are and hope for the best," Dominick said, speaking for the first time. "I can't imagine signing a crew here."

"I can't imagine *how* you could," Dr. Chapman pointed out. "The captives who survive their arrival here aren't allowed to leave, and there are no sailors among them, so far as I know. A ship's crew has two choices when their vessel is taken: turn pirate or die. And one presumes those crews are happy where they are."

"*I* would be," Dickon said. "From what you said, ships going after this Heart of Light don't come back. And speaking of that— where are we to go? We have no charts, no destination . . ."

"Perhaps we are to guess," Dr. Chapman said with ponderous sarcasm. "If we must sail without crew, perhaps we can sail without charts as well."

"We know they cannot mean to simply let us sail free," Dominick said. "I tell you plainly, gentlemen: should we find we can, I will make for Cibola and tell the governor everything I know of this hell pit."

"They can't hang us if we aren't mutineers, right enough. And I've never heard it said that throwing pirates off your ship could be called mutiny," Dr. Chapman said, voicing what they all knew. "As for how the Brotherhood intends to stop it, well, we'll weather that storm when it blows, won't we?"

"That only leaves the sailing," Dickon said dubiously.

Dominick shrugged. "If there is no word by tomorrow noon, I'll go back to the House of the Four Winds to demand answers. Or at least, to very politely request permission to sail," he added with a wry smile.

"If you go, I go," Clarice said. There was no place on earth she wanted less to go, but if Dominick went, she would, too. *And perhaps find out why Shamal didn't want Dominick talking to Captain Fairfax.*

"I would have it no other way," Dominick said warmly. "Well, my friends, let us fill our glasses and raise them before we seek our beds."

Glasses and a bottle were quickly brought from the tantalus, and when every glass was filled, Dominick asked, "Who has the toast?"

"I do." Clarice raised her cup. "To the captain and crew of *Asesino*: *Nous errons où nous voulons*—we go where we choose."

"Hear, hear!" Dr. Chapman said.

Everyone raised glasses and drank.

In the morning, by unspoken agreement, Geordie went ashore and brought back breakfast—and Jerrold Robinson, as well, whom he had found at the tavern. He strutted proudly in his new purchase: a blue coat with a double row of silver buttons.

"It's 'coz I'm Captain Moryet's *personal aide*, like," he announced.

"And you'll make a fine captain yourself someday," Dominick said, forcing cheer Clarice knew he did not feel into his voice. Despite a night's rest he still looked exhausted—and if no one but her knew he feared Shamal's summoning him back into ensorcelled amnesia, she could see that worry plainly.

They gathered in the common room to share bread and cider and cold mutton pies, and Clarice found herself thinking longingly of those few brief days between the mutiny and their landfall. Would she ever again experience such joyful camaraderie and easy friendship?

Will you even live to worry about it? she asked herself bitterly.

Jerrold was delighted to hear they would soon be sailing and insisted on waiting on them as, so he said, "a proper cabin boy should."

"I am glad you are here, for just now I have a delicate job of work for you," Dominick said.

Jerrold practically saluted, and Clarice saw Dr. Chapman hide a smile.

"Anything, Cap'n! Just try me!"

"We need to get the crew aboard," Dominick said. "And while I know Kayin will do his best for us, I would like to make bringing Mr. Emerson back your personal task."

Jerrold blinked, but his enthusiasm didn't waver. "Yes, sir, Cap'n, sir! On the double! Sober?"

That startled an honest laugh out of Dominick. "I don't think we need to go that far, Jerrold. Aboard will be enough."

The crew began drifting back to *Asesino* almost immediately once the word was passed that they were to make ready to sail. The sailors returning to the ship came in ones and twos, but each was accompanied by local people. *To bring them here? Or to watch us sail?* Clarice wondered. Once Mr. Emerson was aboard, Dominick ordered Jerrold to the crow's nest, with orders to keep watch. Both Clarice and Dominick prowled the deck, trying not to fall prey to nerves. The *Horrid Hangman* had sailed as they watched—silently, which meant that her rigging was thoroughly ensorcelled—and now *Asesino* was alone in the harbor.

"Something's about to happen," Clarice said in a low voice. She nodded toward the land.

Men and women loitered in the chandlery dooryard and gathered with ostentatious casualness at the oak tree beside it.

"I see," Dominick said equally quietly. "Perhaps they think we mean to try to run the harbor chain and look to see us drown."

"Perhaps," Clarice said doubtfully. She was certain the Doradans would consider it high entertainment—the question was, why did they think *Asesino* would try it?

She picked up the clipboard with the ship's roster from a nearby barrel as two more men began to ascend the gangplank. Having just checked off Duff Evans and John Tiptree, she peered at the tally to get a count of who was yet to board.

"Ahoy, the *Asesino*! Permission to come aboard!"

It was Edmund Bell Fairfax, captain of *Sirocco* and leader of the Pirate Brotherhood. In the candlelit dimness of the House of the Four Winds, he'd been a dramatic figure. In the light of day, in his jewels and velvets, he looked like something out of a myth. With him were two of the other captains from the House of the Four Winds: Nigel Brown of the *Tamerlane*, and Alec Campion of the *Limerick Rake*. Brown had his tricorne tucked under his arm politely, and Campion was hatless. Bell doffed his hat with a flourish and made an exaggerated bow.

The very model of a modern pirate captain, Clarice thought uncharitably.

"Permission granted," Dominick said, coming up beside her. "I am pleased to see you again, Captain Fairfax. As you can see, we are ready to sail. I was about to come in search of you."

Clarice glanced at the faces of Fairfax's two companions. Both men looked grim, and her heart sank.

"Perhaps we might continue this conversation below?" Fairfax said.

"Of course," Dominick said. "Come to my cabin."

"A lovely place," Captain Fairfax said, gazing around. Now that Clarice was looking for it, she could see he was putting on a show of geniality to cover his unease, and her heart sank further.

"It will do," Brown said. "With a few changes."

"Oh, my dear, always so negative. When life hands you lemons, make grog with them!" Campion said lightly. Of the three of them, Clarice thought he was the least uncomfortable with whatever news the three of them had come to impart.

Dominick seated himself in the cabin's only chair. Clarice went to the tantalus and collected glasses and a bottle. Campion and Brown sat down on the bunk; Fairfax remained standing. Clarice poured five glasses full of port and handed them around, leaving the bottle beside Dominick before taking up a watchful stance beside the door.

"Now that we're all comfortable," Dominick said with only a faint tinge of irony, "perhaps you'll be so good as to tell me why you've come?"

"It's to give you the details about your voyage," Campion said, when it became clear neither of the others would speak. "While of course we appreciate your generous and noble gesture at our little gathering—"

"When you volunteered to bring us back the Heart of Light," Brown added, as if Dominick might have forgotten.

"—there are perhaps some things that remain unsettled," Campion finished imperturbably.

"Such as where we are going, and how we're to find it, and—oh, but I'm sure I need not trouble you fine gentlemen with minor details you have already thought of," Dominick said.

"You will be carrying a passenger," Fairfax said. He sounded as if the words were being forced from him. "These accommodations are to be hers."

"'Hers'?" Clarice demanded sharply, before Dominick could speak.

"The Lady Shamal sails with you," Captain Fairfax said. "Once her baggage has been loaded, you may sail at will."

Clarice drained her glass. *That explains why we have no charts, I suppose. And why she is so confident we will not only go, but come back.*

"I am surprised," Dominick said waspishly. "How can you bear to lose such an *enchanting* companion?"

"Not by choice!" Fairfax blurted.

Campion rose to his feet and put a warning hand on Fairfax's arm. "What my dear Edmund means, of course, is that our days will be dark and our hearts will be heavy until she returns. And that we will trust you to keep her safe."

Captain Brown got to his feet as well, setting his untouched glass aside. "Yes. That's what Edmund means. That's what all of us mean. What else?"

Clarice could almost feel sorry for them. What they were doing was clearly against their wishes, and she wondered if it was magic or simple extortion that forced them to do it.

"What else?" Dominick echoed. "I thank you for this information, gentlemen. Clarence, if you will assemble a work party, I shall vacate my quarters in anticipation of our . . . honored guest."

"Of course," Clarice said.

She'd almost rather stay on Dorado than sail with Shamal.

Not much of a choice.

By the time Clarice had overseen the removal of Dominick's things to the first mate's cabin and had her own possessions moved to the cabin formerly occupied by the Reverend Dobbs, the first items of Shamal's baggage were being brought on board.

Shamal certainly does not travel light, Clarice thought. The porters were the same Ifranes who had loaded *Asesino*'s supplies, supervised by Alumeda Thompson. Boxes and trunks and muslin-shrouded bundles were taken to the captain's cabin, but a number of crates and barrels also had to be—so Alumeda said—stowed below. She remained on deck, and Clarice accompanied Geordie to oversee that work.

"Not a mark or a label anywhere, Mr. Swann!" he said despondently. "And no way to know what's in any of them. How we're to bring up one keg and not another is anybody's guess."

"Perhaps they're all for use at our destination," she said as soothingly as she could.

"We were going to make for Cibola." Even in his distress, he kept his voice low. "But I heard . . . the Lady Shamal . . . she's a thaumaturge, isn't she?"

"Yes, Geordie, I'm afraid she is. A very powerful one." There was no point in denying it; he'd probably heard tales of her while he was ashore. "I don't think you can count on our going to Cibola just yet."

Dominick had told no one but his officers about going after

the Heart of Light, but Clarice kept in mind Dr. Chapman's warn-
ings about gossip.

"Maybe Cap'n Dominick can talk some sense into her," Geordie said hopefully.

"Perhaps he can."

When Clarice reached the deck again, she saw men walking up
the gangplank. Stumbling, rather. Their bodies were gaunt with
starvation. Some supported their fellows as they limped along;
many wore crude bandages. As soon as they gained the deck,
they sat—or collapsed—into the first clear space they could
find.

"You've delivered your charges," Dominick said, white-faced
with fury. "Now get off my ship before I throw you over the side."

"Just as you like, Captain Moryet, sir." The man facing Dominick tugged at the brim of his hat with ostentatious insolence and
shouldered through the men still staggering up the gangplank.
Some fell.

"The rest of Shamal's 'supplies,'" Dominick said to Clarice
with weary fury. "Apparently we are to sail with a full complement after all."

"Captives," Clarice said quietly. That they were being sent to
Asesino as crew—in defiance of all she'd been told of Dorado's
customs—only confirmed what she'd suspected all along: this
"quest" was something they were not meant to survive. Any of
them.

"Tell Kayin to get them belowdecks," Dominick said. "Then
go to the surgery, of your kindness. Dr. Chapman will need your
help. I must make ready to sail. And to see to our passenger's
comfort, when she chooses to board." His voice was colorless.

"Be careful," Clarice said, putting a hand on his arm. She turned
without waiting for his response and made her way below.

Dr. Chapman worked with the quickness of one who has learned his profession in battle. No sooner had he finished with one patient than the next appeared. Clarice's world dwindled to one of broken limbs and ugly wounds. At that, Dr. Chapman was only seeing the worst cases among the fifty-two men they'd been forced to take aboard—he'd sent Geordie and Rogerio to look them over and send those who needed immediate care to the surgery.

"Just thank the Spirits and Powers we haven't seen any sickness," Dr. Chapman said grimly, after dismissing their latest patient. "I'd have to put those ashore to save the rest of us."

"I suppose you don't last long in the stockade if you're sick," Clarice answered dully. She'd known they were looking first for signs of illness. There was no way to quarantine a sick man on *Asesino*, and few resources available for nursing.

"Why haven't we sailed?" she added. She knew Shamal was aboard, for on one of his trips to bring patients to the surgery Geordie had told them that. Only the knowledge that Dominick was vital to Shamal's plans had left Clarice able to concentrate on the work before her.

"Can't until I give the word," Dr. Chapman said. "It's the law of the sea—one even pirates respect." He straightened and stretched.

Clarice moved stiffly to the doorway to summon the next patient. The corridor was deserted. "There's no one out here."

"Then that means we're done." Dr. Chapman picked up a half-full bottle of brandy and splashed some into a tin cup. He tossed it back, then offered the cup and bottle to Clarice.

She shook her head. Right now what she wanted was a strong cup of tea.

"Then you can go and tell the captain we can sail," Dr. Chapman told her. "We're carrying no plague."

Clarice didn't know what she expected to find on deck. Armed men? Dead bodies? But all was quiet. The crew were occupying

themselves with various minor tasks, or simply sitting and waiting for orders. Dominick was on the afterdeck, looking out over
the ship. He looked worn to the bone, and his sun-bronzed skin
held an undertone of gray. The sight of him, alive and whole, made
her giddy with relief and desperately worried at the same time. Was
it Shamal's enchantment that was draining him? Or was it because
he was fighting it?

And if he was, what command was it he was fighting not to
obey?

"Dr. Chapman says we may sail," she said when she reached
Dominick's side.

"Thank you, Clarence," Dominick said, relieved. He took a
deep breath and turned to Kayin, who was waiting nearby. "You
heard him. Let's get out of here."

Kayin turned to the rail and blew a long blast on his whistle.
Suddenly the ship was alive with movement, but not the movement Clarice expected.

They were lowering the boats.

"Can't put on sail at dockside," Kayin said for her benefit. "We'd
go right up on the rocks."

Now Clarice saw the reason for Dominick's insistence on re-
placing the jolly boat they'd lost, for the whole motive power of
the ship was being provided by rowers.

*Twenty-six men in the boats, and even I know we cannot make
sail with those left aboard. I hope we never need to.*

She stood beside Dominick, who occasionally shouted an order
or a correction, but mostly just watched.

"Shamal?" she asked quietly.

"In her quarters. She's ordered her meals brought to her there,
so I do not believe she intends to . . . mingle. She's brought a servant with her to see to her needs. His name is Gregale. A mute."

"Lucky Gregale, he won't have to worry about getting a word
in edgewise," Clarice said waspishly. She sighed. Giving vent to
her temper wouldn't do anyone any good. "Has she told you
where are we going?"

"North. I have no better answer for you, Clarence. She told me to go north, and so I shall."

He must have been fighting Shamal's order until he received Dr. Chapman's all clear. No wonder he looked so drawn!

"Told you . . . or ordered you?" Clarice asked quietly.

"I do not think there is a difference," Dominick answered, equally quietly. "At least she did not say I must sail at once, though Spirits and Powers know I am eager enough to quit this place. But whether that is my will or hers . . . I do not know."

Those were the most frightening words Clarice had ever heard in her life.

Clarice watched from the afterdeck as the jolly boats drew *Asesino* across the sunken anchor chain. The *Vile Vixen* had sailed a few days before, and the *Horrid Hangman* had sailed this morning. Neither had caused the harbor chain to do so much as twitch, but she held her breath until they were across it.

The boats were recalled and hoisted aboard, and the crew leaped to the command "Make sail!" The great sails cascaded down from the yardarms like curtains falling at a play, to boom and stiffen as they took the wind. In that moment, the ship seemed to awaken as if from a long slumber. Once again she was a living thing.

It was a single moment of pure and stainless joy. Clarice clutched the pendant she still wore about her neck. She knew it would probably be the last one.

"I must go below to examine the charts and set our course," Dominick said to her a few moments later. "Will you accompany me?"

"Of course."

The man standing guard upon the door to the captain's cabin was well over six feet tall. He was barefoot and naked to the waist, and his skin was hairless. He stood motionless, arms folded across his enormous chest. The only thing Clarice could compare him to was a statue of some ancient god, for his shoulders were massive and his body was corded with muscle. He resembled such a statue in more ways than one, for he did not look as if he'd ever been out in the sun. But though it was pale, his skin did not seem to be truly fair. Its color had an odd undertone, like the green of weathered bronze.

"Gregale," Dominick said quietly. He stopped beside the door. Gregale's enormous bulk filled most of the passageway. "Get out of the way," Dominick said shortly. "I need to consult with your mistress."

Gregale didn't move.

"Yes, I see, Shamal has given you orders and you intend to obey them." Dominick's voice had a cold undertone of fury. "But you see, you aren't on Dorado any longer. This is my world. And in my world, ships require courses, and courses require charts. And if you don't want to see us founder on the nearest reef I can find, you're going to let me find out where we're bound."

Gregale didn't move.

"Fine! I will see you in hell then. Clarence, does it please you to sail to hell?"

"Absolutely," Clarice said with a wolfish smile.

"Then let us go there. My dear friend," Dominick said to Gregale, "I wish you a very happy life, for as long as it lasts."

Just as he turned to go, the door swung open. "There's no need for such dramatics, dear Dominick," Shamal purred. "Enter."

Freely and of our own will? Clarice gibed mentally. She was sure Shamal had been listening to the whole thing. Why? To judge Gregale's loyalty? Dominick's temper? Or was she simply bored? *It would be nice to know which it is, since our lives are in her hands.*

Gregale stepped aside, and Dominick and Clarice entered. Gregale did not follow, and a moment later Clarice realized why. Large as the cabin was, Gregale could not possibly have fit in here with the three of them. Not now.

Shamal had redecorated.

The desk had been replaced with an ornate dressing table with a gatefold mirror, and a number of ormolu tables were scattered around, covered with expensive—and fragile—knickknacks. Folding screens, their panels covered with painted and embroidered silk, obscured the walls. The floor was covered in thick, jewel-toned rugs, the oil lamps replaced with others that were far more exotic. New curtains hung at the transom windows—which stood open—and the bed had received a coverlet of silk brocade and velvet and was heaped with tiny, bright-colored pillows. It was the most expensive, luxurious, and tasteless thing Clarice had ever seen. *If sorcery had an odor, I'd say this place reeks of it.*

Shamal stood in front of the opulent bed. She had put off all pretense of Wauloisene fashion. Her sole article of dress was a many-layered skirt, but the bracelets, anklets, rings, and the heavy garland of beaded necklaces she wore compensated for her lack of clothing by their sheer quantity. Clarice didn't doubt that each of them was a spell waiting to be cast.

"Where is my chart table?" Dominick asked levelly, ignoring Shamal's nakedness.

The luridly hyperreal clutter of the cabin had been so distracting that it took Clarice a moment to realize it was gone. When Dominick had vacated his cabin, he'd left it in place; it was too large to get through the doorway in one piece.

"It was in my way," Shamal answered coolly.

"I didn't ask you why it wasn't here," Dominick said. "I asked you where it was."

"Oh . . . somewhere," Shamal said airily. "Gregale will show you. But first: I will have the talisman you stole, Mr. Swann."

"You can't steal from the dead." Clarice worked the chain off over her head and hefted the medallion in her palm.

Shamal held out her hand.

Clarice walked forward, smiling. And threw.

The medallion sailed through the open transom.

"I seem to have dropped it," Clarice said blandly. "You're welcome to retrieve it, of course. But surely you won't need it—once we retrieve the Heart of Light?" *And if you think I am handing you an item of thaumaturgy that I have worn next to my skin for a fortnight . . .*

For an instant Shamal's face was transformed by rage. In that moment, only for a heartbeat, she didn't look human at all. Then her face smoothed to mildness once more. "Your clumsiness will cause you harm someday."

"That day is not today."

"You will discipline your man, of course?" Shamal said, turning to Dominick.

The pit of Clarice's stomach turned to ice. Dominick would have to obey any order Shamal gave.

"If he breaks my laws," Dominick answered. "Throwing his own property overboard is not a crime."

"And if I should order you to flog him to death?" From the tone of Shamal's voice, the question was prompted by nothing more than innocent curiosity.

"Then you would have to force me by sorcery," Dominick answered evenly. "As we both know you could. But it is not something that could be kept a secret, and the last master of *Asesino* who beat men to death is dead."

"A threat?"

"A fact. Call it friendly advice."

"And have you other advice for me?"

"No, Lady Shamal. Only questions. If I am to sail due north from our present location, we will run aground within the week. And so I must ask you, how am I to proceed?"

"You are angry with me, my Dominick! That was never my wish." Now Shamal pouted at him, looking contrite and penitent. It was certainly another act.

"Any chance of friendship between us ended when you bespelled me," Dominick said flatly. "You may have what you compel. Nothing more. But I cannot follow your orders if I do not know what they are."

Clarice gazed fixedly at the floor. She would have liked to watch Shamal's face, but she was afraid her own would give too much away. Dominick was playing a dangerous game, confronting Shamal directly with his knowledge of the power she held. Shamal apparently preferred to pretend it did not exist. Why else would she have tangled him in spells of illusion to get him to keep her company? She could have ordered him directly.

But the orders she gave would have told us something she does not want us to know, I think.

"Sail north!" Shamal said, irritated now. "Do so without sinking the ship, or running it aground, or bringing it to the attention of any other vessel. Surely you can do that?"

"Of course, madame." Dominick bowed stiffly. "It would be easier to plot a course if I knew our destination, but I am certain you will remedy that matter in your own good time."

"Get out."

The chart table had been moved to the first mate's cabin—in pieces. The solid mahogany frame had been snapped like kindling, the legs ripped from the top. The charts it had contained were nothing more than carefully shredded scraps. Useless.

"Mr. Emerson will be glad of the additional firewood, at least," Dominick said quietly.

"You play a dangerous game with Shamal."

"I have little choice, Clarence. It was one thing when I was being spellbound to sail on a mad errand. I might have saved the ship and the crew. But Shamal is with us, and the sailors she's presented us with are former prisoners, men who were—who *are*—never meant to make landfall."

"Except back in Dorado. I'd like to think she means us to survive the voyage and return."

"So would I. I have a hard time thinking Shamal has chosen a complicated method of committing suicide."

"When she could just jump into Fuego del Lago any time she wanted," Clarice answered, striving for lightness.

"As we both wish she had." Dominick smiled at her. "But at least I have directions now, such as they are. We'll sail eastward for a couple of days, so as to have plenty of sea room when we turn north."

"And after that?"

"God knows. If we're to be more than a month at sea, we'll need to put in somewhere to take on freshwater and more supplies, and . . . we have no charts. I have the captain's log, and I can take some counsel from that, but if we sail compass north for a month, I cannot say where we will be. The Arktikos, it is said, is a realm of ice. And we cannot sail over ice."

Unless Shamal wants us to. Clarice did not say so aloud. It was gratuitous cruelty to remind Dominick of Shamal's power. "We're in trouble," she said instead.

"You have a gift for understatement."

"I have a gift for seeing danger and not being able to do anything about it," Clarice answered bitterly. "And right now, I see a lot of it. Your crew trusts you. All most of them know is that you sailed into a pirate haven and sailed out again. What the prisoners are telling them now is anyone's guess, but that doesn't matter. What matters, what no one knows but I, is that your crew cannot look to you . . ." She found she could not go on.

"They cannot look to me for protection. Because my will is not my own."

Only one thing could change that. Clarice could no longer afford to wait for some perfect time—which might never come—to tell Dominick the truth.

"Dominick," Clarice said urgently, "there is something you must know. You know that I come from the east, from the Borogynian Principalities, as an adventurer. I took passage on *Asesino* by sheerest chance, but . . . But I am glad I did, because you see—"

A shadow fell across the table. Clarice looked up to see Gregale standing in the doorway. Watching them. Listening.

The words Clarice had been about to say died in her throat. She had always thought she was willing to die for what was right. But that wasn't the same as speaking the words that would cause your own death as inevitably as the fall of a headsman's ax. Worse was the thought of dying for nothing. She thought she might manage to bring about her own death if she could believe it would save Dominick and his crew.

But she couldn't, and it wouldn't, so she ducked her head and said nothing.

"Ah, there you are, Gregale," Dominick said brightly. "Someone seems to have dumped a bunch of kindling in my cabin. Be a useful fellow and carry it up on deck, won't you? And now, I think Dickon will be happier if I go and give him a heading, don't you think?"

"I think I shall go back to the surgery. I must speak to Dr. Chapman," Clarice answered.

The flicker of Dominick's expression said he understood her perfectly. He'd agreed; the officers must be told once they were at sea, and she thought it best to begin with Dr. Chapman.

Dr. Chapman, predictably, was not enthusiastic about the news she brought.

"Insolent puppy! We'd be more than justified in hanging the pair of you. What the devil did you think to gain by hiding young Moryet's enchantment?"

"I don't know," Clarice said wearily. "I suppose we thought that by pretending cooperation . . ."

". . . you would be let to sail away and tell your story to the closest authorities," Dr. Chapman concluded with a snort. "D'you think the Brotherhood wants word of its little haven reaching the words of any authorities?"

"But the island is protected—Shamal is a powerful sorceress . . ." Clarice's protest died to silence at Chapman's glare.

"And I do not doubt Dorado's thaumaturgical defenses would baffle an ordinary man-o'-war, and even the first of the Queen's own thaumaturgical marines that followed. It might well be a long, bloody, messy campaign. But Albion would win, and the pirates would not."

"Which they knew all along . . . ," Clarice said slowly.

"Which is why they handled you and Moryet so carefully. If you showed any sign of understanding the, shall we say, delicacy of their situation, you'd be unlikely to go along with them on the chance of making a run for it. On the other hand, it meant they didn't just execute all of us outright."

"You make it sound as if Dominick and I did the right thing after all."

Dr. Chapman shrugged. "There's hardly a right thing in any of this. We had some luck on Dorado. Let's see if we can stretch it. I don't suppose she told you what breaks the spell? Even a Compulsion spell can be broken."

Clarice glanced at Dr. Chapman in surprise. He was the last man aboard *Asesino* she would have suspected of knowing anything about thaumaturgy.

"She boasted of it. True love."

Dr. Chapman grunted sourly. "Something he's as likely to find on this voyage as unicorn's milk. Pity. How many aboard know what you've told me?"

"You're the only one. Dominick meant to tell you all once we were under sail, but that was before we knew Shamal was to sail with us. Half the crew already knows she's a thaumaturge, so the other half soon will. There must be . . . some explanation made."

Dr. Chapman nodded. "The fewer who know about Moryet's delicate condition, the more likely it is Shamal will believe no one knows, and I expect she'll want to keep it that way. I've never met a sorcerer yet who wasn't arrogant and mysterious in equal measure. Tell Dominick he should say only that she is a sorceress who has commandeered the ship to sail in search of—of whatever this damned thing is she's after."

"I wish I knew," Clarice said mournfully. "You know as much as I."

"That it's all she needs to cast a new set of those medallions? A magical treasure, then. That will be enough for them. You could tell them we were after the north wind's daughter; that part won't matter."

"What does?"

"The fact Shamal means to see us all dead, one way or another. There are too many unanswered questions here for this to fall out any other way. Why would someone with her power need to trick Moryet into sailing after this treasure? If the voyage is deadly, why has she come with us? No, there is something more to this, and whatever it is, it does not end well for us. So the question I have for you is, are you willing to strike a blow for our freedom?"

"Of course," Clarice said with a certainty she was far from feeling.

Dr. Chapman nodded and turned to his medicine cabinet. He unlocked it and withdrew a small brown bottle, small enough to fit in the palm of his hand.

"All we need to hope for now is that the woman eats and drinks like we mere mortals, but I've never known a thaumaturge who didn't. When she calls for her supper, see that you're the one who takes it to her. Pour the contents of this bottle into anything you like—soup, gravy, wine. Don't get any on you—or in you—and throw the bottle overboard afterward."

He held out the bottle. Clarice's hand was steady as she took it from him. *It is poison,* she thought distantly. *It will kill her.* She tried to be horrified at the thought, but she couldn't manage it.

"What will happen to Dominick when she dies?"

"Whatever it is, it will be a kinder fate than what that sea hag has planned," Dr. Chapman answered simply.

Mr. Emerson was grateful for her offer to deliver the tray, for young Jerrold was terrified of Shamal and her servant. It was easy to duck out of sight and find a quiet place to take the tiny bottle from her pocket and pour most of its contents into the wine. Clarice poured the last third of the bottle over the chicken. As she did, the sharp smell of bitter almonds filled the air. Too late to worry about that now. She replaced the napkin and tossed the bottle out a porthole.

Gregale was waiting in the corridor outside his mistress's cabin. He stepped forward and silently held out his hand for the tray.

It was harder than Clarice had imagined it would be to hand it to him. Poison. This was as much a murder as if she'd held a pistol to Shamal's head and pulled the trigger. And she was not a murderer.

But a fighter . . . that I am. Papa always said that anyone who is born to rule must accept the need to fight. For their land, for their people, for what is right. And that is what I was born to do.

For a moment she missed her parents, her sisters, baby Dantan, her *home*, so fiercely it was hard to breathe. But she forced herself to turn and walk away as if nothing had happened at all. She stopped in her cabin to wash her hands thoroughly—first in brandy, then with soap and water—before proceeding to the common room.

Jerrold was setting the table for supper. He was pinch-faced with fear and kept glancing back at the door that led to the corridor in front of Shamal's cabin.

"Hello, Jerrold," Clarice said as warmly as she could. "It's good to be at sea again, isn't it?"

Some of the pinched look left Jerrold's face. "That it is, Mr. Swann. And better if . . . if we were the only ones aboard," he said carefully.

"None of us is happy to sail with a thaumaturge. She gave us no choice, as you saw." Clarice thought of Dr. Chapman's words.

"She has commandeered our ship to sail after treasure, and for the moment we are in her power. But Dominick will do all he can to keep us safe." It wasn't quite a lie.

"But where are we going? What treasure?"

"We sail north at Shamal's direction. What the treasure is . . . that is knowledge she has not shared." Clarice knew this should have come from Dominick, but the opportunity was here, and better not to make the story seem like the unveiling of a great mystery.

"Well, if it's treasure, I guess she wouldn't," Jerrold said thoughtfully. "But the captain will have a plan, won't he?"

Clarice wasn't sure whether to laugh hysterically or howl with despair. First Geordie, now Jerrold—and while it was nice that they had so much faith in Dominick's powers, it did make her doubt their common sense. But the point was to keep everybody calm, not to make them aware of how desperate their situation was. "Of course he will," Clarice said firmly.

The door opened, and Dominick entered, followed by Dr. Chapman.

"Oh, there you are," Clarice said brightly. "I hope you will forgive me, but I have just been telling Jerrold that we are sailing north on Shamal's business."

"To seek a treasure!" Jerrold said. "You . . . you don't think she means to share it out with us, do you, Cap'n? On account of us being the crew and all?"

Dominick's face was utterly unreadable. Clarice could not tell what he was thinking, or whether Dr. Chapman had gotten the chance to speak with him privately. She hoped desperately that he wasn't about to blurt out the one fact Dr. Chapman had wanted kept concealed—that Dominick was enthralled to Shamal's will.

"I doubt it," Dr. Chapman said quellingly. "But I'm sure the tale will be something you can dine out on for the rest of your days. And speaking of dining, what has Mr. Emerson got for us tonight?"

"I'll go and see right now, Dr. Chapman!" Leaving the table only half-set, Jerrold hurried from the room.

"We'll probably starve before he gets back." Dr. Chapman walked to the table to take his accustomed seat. "He'll have to stop and tell his story to every member of the crew."

"And that story would be?" Dominick said, not moving from where he stood.

"Why, only what you mean to tell us here tonight," Dr. Chapman said easily. "That Shamal, a powerful sorceress, has commandeered our vessel to sail north in search of treasure. And as she's such a powerful sorceress, and possessed of an imposing bodyguard as well, you have little choice but to do her bidding. For now."

"Nothing more? Not to any of you?" Dominick asked, blinking a little as he absorbed this information.

"Nothing at all," Dr. Chapman said.

"Very well," Dominick said, moving toward the table at last.

Jerrold had returned with the evening meal by the time the other three arrived. From the sour expression on Kayin's face, Jerrold's gossip had already made the rounds of the ship.

There was roast chicken, new potatoes, two dishes of vegetables, and fresh bread—brought from Dorado, for Mr. Emerson had been too busy getting supper to have the time to bake—and clear turtle soup to begin. The smell of the chicken turned Clarice's stomach, and she toyed with a glass of wine, her soup untouched. Had Shamal drunk the wine yet? Was she dead? Were they free?

"Mr. Emerson will think you don't like his cooking," Dr. Chapman said in a low, meaningful voice, and Clarice forced herself to take a mouthful of soup. *I am a woman pretending to be a man, pretending to be this ship's first officer, pretending to be a pirate, pretending to be innocent of murder . . . I begin to lose track of all the roles I am playing.*

"I'm going to ask you straight out," Kayin said to Dominick. "Is it true we aren't to make for Cibola? We're sailing north?"

"That is where Shamal wishes to go," Dominick said. "So that is where we're sailing. For the moment, *Asesino* is hers."

"It isn't fair dealing," Kayin said. "I never asked to sail with a sea hag. You can stick your neck into a noose if you like, Dominick Moryet, but not ours. I won't let you."

"How do you mean to stop me, Kayin?" Dominick wasn't angry. He sounded weary to the point of despair.

"We changed captains once," Kayin said meaningfully.

"Belay that talk!" Dr. Chapman snapped.

"Fighting among ourselves will gain us nothing," Clarice said.

"And if I take Moryet and throw him over the side, will that gain us anything?" Kayin asked.

"Nothing but the chance to anger the woman who holds all our lives in her hands," Clarice answered steadily.

"Which she didn't, back in Dorado!" Kayin snarled.

"Is that what you think?" Clarice shot back. "She could have had us all executed at any moment—or worse! How do you think Dobbs died—of a bad cold? That was her work. And so is this."

"You mean she killed Reverend Dobbs so Dominick would sail for her?" Geordie blurted out. "But I—my mother—"

"You damned cloudwit," Kayin spat. "You were a dead man the moment you signed aboard this hellsprite. But I'll tell you straight: We'll see Bowling Green before we see land again, you mark my words. If I'd known this was how it would end, I'd have let Sprunt kill us all. It would be an honest death at least."

"I like our situation as little as you do," Dominick said forcefully. "But you knew what you were sailing with while the gangplank was still down. If you wanted to jump ship, Kayin, that was the time."

"And stay on Dorado!?" Kayin demanded.

"Those were your choices," Dominick answered evenly. "And let me remind you: *The pirates don't trust us.* You might be willing to turn pirate, but you wouldn't get that choice. Anyone I left behind would be hanging on that gibbet in the town square by now."

Kayin still looked angry. Geordie just looked scared.

"Captain Moryet is the master of this vessel," said Dickon, unexpectedly coming to the rescue. "He was the senior surviving officer after we were attacked by pirates. Electing him was a lucky chance because he's our rightful master under sea law. Mutiny—again—and it will be for real. No Admiralty court will—"

The door to the corridor flew open with such force that the hinges were torn from the frame and the wood splintered. All at the table sprang to their feet.

"Who has tried to end my life?"

Shamal stood in the doorway, wrapped in an utterly incongruous pink silk dressing gown. Her hair was disheveled, and her face was contorted with rage. She flung the empty wine bottle to the floor. It shattered with a whip-crack sound.

"Must I ask again?" Icy fury had replaced hot rage in Shamal's voice.

Oh, God. Clarice had never believed in the old trope about one's blood running cold with horror until this moment. *I must tell her. . . .*

"No." Dr. Chapman's voice made Clarice jump. The look he gave her was as direct as a shout. *Say nothing.* "You need not ask. It was I."

"Not the boy?" Shamal purred, smiling now. "It was Clarence Swann who brought the tray."

"He had to pass by my surgery," Dr. Chapman said steadily. "I called him in for a moment." He took a step forward. "No one else knew."

"Kill him," Shamal said, looking at Dominick. "Use the knife."

Dominick's face flushed scarlet with the strain of fighting the enchantment, and his entire body shook. But he turned toward the table, and his fingers reached for the knife.

"Good-bye."

From the corner of her eye, Clarice saw the hand-to-mouth movement.

Dr. Chapman dropped to the floor. His cane clattered from his hand. His body thrashed once and lay still. The tiny brown bottle was still in his hand.

Dominick staggered backward. The knife clattered to the table, the compulsion gone.

You cannot kill the dead.

There was a long silence.

Then Dominick broke it. "If poison is going to be a regular part of your dinner parties, Lady Shamal, you must invite me to dine with you from now on." His voice shook. Rage or grief or fear? Clarice didn't know.

"Perhaps I shall," Shamal purred. She smiled mockingly and swept from the room, stepping over the ruins of the door.

"I don't understand," Geordie said plaintively, staring at Dr. Chapman's body in horror.

"Jerrold!" Dominick's voice was sharp. "Get two men to take Dr. Chapman's body to the surgery. And tell Duff Evans we shall need a shroud made."

Jerrold fled, leaving the door to the deck open in his haste. Clarice concentrated on taking deep breaths. Men did not burst into tears, no matter how terrible the tragedy.

He knew. He knew there was a chance the poison wouldn't work. He prepared for it.

In his gruff, blunt way Dr. Chapman had been her friend and mentor. It did not matter that he'd been the one to suggest the plan. Hers had been the hand to administer the poison. But he'd sacrificed himself to save her. He'd suspected—he must have— that poisoning Shamal wouldn't work. There'd been no other reason for him to have poison of his own ready to hand.

But the guilt of standing by and doing nothing while he gave his life for hers was enough to choke her.

"The last words he had from me were in anger," Kayin said brokenly.

"He had forgiven you already," Dominick said softly. "But there was nothing that needed forgiveness. You spoke nothing more than the truth. I have endangered us all. He only tried to save us from my folly." Dominick hesitated for a moment, and Clarice held her breath. "I have endangered us all."

"No," Kayin said. "You gave us a chance. The best chance you could, Dominick. You always have. And if that sea hag means to sail us to the gates of hell, I'll be at your right hand."

"And I," Dickon said. "No matter what course you set."

Geordie gulped and nodded wordlessly.

"And I," Clarice said, reaching out to place her hand on Dominick's shoulder. "To the gates of hell, and as far beyond as you care to go."

Dominick closed his eyes in silent agony. "Such trust—such friendship—I don't deserve— If you only—"

"I know that Dr. Chapman, God rest him, thought you his true captain," Clarice said strongly. "And we will all honor his memory."

Two men came to carry Dr. Chapman's body away.

10

~

To the Body of the Deep

I T WAS late. Only the night watch should have been on deck, but the whole of *Asesino*'s original crew was gathered to see Dr. Chapman to his final rest. The tale had ripped through the ship like a strike of lightning: Dominick had been forced to sail with a sorceress aboard to the destination of her choosing. Dr. Chapman had tried to kill her and died for it.

When the work party had taken his body to the surgery to prepare it for burial, they'd found a letter. A neat confession taking all responsibility, explaining how he would lie in wait for Mr. Swann to bring the tray. How he would send him on an errand while he adulterated the meal.

Lies, all of it. But it might be enough to convince Shamal he'd been telling the truth if she investigated further.

Oh, Clarice, you are assuming she will care about what is true and what isn't! Why should she care about anything beyond her own whim?

At least Clarice could offer up her nursing skills in token of her usefulness. Fifty men were in quarters who needed to be turned into some semblance of working sailors, with a score of minor injuries still to be seen to.

And their ship's surgeon was dead.

Kayin and Dominick carried the sailcloth-wrapped bundle to the ship's rail. Clarice had prepared the body for burial as best she could, and Duff Evans had wrapped it in chain and sewn it into its shroud.

A soft plash, and it was over.

"No one to say the words," Kayin said quietly.

"I will say them." Clarice took a deep breath. She'd heard the service for the dead when they'd put their dead over the side after the mutiny. She'd never dreamed she'd need to say the words herself.

"'We are gathered here to commit the body of Lionel Chapman to the deep, to rise up at the last day when the sea shall give up her dead. On that day the corruptible bodies of those who sleep in earth or sea shall be changed and made incorruptible and raised up again to glory. The Lord bless him and keep him and give him peace. Ashes to ashes, dust to dust. Amen.'"

"Amen," Kayin and Dominick echoed softly. The word of farewell rippled softly through the crewmen gathered to witness.

Clarice stared sightlessly out at the night. She was so wrapped up in her own thoughts it took her a moment to notice Kayin and Dominick were still there, standing a few feet away.

"In a few days, we'll be near enough to Cibola for you to make it there by boat." Dominick spoke so softly Clarice could barely hear. "Take as many of the crew with you as you can. Get a message to the governor. If he will send ships after *Asesino*, those of us who remain aboard may hope for rescue. But at least the Crown will be warned."

"'A few days,'" Kayin said. "She'll be suspicious. Especially after the poison."

"I'll distract her when the time comes," Dominick said. "But I'll need you to do all the rest. Tell me nothing. What I don't know, I can't betray."

"Aye, Cap'n. Leave it to me." Kayin walked away.

"Bear me company, Clarence?" Dominick asked, and she nodded.

She followed him toward the cabin that had so briefly been hers. Gregale still stood guard over his mistress's cabin, an immobile living statue. Dominick recoiled with a grimace. "Perhaps somewhere . . . cleaner?" he asked, glancing at her.

"I believe my cabin is clean enough."

Inside, Clarice lit the lamps, then went to the porthole and locked it open. The scent of sea and flowers filled the cabin. Last of all, she closed and latched the door to the corridor.

"How long can I go on pretending to be my own man?" Dominick asked her, dropping into the chair. "When Shamal ordered me to take up that knife and stab Dr. Chapman to death . . . Spirits and Powers, Clarence, I would have done it."

"She has enchanted you," Clarice said, though it was the coldest of comfort.

"With a spell only true love may break," Dominick said bitterly. "And still you wish me to conceal it?"

"Dr. Chapman felt it would . . . amuse Shamal to think it was a secret," Clarice said carefully, unbuckling her swordbelt and seating herself on the bed. "And that so long as she thought that, she would not display her power over you openly."

Dominick sighed. "I do not know if that plan will work now. We've tried to kill her and failed, and a thing like that tends to make a person feel unloved, as Dr. Chapman—Spirits and Powers keep him!—would surely say if he were here."

"He had, I suspect, some experience dealing with enemy thaumaturges. I think we should follow his advice if we possibly can."

"If we can," Dominick echoed. "Dr. Chapman was well liked. I'm afraid . . . I'm afraid someone will try to finish the work he began. And I— And I—" He covered his face with his hands.

Clarice leaned forward. She could not take Dominick in her arms as she yearned to, so she contented herself with patting his knee. Dominick was right; the crew was terrified of Shamal, and the new hands were an unknown quantity. Something was sure to happen. But Dr. Chapman had also been right. Shamal delighted in trickery and sadistic games. The more they occupied her, the greater the crew's measure of safety.

"Wear your shirt open," she said finally. "Let the necklace be seen, but say nothing about it. The crew will draw its own conclusions. Perhaps, this once, gossip will work in our favor."

Dominick lowered his hands, and Clarice gave way to the impulse to stroke his hair. He was close enough to kiss. Perhaps—

"Dominick, that matter I wanted to speak of earlier. I know this is a bad time, but you must listen, and carefully. You have called me a good friend. I—"

A loud and unmistakable creak came from a floorboard outside the cabin. So attuned by now was Clarice to the thousand noises of *Asesino* under sail that it stood out sharply. She sprang to her feet and flung open the door.

She looked out. Nothing was to be seen, but the deck lamps cast a monstrous shadow onto the wall of the figure that had retreated to the cross-passage for concealment. She stepped back and closed the door. "I think Gregale was spying on us."

"In God's name *why*? Shamal needs but to ask and I will tell her anything I know."

And you must ensure he has nothing to tell her. You nearly told Dominick your secret. She is already suspicious of you—if she asks him to tell her about Mr. Clarence Swann . . .

"But I suppose we must get used to this," Dominick went on. "I never thought I would wish for Sprunt's return, but I do. At least he was merely a villain, and not a monster. But— You had something to say, I think."

"No, I have forgotten."

"Then let us find something to do. I cannot sleep. Can you?"

Clarice shook her head mutely. She didn't want to be alone, either. Not after this evening.

"I would suggest a stroll on deck, save for the fact the night watch would have questions I do not wish to answer," Dominick said.

"Chess, then." Clarice opened her sea chest. She drew out the little traveling board, thinking sadly of the happy hours she had spent playing against Dr. Chapman. "For as you know already, I have no luck at cards."

As she did, her eye fell upon her little diary. It had been safe enough in her locked chest from Samuel Sprunt and Reverend Dobbs. She did not think a stout lock would protect it from Shamal.

The porthole was large enough. Clarice thrust it through and flung it as far as she could. Dominick made no comment on this.

She turned back to him, the little chessboard in her hand.

"I am no chess player," Dominick said, "but our only other option is for me to teach you the principles of navigation."

"I shall teach you chess if you teach me navigation." Clarice sat down beside him and opened the board between them. "It is a game of war, Papa often said."

"Then I shall do my best to learn its lessons."

At dawn, Dominick went on deck to take a sighting, and Clarice departed to the surgery. Dr. Chapman had left several medical textbooks. She doubted she could ever bring herself to perform an amputation, but the one on the treatment of common illnesses found at sea should prove useful. She was deep in a chapter on recognizing the symptoms of voyage sickness—she did not think she could diagnose "irritability," given their situation, but the other symptoms seemed clear enough—when Jerrold tapped at the door.

"Cap'n said you'd be here. Are you going to do for us now?"

"As well as I am able. Let's hope it won't take much."

Jerrold shrugged, unwilling or unable to give an answer, then said, "Breakfast."

Breakfast was as much a council of war as anything else, even though Dominick did not permit anyone to speak about Shamal.

Clarice noticed he'd taken her advice. The beads gleamed like drops of blood against his skin.

"The first thing—no, the second thing—I must do is draw up a watch list," Dominick said. "The first thing I must have is names to put on it. Geordie, Kayin, you've seen the most of them. What do you think?"

"Not a sailor in the lot," Kayin said sourly. "Colonists bound for New Hesperia, most of them. Farmers. A few skilled trades. Carpenter. Blacksmith."

"Better than nothing. We shall have to teach them. How many of them are ready to work?" Dominick winced a little at his unconscious echo of Captain Sprunt's favorite question: *Is he ready to work?*

"A full day's labor?" Kayin asked. "None of them. Ready to learn the ropes, thirty. Maybe."

"Clarence?" Dominick asked. "What do you think?"

"I think we must begin, as you say, with a full roster. I will take that, as I know we saw only the worst-injured yesterday. I shall ask them their professions as well, in case any of that is of use to you."

"Who knows?" Dominick said. "We may find a thaumaturge, or a squadron of Royal Marines."

"I know which I'd rather have," Dickon said quietly. "Sailing without charts. I never thought that day would come."

"We're in open sea," Dominick said reassuringly. "And I've made landfall on unknown coasts before. We won't go aground."

I think you are the strongest man I have ever known, Clarice thought, marveling at his calm. In a deep part of her, something that pushed aside her fear vowed she would be worthy of that strength.

The day was quiet. Even boring. Shamal did not appear on deck. Gregale did not move from his place. Clarice spent the morning seeing the former captives, one by one, in the surgery. She wrote down each name on her clipboard, and of each man she asked the same questions:

Your name? Your age? Where were you born? What ship were you on when you were taken? What is your trade?

The crew had spoken with them freely already; Clarice added her own reassurances and, in some cases, corrected misinformation.

We are not pirates. We are not mutineers. We overthrew our captain, Samuel Sprunt, who was in league with the House of the Four Winds. We have been commandeered to sail after treasure by Shamal, a sorceress.

When the first six or seven had passed from the surgery to the deck, she could hear Kayin's pipe, and the rhythmic boom of a drum as he began to turn landsmen into sailors. Most of the men had been going to New Hesperia as colonists. Many of them had left families behind on Dorado—or seen them slain.

My wife—my daughter—my sister—my boy—what will happen to them?

To those questions, Clarice gave the only answer she could:

You must be strong. When Shamal has what she seeks, we will sail back to Dorado again.

Clarice cleaned and bandaged minor injuries and gave each of them a dose of cod-liver oil, a dram of whiskey, and a piece of preserved lime.

I know it is terribly bitter, but you must not spit it out. Chew it up and swallow it, for it will make you stronger.

She could do little else.

A fisherman, were you? That is good news for us. Tell Kayin when you go up.

You were in service? What did you do there? You have skill in cookery? Tell Kayin so. Mr. Emerson, our cook, will need help.

You were a lawyer? A schoolmaster? You are a seaman now.

She hoped for a doctor, but wasn't surprised not to find one. These were all young men, some barely more than boys. The youngest and strongest of Dorado's human cattle.

You are brothers? Be glad you are together.

She was only halfway through her work when Jerrold came to summon her to lunch.

Go and eat. I will see the rest of you afterward.

When she crossed the deck to the common room, she saw it was full of men resting from the morning's drill. John Tiptree was moving among them with baskets, handing out bread and cheese. There was an open hogshead—the scuttlebutt—and as she passed it, she caught a strong whiff of whiskey.

"And how was your morning, Clarence?" Dominick asked as she entered. The table was already set, and the meal laid out upon the table. There were only five places now.

"Grim. And yours?"

"Busy. It would be funny if our situation wasn't so bad. Half those poor lubbers can't tell port from starboard, and I don't think they believed Kayin when he said he was going to make topmen out of them."

"Can he?" Clarice asked, remembering looking down from the yardarm at the sea so far below.

"Probably not. But he can teach them enough that they'll be some use. I am putting together a watch roster and spreading out our original crew among them. It should do well enough."

"I hope so. Some of them have family, still alive, on Dorado. I have told everyone Shamal means us to sail back there when she is done with us."

Geordie and Kayin entered then.

"Which for all we know, she does," Dominick said. "Where is Dickon?"

"Said he'd as soon stay at the helm," Kayin said. "I don't think he wants to leave young Miles alone."

"Wise," Dominick said. "Until we can be sure of the temper of our new hands. For now, we will go on as we are and hope for the best." He took the lid off the soup tureen. "I hope Mr. Emerson is doing as well for our crew as he is for us."

"Better, so he swears," Kayin said with a faint smile. "Says he means to fatten them like a pig for table."

"I cannot ask for better," Dominick said.

Clarice's work in the surgery continued through the afternoon, until at last she had seen every one of the prisoners. A dozen of them were still too ill to work; Clarice assured them that they would not be thrown overboard (she was by now more familiar with the behavior of pirates than she wanted to be) and made commonsense prescriptions: food, rest, gentle exercise, until she took them from the sick list.

At supper Kayin reported the crew, new and old, was quiet: everyone had worked hard today.

Clarice made her own report: "The rest of our crew have no more useful skills than the others, save that Elijah Sisko is a tailor, and Robert Kinsey is a deacon in the New Church. He was to take his vows when he reached Manna-hattan, he told me."

"Let's hope he won't be as much trouble as Dobbs was," Dominick said.

"I think he is a good man," Clarice said. "He will be on the sick list for a fortnight at least; he was badly beaten while he was in the stockade. By another prisoner, I think, though he will not say. I did ask if the man was part of our company; he says he is not."

"Small mercies," Dickon said. "I cannot imagine what we'd do if we had to call a captain's mast to hear the case."

Clarice looked at Dominick. His face was bleak. She knew what he was thinking: it would be Shamal's will, not his, that would be done if that happened.

"We shall pray it does not come to that," Clarice said firmly.

The long day, and the night before it without sleep, had left her exhausted enough to retire to her bed immediately. She fell into her bunk with a weary sigh. Each day survived was a victory.

Somewhere in the night, a sound roused her from her exhausted slumber. It was so faint Clarice wasn't sure whether she truly heard it. Someone was singing. A lilting, wordless tune that seemed to echo the surge of the ocean over which they sailed. She strained after the sound, telling herself that in a moment, a moment more, she would get out of bed and go in search of the singer.

But the next time she opened her eyes, the light of morning was shining in through the open porthole.

The day began quietly enough, but the halcyon interlude was not to last.

Clarice was on deck. The men were at their drills. Dominick had said they would turn north sometime tomorrow. She knew that the longer they went without danger, the more likely it was the original crew would object to sailing into unfamiliar waters.

Then a musket shot sounded.

She looked first to Dominick—at the helm, speaking to Dickon—and then about the deck.

After another shot, and another, Robert Kinsey burst out of the door to the common room. He was brandishing a pistol. Two more were tucked through the waistband of his breeches.

"It's a duppy, men! It can't be killed! This ship is cursed!"

Clarice began to run toward him. From the corner of her eye, she could see Dominick doing the same.

Gregale loomed behind Kinsey in the doorway—with powder burns across his ribs and marks where Kinsey's shots had struck. But there was no blood.

Kinsey turned, sensing Gregale behind him, and backed away, raising the pistol in his shaking hands. The shot missed, and then it was too late. Gregale reached out and seized Kinsey. Instead of choking him, or battering him, Gregale simply pulled. Clarice heard the grating popping sound as Kinsey's arms were pulled from their sockets, dislocating both of them. Kinsey screamed, a high, anguished sound.

It shocked Clarice from her immobility. She ran forward, drawing her blade. When she reached Gregale, she struck with all her strength. The blade bit deep, with no more effect than the bullets had had. Gregale ignored her.

Kinsey had stopped screaming. His arms were horribly disjointed, the skin turning black with blood, and still Gregale pulled, with inhuman patience and absolute concentration. She raised her sword to strike again—surely Gregale, whatever he was, must die if she could cut off his head?

Kayin grabbed her from behind, dragging her backward to safety as she kicked and struggled.

"Don't—don't—let me go!" she shouted.

Dominick rushed past them, a belaying pin in his hand. He struck Shamal's monstrous, mute servant with it over and over until Gregale released one of Kinsey's arms to catch the pin and toss it aside. Clarice expected Gregale to strike Dominick next, but he simply shoved him out of the way, almost gently, and set his foot on Kinsey's leg. He pulled again, and the arm in his hand came away with a ripping sound. Dominick drew his knife, leaping onto Gregale's back, one arm around Gregale's throat. He stabbed, again and again, into Gregale's ribs—with no effect. Clarice kicked back, freeing herself, and lunged for her dropped sword.

"He can't take all of us!"

Clarice didn't know who'd shouted. But what would have become a rushing mob in the next moment was quelled by the arrival of Shamal.

"Stop," Shamal said. Dominick froze. "Come here," she said, and Dominick moved to her side. She flicked her fingers at Gregale, who picked up Kinsey's mutilated body and moved toward the rail.

There was silence behind Clarice. She did not dare to turn and look. It had all happened so fast.

"I am displeased," Shamal said calmly. "Are you not also displeased, my darling?"

There was a splash as Kinsey's body was thrown overboard.

"Yes," Dominick said dully. "I am displeased, Lady Shamal."

"Bespelled . . . ," someone behind Clarice whispered.

"Gregale has done nothing, yet you allow your men to attack him."

"He didn't know!" Clarice cried. "He was here on deck!"

"The man who attacked your servant is dead," Dominick said desperately. "Lady, have mercy. I beg you."

"There will be an end to this," Shamal said.

Gregale had crossed the deck again to stand at her back. The wounds on his body were plain to see. They would have killed any normal man. Gregale did not even seem to have noticed them. That, as much as Shamal's hyperreal presence, held the sailors at Clarice's back motionless with horror.

"You will punish your crew, Dominick," Shamal said. "You will make your displeasure known. And you will remove all weapons from this ship."

"Yes, Lady Shamal. As you wish," Dominick said hoarsely.

"Begin," she said, and walked back inside.

Gregale followed.

Clarice took a step toward Dominick.

"Clarence," he said, "throw your sword over the side."

"Rush him!" someone shouted. "Throw him over side! Throw them both over!"

"Belay that!" Kayin's bellow could have stunned a charging bull.

Clarice turned to look back. The deck was crowded. *Asesino's* crew and the former prisoners—the latter easy to spot because of their pale skin and starved condition—were mixed together. Some looked frightened. Some angry.

"You all know me." Kayin held a belaying pin in his hand. "And you know Dominick. Bespelled, aye. I don't like it either. But put him over side, and we lose the only man who can sail us home."

"It won't change anything!" Clarice said, adding her voice to

Kayin's. She lifted her sword and tossed it into the sea. "You'll only make her mad! And one of you—"

"I won't sail on a cursed ship!"

Clarice saw someone at the back of the mob scramble to the rail and fling himself into the sea with a shriek. Terrible as it was, the act broke the tension. Several of the crew rushed to the rail to look.

"Any of you want to join him?" Kayin bellowed. "Do it now!"

Clarice went to Dominick's side. He gripped her arm tightly, as if to steady himself. The moment was balanced on a knife's edge.

"No?" Kayin demanded. "Then back to your stations—lively now!"

Slowly the mob broke apart into knots of men. Kayin did not move, still watching.

"You must punish them," Clarice said in a low voice. "What will you do?"

Dominick shook his head as if he were fighting some urging. "Rogerio Vasquez!" he said, releasing Clarice and taking a few steps toward Kayin. "Stand forward!"

After a wait that seemed too long, Rogerio Vasquez disengaged himself from a knot of men and walked the length of the deck. Some of the sailors reached out to him as he passed, but he kept his eyes fixed on Dominick's face.

"You are the armsmaster for this vessel, are you not?" Dominick said.

"You know I am." Rogerio's face had a gray sheen beneath the bronze, and his skin was beaded with fear sweat.

"Then it was by your carelessness that Kinsey was able to arm himself. I am very displeased," Dominick said as mechanically as if he were reciting from a book. "I will make my displeasure known."

"Dominick?" Rogerio whispered. "Spirits and Powers—"

"Take every musket and pistol, every saber and cutlass, every *weapon,* and throw them over the side. The powder and shot as well. Unship the cannon and throw them overboard as well."

"Dominick?"

"You must!" Dominick said urgently. "She has ordered it done, and if you won't do it by my order, you must do it at her will."

Rogerio swallowed hard, the terror on his face mixed now with pity, and said, "I'll see to it immediately, Captain," then turned away.

"If you have not made the surgery fast, now is a good time," Dominick said to Clarice. "Though I'm not sure I'd mind being poisoned."

"Of course," Clarice said, fighting tears. "I'll go see to it. Right now."

Shamal had left it to Dominick to choose what punishment to exact from the crew. Clarice doubted that a week of bread and water was what she'd had in mind, but she'd left him a loophole, and he'd taken it.

That night, by unspoken agreement, the officers joined the crew in the common mess.

Clarice expected attack, or at least abuse—Dominick's secret was out, and the crew would be within their rights to blame him—and his officers—for this hellish disaster. But instead, the atmosphere was as hushed and mournful as a wake. Some of the men wept. Others prayed. Most sat staring silently at the plates of biscuit before them or ate with mechanical indifference.

"Where is Dominick?" Clarice asked in a whisper. Everyone was seated, and she could not see Dominick anywhere.

"His cabin," Dickon answered. "He thought . . . He thought it would be best."

After the meager meal, Kayin called the roll of the ship's company. Ninety-three people had been aboard when they had sailed from Dorado. There were eighty-eight now. Two more souls, both former prisoners, had joined Lemuel Kane (the man who had jumped), Robert Kinsey, and Dr. Chapman in death.

"We will remember them in life as they remember us in death," Kayin said solemnly. "And we will pray for our deliverance. Clarence, will you lead us in a prayer?"

Clarice got to her feet. For a moment her mind was blank, then the words of a psalm came to her unbidden: "'How long will the enemy mock you, God? Will the foe revile your name forever? Why do you hold back your hand? It was you who split open the sea by your power; you broke the heads of the dragons in the sea—'"

Clarice had never been devout, and the words of entreaty seemed a cruel mockery. But as she spoke, they seemed suddenly meaningful. They were still alive, no matter how terrible their situation. And that meant they still had hope.

Afterward, some of the crew gathered in a corner to sing hymns. Geordie went to his cabin and came back with a Psalter and read aloud to any who wanted to listen.

After a while, Clarice got up and went to her cabin.

Two more days.

Dominick did not join them for meals, grim as those meals were. He'd cut the four watches to three: from midnight to dawn, *Asesino* sailed with no hand to guide her, and the crew was forbidden to go on deck.

The night belonged to Shamal. Sometimes, lying in her bunk at night, Clarice could hear her singing.

She was afraid of Shamal as she had never been afraid of anyone or anything before. It had been hard to admit at first, but it got easier. What use were steel and gunpowder against magic? What use were kindness and cleverness and even bravery against malice backed by immeasurable power?

Each morning Kayin called the roll. Each morning it was a few names shorter.

"Tonight at seven bells." Kayin spoke quietly, for her ears alone.

Clarice gazed out at the ocean. It was hard to believe the Hispalides were anywhere within a thousand miles, let alone close enough to reach by boat. But Kayin knew where they were. And if he knew, Dominick must know as well. Tonight Dominick would do all he could to distract Shamal so that some of the crew might escape. Kayin had timed the attempt for the last hour in which the deck would be theirs.

And not hers.

"What must I do?" she asked.

"Go to your cabin and lock your door" was the grim reply.

She paced. Three steps one way. Three steps the other.

There must be something I can do to save us! The single thought was a counterpoint to her steps. *Something—something—something—*

What?

Challenge Shamal to a duel? Her sword was at the bottom of the ocean. There were still knives aboard, for they were vital to the thousand tasks of keeping a ship afloat. Clarice could easily get her hands on a blade.

Would stabbing Shamal work any better than shooting Gregale had?

If only Kayin can get away. Perhaps . . . perhaps she'll run back to somewhere she's safe then.

Even though the safety of Dorado was safety only for Shamal, not for them.

The ship was more silent than usual. Dominick had ordered the sails reefed at sunset, for the glass was falling and he did not wish to sail into a storm with an untrained crew. It must be true—he would not dare a lie that could so easily be exposed—but it was a stroke of luck, for to lower a boat into the sea while *Asesino* was under full sail would have been nearly impossible.

Clarice checked her watch. Almost midnight. She ought to have heard something by now.

She wondered where Dominick was, and what he was doing to keep Shamal's attention from drifting elsewhere. Then she forced herself to stop wondering.

There must be something . . .

There was.

She must go with them.

She didn't want to; Kayin had known that without asking. But of everyone aboard *Asesino,* she was the only one who might walk into the Governor's Palace on Cibola and demand an audience by right of rank and birth. Any thaumaturge could set the spell on her that would prove her words were true. And the governor of Cibola might not believe Kayin Dako, able seaman, but he would certainly believe Princess Clarice of Swansgaarde.

Dominick's life for the lives of all who might fall prey to the House of the Four Winds? The choice was not easy, but it was clear-cut. She shrugged into her coat and picked up her hat. When she opened the door, the corridor was dimly lit and silent. She held her breath, listening for a long moment before stepping out, even though it felt wrong to skulk around the ship as though she were a sneak thief. The weeks she had spent living in this small wooden world had made *Asesino* feel like home. Shamal's presence felt like a usurpation. *If that is so, why, then I am an agent of the Crown in exile,* Clarice told herself, surprised she could make even such a small joke at a time like this. *And together, we shall cast off the usurper and restore rightful rule.*

As she reached the door that led to the deck, she heard the first faint creak of pulleys.

"Gently, lads," she heard Kayin whisper. "Slow and easy."

Carefully she pushed open the quarterdeck gangway hatch and stepped out into the night. The lanterns that should have been burning forward and amidships were dark. The only light came from the lantern portside amidships. Another long creak, as the men gathered there pulled on the ropes, and the jolly boat began to rise from the deck.

Clarice moved to the side, carefully closing the hatch behind her. Another creak of the winch. Another cautious step forward.

Another step.

And then the sound of footsteps behind her, booming loud over the deck. Clarice heard the door rattle as it opened and turned back to see the monstrous bulk of Gregale—a looming shadow against the stars—step out onto the deck.

Then suddenly, there was light.

Branches of violet fire danced among the ship's masts, leaping from mast to spar to yardarm. The wood itself took on a strange illumination, glowing softly as if it were tainted with fox fire. The men clustered by the jolly boat scattered. Some dropped to their knees and began to pray. In the light, Clarice could see that the bottom of the boat stood level with the rail. They had been so close to escape. . . .

Shamal walked out on deck.

Tonight she was dressed like an evil queen from a fairy tale. Her hair was pulled high, to form a hennin made of a hundred interwoven braids from which unbraided hair hung like the fabric of a veil. She was dressed from throat to ankles in velvet blacker than the shadows. Only her face and hands showed, darkly lambent against that sable backdrop.

Behind her came Dominick. He wore neither vest nor coat, and his shirt was open. In the light of the witch fire, the spell necklace was a dark line against his chest.

"I have given none of you leave to depart," Shamal said. "Where were you going?"

No one answered.

"You know of this?" She turned her head slightly as she spoke to Dominick.

"I told them to go," he grated out against his will.

"Where?" she demanded.

"Cibola. Anywhere they could reach."

"And so you hope to thwart my desire? Foolish boy. No one may leave this ship without my permission."

She reached up to lift a string of beads from about her throat. Clarice flinched, but Shamal merely tossed it to the deck. The beads seemed to melt as if they were made of ice, not stone, and in the moment they vanished, the wood seemed to . . . ripple . . . as if the ship lay underwater and Shamal had cast a stone into that water. *She has enchanted all of* Asesino, Clarice realized. *But to what purpose?*

"But I can be merciful. I give you all leave to go. I will hold no one against his will. Go ahead," Shamal said to the men still huddled against the rail. "Lower your boat. Row for your freedom—if you dare."

"No!" Dominick stepped between Shamal and the men at the rail. "What will happen?"

"Why, they will die!" Shamal crowed delightedly. "But they may try it if they choose. Gregale, assist them to lower the boat, if you please."

Gregale took a step forward. Half a dozen sailors scrambled into the boat and began desperately sawing at the ropes with their knives.

"No!" Dominick cried. He ran toward them. Gregale halted and grabbed him as more men clambered into the wildly rocking boat. "Kayin!" Dominick shouted. "Don't go!"

Kayin stopped, one hand on the lip of the boat, then stepped away from it, his face agonized.

The ropes tore apart and the boat tipped sideways, spilling its passengers into the sea before it fell. As it did, Gregale released Dominick. He and Kayin rushed to the rail.

Clarice reached them as Kayin reeled backward with a cry of horror.

"Don't look!" Dominick cried, but it was too late. She'd already seen.

The boat floated hull up in the midst of the sailors. Instead of trying to right it, they thrashed frantically in the water. Some clawed at their throats. Some flailed desperately to reach the side of the ship, mouths gaping as they struggled to breathe. *Asesino* moved slowly away as the men who had tried to leave her drowned in air.

"What are you *doing*?" Clarice demanded, turning on Shamal. "Why are you doing it? Weren't there enough victims on Dorado for you to amuse yourself with? This is madness! What can you possibly want that you do not have already?" Clarice was so furious, so heartsick, that she had gone beyond fear. The magnitude of Shamal's evil made any thought of self-preservation impossible. Dominick clawed at her arm as she stepped forward, and Gregale moved to place himself between her and Shamal.

And Shamal . . . laughed. "Power, my pretty little princess! *Power!* And you're going to get it for me—you, and your chaste and faithful Dominick!"

"But—" Dominick's hand dropped from Clarice's shoulder. He stared at her in confusion.

"You did not know!" Shamal crowed delightedly. "How could you not know? Look at her! She plays the beardless boy well enough—but this is no boy!"

Clarice dared not look toward Dominick. *This is not how I meant you to find out!* a part of her mourned. But she stepped away from Dominick, toward Shamal, and knew that her face showed nothing of what she felt.

"I am Clarice Eugenie Victoria Amalthea Melusine of Swansgaarde. What do you want of me?" she asked, proud that her voice was steady. "I am not the heir. My blood has no power."

"You are wrong, little princess. Your blood has power enough to unlock the gate behind which lies my treasure. Yours—and his.

I have waited long for such as you to fall into my hands," Shamal answered gloatingly.

"Mine? My . . . blood?" Dominick stammered. "But he—she—?"

Now Clarice could let herself turn and look at him. The fox fire still coruscated over the masts; in its light she could see his face was stunned to blankness.

Shamal swaggered forward. "I have told you only the truth each time I spoke," she purred. "That is the price I pay for my power—but there is never any need to tell all I know. And yet, for it amuses me to do so, I shall tell you now. I have said I seek the Heart of Light, and this is truth. You think my power alone would be enough to gain it—do you think I have not seen the suspicion on your faces and heard you whisper in secret? Such a powerful sorceress, you tell yourselves, may have anything she wants for the conjuring. But not this, for the Heart of Light is power absolute. Such treasures go only to the bold and the resolute, and so it is guarded by traps and riddles that have taken me long to solve. And see? I shall tell you all I have learned, and you need not even ask. Here is the secret to gaining the Heart of Light. A virgin, brave, righteous, and steadfast, can see through the illusions that guard the way to where it lies. And royal blood can lift it from its resting place."

It was obvious, from Shamal's gestures, which of them was royal, and which was . . . steadfast.

"The princess was instantly in my power, though she did not know it," Shamal said. "She could not depart Dorado without my leave. She was nothing."

Thank you for that, Clarice thought mulishly.

"But you? A rarer prize. A ship's navigator with the qualities I sought. Any stainless innocent would see through the Heart of Light's illusions. A child, for example. But I discovered—at great cost—that to see through the illusion was not the same matter as sailing a ship through it. And a ship I must have to reach it. You were a gift from the Gods, my darling. And so I made sure of your virtue. Why do you think I spent so many boring hours in your company? And yet you remained . . . incorruptible. Perfect."

It all made a terrible sort of sense, Clarice realized. Virtue was not enough. It must be virtue coupled with seamanship—something she doubted was often seen on Dorado. No wonder the Brotherhood brought the crews of their prizes back to Dorado. It was so Shamal could sort through them in search of the one who could take her to her treasure.

And they'd sailed *Asesino* right to her.

"I'm sure we're both very grateful for your interest," Clarice said into the silence that followed Shamal's last words. "But I have absolutely no intention of assisting you. And neither will Dominick."

"Dominick will do as I bid him to," Shamal said with a feral smirk. "I need his skill and his cooperation, but I have ensured that I have both. As for you, I hardly need your acceptance. Nor do I need your presence. A few days among the rats will cool your tongue."

The air was musty and stank of salt and tar and less pleasant things. Despite the stifling closeness, it was cold. Chill, rather. Chill and damp. Clarice was acutely conscious that ocean was only a few inches away, on the other side of some wooden planks that suddenly seemed far too insubstantial to hold it at bay.

She closed her eyes tightly and forced herself to do more than simply sit and gibber—though she thought that was an entirely sensible reaction to her situation. Gregale had placed heavy manacles on her ankles and wrists, and another length of chain about her waist, and then around her a length of the rope that filled the orlop. She was not only thoroughly imprisoned, she was weighted down by so many chains she could barely move.

She could not think of anything she could have done differently. Or if she had, that it would have made much of a difference.

She might never have taken passage on *Asesino* at all. Never met Dominick. Never fallen in love. She could be in Cibola at this very moment. But that would be an accident of circumstance, not a response to danger.

If she'd somehow found some way to stop the mutiny, Samuel Sprunt would have sailed them into Dorado, and she and Dominick would still be in Shamal's hands.

If she'd told the crew immediately about the spell Shamal had cast over Dominick, they might have tried to make a run for it. *Asesino* would have foundered on the harbor chain if they'd tried to sail to freedom, and she doubted it was possible to hide on Dorado.

She could have taken a musket and shot Shamal the moment they were clear of the harbor. Or jumped overboard. Or rather, she could have *tried* to do either of those things and likely have been thwarted by Shamal's magic or Gregale, or both.

And now I will die, and Dominick will die, and Kayin, and Dickon, and everyone aboard Asesino, *and Shamal will gain the Heart of Light, and I do not know what it is or what she means to do with it, but I suspect it will make her career as a pirate queen seem harmless and wholesome. And there is nothing at all I can see to do about any of this. I cannot free myself. And I cannot free Dominick. . . .*

She did not know how long she sat alone in the dark. Long enough to have to lecture herself sternly that nobody died of thirst in a few hours, and that even if she did, it would probably be a good thing, under the circumstances.

There was a light.

At first it seemed like some trick played on eyes weary of staring sightlessly into the darkness. But it grew stronger, until she could make out the dim shape of the ship's ladder, and she could finally see, dimly, the vast coils of hempen cable that filled the whole of this cramped and fetid space.

It occurred belatedly to Clarice that anyone who was brave

and clever enough—and who had overheard Shamal's speech—would know that the easiest way to thwart Shamal's plans was to come down here and end Clarice's life.

"Hello," Dominick said in a low voice. "Don't be afraid. It's only me."

He held a lantern in one hand and a bundle in the other as he picked his way carefully over the rope cables.

"Dominick!" Clarice said as soon as she did not need to raise her voice for him to hear her. "What are you doing down here? If Shamal finds out—"

"Nothing will happen. She needs me to get where we're going. And since she hasn't forbidden me to come . . . here I am."

He set the lantern on the deck and knelt down beside Clarice. The bundle in his arms contained several blankets, a flask of water, a bottle of brandy, and food. "I thought you might—"

"Yes, thank you."

There was an awkward pause.

"I kept trying to tell you. Ever since . . ." *Ever since she told you what would break the spell.*

"I, ah . . . I suppose it's for the best. That you . . . aren't a boy, I mean." There was another, longer awkward pause. "I . . . I'm glad you aren't a boy."

Despite the danger, the horror, the utterly terrible ridiculousness of the situation, Clarice felt like laughing. "Thank you," she said gravely. "I'm glad I'm not a boy, too."

"Are you really a princess?" Dominick burst out nervously. "Oh, of course you are, I'm an idiot. You wouldn't be chained up down here if you weren't. And then there was that brooch you showed me. . . ." Another awkward pause. "Gregale has the keys; I can't get them. I'm sorry. But do I call you Your Highness or Your Grace or—"

"Call me Clarice. It's my name. Or Clarence, if you prefer. I have gotten used to it, you know."

"But you're a princess!" Dominick said insistently, and Clarice's heart sank a little. When he said "princess," Clarice knew he was thinking of a princess like Queen Gloriana's daughter, Isabet, someone born to rule an empire.

"I'm not much of a princess," Clarice said hopefully. "Swansgaarde is a tiny little duchy that isn't even on most maps. Even the whole of the Borogynian Principalities aren't on them. I know. I've looked."

"But you were born in a castle! And I am only—"

"A member of an important merchant family," Clarice said firmly. "Or you would have been if Barnabas Bellamy hadn't stolen your fortune. And it is a very small castle, I assure you. Scarcely rating the title of *manor house* by the standards you know."

"Very small?" Dominick asked after a long pause.

"Almost infinitesimal. Why, for all I know, your old home was larger."

He reached out as if to touch her hand, then drew back. "I suppose what you told me about yourself was all . . . a story?" he said at last.

"That my father was a law clerk, and the rest? Well, Papa does spend more time in court than he likes, but . . . that part was not true. But I ride and play chess and fence, just as I told you. Everything I told you about *me* is true. And I left home to seek my fortune. That part is true as well. I have eleven younger sisters, you know. I fully intended to become a swordsmaster. *Mistress*. Well, I hadn't made up my mind—"

"Eleven!" Dominick exclaimed, sounding astonished. "You must be very glad to live in a castle. Even if it is . . . infinitesimal."

"And one brother. His name is Dantan, and he will be duke after Papa—but not for many years, I hope, for he is only two! And perhaps Papa will abdicate, when he is older, and spend the rest of his life fishing, as he has always sworn he means to. . . ." She found herself speaking to Dominick of her family, a family not grand, like Albion royalty, or fearsome and distant, like the kings and queens of Cisleithania, but just . . . her family. "Anise is the next eldest. She is the thaumaturge of the family, while Talitha is more venture-some than I. It is Damaris who is the bloodthirsty one, though. She is six. Oh . . . she is seven now. But she would certainly make short work of this Pirate Brotherhood, if she were let."

"It sounds like you have a wonderful family," Dominick answered wistfully. "I can't imagine how you could leave them."

"I could not stay in Swansgaarde for the duchy cannot afford a dozen dowries, and there is no work for me there. I could not sit in a garret doing embroidery all day—even if I could do embroidery in the first place!—and I have no taste for army life, though I think Jennet does. And we have no army, in any event. Really, the one thing I am good at is swordplay."

"You could have married a prince. Or . . . a duke?"

She laughed. "I would have had to marry into one of the other principalities to do that, and there is the matter of a dowry that I do not have. And I have known most of their young men since we were children, and if I were to marry, I . . . I would rather marry you, Dominick, if you were to ask me. I know I have no reason to—"

Her heart thundered, and her cheeks felt hot. She had not meant to say it so abruptly, dropping the declaration into the middle of a conversation so much like one Clarence could have had with Dominick. But if the events of recent days had taught her anything, it was that there was no time to spend in working into things in some tactful, polite way. The people who had written those manuals of etiquette and deportment had not been under a sentence of death at the time.

For a moment she thought he would recoil in shock. Disgust. Worst of all, he might babble some polite lies about being only able to think of her as Clarence and not Clarice, and while it was flattering of her to declare such an interest in him, he could never . . .

But instead: "I love you," Dominick blurted out. "I thought—You were Clarence, you see, and I thought it was friendship—only friendship—and you would leave when we . . . if we ever got somewhere, and . . . the sea is a hard mistress if you do not love her. I could not ask . . ."

"If you had, I would have said yes," Clarice answered softly. "I might have said yes even if you did not ask, you know. I have loved you for a long time, I think."

"I'm glad," Dominick answered simply. For a heartbeat, nothing else in the world mattered. Dominick loved her and knew that she loved him, and for that brief instant there was nothing but joy.

But it could not last, for love was not as urgent as survival.

"I would be gladder if we weren't all about to die," he added. "I wish I knew what Shamal is after."

"Hasn't she already told us? This . . . mystic treasure of hers. Dominick, she's said you're the only one who can see where you must go to reach it safely. You . . . When the time comes, you must sink us."

"If I could, I would do so gladly. She has but to order me to reach our destination safely, and I will have no choice but to obey."

"Because you are bound by a spell only true love can break."

"Spirits and Powers," Dominick said softly. "Is it as simple as that?"

"If you love me as I love you, it is. Come. Lean close to me and I'll take off that damned necklace. These blasted chains are so heavy, I'm afraid I'll just knock you unconscious with them if I reach up to you."

"Let me help." He leaned toward her and picked up the heavy length of chain between her manacles, lessening the weight dragging on her wrists. But instead of leaning down so she could reach the back of his neck, he closed the distance between them.

Though not Clarice's first kiss, it was the sweetest by far. And the most painful. It made her wish even more keenly that it were happening in ordinary time, when the two of them were free to be selfish and think of nothing but themselves.

But when she opened her eyes, the first thing she saw was Gregale, looming over Dominick's shoulder.

Her first instinct was to recoil; her second was to snatch at the spell necklace around Dominick's neck. When she tensed, Dominick drew back, glancing over his shoulder. He shook his head fractionally as he pulled away.

He was right. She knew that, maddening as it was. Show Shamal this spell was broken, and she would only enchant Dominick again. All spells contained the way to end them—but what if the new one required something unobtainable, such as water from the Temese River?

But, oh, it was so *hard* to let him go!

"Rest well . . . Clarice," Dominick said, getting to his feet. "I will come back as soon as I can."

"Spirits and Powers go with you, Dominick," Clarice answered softly.

Gregale retreated, and Dominick followed him. Clarice listened until the fading sound of their footsteps was lost in the sighing and creaking of the ship. At least she had light; Gregale had come to collect Dominick, but he'd left her the things Dominick had brought. She hefted the lantern to see how much oil it contained. As she did, its light caught a gleam of metal where no gleam had been before. Her arms aching with strain, she held the lantern as high as she could.

It was a ring of keys.

Dominick did not leave them. He would have freed me immediately. But . . . why would Gregale *seek to free me?* Gregale could certainly have dropped the ring of keys without her noticing at the time, but it beggared belief that he could have dropped them *by accident.*

He meant her to get free.

Why?

She didn't know. But she knew she could not afford to waste this chance.

It took her most of an hour—as closely as she could judge—to get her hands on the keys, and her muscles were trembling and aching by the time she had her prize in her hands. Panting with triumph, she unlocked her shackles, her manacles, and the padlock that secured the length of chain around her waist to the hawser cable. She was free.

I need somewhere to hide. Somewhere no one would find her. Dominick might no longer be compelled to do what Shamal ordered, but he must pretend he was or risk being bespelled again. And the crew knew that the penalty for disobeying Shamal's orders was a gruesome death. She could trust no one. Shamal herself had said so:

"Royal blood can lift it from its resting place."

Shamal had said nothing about keeping Clarice alive until they got wherever they were going. A jug full of her blood would probably be as much use as she was. More, once Shamal was tired of playing games.

Clarice got cautiously to her feet and collected the blankets and the supplies Dominick had brought. She tucked them under her arm and turned the lantern down as low as she dared. After a moment's debate, she returned the ring of keys to the place on the deck where she'd found them. They were useless to her, and Gregale might come back for them. *And maybe he'll put them back where he got them from. Or maybe he'll tell Shamal I've escaped. I am so tired of not knowing what's going on!*

The deck above was not full by any means, but the provisions had been stored near the ladders for easy access. They made a fine hiding place. She made herself a nest between the aft bulkhead and a pile of sacks (potatoes, turnips, and carrots). She wrapped herself in the blankets and forced herself to eat and drink a little. She doused the lantern and made sure it was where she could find it by touch if she had to.

Then, at last, mercifully, she slept.

———

She was ruthlessly jarred awake by the motion of *Asesino*. Before she knew what was happening, she was sliding down a steep slope that had been level deck when she'd fallen asleep. She hit something with a thump, only to be tossed back the way she'd come in the next moment. This time she found a handhold—the ropes securing the pile of sacks—and clung to it desperately. *Pitch, yaw, and roll,* she thought dazedly as she clung to the ropes. She remembered a midnight conversation in happier times, with Dominick explaining the mechanics of a ship's movement along its three axes: linear vertical, linear lateral, and linear longitudinal. He'd said then that if she was lucky, and the sea remained calm, she would experience no more than two of them at once, but right now, *Asesino* seemed to be wallowing from side to side even as it seesawed stem to stern and bounced up and down. In the absolute darkness, this was frightening.

She did not know whether this storm had been raised by Shamal for her own purposes or was something she could not quell (terrifying as that possibility was). At the sound of new and louder crashing, she scrabbled one-handed for her spellmatch, praying it had remained in her pocket through all that had gone before. It did not give as much light as a lantern would, but her lantern, and everything else Dominick had brought her, was lost in the shifting mass of cargo. Holding the precious light source as high as she could, she saw crates slide across the deck—or tumble from their resting places at the top of their stacks. Clarice realized that she was in danger of being crushed if she stayed in the hold.

With only the spellmatch's faint light to guide her, she lurched and staggered along the deck, seeking some haven that would not expose her to discovery. At last she reached the ladder to the middle deck. The balusters would protect her. She doused her spellmatch and tucked it away and braced herself as best she could.

For what seemed to be an eternity, she clung, dazed and weary, to the ship's ladder. It took all her strength, and the effort left her battered and bruised. But at last *Asesino* seemed to reach some accommodation with the weather. The ship continued to groan and shudder, but the ship was no longer being tossed about like the toy of some fractious child.

Once she was certain this condition was not just temporary, Clarice fumbled for her spellmatch again. At least it gave light enough to let her pick her way across the deck.

I have to admit, if one is attempting to hide from a search, a ship is not a good place to attempt it. Especially when I have no idea if we may sink at any moment.

But where should she go?

The sound of approaching voices left her no time for debate. She hurried as quickly as she could to the farthest corner of the hold and doused her spellmatch, praying that those who approached would not stay long.

"—quick look, Mr. Evans." She recognized the voice. It was Geordie Lamb. The man with him must be Duff Evans, ship's carpenter. "To see if we're taking on water."

"And what would it matter if we were?" Evans answered harshly. "Blown to the bottom of the sea in a storm is at least a natural death. No, Geordie, you're wasting your time, and so am I. I'm for my bunk. If you're smart, so are you."

"But, Mr. Evans!" Geordie cried, his voice almost a wail. "Kayin said—!"

"If Kayin Dako wants to know the state of the hull, he can come and look himself. Good night, Geordie."

Silence again.

"What shall I do?" Geordie said, and Clarice could imagine him wringing his hands. "What if we *are* taking on water? We could be in Bowling Green before we thought to man the pumps."

I must trust someone, Clarice thought. And Geordie Lamb was the most harmless person aboard. She pushed herself out of hiding.

Geordie caught the sight of movement in the shadows and

raised his lantern high. "Who . . . Rats? If you're a rat, get back to your hole. Not even rats can leave this ship now, I wager."

"It's me, Geordie," Clarice said in as loud a whisper as she dared. As she hoped, Geordie came toward her, and she was able to forestall his loud exclamation of delight at the sight of her.

"But— How did you get out, Mr.—? Miss—? I swear, all these weeks, I didn't have any clue you weren't a mister instead of a ma'am, and I only hope you didn't take offense at any of our horseplay. On account of being a female, and . . ." His words staggered to a stop, and he gazed at her in shy confusion.

"Of course I did not," she assured him warmly. "And I am just the same person as before, I promise you, and I hope you are still my friend. But what's going on? I was able to work myself free— but then the storm hit. . . ."

"It was a terrible thing, Mr.—Miss—"

"You must call me Clarice. It is my name, you know."

"Miss Clarice."

As she'd hoped, he needed little prompting to tell her what had happened after she'd been imprisoned. Once Gregale had taken her below, Dominick had ordered prayers said for the dead. "He came down and said them with us. And said the crew might kill him if they wished, but Shamal would send the ship to the bottom if they did. Faced them all down, cool as anything. He said, on account of everything, there was no point in going on with the punishment and ordered Mr. Emerson to give the crew anything they wanted in the way of victuals. And Mr. Emerson, he did— and he unlocked the liquor stores and threw the key overboard, too!"

"Good Lord," Clarice said inadequately. She wondered for a moment what exactly Shamal had thought would happen once she'd all but told every soul on the ship that it was only a matter of time before she killed them. Terror could not motivate when hope was dead.

"Then at dawn the storm blew up. It was terrible," Geordie

said. "The sky turned black, and Dominick ordered all hands on deck, and Kayin said it was our only chance to come through alive. But Ned Hatcliff said it didn't matter and we were a ghost ship now. Dominick went up into the rigging his own self, and that shamed enough of 'em into slinking out of their holes before he had to cut the mainsail free. But we're going where the sea sends us now, Miss Clarice, and who knows where that is? To hell, they're saying. You—you don't think that's so, do you?"

"No, I certainly do not. And I will tell you something else, Geordie. Shamal isn't as smart as she thinks she is—and she isn't as well loved as she'd like. We still have a chance. But we must be prepared to take it."

Geordie's face lit with desperate hope. "Do you think so?"

"I don't think so. I *know* so," she answered with all the conviction she could muster. "You must tell the crew. There is still hope for us to come through this alive. I swear it."

"Your word as a—as a princess?" Geordie asked, stumbling a bit over the words.

"My word as a princess of Swansgaarde," Clarice answered firmly. "And you must tell them so. Tell them I said so—you were supposed to check the ship for leaks, weren't you? That means the orlop, too. Well, tell them you spoke to me. You needn't say where."

"But you aren't down there now," Geordie said, sounding confused.

"No. That is part of my plan. You must find me a place to hide."

She watched as he thought for a moment, hoping she'd made the right choice. But the crew must have hope. And with Dominick free of enchantment, they had a chance to survive.

At last Geordie's face cleared. "I know just the place! Come with me. I'll take you there."

The two of them ducked into the tiny cabin on the floor above, and Geordie closed and bolted the door. "It's the purser's office.

Mr. Foster's it was, and I don't need it. So you can just stay here, and I can bring you things. Food and, and blankets, and—I can tell Dominick where you are."

"No!" Clarice said instantly. "Don't tell anyone. Just . . . go on about your normal duties."

"Yes, Miss Clarice," Geordie said dispiritedly. "Whatever normal duties are these days."

"I wish I knew. But tell the crew: Do not despair. There is hope."

She hoped the promise she'd made was one she could keep.

11

~

THE KINGDOM OF WINTER

THE PURSER'S cabin was windowless, but Geordie had left her his lantern. He returned a few hours later with a bucket, a pitcher of water, and several pieces of hardtack. No hot food was to be had while the storm was raging.

"It's like nothing I've ever seen in these waters," he said. "There doesn't seem to be any end to it. If it doesn't blow out soon . . ."

He didn't finish the sentence, but he didn't need to. Whatever it was that would happen, it would be something bad.

"Have you seen Shamal?" Clarice asked.

Geordie shuddered. "Standing in the bow. Just like she's been since dawn."

After a long pause, Clarice asked, "And . . . Dominick?"

"At the wheel. He sent Dickon below. I don't know why he's there, Miss Clarice. He can't hold her. No one could."

He's there because it's all he can do. "He'll do what he thinks is best for all of us," Clarice said aloud. "Now go before you are missed."

Hours passed. Time enough for day to turn to night again, for Clarice to exhaust herself with fretting. She could not even pace, for the ship still tossed. At last she curled up in the "bottom" corner of the cabin, her cheek upon her knees, and tried to rest.

It was not sound that woke her, but stillness. She placed her hand upon the bulkhead. She no longer felt the constant vibration she'd felt during the storm.

It was over.

She got to her feet, suddenly realizing how cold she was. Her breath smoked on the cabin air. She tugged her blankets tighter and hugged herself against the chill. Was this some new sorcery of Shamal's?

Freezing all of us to death is a stupid idea, but I really don't expect logic from her, Clarice thought bitterly. She crept to the door and listened. Silence. Her heart in her throat, she opened the door the barest crack.

The corridor beyond was deserted. It was even colder outside than in the tiny purser's cabin. Daylight shone weakly through the hatch gratings, but it was the wrong color. Even the dawn light should be golden in the Hispalidean Sea. Not . . . gray.

Am I the only one left alive? It seemed frighteningly possible. She had to know. She opened the door wider, listening intently.

Nothing.

The crew quarters were deserted. Bottles littered the deck, and the air stank of spilled liquor and beer. In the storm, someone who wished to die would not even need to nerve himself to jump overboard. All that would be needed was to release a handhold and let the sea . . .

No! I will not believe that without proof!

When Clarice reached the deck, she saw why no one was below. The remains of the ship's company lined the railings, staring silently out at . . .

Nothing.

Not even the ghost of a shadow marked the position of the sun in the sky—if there was a sun at all. Ice crusted the rigging and frosted the deck. All that could be seen was a gray and formless mist.

As quietly as possible, Clarice retreated to the deck below, and for the next three days she became a ghost aboard a haunted ship.

From eavesdropping, Clarice knew *Asesino* carried full sail, even though she sailed through impenetrable mist. Clarice's absence had been discovered, but the searches conducted for her were lackadaisical at best. The crew huddled around the chimney and the stove in the galley to drink and pray—and to read out the ever-lengthening list of the dead. They had run out of coal for the stove long before and now burned any wood they could scavenge.

I must risk seeking out Dominick. I pray Shamal has not done something worse to him than what she has already done.

When the *Asesino* stilled with what passed now for night, she crept up on deck. The superstructure of the ship groaned under a freight of ice. It shone with strange brightness in the wan light of the ship's lamps, the whiteness of the frost and the ice limning the once-familiar structure of the ship and rendering it strange. The air was as cold and arid as if Clarice stood on the surface of one of the glaciers in the mountains that surrounded Swansgaarde, and she tried to imagine a storm so savage that it could blow them all the way to the Arktikos in only a few days.

Neither moon nor stars were to be seen. Even the surface of the ocean was invisible. The absence of context reduced *Asesino* to a simulacrum of a real ship sailing against a painted backdrop onstage in some theater of the damned. Clarice looked up toward the afterdeck, but it was as deserted as the rest of the ship. Everyone was huddled around the galley chimney for warmth. Everyone but Dominick. And Shamal.

And Shamal cannot be as powerful as she wants everyone to believe, can she? She would not need a great hulking brute of a bodyguard such as Gregale if she were.

With that hopeful thought, Clarice hurried down the ladder. If Dominick was in the first mate's cabin, she could not reach him without being seen, for that door was in clear sight of Shamal's, and Clarice could only assume Gregale still stood guard. But Dominick had done all he could to avoid the first mate's cabin since Shamal had come aboard, and Clarice thought she knew where he might be instead.

She reached the door of her own cabin and tried the latch—the door did not open—then tapped as softly as she could, praying Dominick would not simply ignore the sound.

When he opened the door, his face went blank with surprise for a heartbeat. Then he swept her inside. "Clarence—*Clarice*!" He enveloped her in a fierce embrace. "Where were you? What happened? How—"

"Gregale," she answered, latching the door securely. The tiny space was barely warmer than the corridor outside. "When he took you away, he left the keys to my chains behind. Intentionally, I think." Clarice moved back into Dominick's arms, as much for warmth as for comfort.

"But why?"

"Perhaps he is compelled to serve her just as you are. Perhaps he, too, is fighting back in any way he can."

"I wish he'd break her neck," Dominick said feelingly. He led Clarice over to the bunk and pulled its blanket around both of them. "I've spent the last three days sailing in circles, but I can't stall Shamal much longer."

"I'm surprised you've been able to stall her at all."

"It was easy enough." Dominick grinned at Clarice and held the necklace out to her. She reached out to touch the string of beads. They were hard and real beneath her touch. "Why should she imagine I could lie to her?"

"I—but—" It had worked! No more absolute proof of love could be found outside of a fairy tale. But there was no time to plot a happily-ever-after yet. "Didn't she *notice*? I mean, it's magic."

"I don't know. For that matter, I've been waiting for her to yank you up on deck with some spell ever since she found out you'd escaped. Maybe she can't. Maybe her magic's . . . gone."

"Or maybe she's saving it up for what comes next," Clarice said grimly. "You say you've been stalling her, but—where are we going, Dominick? What do you see?"

"Ice," he answered softly. "Gray sky, gray sea—and mountains of ice floating over it like a vast flotilla of ships. That is bad enough. But beyond them, there is a ring of icy pillars. I have sailed all around it. At its center there is some . . . structure."

Clarice waited, but he did not elaborate. "It is our destination?"

"I cannot imagine we have any other," Dominick said grimly. "And to sail between the pillars to reach it would be tricky enough—but to do it with an unwilling crew . . ."

"*Unwilling* seems a mild word for it," Clarice said dryly.

Dominick laughed bitterly. "She's given them nothing to live for. I would have sunk us a dozen times these last days but for the hope you've given me, mad as it is. But even if Shamal were to vanish tonight like a soap bubble, I do not know how I could save us. We are in no waters I know. That storm . . ."

"Blew us here, and we must believe there is some way to sail home again. But for the other . . . you must speak to her, Dominick."

"To *Shamal*?" It was clearly the last thing he'd expected to hear.

"You must tell her that if your crew has no hope, they will send *Asesino* onto the ice. She can say she'll give them their lives as a reward for bringing her here."

"She won't," Dominick said simply. "She means us all to die in this frigid arctic waste."

"And we will, if the crew do not believe they have at least a chance of survival. If she will not—or cannot—tell them herself, get her to agree that you may say it in her name."

Dominick nodded reluctantly. "I'll go to her in the morning. But . . . what of you? She's going to kill you—"

"Certainly she means to. So we must find a way to make her

put it off until the very last minute. So tell her this: I have come to you hoping to save the crew. Tell her I said I would trade my . . . compliance . . . for their lives. I imagine it is what she thinks a proper princess would do."

"It is. Clarice . . . would you?"

I would trade my life for yours, my love. In a heartbeat. "If this plan works, I won't have to," she answered simply.

When the first rays of dawn shone through the porthole, Dominick got up from the bed where he and Clarice had huddled, chaste and shivering, through the night.

"By tonight it will be over," Dominick said, kissing her on the forehead. "And we shall be warm. Or dead."

"I prefer warm."

Dominick smiled.

A few minutes later he was back, and Shamal was beside him. Today she was clothed neck to toes in a heavy fur robe that gave Clarice an unworthy pang of envy. The only unchanging thing about the sorceress was the mass of beads about her throat. *She always wears them,* Clarice thought. *I wonder . . .*

"So, my pretty princess, here you are," Shamal said. "I trust you have not . . . despoiled . . . my Dominick?"

"Ask him," Clarice said, feigning sulkiness. "He's the one who has to tell you the truth."

"Why so I did, and so he has. And you are willing to trade your life for those of a boatload of jail sweepings? How very noble of you."

"Will you?" Clarice asked urgently. She must convince Shamal the survival of *Asesino*'s crew was all she was thinking of, or Shamal would not even keep her alive for another hour. "Once you have what you want, their lives will mean nothing to you—"

"Why, so they will not!" Shamal said gleefully. "And so their brave and noble captain will tell them they are to live—won't you, my darling? And all will be well."

"Is it true?" Clarice asked. Not because she thought Shamal would tell her if it weren't, but because it was something a woman sacrificing her life would ask.

Shamal laughed. "I promise you, by tonight this ship will sail waters filled with treasure enough to make a thousand men rich as kings—and I desire none of it! Now, you have had the truth from my own lips. Come. You have a promise to keep."

It was nearly an hour before the whole of the ship's company were gathered on deck. Clarice was glad to see Kayin in the front rank, for the mood of the crew was, well, *mutinous*.

Clarice, Shamal, and Dominick stood at the poop-deck rail, with Gregale behind them. All Clarice saw was gray mist. She shivered in the bitter air and wondered what Dominick could see.

"Gentlemen!" Dominick said, once the crew was assembled. "I have good news! Today we reach our destination! To do so I shall need all your skill, for it will require a neat bit of sailing and some split-second timing."

"And why should we?" Ned Hatcliff demanded, shouldering to the front of the crowd. "So we can freeze for a few more days before we die?"

The mutterings of the crew grew louder, and the sound was ugly.

"No!" Dominick shouted. "To gain your lives—and fortune as well! Hear me out! The Lady Shamal will release us once she has her treasure! She has sworn it! All we must do then is sail south—to freedom!"

For a long, tense moment there was nothing but silence, and Clarice began to fear that the lie would not work.

"Cap'n's saved us!" Jerrold whooped. "Three cheers for Captain Moryet!"

The cheering was ragged. But it came.

Clarice clutched the railing before her with hands that had gone numb with cold. Mr. Emerson was heating the galley as if it were a blacksmith's forge, and each time they came about, smoke from the chimney blew over the deck.

It was like trying to guide a blind horse over a steeplechase. Again and again they tacked awkwardly into position, following Dominick's shouted orders. Four times he'd ordered *Asesino* to veer off at the last possible moment. Each time he did, those on deck slipped and skidded helplessly, for the deck was covered with ice. Two of the riggers had fallen to their deaths. She did not need seamanship to know the crew was tiring. Willing or not, this was brutal labor.

Shamal stood upon the bowsprit itself, a second ship's figurehead. Clarice could not imagine how she kept her place. Magic, perhaps. Clarice glanced toward where Dominick stood, muffled in a heavy greatcoat. His hair, his eyebrows, even his lashes, were crusted with ice. He looked like a statue, not a man.

"Kayin! Bring us about!" he cried. The orders were relayed yet again, adjustments made to follow a line only Dominick could see. Clarice saw his lips move as he whispered to himself, *This must work. We can't survive another try.* He struggled from his greatcoat.

"Dominick!" Clarice cried. "What are you doing?"

"They can't see!" he shouted. "I can!"

On the main deck he stopped to kick out of his boots, then began to climb, shouting orders as his crew struggled to obey. She strained her eyes at the mist, but there was nothing to see.

Once more *Asesino* leaped forward into nothingness. Suddenly there was a grinding crash and a terrible scraping sound. Clarice clung grimly to the rail as chunks of ice sprayed onto the deck along the starboard side. Lines fouled and were torn away, sails collapsed . . . and then . . .

Light!

Clarice blinked. The light was weak, but it was true sunlight at last. Behind her she heard Shamal give a crow of triumph as she leaped down from the bowsprit to the deck.

The wind had died to nothing more than that created by their own motion. Clarice gazed around, hugging herself tightly. The air was so cold each breath cut like knives.

But at last she could see what Dominick had seen all along.

They were within the ring of ice pillars. And at its center, what must surely be their destination: an ice mountain to rival the Swanscrown. The whole surface of the eldritch structure was carved. Clarice could not decide whether it was the most beautiful thing she had ever seen—or the most horrible.

We are not supposed to be here.

She didn't know where the thought came from, but if it had been within her power, Clarice would have fled as fast as she could.

"Snakes! The water is full of snakes!"

Jerrold's scream jarred Clarice out of her half trance. She stared up at him; he was pointing over the side of the ship and shouting.

"Get down here!" Dominick shouted. He suited his own action to his words, scrambling to the deck and then toward the rail. "Every hand on deck! Now!"

"Ah . . . but they are helpless without their king," Shamal whispered in Clarice's ear. "They dare not cause him harm."

Clarice hadn't heard her approach and stifled a yelp and turned. "Their . . . king?" Clarice stammered.

Shamal's eyes sparkled with glee.

"We can't lower the boat," Dominick said, running up the ladder to the afterdeck. "Look down."

Obediently, Clarice peered over the rail. At first, she saw nothing but water—then something shadowy and pale rose up through the depths, stopping perhaps a fathom below the surface. The ice-pale serpentine body was larger around than the water casks in the hold. She recoiled with a hiss of dismay.

"There are hundreds of them out there," Dominick said. "You can see it from the rigging. They're swarming around the ship."

"We shall have to sail closer to the temple, then," Shamal said from where she stood. "It is not far."

"Does this look like a horse?" Dominick said in exasperation. "You're on a ship—and there's no wind. Without wind, we drift."

It was true. Clarice glanced up. *Asesino*'s sails hung slack.

"Once our momentum's gone, we'll be at the mercy of whatever currents there are in this place," Dominick said.

Clarice looked back over the side. *I don't think we'll get the chance to find out.* All around them the gelid water was roiling with the movement of sinuous bodies. Lattices of ice were spreading from the bobbing chunks of ice scattered across the water, racing across the surface with unnatural speed. In scant heartbeats *Asesino* would be icebound, caught in ice as if it were a fly caught in amber.

"Kayin," Dominick said. "Get the men—"

The ship suddenly rocked violently. A long, thrumming groan from *Asesino* herself came as something large—very large—scraped along the hull.

"Gregale! Do you think to betray me?" Shamal cried in fury.

"What's happening?" Clarice asked Dominick.

"I don't know, but I think we might have been safer out there in the fog," he answered in a low voice. Hard upon his last words, the ship was rocked violently again. "Kayin! Everyone below! Now! Those things are big enough to capsize us if they keep that up," he said quietly, as Kayin moved to rally the crew and chivy them below. "In that water, we'll freeze to death in minutes."

Clarice took his hands. "If that's what happens . . ."

"Stop them! Stop them at once! I order it!" Shamal cried. She seemed to realize she was being observed, for she gave Clarice a venomous look. "Or perhaps they require a . . . sacrifice? Dominick, my darling, you have served me well. Now climb over the railing and jump into the ocean."

Dominick did not move.

Shamal's eyes narrowed. "Dominick!" Shamal cried. "Throw yourself into the sea! I command it!"

Clarice looked up and met Gregale's gaze. The creature was staring straight at her, his dark eyes imploring.

"They are helpless without their king. They dare not cause him harm."

Every time Shamal has cast a spell, she's used one of her necklaces.

There is no more time.

Clarice lunged across the icy deck, straight for Shamal. She struck her full force, skidding on the ice and clawing at Shamal as she dragged her to the deck. Shamal writhed like a maddened animal, opening her mouth to shout commands Gregale would surely be forced to obey. Clarice ducked her face to protect her eyes from Shamal's clawing nails as she wrestled with her and concentrated on only one thing.

The beads about Shamal's throat.

Clarice's hands were stiff and clumsy with cold. The strands burned her fingers as if with fire; it was like grabbing a handful of razors. Clarice gritted her teeth and endured. Shamal bit and scratched and clawed at her, but Clarice ignored it all. The beads. That was the important thing. Get the beads.

A few of the necklaces broke, but Clarice could not get a grip on the whole mass of them, and her hands were wet with blood from a thousand cuts. In the cold it froze even as it welled up.

"*Gregale!* Gregale, I command you—!"

Then Dominick was beside Clarice, and his hands were beside hers, ripping at the necklaces, scattering beads everywhere.

Shamal arched her back, writhing against the icy deck. "Kill them! Kill them all!" she shrieked in a high, wild voice.

Dominick dragged Clarice to her feet and away, backing toward the railing. It would not save them. Nothing could. Ice climbed up the hull, holding the ship so utterly still that Clarice and Dominick both staggered with the loss of the familiar motion. Clarice looked toward Gregale.

He had not moved from where he stood. Now he smiled, holding Clarice's eyes, and nodded, once.

Shamal rolled to her knees and scuttled away on hands and knees. Her face and neck were daubed with blood from Clarice's lacerated hands. Loose beads covered the deck and clung to her furs like drifts of rainbow snow. She groped at her neck, feeling for the necklaces. More beads spilled through her fingers as broken strands came free. Bright bits of magic fell to the deck, their enchantment fading like dying sparks. Her mouth worked, but no words came out.

Gregale flung back his head and howled. The sound silenced the shouting of the crew on the deck below, drowned out the crackle of the forming ice. He raised his fists to the heavens and shouted in triumph, a sound louder than any human throat could produce.

"No, no, no, no, *no*—!" Shamal screamed, her voice raw with terror.

Gregale's body warped and lengthened like a piece of rubber. He burst the seams of his garments and arched backward, his spine curving impossibly.

"No! You'll kill us all! No! Gregale, don't! I love you, I do, I always have—*please*—" Shamal babbled.

"The ladder. Quickly. We must get below," Dominick said. "It is our only hope."

They reached the main deck. Ice continued to thicken and spread with unnatural speed, pushing between the gaps in the rail and spreading across the deck. Behind them, Shamal continued to rave: threats, promises, pleas . . .

Clarice dug her fingers into Dominick's arm, heedless of the pain from her reopened wounds, and turned back. She had to see. The thing that had been Gregale was a monstrous column of glistening scaled flesh. As she watched, it fell backward over the railing. A heartbeat later ice and water sprayed everywhere as Gregale surfaced again.

He had completed his transformation. His head was long and tapered, his body as big around as the hull of *Asesino*. Pinprick black eyes glinted balefully, and his body was covered in scales that were all the iridescent colors of northern ice. The terrible jaws gaped open.

Clarice heard the hiss of his exhalation, and the cold of it burned her skin like fire, making it impossible to breathe. The air was filled with flashes of green and violet fire. Shamal was fighting back with all the sorcery left to her. It was useless.

The ice drake—the King of the Northern Serpents—reared up. His body arched, and the head dived toward the deck. Clarice gave a blurt of horrified laughter—he looked just like a goose diving at a tasty bug.

There was a scream, then silence. Gregale reared back again, with the body of his captor and tormentor crushed between his jaws. Blood stained his glittering scales.

Then he flung himself into the sea. *Asesino* rocked violently, the ice holding her cracking with sharp gunshot sounds. Dominick slipped and clawed at the ice-covered deck, leaving bloody smears against wood and ice as he fought to get the two of them to safety.

The seething mass of serpents rose up under *Asesino,* and she jerked and thrashed like a rat caught in the jaws of some gigantic terrier as she fell from one coil to the next. Clarice slid the length of the canted ice-covered deck and hit the afterdeck housing with a bruising thump. A moment later, Dominick landed against her. She could hear screams from the men below, and imagination brought her a lightning image of the stove and ovens spilling their flaming contents across the decks.

The wind began to rise. The sky went dark. Dominick was shouting something she could not hear, clinging to her desperately as *Asesino* was flung at the ring of pillars. Ice sprayed across the deck like shrapnel, and then they were through.

The prow crashed back into the icy sea, and the gale struck full force. The sails filled with a crack, and the timbers sang in protest. Rain, sleet, and hail struck with stunning force. Balls of ice made drumming sounds against the deck, audible only for an instant until the sound was drowned in the scream of the wind through the rigging.

Waves crashed over the deck as *Asesino*, full rigged and helpless, was seized by the storm. The deck tilted sideways, nearly vertical, and the portside rail sank below the surface of the sea. A moment later the ship was flung back the other way.

Dominick clawed his way along the railing, dragging Clarice with him. Water poured across the deck and down through the hatches. Clarice was drenched, blinded, deafened, her hands so numb she could not tell whether she clung to Dominick or not. She shouted his name and could not hear the sound of her own voice.

They reached one of the masts and clung to it desperately. Dominick sawed one handed at a drum-taut line. She felt a length of rope being passed around her body. *He is tying us to the mast,* she thought dazedly.

But no. Not both of them. Through salt-blinded eyes, she saw Dominick move away from her and begin to climb the rigging. She gasped and coughed, gagging on seawater, struggling against the rope that bound her.

Then Kayin appeared, dragging himself across the wildly pitching deck. He was not alone. Impossible as it seemed, the crew of *Asesino* was rallying. They fought their way across the deck, armed with axes and knives. Clarice watched in numb incomprehension until the first of the great sails ripped free, carried away by the tempest.

With the sails gone, we have a chance.

She did not know how long it was before she felt a body pressed against hers. She struggled dazedly to cling to the mast until Kayin and Dominick pulled her away.

"Clarice! Clarice!" Dominick had to shout to be heard over the shriek of the wind. "Come below!"

We've won, she thought giddily, as the three of them staggered to the ladder.

The storm blew for three days. Clarice manned the pumps beside every able-bodied man left aboard. She cut the laces of her corset so she could work, tore the sleeves from her shirt to bandage her bleeding hands, pushed her body past the limit of its endurance. Dominick pushed himself harder than anyone else, taking his turn at the pumps, moving among the crew speaking words of encouragement.

"A miracle has brought us this far, Clarice," he said. "We must provide the rest of the miracle ourselves."

"Not a miracle," she answered. "Gregale."

"Next time I see him, I shall have a word about his taste in rescues."

She worked the pump until her strength gave out, dropped to the deck for a too-brief rest, then returned to the work again. It was all they could do now: try to pump the water out faster than it came in. She didn't know whether the storm was of Gregale's making, or something he couldn't prevent, or if he simply hadn't cared once he'd been freed. And she was too exhausted to care.

"Wake up." Dominick was shaking her. "Wake up. We're alive. And . . . Shamal told the truth."

The name brought Clarice instantly awake. "She's here?" Clarice sat up quickly. Every muscle screamed in protest, and she groaned, squinting at her surroundings. All around her, the crew lay as if dead, but as she watched, she saw a body move in sleep and heard a sudden racking snore. The pumps stood silent. Everything was silent. *Asesino* was rocking gently, as if at anchor, and Clarice realized she was actually warm for the first time in days.

"Still dead," Dominick said. "But . . . come and see."

"Shamal told the truth?" Clarice said groggily. "About what?"

"Come and see."

He lifted her to her feet. She staggered to the nearest keg and plunged the tankard into it, drinking thirstily. The bandages on her hands were frayed and grimy, spotted with blood where blisters had burst. Her hair clung stickily to her face like seaweed. She winced as she raised her hands to her face to push it back. She turned back to Dominick.

"We're alive," she said hoarsely. On aching, unsteady legs she followed him to the ladder.

"The storm blew out last night. At that point even I didn't care what happened next. But it's morning now."

It was just after dawn. The sky was a stainless tropical blue, and the wind was soft and warm. In daylight *Asesino* looked even more like a wreck—masts sheered away, railings splintered, and even hatches gone. But Clarice took all that in with one brief glance because of something even more important than the precarious state of *Asesino*.

They were surrounded by ships.

12

THE GRAVEYARD OF LOST SHIPS

SOME, LIKE *Asesino* herself, were mastless and storm racked. Some foundered barely above the waterline. Some looked nearly whole.

All were deserted.

"But what is this place?" Clarice asked, her voice barely above a whisper. "And how did all these ships get here?"

"A legend." Dominick's voice was as low as her own. "The Graveyard of Lost Ships."

"A graveyard?" For a moment Clarice wondered if this was Shamal's last cruel trick. "We aren't . . . dead . . . are we?"

"Different sort of graveyard." Dominick leaned over the rail to peer down into the water. "No spirits in it—and no magic, either. Just wind and currents. See, sometimes a ship gets lost—in a storm, like we did. She drifts into a place where there's no wind. And there she stays."

"One, maybe," Clarice said dubiously. "Or two, perhaps. There must be hundreds here."

"And more down to Bowling Green. Look there." He pointed.

The water was clear enough that Clarice could see, down below, the remains of another ship, its shape blurred with streamers of green.

"So," Dominick went on, "ships start to all collect in the same place. And after a while there's so many ships together in one spot, and some of them half-sunk, that they attract more. That fine lady, over there, say. I'll wager you she hasn't been under sail in a century, maybe more."

"But—" Clarice wasn't sure Dominick's explanation made any sense, though he seemed to be perfectly satisfied with it. "Are we lost?" She took a step closer to him.

Dominick put an arm around her shoulders. "I will know to-night, should the sky remain clear. Without instruments I cannot know to any degree of accuracy, but . . ."

"But we are alive, and here—and free!" Clarice was only now beginning to believe it. To believe *in* it—freedom and safety after so long a time spent passing from one disaster to the next. "We're safe."

Dominick laughed a little. "Safer than we were, though how safe we are I cannot say. We must have supplies—there are repairs to make—we must search the ship . . ."

"We're *safe,*" Clarice said insistently. "Safe! And very very damp," she added with a rueful laugh.

"That, at least, is a matter easily cured. If we have nothing else, we have sun." He stripped off his shirt and spread it over the rail, then sat down on the deck. "I cannot say if your boots will survive, but I can say it is better to have them off than on."

"Easy for you to say," Clarice grumbled. She fumbled with the buttons on her vest and pulled it free. There was a bright flash— her brooch was still pinned into the lining. She fumbled it free and pinned it to the ragged remains of her shirt. By the time she'd struggled out of her boots and her stockings, her shirt was nearly dry. She wiggled her toes, relishing the feel of warmth.

It felt so strange to her to be with him without secrets between them, and no more enemies to fight. When he took her hand to help her to her feet, it startled her for a moment, but he smiled at her as if the two of them shared a secret joke, and Clarice smiled back. At last, for the first time, this was something they could do. Openly. Without fear.

"Come on," he said. "We should rouse everyone and get them up on deck where it's warmer."

And find out who has survived.

Twenty-two souls, of the ninety-odd who had sailed from Dorado, had survived. Some had been swept overboard. Some had been trapped below and drowned. Only ten of *Asesino*'s original crew had survived. Kayin, Geordie, Jerrold, and Mr. Emerson were among the survivors.

Dickon Greenwell was not.

"He died in the storm," Dominick said quietly. "He went forward to lash the helm. He saved us all."

"I am sorry," Clarice said quietly. "He was a good man."

"They were all good men."

By late that morning the survivors had searched the ship and had brought up the bodies of the dead. All were consigned, with as much ceremony as *Asesino*'s weary and injured crew could muster, to the sea.

The galley was a total loss—most of the chimney was gone—but most of the provisions in the hold, including their precious casks of drinking water, had survived. Mr. Emerson built a fire on deck, and by midday the survivors were eating their first hot meal in many days.

"What now?" Clarice asked. It seemed she had been asking that question for longer than she wanted to remember. *What now? What next?* Each time, lives and fates had depended on the answer.

"Now we eat, and rest," Dominick said, sitting down beside her and offering her the bowl he held. It held a pottage of salt beef and potatoes. Clarice dipped her hand into it and liberated a chunk of potato. She was sure she'd never tasted anything so delicious in her life. "I do not think any of us is good for much else today."

"And then?"

"Wait for the sky to grow dark. So we can find out where we are. Find something we can sail home in—if home is to be found." Dominick pitched his voice low. "Not *Asesino*. Even if she were whole, we have not enough crew to man her."

And then? But Clarice did not want to ask that question just yet. She knew the important part of the answer already.

Whatever came next, she and Dominick would face it together.

And so, the survivors made a castaway's holiday on the deck of their ruined ship and awaited the appearance of the stars, which would truly tell their fate. Bottles were passed about, and songs were sung. Every now and then a few of the men would go scavenging about the ship, bringing their finds up on deck to dry. Soon the main deck was covered with mattresses and blankets; even a few items from Shamal's cabin had found their way topside. Clarice lay dozing on a blanket. She'd received a few curious looks—everyone knew she was a woman now, after all—but in general, the crew seemed to feel she was one of them.

As do I, she thought. *Not Princess Clarice of Swansgaarde, not Clarence Swann of nowhere in particular. Just . . . Clarice, now.*

It was enough. It was more than she'd had.

She woke from her doze when Dominick moved.

The sun had set, and the evening breeze was cool. A few of the ship's lanterns had survived, miraculously intact, and were set about the deck in whatever places could hold them. By their light she could see Kayin and Miles Oliver already standing in the center of the deck.

"Kayin!" Miles said. "I see—"

"We all know what you see, young fellow," Mr. Emerson said sharply. "It's for the cap'n to announce it."

"Captain of very little, Mr. Emerson, but I thank you regardless." Dominick walked to the center of the deck.

All around them, the crew—for those who had been sleeping had clearly been awakened to view the night sky—looked heavenward. So did Clarice. The stars meant nothing to her, though she knew they must to anyone who lived by the sea. If they meant anything at all . . .

But they must, for if they had not, the mood of the men would be very different. Familiar stars, then. That was good. But it was Dominick who must sail them home.

"There is the Cross, and there the Dragon's Tail. And so this is the Hispalidean Sea—as you all know," Dominick said, turning to face his audience. "We do not have clock or compass, but men sailed long before such were invented! Tomorrow I shall make a cross-staff, and with a few sightings, I shall know precisely where we are. And surely, in all of this, we can find something to sail home in?"

"That we can, Captain!" Kayin said.

"If it's a raft we build, why, I'll drive the nails myself!" Duff Evans announced.

"And sail home!" Geordie cried.

"Home!" Jerrold shouted, and soon everyone was shouting that single word, over and over, like shipwrecked men sighting land at last.

Home.

But before they could sail home, they must have a ship.

"I'm not really sure what we're looking for," Clarice said.

She and Kayin were standing on the deck of a ship two away from *Asesino,* one of the few they could reach without a boat.

The galleon was riding high in the water—which meant it was seaworthy—but it was far too large for their purposes.

"Anything we can use, Miss Clarice," Kayin answered. They'd already found one of the things they needed most—the captain's gig was on deck and intact. To lower it into the water would require ropes and pulleys to be brought from *Asesino*, and they'd need to gather the whole crew together to winch it down. "It's salvage, you know. Everything here is free to anyone who can take it."

"I wonder why pirates waste their time attacking shipping, in that case, if all this is here for the taking."

Kayin grinned at her. "Folk have been looking for the Graveyard of Lost Ships since Cap'n Ulysses sailed home from Troy."

She was kept from pursuing her argument by Jerrold's return.

"Kayin, there's something in the hold I think you need to see." Jerrold held out his palm, holding something round and gold. A brooch. Sunlight struck green fire from the jewel in the center and turned the diamonds around the edge into a blaze of light. "The hold's full of this stuff. Chests and chests of it!"

Shamal said we would sail waters filled with treasure enough to make a thousand men rich as kings. She might have been telling the truth about that icy temple; we will never know. This is enough truth for us.

The three of them stood in the hold. Light filtered down from a hole in the decks above—enough that the lantern Jerrold held wasn't necessary. Enough to show them broken chests spilling gold coins and jewelry across the deck.

It is like something out of a storybook, Clarice thought numbly. The treasure room at Castle Swansgaarde seemed suddenly paltry by comparison. She picked up a rope of pearls. The string broke even as she lifted it, but the clasp that had once held them was set with a sapphire as large as her thumbnail.

"There's tons of it," Jerrold said, sounding bewildered.

"Where did it all come from?" Clarice asked.

"Everywhere." Kayin picked up an ornate chalice that had surely been meant to decorate some church's altar. "Might have been an Iberian treasure ship. Or a pirate. Whichever it was, it's our fortune, true and certain." He tossed the chalice back into the heap from which he'd taken it.

"You don't sound very happy about it," Clarice observed.

Kayin made a face. "Hard enough to get everyone to work now. Show them treasure, and they'll go mad drunk on it."

"We could swear to keep it secret," Jerrold said tentatively.

Clarice shook her head. "Secrets among us would be a very bad idea, I think. And what if someone finds treasure aboard another ship? No. We shall tell Dominick when we get back, and we shall all make a pact: When we sail from here, we will carry as much treasure with us as we can. And we will divide it equally among us all."

"Good." Kayin nodded in satisfaction. "And I'll remind those lubbers that diamonds and suchlike may dazzle, but"—he plucked the brooch from Jerrold's hand and tossed it back into one of the piles—"gold coins spend better with less history to 'em."

As Clarice had suspected, theirs was not the only ship that had been carrying a cargo of treasure. Dominick's search party had found much the same, and as Kayin said, everyone, even the former prisoners, were giddy with the thought of such wealth.

"Although the ship's boat is far more useful in our present circumstances," Clarice said.

"All things considered," Dominick agreed. "I hope she's sound. I want to take a look at that brigantine I spotted today."

The two-masted brigantine was too far away to reach except by boat. She'd taken on a lot of water, but Dominick thought she looked sound enough, and if they could row one of the pumps over to her, they could pump her dry and caulk her leaks. Then it would be a matter of contriving enough in the way of sails to be able to . . . sail her. That news had begun the evening meal, though even the knowledge that they could escape the Graveyard of Lost Ships was eclipsed by the discovery of the treasure that it held. The mood was festive: not only were they going home, they were going home as rich men.

As good as the promise of wealth was the promise of justice. Clarice remembered Dr. Chapman's conviction that the Royal Navy had thaumaturges powerful enough to break Dorado's enchantments. And now that Shamal was not there to renew them, with her dead, all that protected Dorado was the spells she—or someone— had already woven upon it.

I wonder what the Heart of Light was. I wonder what Shamal would have done with it if she'd been able to gain it. Whatever it was, it was something so powerful that she no longer needed Asesino. I don't think she would have just gone back to Dorado. I suspect the Brotherhood knew that. They did not want to let her sail, but they could not stop her, either.

"Now, lads, a word." Emmet Emerson stood to take center stage. "We're going home, right enough. And now we're all going home as rich as kings. But there's a right way and a wrong way to go about it, look you, and I'm here to offer up a friendly word of advice, as it were, about the right way."

This was something the crew would take from one of their own, whereas coming from Dominick, they would resent it. It didn't matter that Dominick was as ragged and penniless as they were; he was their captain, and the acceptance of that authority meant an unconscious assumption of resources and even wealth they could never possess. Now Mr. Emerson told the crew what Kayin had told her: Coins could be spent. There were enough of them here to sink the little brigantine they hoped to sail home in. It was foolish to try to bring it all—and twice as foolish to bring jewels of a price that would only attract the wrong sort of attention. And what they brought away with them would be divided equally and openly.

"If any man jack of you knows how to sell a diamond necklace without getting cheated in the dealing and having your throat cut afterward," Mr. Emerson said, "sing out. And think on this: You'll have to say where it came from, won't you, if you show up with one of these here golden chalices or suchlike? And it won't be your mates asking, to buy you a round after you've spun your yarn. It'll be the portmaster, or the governor, or the guild. And they'll be very particular about your answers."

Clarice heard a low mutter among the crew as they spoke among themselves, but the overall tone seemed to be one of agreement. "Would they really prosecute us?" she asked Dominick. "Kayin said everything here was lawful salvage."

"True enough," Dominick said. "Everything here is any man's for the taking. These ships are long abandoned, and under the law of the sea, they and their cargoes belong to whoever claims them. But this is treasure enough to buy kingdoms."

"And treasure drives men mad," Clarice said. For a moment she was back in Dr. Chapman's surgery, showing him the key to the House of the Four Winds for the first time. "But won't they talk about this? About where they've been?"

"Of course," Dominick said, sounding surprised. "And no one pays any attention to the yarns a sailor spins. That this one is true won't matter in the least."

"I suppose it won't. It's a very good story, too. Sorceresses and sea serpents and pirates . . . Do you think the governor will believe us? Those poor captives! And the Ifrani taken as slaves. Surely they all deserve to go home again?"

"Yes," Dominick said grimly. "And I will do all I can to make sure the governor takes us seriously when we arrive at Cibola."

"I hope so." The story Matthew Pratchett had told her still haunted her. He might have made a home for himself on Dorado, but she wanted him to have a choice.

"But can't we take even a little souvenir, Kayin?" Geordie Lamb's voice was raised above the murmur of quiet talk. "My mother would so admire one of those brooches—"

"Cloudwit!" Kayin said roundly. "She'll have you alive with your pockets full of gold—you can buy her a dozen brooches."

"Something she can actually wear," Clarice murmured to Dominick.

He chuckled. "What about you? Doesn't the thought of the jewels tempt you?"

"They're a good deal grander than anything Swansgaarde has to offer," she said dryly. "I hope someday to convince you of that. I am a mere traveling swordsmaster, as I have told you."

"Or swords*mistress*. You told me you had not quite made up your mind, as I recall. But it might take some extraordinary persuasion to convince the governor of Cibola to marry me to . . . to a beardless boy with violent tendencies." He put an arm around her, and Clarice nestled comfortably close.

"Swordsmistress it is, then," she said comfortably. "I hope you can find a use for such a one on the fine new ship you will undoubtedly buy with your treasure."

"Master of arms," Dominick said at once. "Only . . . I think I shall keep the brigantine, if she is seaworthy. She will certainly need careening as soon as we are somewhere we can beach her, but I can refit her with my share of the treasure—"

"With *our* share of the treasure."

He hugged her. "With our share of the treasure. Geordie will wish to go home, I know, but perhaps Kayin will stay."

"As a proper first mate this time."

"Yes! There's a living to be made in sailing among the Hispalides. And to New Hesperia as well, for its coast is not far."

"And you shall own her outright, and—I can't just keep calling the brigantine *her*," Clarice complained. "What's her name?"

"She hasn't got one yet. The escutcheon was too weathered to read, so she has none. We must name and christen her before we sail, of course. But I want to choose a proper name for her."

"I thought it was bad luck to rename a ship."

"It is worse luck to sail a nameless one. For how would Father Neptune know we were proper sailors if we could not tell him the name of our ship? It will all be done properly. You'll see."

They spoke long into the night of their plans for the little brigantine, and for the future.

It was nearly a fortnight before they were ready to sail.

It took two days to pump the water from the brigantine's hold and to empty it of the rotted remains of her cargo. That was nasty work; the sludge the pumps couldn't handle they carried out in buckets, but when she rode high in the water once more, they were able to tow her alongside *Asesino*. Then the real work began. There was inspection and caulking to be done—another tedious, nasty job involving oakum and hot pitch, supplies to transfer to the new ship, barrels smaller than *Asesino*'s hogsheads found to carry the new ship's stores of water, tested, scrubbed to sweetness, and filled. But their most pressing need was new sails. Clarice and many others spent hours sitting cross-legged on deck, pushing a long, curved needle through heavy thicknesses of canvas. And slowly the brigantine woke to life again.

But it was not a time of unending toil. It was impossible to work the crew from dawn to dusk, and to his credit Dominick didn't even try, so some afternoons he and Clarice would take the gig and simply explore the sea of lost ships, just the two of them. Something about so many decayed, abandoned ships— some bearing the marks of storms or battles, some half-consumed by fire, some so nearly submerged that the disaster that had brought them here could not be determined—was both grand and a little sad.

It gave her hours to spend with Dominick, and if their courtship had been backward, beginning with an introduction and a proposal of marriage, they made up for it now, with long, lazy hours spent telling one another the stories of their very different lives.

"You know," Clarice said one afternoon, "when we reach Cibola, we shall all be quite wealthy—and I'm sure the governor will be grateful for the news about the House of the Four Winds. You could go back to Albion. Take Barnabas Bellamy to court and regain your rightful inheritance."

"I know his path and mine must cross again at some point," Dominick answered slowly. "For I suspect he was complicit in the disappearance of the ships Sprunt sailed for him. The Cornhill Society will certainly want to know one way or the other, for they have paid out the assurance on the lost ships. But I do not want his company—for it is that now, and not the one my father started. I would either have to spend my days behind a desk or trust a partner to manage matters for me ashore, and I do not think I can ever bring myself to do so. Besides"—he strove for a lighter tone—"what would I do with such a fleet? Would I have to sail it to the ends of the earth to bring back wealth so that a beautiful princess would look favorably on me?"

"You know this princess already does," Clarice answered, smiling.

And at last the day came when the ship was ready. They had spent the day rigging her, and now she rode at anchor, her sails reefed, as shipshape as they could make her.

The treasure was already there: six barrels full of gold coins, carefully chosen and gathered in between other tasks. Each coin had been counted out carefully by Kayin as they all watched, to be sure the whole would divide exactly among them, just as they'd planned. The load was heavy enough to make even the most avaricious souls glad they were not carrying more, and Mr. Emerson warned everyone, once again, against the trouble they'd get into by smuggling away a ring or a brooch or a pendant as an additional reward.

Clarice had thought they would move aboard her at once. They'd spent the whole of the day aboard the—still-nameless—vessel, and the brigantine was now ready for occupancy. But they'd returned to *Asesino* to spend one last night aboard her.

"You can't go about on a ship with no name, Miss Clarice," Jerrold told her earnestly. "It's fair unlucky, it is. We'd never make port if we did!" He gestured theatrically as if to illustrate the magnitude of the possible disaster.

"Well, then, we shall have to name her, won't we?"

"Course we will! Going to baptize her at sunrise, all right and proper."

Clarice wondered what name it would be. Dominick had claimed the privilege of naming their vessel, but he'd refused to tell anyone the name he'd chosen.

That night, for the first time since they'd come to the graveyard of lost ships, a watch was set, for the new ship would be launched at sunrise, for luck.

When Dominick shook Clarice awake, the sky was still dark. "Come on. It will be dawn soon."

She dressed quickly—a matter of putting on her boots and her coat—and scrambled down the rope ladder that bound the two ships together. It would be the last time.

I shall miss you, she thought, gazing up at *Asesino. Sleep well, my friend.*

Soon they were all gathered on the deck of the brigantine. Dominick stood aft, surrounded by a number of bottles of rum and brandy. For all its impromptu seeming, Clarice sensed this moment was solemn.

He stood in silence, facing east, until the first line of light appeared upon the horizon. "Cast us free," he said to Kayin.

Kayin cut the knots that tied the two ships together and flung the ropes over the side, then came to pick up a bottle. Geordie and two men from *Dorado*—Cecil Mild and Hume Lewis—did the same, taking places by the railing as close to the cardinal points of the compass as possible.

"Great Father Poseidon, we offer these libations to you and your court." Dominick picked up a bottle and drew the cork. He took a mouthful, then poured half the bottle onto the deck and the rest into the water before tossing the bottle overboard.

"Great Eurus, exalted ruler of the East Wind, grant us permission to use your mighty powers in the pursuit of our lawful endeavors, ever sparing us the overwhelming scourge of your potent breath," Kayin said. He uncorked the bottle he held and took a mouthful, then poured the rest over the side.

"Great Notus, exalted ruler of the South Wind, grant us permission to use your mighty powers . . ." Now it was Hume Lewis who spoke, repeating Kayin's gestures.

Cecil Mild begged the favor of Zephyrus, ruler of the West Wind, spilling the liquor carefully upon the railing itself as he poured his libation to the deep.

Geordie called upon Boreas, ruler of the North Wind. ". . . and ever spare us the overwhelming scourge of your frigid breath," he finished fervently.

"Amen to that, I says!" Mr. Emerson said roundly.

By now the whole sky was a deep blue, and golden fire lined the eastern horizon. But the ceremony was not yet finished. Dominick opened two more bottles and began to pour—one to the deck, one into the sea.

"O Father of Oceans, Lord Poseidon, today a ship is born. We who venture upon the surface of your vast domain commend her to your care and implore you in your graciousness to take unto your records and recollection this worthy vessel hereafter and for all time known as . . . *Sea Swan*!"

"Three cheers for the *Sea Swan*!" Jerrold shouted. "And for Clarence—I mean Clarice—Swann!"

When the cheers had died, Dominick came to where Clarice stood—blushing in embarrassment and delight—and took her hand.

"Kiss the lady, will you, Dominick?" Kayin shouted.

"Give our swan wings, Kayin, and I shall." Dominick put his

arm around her shoulders. "I wanted to give you something no one else could."

"It is the greatest gift I have ever received."

The sails were raised into position. The ship began slowly to move forward. The men paused briefly to cheer, before leaping to their posts, all their thoughts now of home.

And as the little ship surged as if she were eager as Clarice to start her journey into her new life, the wind of her passage caressing them all, and the sun shining down on them like a benediction, Dominick kissed Clarice, and no woman before or since could ever have been more thoroughly kissed.